'An excellent read! So original and clever that I was
completely absorbed . . . Gripping . . . and twisty
with an unexpected ending. Phenomenal.'
Claire Douglas

'Emma Curtis is the queen of the
unputdownable thriller.'
Nuala Ellwood

'A dark, gripping page-turner.'
Sarah Vaughan

'A twist that almost made me miss my flight.'
Jane Corry

'Filled with drama and twists that exploded
on to the page at every turn.'
Lauren North

'A tense and utterly engrossing story.'
Tammy Cohen

'Starting from a brilliantly twisted premise,
the tension simply doesn't let up.'
Nicola Rayner

'I loved it from start to finish.'
Phoebe Morgan

www.penguin.co.uk

By Emma Curtis

ONE LITTLE MISTAKE
WHEN I FIND YOU
THE NIGHT YOU LEFT
KEEP HER QUIET
INVITE ME IN

and published by Black Swan

Invite Me In

Emma Curtis

BLACK SWAN

TRANSWORLD PUBLISHERS
Penguin Random House, One Embassy Gardens,
8 Viaduct Gardens, London SW11 7BW
www.penguin.co.uk

Transworld is part of the Penguin Random House group of companies
whose addresses can be found at global.penguinrandomhouse.com

First published in Great Britain in 2021 by Black Swan
an imprint of Transworld Publishers

A CIP catalogue record for this book
is available from the British Library.

ISBN
9781784165260

Typeset in 11/14pt Sabon by Jouve (UK), Milton Keynes.
Printed and bound in Great Britain by Clays Ltd, Elcograf S.p.A.

The authorized representative in the EEA is Penguin Random House Ireland,
Morrison Chambers, 32 Nassau Street, Dublin D02 YH68.

Penguin Random House is committed to a sustainable future for
our business, our readers and our planet. This book is made from
Forest Stewardship Council® certified paper.

This book owes a huge debt to my wonderful friend David Fraser, who allowed me to pick his brains about living as a paraplegic, and who read and fact-checked the first draft for me. As a trustee of Back Up, over the years David has helped many newly paralysed men and women adjust to life in a wheelchair. Everyone's experience is different and my character Martin Curran is just one man, but it was so important to me to get it right.

www.backuptrust.org.uk

1

The room is filled with summer sunshine. It falls through the two sash windows in great shafts, warming the unsanded floorboards and making the freshly painted walls gleam. The tiler, at work in the bathroom, is listening to a 1980s station on the radio. It's playing 'Hold Me Now' by the Thompson Twins. He likes the eighties stuff; the music my father used to listen to.

I dreamt about Dad last night for the first time in months.

My arm rises and falls to the beat as I apply a fresh coat of paint with the roller. My hips and shoulders move in time too. When I'm done, I stand back to admire my handiwork.

This flat has been a sanctuary. I expect that's why I had the dream; because the renovation is almost complete and it'll be rented out soon. Just this room and the carpeting, and then I'm done and it won't be my sanctuary any more. It'll be someone else's. Martin felt like a safe place once, two arms to enfold me, when I was too young to realize I had taken the easy option, that I needed to do it for myself. And now it's too late; I'm trapped.

Flat 2, 42 Linden Road. I spotted the 'FOR SALE' sign on the walk to Lucas's school two months ago, viewed it the same morning and then convinced Martin it would be a sound investment. The four flats we currently rent out are modern, trouble-free boxes; this would be our first fixer-upper. Martin didn't take much convincing; after all, it's a lot closer to home than the others. A five-minute drive or a twenty-minute walk. He's happier when I'm close by.

I check my phone. Twelve fifteen. Time to start cleaning up. Martin likes lunch at one on the dot, and he likes us to have it together, even if it means interrupting my day.

I push the lid back on the paint pot, take the roller, paintbrush and tray into the kitchen and turn on the taps. Paint ripples through the stream of warm water as I press it out of the foam. It swirls down the drain. I repeat the process until the water runs clear. Down below in the narrow strip of a garden, a workman puts the finishing touches to the decking. What had been an overgrown mess used as somewhere to dump unwanted household items is now a low-maintenance urban oasis.

Unaware of me watching, the workman straightens up, rolls his shoulders, then walks back to the house and pulls a Peroni out of the small cooler bag he's left at the bottom of the stairs. He turns to look at his handiwork, raising the bottle to his lips, one hand rubbing the back of his neck as he glugs it down. My hold on the paintbrush tightens.

The doorbell rings. Startled out of my trance, I drop the paintbrush, turn off the tap and go downstairs. I expect it's a delivery.

2

There are events in all our lives that trigger change. Sometimes it's a tiny thing; a missed connection on a journey. Sometimes it's huge; a car crash, a death. You can wake up in your bed, yawn and glance at the clock, get up and put the kettle on, not knowing that at some point on this ordinary day, life will take a different course. For Martin, it was the moment he left the pub. If it had been even thirty seconds earlier or later, things would have been very different.

I'm standing in the cramped entrance to the flat, holding open the door, looking up into the smiling face of a stranger, and I don't know, I don't have a clue that this is my fork in the road, or that the choice I'm going to make is crucial, that people's lives are in the balance. What I say, what I do, what I sense.

The man standing on the doorstep is empty-handed.

'Hi?' I say, turning the greeting into a question.

'Hello,' he replies. 'I'm your new tenant.'

2

Did I miss something? A message from the lettings agent? I feel flustered and mildly embarrassed.

'I'm so sorry, but the flat won't be available for another two weeks. How did you know it was a rental?'

'Oh shit, I was only joking,' he says. He thrusts his fingers through his already mussed hair and scratches his scalp. 'I've just been in Hooper's. They didn't have anything suitable to show me, but they mentioned this place was coming up.' The big friendly smile dims. 'I'm sorry, this was inappropriate. I'll go away.' He pauses, perhaps waiting for me to say something. 'It's only . . . This is exactly where I want to be. I know it's cheeky, but I wanted to get in before anyone else did.'

Do I tell him to hang on until it's officially advertised? I should be leaving but his face is so earnest and warm. What could five minutes matter? I open the door wider, standing back. 'I'm on my way out so it'll have to be quick, but why don't you come up and I'll give you a sneak preview. It's not finished so you'll have to excuse the state it's in, but at least you'll know if you like it, and then, if you're still interested, you can be first in the queue.'

He looks uncertain. 'Is that OK? I mean, you don't know me from Adam. I could be a serial killer.'

'I hope not. But I'm not on my own. There are workmen here so I think I'll be all right. My name's Eliza, by the way, Eliza Curran.'

'Dan Jones.'

'Nice to meet you, Dan. You go first.'

'OK. Well, thanks. I appreciate it.'

He goes upstairs and heads straight into the sitting room where the pot of paint is still standing on its piece of newspaper. The wall colour is soft and inviting. When I first walked round the flat, even when it was covered with garish floral wallpaper and disintegrating brown carpet, I'd felt embraced. The flats on Linden Road are Edwardian, built around 1910, so the proportions are generous, graceful even.

He pokes his head into the bathroom, says a cheery hello to the tiler and admires the greenish-blue bevelled tiles. In the kitchen there's a table, big enough to squeeze four people round. Sometimes I've allowed myself to imagine living here with the children, how I'd arrange things. It's tiny compared to our house, and there wouldn't be much money, but we'd be cocooned and happy, there'd be no pressure, no stress, no need to be constantly alert. Most of all, I would be in control, not Martin. It's only a dream. In reality there would still be stress.

'Oh, wow. It's perfect.'

I glow with the pride of a child getting a good school report. I haven't felt this sense of ownership with our other flats; they've merely been a means to an end, a financial transaction. Linden Road is different. Linden Road feels like a friend.

'This is great,' Dan says, making a beeline for the windows and peering out into the street. 'And there're two bedrooms, aren't there?'

'Yes, but the second one's more of a single. Were you hoping to flat-share?'

'No,' he says, turning away from the window. 'It's only me, but I'd like a study. I work for myself.'

'We could fit a desk in, with a single bed. It might be a bit cosy.'

'That wouldn't matter.'

Things are moving too swiftly and I pull back. 'Obviously, it'll be subject to references and a credit check.'

'You can't be too careful,' he agrees.

Dan is wearing a T-shirt and scruffy jeans with rips in the knees, which gives me pause. A self-employed tenant is a risk. Martin won't like it. His ideal would be a young professional, or a couple, who would take care of the place. It's the first time I've thought about my husband since Dan arrived, and with that thought his presence descends like a weight on my chest. I really should be leaving, but something about Dan makes me want to continue chatting.

'What do you do for a living?'

'I'm that conversation stopper, the tech support guy,' he says. 'But I also design websites and marketing material. I write copy for businesses and advise them on content as well. And I create 3D floor plans for developers. A bit of everything.'

'Gosh. I wouldn't know where to start with that. You must be very clever.'

'Highly intelligent,' he says. His smile is contagious. 'Practically a boffin. What about you?'

'Averagely intelligent.' Did that sound arch? Oh God. It did.

He laughs. 'I didn't mean that. Is this place a one-off or are you a serial landlady?'

'Oh, I, we . . .' I stammer. 'I mean, my husband and I own several flats in the town.'

His gaze drops to my ring finger.

'Nice business to be in.'

'So your income is regular?'

'It is, part of it at least – I'm on a retainer for a couple of clients. I can show you my bank statements if that would reassure you.'

'Don't worry, Hooper's will do that.'

'Seriously though, I want it.' There's that infectious grin again. 'What do I have to do to stop you putting it on the open market?'

I notice that his hands move a lot; rubbing his face, the back of his neck, touching his hair, his nose. Occasionally he shoves them into his pockets in an effort to keep them still.

'Let me talk to my husband first. If you give me your contact details, I'll let you know tomorrow. It would be helpful to have a tenant ready to move in immediately.'

I sneak another look at my watch. Shit, Martin's

going to be furious. 'Listen . . . I don't want to be rude but I really must . . .'

'You have to go.'

I smile. 'Yes.'

He moves towards the landing. 'I'll go back to Hooper's and do this officially. I'm sorry I approached you like that. I should have thought it through.'

'It's fine. Really.'

It's not. I'm seven minutes late. I show Dan to the door, hold it open for him. He steps outside then turns to me.

'You've, um . . .'

He touches my face, picks a dried blob of paint from above my right eyebrow. I flinch at his touch, the unexpected warmth of his fingertips.

'Good to meet you, Eliza.'

Then he's gone. I run back upstairs and into the spare bedroom, get out of my overalls and into my jeans, hopping around as I slip my trainers on at the same time. I scoop up my bag and keys, run back down and jump in my car.

3

Coming from the morning spent in a pretty period flat, walking back into our modernist house always jars. I never seem to get used to it. The stark concrete exterior of Winterfell is unwelcoming after the friendly red brick and cream woodwork of Linden Road.

Inside the front door I instinctively stop to listen. The house is quiet; my three-year-old daughter is with her au pair at the One O'Clock Club, my son is at school. Without them the spaces feel hollow.

'Martin,' I call, my voice sounding echoey. 'Sorry I'm late.'

I walk into the kitchen and put my bag down on the island. Martin is sitting outside on the terrace, the *Financial Times* spread open on the table in front of him. I join him, but when I bend to kiss him, he jerks his wheelchair back and slaps me.

I press my palm against my cheek to draw out the sting. 'I'll get lunch on.'

'You do that.'

I walk back inside. I whisk up four eggs. I make a salad dressing. I heat a pan and drop a knob of butter into it, watching it melt as I tip the pan to and fro over the heat, swirling it around. Life is a series of bargains. Battles you win, losses you accept. Martin loves me and gives me so much, but his love is like a protection racket. I pay every day so that my children are happy, so that my past remains buried, so that I can maintain my friendships and feel secure.

'He just walked up and rang the doorbell?'

Ten minutes later and he's acting as though nothing has happened. But that's the way Martin operates. He's like my father was, in that there's no apology and normal service is expected to resume immediately. No dwelling, no crying, no sulking.

But my face still stings.

I told him about Dan. I thought about not saying anything, letting Dan go through the normal channels as though we had never met, but that would have involved asking him to tell a lie, which would have been unfair, not to mention risky. Martin would be bound to find out.

I divide the omelette in two with the edge of a spatula and ease the pieces out of the frying plan and onto heated plates.

I wanted to see what it felt like to say Dan's name out loud too, if truth be told; a touch, even fleeting, from a charming man, is not something that happens to me every day.

'I know,' I reply. 'It does sound odd. It was a spur-of-the-moment decision. He was trying to steal a march on other candidates. I think he was embarrassed when he realized it wasn't the done thing.'

Martin helps himself to salad. He does it with aplomb, lifting it high out of the bowl before dumping it onto his plate. Then he fishes with the salad spoon for slices of avocado and cherry tomatoes.

'What did Susie say?'

I'd called our lettings agent from the car, wanting an explanation before I got home.

'She was apologetic. He'd come in off the street and asked to see what they had. She couldn't show him anything he liked, so she mentioned Linden Road. She told him which flat though, which she shouldn't have done.'

'Stupid cow,' Martin grunts.

'She was trying to be helpful.'

'For all she knew he could have been a psychopath.'

'He seemed perfectly pleasant. He was so enthusiastic about the flat.'

I pick at my food. The omelette is perfect, but it's hard to swallow when you're trying to hold it together, to get the balance right. Humility, but with a touch of spirit. Too much humility and I irritate him; too much spirit and I make him angry. He doesn't like me to be pathetic, but he doesn't like me to be combative either. You'd think after ten years of marriage I'd have it down. Martin is a good-looking man, broad-shouldered with thick black hair and a strong jawline; his effect on me was instant when I first laid eyes on him. In his mid-thirties he is still handsome, but the lines between his eyes and at the corners of his mouth have deepened. When he smiles though, his eyes crinkling, he is irresistible. I see women react. Men too. I don't get many of those smiles directed at me these days.

11

'Eliza, he showed up unannounced and said, "I'm your new tenant." You don't think that's creepy? What I can't understand, what really beggars belief, is that you let this man in.'

He cocks his head.

'OK,' I concede. 'If someone else told me the story, I would think it was creepy, but it didn't feel it at the time. Besides, the workmen were there so I wasn't putting myself in any danger. I'm not an idiot.'

Martin purses his lips. 'That's debatable. You know what we said. We don't take on a tenant we have even the smallest doubt about, no matter how good-looking.'

I falter. 'I never said he was good-looking.'

'Well, is he?'

I get up, needing to move, and take our empty plates to the sink.

'Not particularly,' I say over my shoulder. 'He's just a regular bloke. He had a friendly smile.'

Martin leans back and regards me. 'Oh, well, in that case . . .' he sneers. 'Get rid of him.'

'I as good as told him he could have it.' My voice rises.

'Well, you're going to have to un-tell him.'

I come back to the table. 'I promised . . .'

He pulls me sharply onto his lap, and starts to massage the back of my neck. I struggle not to recoil from his touch as the pressure gets more painful. He says in a low voice, 'I don't care what you promised. You're going to have to disappoint him.' He grips my neck tightly, so

12

tightly that I can't take a breath. 'You're good at being a disappointment.'

He releases me, and pushes me away. As I walk out of the room and mount the staircase, I hear his laughter. It is so important for Martin to win.

4

'How thrilling,' Ali says, as we stroll through the school gates and out into Carlton Road.

Highfields Primary School is carved out of two grand Victorian villas knocked together on the corner of the main artery through Hasleford. I glance back at the building for a final wave at Lucas but he's already deep in conversation with Briony, Ali's eldest.

'Hang on.' I unhitch Joy from the railings, because Ali has walked straight past her dog. Leonie, Ali's three-year-old daughter, is leaning out of her pram, twisting round anxiously.

Ali reaches back for the lead with a self-deprecating laugh. 'Damn pregnancy brain. I'm sure you can get Martin to change his mind.'

Ali Gordon is my sister-in-law, and best friend. She's on maternity leave and due to have her third baby in two months' time. She gets tired easily and has piled on the weight, but despite this, I have no doubt she'll be back at work three months after she's given birth. Ali has a way of saying 'I'm absolutely fine' that will get her into trouble one of these days.

'I don't know,' I muse. 'Maybe he's right. You have to be so careful with tenants. It can be really hard to get rid of the bad ones.'

'You must be a pretty good judge by now.'

We amble along at Ali's current snail's pace, and turn into Boundary Road where we've agreed to stop for a coffee before going our separate ways. Hasleford is thriving. It had its heyday in the sixties and seventies, declined in the eighties but has seen a revival since the millennium, discovered once again by young families. Boundary Road has a good end and a bad end. The bad end is run-down and litter-strewn; the so-called good end has pretensions. Expensive butchers and fishmongers have moved in, as have cafés dedicated to indulging children, like my daughter's favourite, Boiled Eggs and Soldiers, and expensive clothes shops for well-to-do mummies. Even the charity shops are aspirational, their clothes curated rather than hung haphazardly, one of them dedicated to vintage clothes and accessories.

Ali chats about this and that while my mind wanders. Has Susie from Hooper's broken the news to Dan yet? I feel rotten for getting his hopes up, but it's not like I owe him anything. He's a total stranger and, as Martin said, who does what he did?

Ali prods me. 'Am I boring you?'

'Sorry, I was miles away.'

'Something wrong?'

She takes my arm and gives it a squeeze. I've never been a touchy-feely person, but Ali is.

'No. It's nothing. Just life.'

'Well, God, I wouldn't want to be married to my brother.'

I laugh, because she's only joking. She worships Martin. She has no idea that I'm unhappy, that I fantasize about leaving him, that the fear of what he knows about me and what he could do with that knowledge is all that ties me to him now. I look at the way Joy is tripping daintily along at Ali's feet. Perfect trust. I'm jealous of a dog.

I'm about to reply when a man whips past, yanking my bag off my shoulder so violently that the leather strap scratches my arm. Ali lets out a shriek, startling Leonie and Joy.

'Hey!' I shout.

I charge after him but he's too quick for me, dodging through the pedestrians. As I bend over, crippled by a stitch, I realize an onlooker has given chase. He grabs him by his shoulder, whirls him round and pins him against the door to the flats above a craft shop. I jog up to them, panting. The mugger looks about forty, with skinny limbs and hollow cheeks. His face is weathered, his eyes bloodshot and weepy. I'm surprised he found the energy to mug me.

I break into a helpless smile when I see who my saviour is.

'Dan! Thank you so much.'

Dan is out of breath too. He grins as he hands me my bag. Our fingers touch briefly.

'That's my cardio for the day. What do you want me to do with him?' He palms his phone, his thumb poised to swipe.

'I don't know.'

He looks pensive. 'He's desperate, poor fellow. But if

you want to press charges, I can call the police. It's up to you.'

'That was impressive,' Ali says, using the pram to push her way through the crowd, her flyaway hair escaping its clip, her voluminous dove-grey linen dress making her look like a ship in full sail. The crowd melt back for her. 'Are you OK?' Joy jumps up at the man, and Ali jerks her lead.

'Never mind me. What about you?' I look her over with concern. What if this shocks her into labour?

'I'm fine, really.'

'You should sit down,' Dan says. 'Why don't you go into Nico's?' He indicates the café a few doors down. 'I'll get you a glass of water.'

'Don't fuss.' Ali looks at me, her eyebrows raised, and I remember my manners.

'Ali, this is Dan.' I feel unaccountably coy. 'Dan, this is Ali.'

It all feels very formal and strange, what with Dan restraining a trembling wraith of a human being.

'Poor chap,' Ali says, bending over the pram to check her daughter hasn't been traumatized. Leonie seems unfazed as she gazes up at them, her thumb in her mouth.

Ali works for the local council and has a strong social conscience, unlike Martin who has little sympathy for those living in deprivation. It's sometimes hard to believe they're related.

'Shall I call the police?' Dan says.

I pause. The man looks sullen, but at the same time pathetic and vulnerable. I have some idea what that feels like.

'Let him go,' I say.

Ali smiles her approval and Dan gives me a nod, and I feel a little glow inside from their approbation. It's for the best. If the police get involved, this is going to turn into something. Martin will overreact. It'll be my fault in some way. Not paying enough attention.

I open my bag, take out my purse and extract a ten-pound note. 'Get yourself something to eat,' I say.

Dan queries my decision with one eloquently raised eyebrow, then releases his captive. The man pauses, stuffs the tenner into his jeans pocket, then walks off without a word of apology or thanks.

'That was kind of you. Not many people would have done that.'

I brush Dan's compliment aside. 'Did Hooper's get in touch?'

'Yeah.' His mouth twists in an awkward attempt to smile.

'I'm so sorry.'

'Don't worry about it.'

'It's my husband. He likes things done by the book.'

'Well, he's right. I don't know what I was thinking. I'm seriously embarrassed about the whole episode, so let's forget it happened.'

'Where were you?' Ali asks him. She's been watching the exchange with interest. 'You came out of nowhere.'

'I was getting some work done in Nico's. I saw it happen and acted on instinct.' He grins. 'I'd better go. I left my laptop on the table by the window. If it's stolen, that will be the icing on the cake as far as my life is concerned.'

'Well, thank you,' I say. 'Thank you so much.'

'*De nada*. Nice to meet you, Ali.'

His smile slips as he turns to walk back to Nico's. There's a sadness about him that makes me want to call him back.

'Bloody hell,' Ali says. 'He's easy on the eye, isn't he? I'm not surprised you wanted to offer him the tenancy.'

'What?' I blush, caught out. Dan hasn't been far from my thoughts since I met him. 'Don't be daft. God, I can't believe that happened.'

'You owe him now.'

I look after Dan, noticing the way his shoulders are hunched forwards. 'Do you think so?'

'He could have had a knife,' Martin says.

'If he did, I didn't see it.' I don't want Martin to see how shaken I am, in case he decides to curtail my freedom even more than he does already. The only reason I've told him is because I want him to change his mind about Dan. 'It was an opportunistic mugging. And I got my bag back, thanks to Dan. Martin, couldn't you—'

'Ali and Leonie could have been hurt, have you thought of that? And what if you'd had our children with you?'

'He needed a square meal, not the entire Hasleford Constabulary after him,' I say, making light of it. 'I don't think he would have harmed them. It honestly wasn't that dramatic. We were never in any danger.'

My phone vibrates, and I glance at the screen.

'The electrician's outside the flat. I've got to go. Can

we just do Dan the courtesy of interviewing him? He deserves that, don't you think?'

'I'll see him,' Martin says. 'But I'm not making any promises.'

His smile is perfunctory as he beckons me over. I rest my hands on the arms of his wheelchair and kiss him. As soon as I shut the front door, I wipe the kiss away. That is not what wives are supposed to do. It feels significant somehow; a moment I'll remember because it marked a change in me.

5

Dan turns up at our house at the stipulated time the following Saturday morning. His finances have checked out, his character references – from one of his clients and a magistrate; a long-standing friend of the family – are glowing, and there are no county court judgments against his name or complaints from previous landlords. Susie assured me he'd had the platinum treatment.

The children have been promised a swim if they're quiet and well-behaved. With six-year-old Lucas this is a given; with Aurora, well, I'll have to wait and see. I feel a weird tightness in my diaphragm at the prospect of seeing Dan again. It has less to do with his heroics and more with the way he picked specks of paint off my face without asking. Without that, I don't think he would have registered so strongly. But still, it was nothing really. I'm sure it was nothing to him.

If Dan is surprised when he sees Martin's wheelchair, he doesn't show it. He nods a greeting and takes a seat at the kitchen table while I fiddle nervously with the coffee machine. He's dressed for the occasion, in as much as he's wearing a proper shirt rather than an over-washed T-shirt. Same ripped jeans.

Martin looks him up and down swiftly. Aurora, always anxious not to miss out, picks this moment to fling herself at her father. I call upstairs to Isabel, our au pair. She runs down, smiles at the men and wishes them a good morning, in her lilting French accent.

Isabel Gardin has a little more personal allure than I'd normally be happy with in an au pair, but good au pairs are hard to come by these days, and she is good, willing to clean as well as look after the children. She's been with us for six weeks. She is twenty-one years old, naive but also knowing. She has ambition. She's perfecting her English with us, then she intends to live in Paris and work in fashion. Martin tolerates her, like he's tolerated all our au pairs, with reasonably good humour and a tendency to tease.

Aurora sticks her thumb in her mouth. She stares unblinking at Dan.

He grins at her. 'What's your name?'

Aurora takes her thumb out of her mouth. 'Orwa.'

'That's pretty. How old are you?'

'Free. How old are you?'

'Aurora,' Isabel admonishes. 'That is not polite.'

'It's all right,' Dan says, chuckling. 'I asked her, after all. I'm thirty-three.'

The number is incalculable to my daughter. She would have been more impressed if he'd said ten.

'Not too old, not too young,' Isabel comments, flicking her hair.

22

Too old for you, I think, then tell myself off for being judgemental.

'Let's go play, *mignonne*,' Isabel says, scooping her up and kissing her plump cheek.

Aurora giggles and kisses her back, and I suppress a spurt of jealousy. I want her to love my children, after all.

'I thought you were younger,' Martin says, looking pointedly at the rips exposing Dan's knees. Martin doesn't like anything that smacks of a casual attitude to life and work.

'Good genes, I suppose,' Dan says cheerily.

Martin grills Dan for the next half-hour, asking where he's from – Sussex – and what his parents do for a living – homemaker and company director – and to my relief seems OK with his responses. I allow myself to hope this man will win my husband over.

'So what brought you to Hasleford?' Martin asks.

Dan flashes me a smile. I'm surprised when my belly does a little flip.

'Oh, you know, I'd been working in Canada. When I came back to the UK, I tried London, but after seven years in Vancouver it didn't suit me. I moved here about eighteen months ago because of a girl. I thought we'd get married, have kids, the lot, but that relationship ended recently. Hasleford has grown on me. You get a lot more for your money. In London I'd have a studio flat in a dump. Here I can have a beautiful two-bedroom flat around the corner from the shops and the station and a spit away from open country. Can't ask for more than that.'

'So you know people here already? You have friends?'

'Martin,' I say. 'You have no right to ask questions like that.'

'That's OK,' Dan says. 'After what I did, your husband has a right to check I'm not a nutcase no-mates loner.'

Martin looks irritated. I attempt not to wince, but Dan has patronized him. Martin will remember that.

'I do have friends in the area,' Dan says, seemingly oblivious. 'As I said, I don't have a girlfriend, but if I meet someone and want her to move in with me, I'll introduce you, and if you're happy, we can get a new tenancy agreement drawn up. Can't see it happening any time soon though.'

His eyes darken, but the smile remains in place. He's been hurt. I want to say something sympathetic but stop myself; this is a conversation between landlord and potential tenant, not a new friendship. Martin wouldn't like me making it personal.

'So,' I say, 'I take it you're still interested in Linden Road?'

'If you'll have me.'

There's a subtle change in Martin's expression. 'You're all right for the next couple of weeks while we finish the work?'

'Yeah. But I'm on a mate's sofa, so the sooner the better. So, what's the next step?'

Martin stares straight at him, then he smiles. 'Hooper's can take it from here. I'll give them a call. I hope you'll be happy there.'

There's an infinitesimal pause, as if a subliminal message has passed between them, and then Dan stands up to indicate he's leaving and it's all friendly smiles again.

As Martin leads Dan across the hall, he points out some of the features of the house and Dan is suitably impressed. When he arrived he would have thought nothing of the fact that the elegant, sloping forecourt is flush to the threshold, or that the doorways are wider than is conventional. He wouldn't have noticed the lift discreetly concealed behind a door, or the fact that one of the two top-of-the-range electric Audis parked on the driveway has been modified. That's the whole point. You have to look closely to see that allowances have been made for Martin's disability.

On the lower ground floor, there's a gym where Martin does weight training, a massage room and a swimming pool. He swims thirty lengths most days; at dawn if he wakes early, or in the late afternoon. He doesn't have any fancy gadgets for getting in and out of the pool. To get in, he locks his wheelchair about two feet from the side, at the corner of the shallow end. He has a cushioned mat that he places in front of him and to the right. He leans down and places a hand on the mat to create a bridge, and then transfers himself. Once he's in position he goes in head-first. He wears diving socks to protect his feet from abrasions, but also because his legs tend to drift and the socks give some buoyancy. He hasn't used a floatation belt in years. Getting out is harder, and he tried several ways before he found the one he was most comfortable with. With his back to the corner, he puts his hands on the side, sinks down then pulls himself up. Once he's correctly positioned on the mat, he unlocks the wheelchair, moves it round behind him, locks it, pulls up his legs, leans them against the front of the chair, and heaves himself up using his legs for extra support.

On the face of it, this house has everything. All it lacks is a beating heart. It's not so bad when the children are around, but when they're out it feels emotionally unreachable. To me at least. Martin won't hear a word against it.

'This place is awesome.' Dan says. 'How old is it?'

'It was finished four years ago,' Martin says.

'You commissioned it?'

'I designed it. With the help of an architect, of course. But yes, it was my vision.'

The architect in question is Pete Gordon, Martin's brother-in-law and closest friend. He is Ali's husband.

Dan whistles through his teeth. 'I'd love to see round it one day. Do you ever open the house to the public?'

'No,' Martin says, 'it's an invitation to criminals.'

A shadow crosses his face. Before we built Winterfell, we rented a single-storey house outside town. One afternoon, while I was out, Martin opened the door to a man in a balaclava who pushed his way in. The intruder tipped Martin out of his chair, then calmly wandered around helping himself. He laughed at my husband, stranded on the floor, his wrist broken, his face bruised, and let himself out having loaded up his van. But it wasn't the items he took that devastated Martin, it was the wholly unnecessary humiliation.

Winterfell is as secure as it could possibly be without

turning the place into a fortress. The front door is made of steel and there are security shutters and cameras positioned at every corner, scanning the grounds and the street beyond the gate.

'Are you interested in architecture?' Martin asks.

'I'm interested in anything to do with cutting-edge design. From houses to commercial developments, to space travel. I love exciting projects. This place is deceptive. I only saw the space and felt the dynamism. I wouldn't have guessed the owner was in a wheelchair.'

'That was the plan,' Martin says.

'And I love all the concrete. It's an amazing material. You'd think it would make the place feel cold but actually it's so textured that it gives it that extra dimension. It makes you want to touch it, doesn't it?'

'It's also one of the most energy efficient materials,' Martin says. 'We're practically carbon neutral here.'

Isabel comes out of the playroom, her denim jacket casually hooked over her shoulder with a finger.

'It is OK if I go now?' she asks, making a play of checking the time on her phone.

There are subtle changes in her appearance. It's like a spot-the-difference competition. Her hair is down and brushed, she's applied mascara to her eyelashes, and she's undone another button on her shirt.

Her timing is impeccable. Almost as though she's been listening out for Dan's departure. And who can blame her? Dan is attractive and she's complained about the lack of boyfriend material here. She has a point. This is a very family-friendly area – there aren't many eligible bachelors around.

I shift my gaze to Dan to see how he's reacting to Isabel. He is watching her, but then he turns and catches my eye instead.

'Yes,' I say to her, somehow feeling like I've won a battle neither of us knew we were fighting. 'Have a lovely afternoon, and thanks for this morning.'

'Which way are you headed?' Dan asks.

Her eyes sweep him. 'To the station. I am meeting my friends in London.'

'Cool. I'm going in that direction. I'll keep you company – if you don't mind, that is.'

'You can walk where you like,' Isabel says.

They don't see – or perhaps they ignore – my wave as they stroll down the path, side by side, Isabel laughing, her bouncing, shiny hair catching the sun.

'Jealous?' Martin enquires.

My stomach knots. 'Not at all.'

'Who was he?' my son asks suspiciously. I hadn't seen Lucas standing in the door to the playroom, Aurora beside him. I hope they didn't hear.

'Just someone who wants to rent the new flat. Thank you for being so good and quiet.'

'He's tall,' Lucas says.

'He can't help that,' I say, ruffling my son's hair. 'Go and get your swim shorts on. I'll be ready in five minutes.'

'Yes!' He punches the air. 'He smiles a lot.'

'With his teeth,' Aurora says.

'Like a big old crocodile,' Martin says, reaching to grab her. He plonks her on his knee and pretends to bite her arm. She squeals and wriggles round until she can wrap her arms around his neck.

'You're not a crocodile, Daddy.'
'What am I then?'
'You're a nice man.'
He looks up, triumphant. Out of the mouths of babes.
I wish he was the man they think he is.

6

It's a searing morning, the last day of June, when Dan moves into 42 Linden Road. I'm already there, watching from the front window, breaking into a smile when he pulls up and manoeuvres a U-Drive van into a tight parking space.

I put the door on the latch and go outside, feeling unaccountably shy. I've seen Dan several times since our first meeting, but I still feel an illicit excitement about the prospect. It's silly; I haven't felt this way since I first met Martin, who was with someone at the time and thus should have been out of bounds. The knowledge that it was wrong, that I ought, in all conscience, to have avoided him but couldn't, honestly couldn't, stop thinking about him, imagining the impossible, was so delicious. I chide myself. Dan is not interested in me like that. He's just my tenant and I'm sure all he sees is a landlady, a married one. With that humbling thought, I greet him.

'What a lovely morning.'

Dan looks up at the sky, as if he hasn't noticed, and smiles. 'A good omen.'

'Shall we get you checked in?' I say. I will not smile

too much, or play with my hair, or look him too long in the eye. There are so many things to think about, so many potential ways to inadvertently show that I have a bit of a crush, that it's hard to form sentences. 'Then I can leave you in peace.'

He signs the inventory, I quickly run through meter readings, the burglar alarm, appliance serial numbers, central heating instructions, and then I hand over the keys.

'Shall we crack open the bubbly?' he asks, his eyebrows raised, his smile crooked and boyish.

He opens a wall cabinet and takes down two glasses, hanging them upside down between his fingers. We always leave a bottle of champagne in the fridge for new tenants as a gesture of goodwill.

I shake my head even as my pulse races. I think about Lucas and Aurora. I think about failing them. I think about how hard I've worked.

'Save it for when your friends come round.'

'Nah. I'd rather do it now. Savour the moment.'

I swallow. He's going to open it. I rest my hand lightly on his wrist to stop him twisting the wire that holds the cork in place. His skin is warm and rough with hairs; the muscles move under my fingers. I drop my hand, embarrassed to have touched him, hoping he doesn't read anything into it.

'I don't drink,' I say. 'I'm an alcoholic.'

Dan doesn't comment; he merely returns the bottle to the fridge and runs cold water into the glasses.

'What shall we toast to?' he asks.

My diaphragm relaxes.

'A trouble-free tenancy?'

He hands me a glass. 'Too boring. To surprises.'

'Surprises?'

'You were a surprise.'

I blush. It's the nicest compliment I've had in ages. Martin's compliments are meaningless and are often a subtle taunt or a way of underlining his point.

'Shall we go outside?' Dan adds before I can ask what he means.

I glance at my watch. 'Ten minutes, then I really must go.' I unlock and open the back door. 'And don't you have work to do?'

'I've given myself the day off. There's no hurry.'

Not for him. I told Martin I'd be back by ten and I've no excuse to be out any longer; no shopping to do, no other tenancies to deal with. It's twenty-five to now. I can't afford to be late again so soon, particularly as the delay would involve Dan for the second time.

At the top of the wrought-iron steps, tendrils of ivy wind through the banister and the heady scent of a rose the colour of ripe peaches fills the air. At the end, where the garden catches the afternoon sun, there's a small barbecue and a bistro-style aluminium table. You can't hear the traffic from here; only birdsong, and the sounds of domesticity coming from open windows along the backs of the houses.

I take my jacket off and carefully hang it over the back of a chair.

'So tell me about you,' Dan says, stretching his legs out to the side.

'There's really not much to tell. I went to school, went to uni, went travelling, met Martin. I found a job and we got married. Then he had his accident and everything changed.'

My life summed up in four sentences. I'm so used to glossing over the details that it costs me nothing to do it with this man.

'God. Poor chap. He's done astonishingly well.'

I smile. 'He certainly wouldn't appreciate being called a "poor chap". He's proud of what he's achieved since it happened. I don't know anyone else with his determination.'

I don't tell Dan that when I got the call, I thought Martin was dead and that for one shameful second I felt relief. But he didn't die, and I didn't want to be the woman who jettisons her husband when he's no longer able-bodied. I tied myself to him out of pity and pride. And cowardice. And, as it turns out, he has proved himself more than capable of looking after us all. It's just that I don't want him to any more. I realize now, with a sense of despair, that the feelings I seem to be developing for Dan are probably more to do with Martin than the man himself. It's like I'm drowning and reaching out to the first person to float by on a life raft.

'You must have been terrified,' Dan says.

'I was, but I underestimated him. Martin isn't an object of pity. If anything, people envy him. The children have never known him any other way.'

'I admire him. Not many men would have achieved as much as he has in such a short space of time. But he has that dynamism, doesn't he? That can-do attitude. I'd love to meet him again sometime. Talk to him.' Dan laughs. 'Maybe some of that magic could rub off on me.'

I nod in response. Admiration is probably the only positive feeling I have left for my husband.

'With Martin, you have to show that you're willing to grasp the nettle. He has no time for people who stand at the edge watching others do the work. He's a self-made man.'

'It seems to me you've achieved a lot too.'

'Thank you. But it's really Martin. I've just come along for the ride.'

'Oh, I doubt that.'

I smile. Let him think what he likes. I'm enjoying the moment. Martin doesn't know I'm sitting here. He doesn't know I feel a million miles from him, temporarily free, talking to an attractive man who appears to like me. It might be that Dan Jones is the kind of character who makes everyone he meets think he enjoys their company above all others, but I don't care. It's a relief for once to be with someone who doesn't pick apart everything I say.

'You shouldn't put yourself down. I think you're remarkable.'

'You know nothing about me.'

'No, I don't. But I have a sixth sense for people who step up to the mark.'

I put my glass down slowly. He's talking about me being an able-bodied woman with a handicapped husband. He's not the first to subtly infer that I must be a saint to stay. Much as I dislike my husband, I will defend his abilities to the hilt.

'I should go.'

His face falls, then he laughs out loud, throwing his head back. 'Oh shit. I've said the wrong thing. I do it all the time. My sister called it foot in mouth disease. I don't know what I said to offend you, but I'm truly sorry. Again.'

My phone pings. It's Martin, wanting to know if I'm on my way home. I stand up and Dan follows me to the steps.

'Thank you for being my first guest.'

Our eyes meet and something slowly spirals up through my body, a light, twisting thing, like smoke from a cigarette. I feel self-conscious so I say the first thing that comes into my head.

'You and Isabel seemed to hit it off.'

'Isabel?'

'My au pair.'

'Oh, yes. She seems very nice.'

'Just nice?'

He cocks his head, looks at me until my cheeks burn. 'What are you angling for, Mrs Curran?'

'Sorry,' I stammer out. 'None of my business.'

35

7

The children have gone to bed and Martin and I are in the garden making the most of a balmy evening. Martin is on a call. He's talking to a client; it doesn't matter that it's the weekend, money doesn't kick back.

I get up from my chair and wander to the far end of the lawn with my glass of elderflower pressé. Beyond the lawn is the wild area where the children have their treehouse and a stone path winds through shrubs to the compost heap at the back. It's shady and mysterious. I follow the path, thinking about the rejected champagne with a mixture of pride and despair. It wouldn't have ended well. I'd have drunk most of the bottle and made a fool of myself with a man I barely know. I did well and I need to keep that thought in my mind.

Martin's voice rises. He's animated, as he always is when he's showing off his knowledge and expertise. I used to find it sexy. Now it's merely something else to be endured.

A movement makes me glance up at our bedroom window and I frown, wondering if one of the children is in there. It's Isabel. What's she doing? She doesn't have any reason to be in our bedroom. I keep it clean and tidy myself. I'm about to investigate when the gate buzzer sounds. Martin's still yakking. Without looking at me, he flicks his finger in the direction of the house. I go inside and check the monitor and involuntarily smile. It's Dan. How odd. I wonder what he wants.

I press the buzzer then sweep my hands across the front of my skirt, and pull my stomach in. I feel terribly nervous. It's the idea of being with Dan and Martin at the same time, of accidentally alerting Martin to the fact that I fancy our tenant.

'Hi,' Dan says, striding across the forecourt as I open the front door. 'Is she ready?'

The penny drops.

'I'll give her a shout.' I leave him standing outside and go to the bottom of the stairs. 'Isabel! Dan's here!'

'*Deux minutes*,' she calls back. 'Tell him to wait please, Eliza.'

I scowl, irritated, but I pass the message on, although Dan will have heard it. I feel very stupid.

'Come in,' I say, doing my best to sound like a land-lady, not the woman he entertained in his garden. Our conversation became personal; I wasn't imagining it. But maybe I misread the signals. It's been a while. 'You can wait for her in the garden. Beer? There's only alcohol-free, I'm afraid.'

I lead him through to the kitchen, wondering why this is so crushing. Just because I saw him first doesn't give me ownership. I reach into the fridge for the beer, and manage to drop the opener. Dan bends and picks it up, takes the bottle out of my hand and pops the lid.

'Everything OK?' he asks. 'You seem nervous.'

'Not at all. It's just that Martin doesn't particularly like people turning up out of the blue.'

'Ah. That's understandable, but Isabel knew.'

'Of course. She should have said something, but she probably just didn't think.'

We step outside. Martin swivels his chair round when he hears us, finally off the phone. His expression isn't welcoming.

'Don't worry.' Dan sounds friendly and relaxed. 'I'm not after a new lightbulb.'

'Dan's come for Isabel.'

'Oh, right.'

He offers Dan a chair and we sit down, all of us facing away from the house, as if we are an audience for a play about to take place on the lawn. Dan is between Martin and me, his hand curled round the bottle. He leans back and breathes a contented sigh.

'This place is a sanctuary,' he says.

'We think so,' Martin says.

'It was so stiflingly conventional where I was brought up, everyone the same, curtains twitching. It was all about where you got your cushions and keeping up with the neighbours. You've done what you wanted, and sod the John Lewis catalogue.'

'Exactly,' Martin says, practically purring. I'm impressed. Dan has worked out exactly where Martin likes to be scratched. 'If you want to get anywhere, you need to make a conscious decision not to be afraid to surprise people. We are hard-wired to provide what our fellow humans want and expect. If you do something they don't want, and don't expect, you confuse them, but you can also delight. The trick is to have absolute faith in your own decisions. Any self-doubt and people become wary. But you aren't ashamed of showing enthusiasm. I like that.'

'Where are you taking Isabel?' I ask.

Even though she's an adult I feel responsible for her. She comes from a tiny village. She told me that she had been in a relationship since she was fifteen, but that they had broken up when she came away, because he wanted to get married and she wanted an adventure.

'The Duck and Drake.'

'It'll be heaving,' I say.

The pub is on the river, and a favourite with the locals. We go there from time to time.

'We'll cope.'

Dan's foot shifts against mine. I go rigid, aware of my entire body, of my nerves crackling, my muscles tensing, the hairs on my arms standing up. He's wearing shoes; I'm barefoot. It might be that he hasn't realized. I move my foot away. There's no repeat, so I give him the benefit of the doubt.

'Isn't she a little young for you?' Martin says.

Dan waits before he responds. I'm not sure if that's because he's shocked by the intrusive nature of the question, or because he's as measured as my husband.

'Probably,' he says. 'But she asked me. It would have been rude to say no.'

Martin stretches his hands above his neck. 'I consider myself in loco parentis where Isabel's concerned.'

Dan smiles. 'It's just a drink, mate. It's cool.'

Isabel appears, smiling shyly. She's wearing a kingfisher-blue cotton summer dress with scalloped shoulders that brings out the colour of her eyes. It's demure, but at the same time provocative. A gold chain with her star sign, a golden crab, hangs around her neck, drawing attention to the curve of her breasts. Another gold chain is looped around her right ankle. That's why she was in my bedroom, I realize. She'll have wanted to look at herself in the full-length mirror. She should have asked, but it wasn't an unacceptable invasion, just thoughtless. I might have a word with her about boundaries.

'You look lovely, Isabel. Doesn't she, Martin?'

Martin grunts then pushes his wheelchair back. 'Very pretty. Take good care of her, Dan.'

'Oh, I will.'

Isabel is gazing at me, an odd gleam in her eye that I don't like, then she shifts impatiently. '*On y va*, Dan. Let's go. You two be good.'

I smile. How can she live in our house and be so unaware? But perhaps she isn't. Perhaps she's mocking us.

'Hang on,' Martin says. 'That reminds me. I've got something for Isabel. You too, Eliza.'

He pushes himself into the house and comes back with an Amazon package. 'They arrived today. After that incident in Boundary Road, I thought you should both have some protection.' He opens the box, takes out two personal alarms and hands one to each of us.

'Thanks,' Isabel says, looking at it dubiously. 'But I think I am safe with Dan.'

'Take it anyway. I'd feel better knowing you have it.'

They leave. I lift my glass to my lips. The elderflower

has warmed and tastes overly sweet. A wasp investigates, and I wave it away. It returns and alights on the edge of the glass, wings twitching in anticipation.

'That was thoughtful of you,' I say.

Martin puts his hand on my knee and I let it rest there. I make myself focus on the fragrance of the evening, the warmth, the birds, the calm. Breathe. Ignore the weight of his hand. Breathe. Behind us the house rises dark and geometric, a modern palace, designed to protect, to secure. To hold.

'Does it bother you?' Martin asks.

'What do you mean?'

'That he prefers her.'

I sit very still. A squirrel jumps from the apple tree onto the wall and scuttles along it, pauses to peer at us then goes on his way.

'Why would it bother me? What about you? Are you jealous of him?'

'Don't be ridiculous.'

'Well, don't you be ridiculous either then. I'm going to have a bath.'

I push my chair back abruptly and stomp upstairs. Ten minutes later I look out of our bedroom window. Martin hasn't moved. I get into the bath I don't even want, and sink slowly into the hot water. You have to face your demons, Martin says. He is good at that; in a combative situation he steps up, not down. Fight not flight. Even in the aftermath of the accident, he refused to give in to self-doubt and fear; although it was there, I know it was. In the aftermath of my father's death I knew little else. I had spent my childhood in a state of anxiety, constantly alert to threat, and when that threat was taken away, I was left with something else; a sense of failure. Why had it been death that got the better of my father, and not me? It took years. Now it's all packed away, door after door closed on it. Sometimes I take a peek, just to test my resilience, but facing my demons has never really helped. The only thing that has ever obliterated them is alcohol.

8

Isabel stays up in London with her friends on Sunday so it's Monday morning before I get the chance to ask her about her date with Dan.

'Good weekend?'

'Super,' she says, extending the *e* and rolling the *r*.

'So, what did you think of the Duck and Drake?'

'Pretty. We sat on the riverbank.'

'Do you like him?' I put down the cup I've been holding, and give her an encouraging smile.

'I think so, yes.' She blushes faintly. 'He is funny. And handsome. He is not like my boyfriend was. He is mature, no?'

'He's a lot older than you, Isabel.'

'The same age as you, I think. But it does not matter in a man.'

I raise my eyebrows, but she doesn't notice, or if she does, she doesn't care that what she said was borderline insolent.

'I like it,' she burbles on. 'He has experience, and he is so . . . how do you say it . . . *confiant*. Ah, *merde*.'

'Confident,' I supply. 'Self-confident.'

'Yes. We had fun.'

'And, er, are you intending to have more fun, with him?'

She looks me in the eye, and smiles. There's definitely a challenge there. She likes the idea that I might be attracted to him but no match for her. The arrogance of youth. I wonder whether she pities me, whether she thinks Martin casts a lascivious eye over her too. Almost overnight I've become hyper aware of Isabel as an inviting package; that gorgeous young body, that pretty face with its big blue eyes, freckled nose and flirtatious smile.

'Just be careful,' I say.

'Oh, Eliza,' she laughs, making me feel ancient. 'I can look after myself.'

I call after her as she sashays off. 'Can you get the kids' teeth brushed? Lucas, run upstairs with Isabel now. I don't want you to be late.'

Ali and her girls come home with us after school. When the kids have been fed, Isabel puts on a Disney show-tune CD and dances with Aurora and Leonie while Lucas and Briony, wearing fluffy bedsocks, take turns pulling each other around the polished concrete floor. Aurora asks for this CD most days. We only have ourselves to blame. It was short-sighted of Martin and me to give our daughter the name of a Disney Princess, unwittingly selling the idea of happily ever after. I believed in handsome princes once, someone who would rescue me, and look where it's got me. I was a fool to think I could escape my childhood nightmares through marriage.

There is something in the way Isabel plays with Aurora when I'm there to witness it that irritates me. It's as if she's saying, *Look how much your daughter adores me.* Maybe I'm imagining it, but it feels passive aggressive.

Ali is stretched out on the sofa, a criminally expensive and uncomfortable Swedish designer piece – Martin's choice – a mug of tea beside her, her feet up, her hand resting on the steep incline of her pregnant belly.

'Budge up,' I say, and Ali shifts her bare feet to make room. We watch Aurora and Leonie jump about with abandon whilst Isabel slinks her way around the room. She moves in a way I can only describe as *undulating.* Ali gazes at her for a moment then sends me a mischievous look, raising her eyebrows.

'She's a very expressive dancer,' she mutters.

I almost snort with laughter. 'That's one way of putting it.'

I watch Isabel. Her eyes are bright, her cheeks flushed.

'She's started seeing someone,' I say, quietly enough not to be heard above the music.

'Oh, really? Have you met him?'

I pause, something obstructing the words. 'It's our tenant.'

'Oh, the ninja!' Ali laughs loudly and Isabel looks our way. 'Is that going to be awkward?' She speaks into her mug.

'I hope not.'

'Do you mind?'

I give the question some thought. 'Not really. I mean, she does get on my nerves sometimes, but I'm glad she's happy. Are you organizing some help for when this one arrives?'

Ali makes a face. 'Probably not. Our house is so small and chaotic. They'd run a mile. Mum will help.'

Martin and Ali's mother, Kate, lives about forty minutes away.

'You could share some of Isabel's hours. I won't need her so much once Aurora starts nursery in September.'

Ali picks up another flapjack, takes a bite and brushes the crumbs off her front.

'That's very kind of you, and it would be great. I'll pay for her time, of course.'

'You don't have to do that. In fact, you would be doing me a favour. Isabel can look after all the children here in the summer holidays too. It'll make life a lot easier for me if Aurora and Lucas are entertained.'

'I want to pay my fair share. I don't want to take advantage.'

'But you wouldn't be. You never do. I don't know what I'd do without you. You were so incredibly kind to me when Martin was in hospital. I would have fallen apart without you.' I ought to add 'and Pete', but I can't bring myself to. I move on before she notices. 'I won't take no for an answer. We'll set up a schedule. Save your pennies for the newbie.'

Ali closes her eyes, breathes in and out, her hands on her stomach.

'Are you OK?'

'Braxton Hicks. They'll pass.'

She goes quiet after that. I try to talk to her, but get monosyllabic replies.

46

'Have I offended you? I have, haven't I?'

She flushes and flaps her hands, as if she's trying to bat away the question.

'No, of course not. Don't look so mortified. I know you only want to help. I'm being over-sensitive. It's just that if I share your childcare without contributing financially, Martin won't let me forget it. Or Pete, which is potentially more of a problem.'

I cringe, knowing that there's some truth in that, at least where Pete is concerned. 'Martin adores you both and you know it. Let him help if he wants to.'

A phone pings. Ali and I glance at our phones. My screen is blank. Isabel takes her mobile out of her back pocket, reads a message, then looks at me.

'Are you OK if I finish now? Dan is here.'

'Yes, of course. Enjoy yourself.'

'Can I ask him to come in? I need to get changed.'

'Do whatever you like. This is your home too.'

I compose myself as she darts upstairs. At least there isn't the added element of surprise this time. Isabel has mentioned their date more than once today.

'Has she read *Keep Him Keen for Dummies*?' Ali whispers.

'Very funny,' I whisper back. Then I add, 'Probably.'

'Hey.' Dan strolls in.

He glances at me but I look away, at Lucas who is sitting on the floor trying to cuddle Joy, who strains away from him, scrabbling her paws against his chest, much more interested in the new arrival.

Just after Dan, Martin pushes himself through the door. He takes in the scene: me and Ali, the little girls,

Joy sitting at Dan's feet, regarding him slavishly. Dan with his thumbs hooked into his belt, embracing us all with his wide smile.

'Daddy!' Aurora squeals, running to him. Joy jerks her head round and gives a polite woof but doesn't leave Dan's side. 'We did dancing!'

'Is that what the noise was? I thought a herd of baby elephants had got in.'

Leonie and Aurora fall about laughing.

'You're here to see Isabel again, I assume?' Martin asks Dan.

'Yes, we're going for an early supper, then the cinema.'

'Two dates in as many days. You certainly don't hang around.'

'You don't have to worry,' Dan smiles. 'It isn't serious.'

'Maybe not for you, but I for one don't relish the idea of a miserable au pair mooning round the house because you haven't replied to her texts. It's Eliza and me who'll have to pick up the pieces when it all goes wrong.'

'Isabel's a grown woman,' Dan says. There's a sliver of steel in his voice. 'She can make her own choices.'

Martin's eyes narrow. 'Isabel is here to look after my children and help my wife. I don't want her distracted.'

There's an uncomfortable silence. Ali is looking from Dan to Martin. She has a nose for an awkward situation. She reaches for Martin's hand.

'OK, Grandpa. Isabel is old enough to look after herself. If she gets her heart broken, that's part of growing up. And you never know,' she says, with a sly look Dan's way, 'the boot might be on the other foot. Who's going to pick up the pieces for you, Dan, if Isabel breaks your heart?'

'Ah, no one,' Dan says. 'Unless you're offering.'

'Ha ha,' Ali says. 'Good luck to both of you.'

Martin looks as though he's about to object, then his shoulders relax and he smiles. 'Sorry, mate. You're right, it's none of my business. Why don't you and Isabel have supper with us on Saturday? You and Pete too, Ali.'

My eyes fly to Dan's face. For a second his expression changes. He has the panicky look of a teenage boy for whom things are moving too fast.

'Whoa,' Ali laughs. 'Bit intense. Give them a chance, poor things.'

'It's cool,' Dan says. 'He's calling my bluff, aren't you, dude?'

Martin arches his eyebrows, but Dan only laughs, his equanimity restored.

'I'm up for it if Isabel is.'

'Brave man,' Ali says. 'He's got your measure, Martin.'

I think she could be right. No one else would dare call Martin 'dude'. Dan Jones interests me more and more.

Isabel swings into the kitchen in a pretty summer dress, a denim jacket over her shoulders. We all admire her, as if we're admiring our children; but she's not a child. She's a woman, and a desirable one at that.

'Martin and Eliza have invited us for dinner on Saturday,' Dan says, 'what do you think?'

'No pressure,' Ali laughs.

Isabel's eyes widen. 'Oh, we would love to, wouldn't we, Dan? I can help with the cooking if you want, Eliza.'

'No, no,' Martin says. 'It'll be our pleasure.'

'Martin,' Ali says after the front door has closed behind them. 'You are unbelievable. Right. I should get

49

my lot home.' She struggles to heft herself off the sofa, and I take both her hands and pull. 'Thanks. Oof. I'm going to need a crane soon. See you both on Saturday. I can't wait to see how this turns out.'

She is not the only one.

9

Saturday evening rolls round. I kiss the children good-night, easing them back under their duvets, and leave the room, closing the door behind me. The whispering starts immediately. I walk away smiling. They could have a bedroom each but neither of them has shown any inclination for it yet.

Delicious smells reach me from the kitchen; tarragon and onions, garlic and spices. We are having some elaborate Ottolenghi recipe. Martin likes to show off and always cooks when we have guests. The tradition began as an act of defiance – Martin telling us that he could still do things that enrich our friends' lives, that he could still carry some of the burden for his beloved wife. There's no doubt that it impresses, but then everything my husband does is with that aim in mind. Never underwhelm.

I open my wardrobe, not sure what to wear. It would be wrong to dress up too much, seeing as Ali can't. Isabel will no doubt look gorgeous, but I refuse to compete with a twenty-one-year-old. I tug a black dress from its hanger. It has a fitted top and an A-line skirt that swishes pleasingly around my thighs. Who needs dewy youth when you have sophistication?

I go downstairs. No sign of Martin. I open the wine cooler. I can't help it. Bottles of wine are ranged on the normally empty racks, bought by Martin for tonight. I rest my hand on a Pouilly-Fumé, conjuring up its aromatic taste on my tongue, its tide of coolness flowing down my throat. I glance disdainfully at the lower shelf with its ranked bottles of sparkling water.

'Don't even think about it,' Martin says, pushing himself into the kitchen.

'Just getting used to looking at it,' I say, closing the cooler door. 'Desensitizing.'

Martin's eyes skim my body and I catch the slight lift of his eyebrows.

'What?' I ask.

'Didn't you wear that to my father's funeral?'

I tense at the hint of disapproval. 'Yes, but I didn't buy it for that. I bought it to wear at Ali's thirtieth. It's Joseph,' I add, as if that makes all the difference. I look down, smoothing my hands over my hips. 'I didn't want to overdress.'

'I don't want you to either, but I would like to show you off.'

Martin rolls his shoulders. Not having the use of his legs means that his upper body holds all the tension. In the evenings we often sit in front of the television with me kneading his shoulders and neck. I've developed muscles in my fingers that I never knew I had.

'Show me off to who exactly? Pete and Ali know me

well enough not to care if I wear a sack, and Dan's only interested in our au pair.'

Martin leans back in his chair and regards me. My palms itch and sweat.

'Do you think I don't care? It's not much to ask, is it? For my wife to look her best.'

'I thought I looked nice.'

'Nice?' He manages to imbue the word with contempt. 'You're an extremely beautiful woman, Eliza. Why play it down? Why don't you enjoy being noticed? Most women would.'

I could say, *Because you'll only complain about it later*, but I don't dare. I could also say that I'm worried about Isabel thinking I'm trying too hard for Dan and that would be true too. Dan has started seeing Isabel, but I don't sense his heart is in it. If it was there would be a frisson between them, and there isn't, or none that I can detect.

'All right, I get the point. I'll change.'

I move like an automaton to the door. Martin loves me, I know that. The trouble is that his need for control, only hinted at when we met, has gone into overdrive in the years since the accident. Nothing is beyond his attention. What starts with a perfectly reasonable request, given Martin's circumstances – say, keeping the floor free of clutter – sends spores throughout the rest of the house and our lives. The children must not leave their bedroom untidy or their toys out. The children's supper must be eaten and cleared up by 6.30 p.m. No item of clothing should be slung over the back of a chair even if it's going to be worn later. Keys on the key hook.

Children's DVDs back on the shelf. For every infraction between ten and fifty pence is deducted from that week's pocket money, depending on the severity of the lapse. Not that Aurora gives a fig about that. Lucas does though.

I change into a midnight blue dress that stops well short of my knees. It has a low neckline and elbow-length sleeves and is very slimming. I bought this dress once I'd lost my baby weight. I remember trying it on, turning slowly in the changing room, feeling sexy for the first time in over a year. Now I'm not sure I want to look sexy. I just want to look like me.

Martin's face registers approval, but when I open the door to Ali and Pete, I can't help thinking I should have listened to my gut. Ali is wearing another of her linen tents and still looks uncomfortably hot. Despite her initial enthusiasm, I have a feeling she'd rather be sitting in front of a good film with her feet up on the sofa. Pete hands me a bottle of red wine, which I briskly pass to Martin. Dan arrives shortly after them, ruggedly handsome in a red and white cotton shirt with the sleeves loosely rolled up and jeans without rips in the knees. He's carrying a bunch of pink roses. I take them off him, bury my nose in them to hide my blushes, and breathe in their scent.

'Thank you. They're beautiful.'

'Dan, this is Pete,' Martin says. 'My oldest friend, and the genius who brought my vision to life. He literally got the stuff out of my head and onto the drawing board.'

Pete stiffens. The designs for Winterfell were as much his vision as Martin's. As far as he's concerned it was a collaboration with a client; he wasn't a cipher, purely interpreting Martin's back-of-the-envelope scrawls. They discussed everything together. I see a glance pass between Pete and Ali, but he says nothing. If he feels slighted he should stick up for himself.

'Pete. Dan. Dan's our tenant, but he's also a tech whizz.'

'I suppose you could call it that,' Dan responds. 'I'm a digital designer.'

'You should talk to him about the Pitfield Group's website, Pete. It could do with jazzing up. It's far too basic for a firm that aspires to be seen as cutting edge.'

'Shall we go outside?' I say, giving my husband a warning look.

The garden is at its best at this time of year, its borders bursting with colour. Everything has been chosen to attract insects, from the sculptural piles of logs to the flowering plants. There are lavenders and purple echiums, poppies and salvia, campanula and foxgloves, and many more besides. It's deliberately untidy, with dandelions left to seed, roses clambering up the walls and billowing over the fence. Even the lawn has been allowed to sprout daisies and buttercups and gets cut long only once every three weeks. Martin initially wanted something more formal, to reflect the sharp lines of the house, but the children changed all that. Now he's a wildlife enthusiast and there are bird boxes and feeders in the trees beyond the lawn, where there used to be a small orchard. It's shady and cool; a mini ecosystem.

Five minutes later, as if she's peeked to check it's the optimum moment, which I think she probably has, Isabel makes her entrance in a white dress. She walks as though she's floating across the terrace from the annexe, where she has a bedsitting room and bathroom, a character from a romcom, tendrils of hair falling around her neck. She literally takes the men's breath away.

'Oh God,' Ali whispers. 'Were we that young and lovely once?'

I smile and try not to look at Dan's reaction. How could he not prefer this girl to me? She's young, carefree, single and gorgeous, and has an enchanting French accent. I have got to shake off this thirst I have for him. It's undignified.

At that precise moment Dan winks at me. I blush with pleasure and hope no one else saw.

'So, Dan, would you like a guided tour?' Martin asks once everyone has a drink in their hand.

Dan jumps at the chance, and I can't help myself; I come too, ignoring the look Martin sends me. Leaving Isabel and Ali chatting together, Pete, Dan and I take the stairs and meet Martin on the landing. We start with the master bedroom. Like the rest of the house, its interior is bare concrete with spots set into the unpainted ceiling. My dressing table is a slab of concrete. The far wall boasts floor-to-ceiling windows that slide open onto a large balcony. There are warm touches; my dressing-table stool upholstered in fuchsia pink that Martin only agreed to after I went out and bought it, a large cream rug covering most of the floor, and a faux fur bedspread. The huge bed with its upholstered headboard is conventional. There's no bar to help him on and off, no visible emergency button, just a phone on the walnut bedside shelf, a digital alarm and the book he's reading – currently a political biography. The room is somewhere to repose. It's all very zen.

The men discuss the leaps forward in residential engineering and I can't help but notice that, although this isn't Dan's area of expertise, he has plenty to say on the matter. Pete and Martin let him have his head, but I worry Martin will mock Dan for it later.

We inspect the bathrooms and dressing room and somehow or other, though not through any effort on my part, rearrange ourselves so that Dan is standing so close to me I can feel the hairs on his arms creating static against mine. I edge away, frightened by the intensity of the feelings it engenders. I haven't felt like this since those early days with Martin, before he was mine.

From somewhere outside the room, Isabel calls Aurora. That's followed by the sound of padding footsteps on the landing.

'His and hers bathrooms, and a dressing room for Eliza,' Martin is saying. 'Let me show you something clever. It was Eliza's idea.'

We follow him into the dressing room. Martin presses a button on the wall; two doors open at the top and a metal arm hung with my shirts slowly swings out and down.

'Ingenious,' Dan says. 'Somewhere for Eliza to hide her secrets.'

In the silence that ensues I become aware of a small person at my side, insistently tugging at my dress.

'Sweetie,' I say, picking Aurora up. 'You should be in bed.'

She shakes her head and whispers insistently. 'I want to tell you somefing.'

Pete wanders over to the window and looks out. I feel Aurora's hot breath against my ear as she tells me she loves Dan.

'Eliza and I don't have secrets from each other,' Martin says.

Isabel is beside me. 'Come, *mignonne*. Bedtime.' She raises her arms and Aurora reaches for her.

'It's fine,' I snap, hanging on to my daughter. 'I'll take her back to bed.'

'Give her to Isabel,' Martin says. 'You need to look after our guests.'

'Isabel is our guest,' I remind him.

He extends a hand. 'Of course you are. Force of habit, Isabel. I apologize.'

'Don't worry,' she says. 'I'll take her. Eliza is the hostess.'

As the lift doors close on Martin, and Pete goes downstairs to check on Ali, Dan touches my arm. It acts like an electric shock. I jump.

'Sorry,' he says. 'I shouldn't have said that.'

'It's fine.'

'Is it true?'

'Is what true?'

'That you don't have any secrets from your husband?'

Isabel comes out of the children's bedroom and

quietly closes the door. I frown at Dan then shake my head and walk downstairs.

'There's an annexe,' Martin says, once we've explored the rest of the house. 'It's accessed through the utility room but it also has a separate entrance outside. It means our au pairs can come and go as they please.'

'You are not taking people in there,' Isabel says quickly.

I smile reassuringly. 'Don't worry. No one's going into your room.'

'I'm surprised there isn't more Smart wizardry,' Dan says. 'Weren't you tempted, Martin? It's staggering what a house can do these days.'

'That shit,' Martin says scathingly. 'We've kept the potential open, of course, we'd be idiots not to; but most of it isn't activated – we use it for things like the lighting and the security measures; the irrigation system. The more I do for myself the better. I don't want to sit in this chair and atrophy. Opening doors improves my flexibility. I don't need a machine to do that for me, and I don't want some fucking robot telling me when the milk's run out. Nor do I want someone in Russia hacking in and messing with my head.'

Dan catches my eye and I smile.

'So you switch your own telly on?' he says.

'Yup. Aren't I the hero?'

Dan laughs and I do too. Pete looks mildly irritated.

'I can give you a little demonstration,' Martin says, pushing himself into the kitchen and picking his phone up from the side where it's been on charge. We follow him obediently. 'When it comes to security, *intelligent* beats a key or a switch on the wall. Here we go.' He swipes and taps. Immediately, the shutters descend throughout the house. For the uninitiated, it's a shock.

'*Bordel de merde!*' Isabel shouts furiously. 'Open them. I am claustrophobic.'

'Martin?' I say tentatively.

'Oh, for God's sake, Martin,' Ali says, making her way to Isabel's side. 'Stop messing around. It's not Halloween.'

'Your wish is my command.'

I can hear the self-satisfied smirk in his voice. The shutters clank into gear and start their slow rise. Then Martin's mobile rings. He turns away from us and quietly reels off a code, tells Fortress, our security company, that it was a demo and signs off.

Isabel is gasping, white as a sheet, her arms wrapped round her body.

'Breathe,' Ali tells her calmly. 'It's OK. You're going to be fine. Breathe with me. Slow it down. That's right. Nice and slow. In two, three, four. Good girl. Now out two, three, four. And again. Dinner smells good, doesn't it? What are you cooking, Martin?'

'Cardamom chicken with yoghurt and almonds. Why don't you take her outside? She looks like she could do with some air.'

'You should not do that without telling people,' Isabel says.

'Don't be wet,' Martin says.

I admonish him with a look, but he just rolls his eyes.

Fury comes off Isabel in waves. 'What do you know about it?'

'About claustrophobia? Ask me that when you've been stuck in a hospital bed for six months, dear.'

'Apologize,' I hiss. 'That was unfair.'

'She's right, Martin,' Ali says. 'That was a stupid thing to do.'

Martin apologizes with surprising grace, but Isabel remains sulky and silent. She's used to unqualified admiration from men. I'm only now realizing that she's a little spoilt. And as someone who wasn't the spoilt darling of a doting father, I feel good about that revelation. Superior even. I have resilience and patience and I have survived. Isabel is nothing. A piece of fluff who will be gone in a few months.

'You could have warned me,' I say as I plate up.

'Where's the fun in that?' Martin asks.

I give him a tetchy smile.

Outside Ali is still with Isabel, distracting her with gossip as she recovers. It doesn't escape my notice that Dan has shown little concern for his date.

10

The seating is arranged so that no one is sitting next to their partner, which means I'm between Dan and Pete. The garden table is large enough to seat ten, so we aren't pressed up against each other, but I'm still uncomfortably aware of Dan's presence inches from me. It's an unnervingly pleasant discomfort. Isabel's beauty no longer feels so dangerous.

I periodically refill my glass with sparkling water. Food is the only thing that dulls the craving for alcohol, so I eat slowly, savouring each mouthful, making it last, trying not to watch hungrily when someone else's glass is topped up with wine. From time to time Martin catches my eye. He knows what this does to me and is willing me to be strong. It's at times like this that I remember how we used to be together, the symbiotic nature of our relationship, not needing words to understand each other.

Isabel grows quieter as the men's volubility increases. We are all so much older than her. When I happen to glance her way, she's staring straight at me, a small frown buckling the space between her eyebrows. It's only a split second, then her brow clears and she smiles. Ali takes pity and probes her about her life back in France. She's the daughter of an electrician and a teacher, an only child and loves horses, but not enough to keep her in rural isolation. She becomes quite chatty, telling Ali more than she's ever told me.

Dan seems more interested in Martin and Pete than Isabel. Pete is pissed, which means he's studiously ignoring Ali, in favour of being one of the lads. Martin is holding court. I sense an element of competition for his favour. My husband's perfect scenario. He can bask in the warmth of their admiration to his heart's delight.

Without warning, Dan's hand is on my thigh. I cannot breathe. I dart a glance at Martin. He's smiling his inscrutable smile. That means he's drunk more than he normally would. He won't have noticed anything.

'So, Eliza?' Dan asks me. 'Do you have any siblings?'

'I have a twin brother.'

'That's so interesting. Do you see much of him?'

'I see him from time to time. But we're not as close as we used to be.'

'Why is that?'

'No reason. We just drifted apart. His lifestyle is very different from mine.'

'What my wife is trying to say,' Martin says, waving his knife, 'is that she sees Sam when he wants something. My money, usually. He's a waste of space.'

'He's my brother.'

'Twins are different, aren't they?' Dan says. 'You hear stories about them feeling each other's pain. I've always found that fascinating.'

He finally takes his hand away and raises his glass to his lips. My heart has gone berserk.

'Sam's not so bad,' Ali says. 'He's just a little lost.'

She smiles at me and I smile back gratefully. Ali is one of the few people I mix with that my twin actually likes and trusts.

'What about you?' Dan asks Martin. 'Let me guess. You're an only child.'

Martin and Ali burst out laughing.

'Ali is Martin's sister,' I explain. 'Sorry, I just assumed you knew.'

'Interesting that you thought my brother was an only child though,' Ali says. 'Why would that be?'

Caught on the spot, Dan smiles. 'All the signs are there. Over-achiever, fiercely independent, used to getting his own way, always right.'

Ali laughs out loud. Martin looks prim. I watch Dan watching them. He's satisfied with himself.

'I am an only child,' Isabel pipes up, and Pete, entirely out of character, puts his arm around her shoulders and gives her a quick hug.

'Ignore them,' he says.

We've had pudding, and I'm pleased to see everyone's practically licked their plate clean, seeing as it was my contribution. Ali surreptitiously glances at her watch, yearning for her bed. Pete's worked his way through at least a bottle of wine on top of the beer he had when they arrived. Dan hasn't touched me again, but I've been catapulted into unknown territory and I don't know what to do.

'It's getting chilly,' I say, pushing my chair back. 'Why don't we go inside?'

'I think it's probably time we went home,' Ali says.

She nudges Pete, who doesn't react except to dart a glance in Dan's direction. I realize that he has no intention of leaving Dan and Martin in a cosy, mildly pissed tête-à-tête.

'Pete,' Ali says. 'I'm shattered.'

'It's only eleven, darling. Millie won't mind. More money for her.'

I notice the look that passes between them; Ali's remonstrating frown, Pete's defiant glance.

'Quick coffee?' Martin says. 'I know you're tired, Al, but when number three arrives you won't be getting out at all. Make the most of it.'

She wrinkles her nose, but Pete nods. 'Coffee would be great.'

I can't believe he's being so selfish or that Martin is encouraging him. Coming to Ali's rescue, I chivvy everyone into the drawing room where the sofas, which I insisted on choosing, are soft and springy. Martin uses the iPad to set the lighting to intimate, and chooses background music. Ali sinks back into the cushions with a small sigh of resignation. Ten minutes later, when I return with the tray of coffee, she's closed her eyes and someone has thoughtfully covered her with the cashmere blanket I keep folded over the arm of the sofa.

'Where did you and Martin meet?' Dan asks.

'India,' I say, handing him a delicate china cup. 'I'd left home in search of adventure.' I smile to show that

I'm being ironic. 'Martin was killing time before he took up a job in the City.'

'We all kill time when we're young, don't we?' Martin says. 'It's only later we realize what a mistake that is.' He shifts his back slightly. 'India was amazing though. Meeting Eliza was the best thing that had ever happened to me.'

He glances over at me and holds my gaze. It was special. I feel no resentment when I look back at that time. He helped me move away from the past and into the future. My mistake was to stay with him, rather than use the holiday romance as a launch pad.

Martin digs his fingers into the curve between his neck and shoulder. If we were alone, I'd do it for him.

'You know when you've found the one,' he says, dropping his hand when he sees me watching. 'I had no intention of letting her go.'

'It was a surprise to everyone,' Pete says. 'What with your well-earned reputation for not sticking around. Broken hearts strewn in your wake.'

'In my defence, I was a young man. Sowing my wild oats.'

'Of course you were,' Pete agrees. 'And you've been dedicated to Eliza ever since.'

'Was it love at first sight?' Isabel asks.

'Sort of,' I say. 'Martin smiled and something just kind of fell into place.'

That much is true. But our love story was not without collateral damage.

'What about you and Ali, Pete?' Isabel says. 'How did you meet?'

Pete looks fondly at his dozing wife, and in doing so

66

avoids my eyes. 'We've known each other forever, but Ali was always just my mate's little sister. It was only after Martin's accident that we became close.'

'So, Dan,' I say, my eyes anywhere but on Pete's face. I feel hot with shame. 'I remember you saying you spent time in Vancouver. Did you enjoy it?'

'It was a great experience. I lived in Mount Pleasant, which was cool, and worked in IT services which wasn't. Being a glitch fixer is pretty much the same whatever part of the world you're in.'

'Tech experts will always be in demand,' Martin says.

'There is that. I can work pretty much anywhere. Whereabouts were you in India?'

I can't help thinking he sidestepped talking about himself neatly, but I'm an expert in that so I'm in no position to criticize. 'A village called Anjuna. It's in North Goa. On the coast.'

'It is romantic, no?' Isabel says. 'Mostly holiday romances end when people go home.'

She doesn't look at Dan, but casts her eyes down. I see his expression though. A brief shuttering, before he changes the subject.

'So here's an idea.' He drops a couple of brown sugar crystals into his coffee and stirs. 'Why don't you design bespoke homes for paraplegics? Target wealthy clients, people like you who don't want to compromise on style even if it suits their needs better to do so.'

'Nice pitch,' Pete snorts. 'Came up with that in the shower this morning, did you?'

I glance at Pete in surprise. Martin doesn't say anything, but he's nodding thoughtfully.

'Sounds interesting,' I say.

'Yeah. And good ideas generally filter down, so the hope would be that developers catch on and in time you would get better quality, more interesting and attractive accessible housing where it's needed the most. But Martin would lead the change from the top by doing something radical.'

He's good, I'll give him that. He seems to have the knack of discovering what makes people tick. It crosses my mind that he would make an excellent conman.

'What do you know about it?' Pete asks.

'I've done some basic research,' Dan says, refusing to take offence at Pete's dismissive tone. 'Googled it. Apparently someone is paralysed in this country every four hours. That's a rough statistic, but it shows there's a need. And,' he says, smiling at his audience, 'I think I've found the perfect property.' He pauses, making sure he has our undivided attention, which of course he does. Apart from Ali. In the silence her soft snores are clearly audible.

'So, I was on a cycle ride, just kind of following the river, seeing where it took me. There's one bit where there's a stretch of houses with moorings, so the path loops behind them and connects with the road. There's an auction sign outside a bungalow. The house is pretty shoddy – it doesn't look like it's had a coat of paint in forty years – but the piece of land, that's really nice. There was obviously no one living there, so I had a mooch round the outside. You could demolish the house and build something fantastic. The view across the river is spectacular.'

Martin's eyes glint. Dan has played a blinder.

'Don't go anywhere,' Dan says. 'I need to pee.'

He jumps up and leaves the room, and Pete raises his eyebrows.

'Pleased with himself, isn't he?'

'He is not pleased with himself,' Isabel says sharply. 'He has good ideas. You should listen to him. Maybe it would help you.'

Martin laughs loudly. 'Quite right, Isabel. You're being boorish, Pete.'

'So we can't have a laugh?' Pete says.

'Not at the expense of my guests,' Martin says. 'No.'

Dan comes back in and sits down. 'What did I miss?'

'Email me the link,' Martin says to him. 'You've made my mouth water.'

'Cool. I might not have the money to fund something like that, but I would dearly love to be involved if you did go for it. Development is something I'd like to branch into eventually. I can do concepts and visuals; I can see the big picture.'

'That is what an architect does,' Pete says unpleasantly. 'I suppose that's one of your many skills too.'

'Relax, mate. It's only an idea. You don't need to be an architect to be able to design the overall look of a house.'

I can feel Pete fizzle with barely suppressed anger. I glance at Ali, but she's slept through it. Even though he's smiling and alert, I can tell from the increasing strain in Martin's eyes that he's in pain and would like everyone to go. I start picking up empty coffee cups as a hint, and

Dan stands up and stretches, revealing the toned stomach beneath his shirt. I look away.

'It's late. Time I headed off,' he says.

Ali opens her eyes, startled, then sits up and peels off the blanket.

'Can we go home now?'

I laugh. 'Of course you can, darling Ali.'

Before Pete can do anything about it, Dan reaches for Ali's hands, pulls her up off the sofa and steadies her with a hand under her elbow. I glance at Pete's face and clock his fury.

In the bustle at the door, Dan's lips graze my cheek. He whispers, 'You smell incredible.'

I flush as he turns to Isabel to say goodbye. Dan's hand rests lightly on her upper arm as she reaches up to kiss him. To me it looks as though Isabel is the one doing the embracing, Dan merely the polite recipient. But I could be seeing what I want to see.

I slip off my shoes with a sigh of relief and put them on the stairs to be taken up to the bedroom, then tell Isabel to go to bed and start cleaning up. I'd leave it till morning, but it's one of the rules. I wish Martin would go to bed so that I can think about the evening and the strange tensions running through it. Remembering Dan's hand on my thigh and his words at the door with a happy shudder, I feel more exultation than I do remorse at the disloyalty to Martin.

'On reflection,' Martin says, yawning, 'you were right.'

'About what?'

'About what you're wearing. It was too much. The black dress would have been better.'

I want to speak, but I content myself with a curt nod and bang a saucepan down in the sink before aggressively squirting washing-up liquid into it, burning with shame. Too much? What did the others think? Is that why Dan made a pass?

He takes my hand. 'Don't be like that. I wasn't getting at you, I was apologizing for pushing you into what was a wrong decision.'

My body is stiff with anger and mortification; I won't let him pull me close. I don't want to sit on his knee.

'You still looked gorgeous. Pete and Dan couldn't take their eyes off you.'

That makes me cringe. 'That's rubbish and you know it.'

'You'll always be the most beautiful woman in the room to me.'

'Not when Isabel is around.' I scrape the leftovers into the caddy and rinse the plate.

After a pause, Martin says, 'I'm not convinced by those two as a couple.'

'What do you mean? She's besotted with him.'

'That might be true.' He gives me a self-satisfied look. 'That man is an opportunist, and he thinks he's worth more. He's using her as a way of getting close to me.'

Not you, I think, in a moment of recognition. It's me. Dan is using Isabel to get to me.

* * *

71

Before I go to bed, I open the children's bedroom door and step quietly inside their room. They are sleeping so peacefully, Aurora on her right side, Lucas on his left, so that they're facing each other across the gap. Oh my god, the damage I could do if I allowed myself to be swept away.

11

'Eliza! Wait.'

I stop outside the school gates, bracing myself. Pete is striding towards me.

'Thanks for supper,' he says. He fishes around in his pocket and hands me a postcard. 'Ali asked me to give you this.'

It's a Matisse, and on the blank side she's written, *Lovely evening, delicious food, and interesting company! Ali xxx*

'How is she this morning?' I ask, wishing I hadn't hung around chatting in the classroom. I could be well away by now.

'Hot and bothered. She hates this sort of weather at the best of times.'

'I'll look in on her later.'

'Thanks. She'd like that.'

From the other side of the street, Amanda Kelsey waves. In desperation, I beckon her to join us but she shakes her head and indicates her jogging bottoms and bright pink stretch top. I don't particularly like her; she's condescending to me and possessive about Ali. I have a suspicion she thinks Ali only puts up with me because I'm family, whereas Amanda is chosen for herself. The galling thing is, she isn't entirely wrong. Ali is my friend because she's my husband's sister. In moments of insecurity, I've wondered if she would have made the effort if it had simply been a case of our children attending the same school.

Pete and I walk along in silence. A minute passes, then we both speak at once.

'I wanted to catch you,' Pete says.

'Have you got much work on? Sorry,' I add, practically tripping over my tongue. 'Go on. What did you want to say?'

He walks a few paces, hands stuffed into his trouser pockets, head down as though he's looking for something on the pavement. There's an air of disappointment about Pete. In the years since the accident, Martin has forged ahead, entirely on his own energies and scrappiness, whereas Pete has struggled. As a partner in an architectural firm, apart from Winterfell most of his work involves home extensions of one kind or another. It's not what he talked about when I first knew him. Back then he had been full of himself. He was going to be a millionaire by the time he was thirty.

I have never really understood the attraction between Pete and Ali, but I expect it was to do with the intensity of those days when Martin's life was in the balance. They were there for each other; the best friend and the sister. I remember that so clearly. I was the wife but I mattered less. I didn't mind, I understood. But they made me feel isolated in my grief. Until, of course, Pete didn't.

'It's about your tenant.'

'Which one?' I ask, although I know the answer perfectly well.

'The one I met on Saturday night.' He says impatiently. 'The one sucking up to Martin like his life depended on it.'

'He was just being friendly.'

'Don't be naive. It made me sick to see his hands all over Isabel. What does he think he's playing at? Fucking cradle-snatcher.'

I think about Dan's hand on my thigh. It jerks a response out of my body, filling me with heat.

'You're very angry,' I say hurriedly. 'Is this really all about Dan?'

'What else would it be about? He's schmoozing you and trying to get into your au pair's knickers.'

I grimace at his crudeness. 'Do you have to?'

'Well, isn't he?'

I don't answer.

'He's after something from Martin. I mean, honestly, just happening to cycle past that place? Don't make me laugh – he was on the lookout for something; trying to ingratiate himself with Martin, and at my expense. What's he done anyway? Mid-thirties, unmarried, renting a flat. The man's a leech.'

I laugh. 'You're over-reacting. Martin barely knows Dan, but he's not an idiot. He won't let himself be taken advantage of and he would never jeopardize your friendship. You have nothing to worry about.'

The truth is, Pete doesn't want anyone else infiltrating our tight circle, but all he'll achieve by being heavy-handed is to damage it. Martin would be livid if he thought Pete felt the need to protect him.

'I know I should believe you. But the way he is with Martin – teasing him, winding him up, and Martin takes it. No one apart from my wife gets away with that. Am I really the only one who can see it?'

'See what?'

I do have some sympathy, despite my exasperation. Martin is brilliant at playing people off against each other; he does it to me often enough.

'See that the man is a fraud. Christ, you're all taken in by his shiny smile. Even my wife. He is not what he seems, Eliza.'

'He's exactly what he seems,' I counter. 'You're getting this out of proportion because you feel threatened.'

'And I'm right to feel that way.'

We look at each other silently.

'Well, don't say I didn't warn you,' Pete says, starting to walk faster.

I strive to keep up with him. 'You have to understand.' I'm aware that I need to be circumspect here. 'Martin might seem confident and in control, but it takes an enormous effort to carry that off. He may not show it, but he is afraid. It's like he has to keep up the facade at all costs; to be the invincible Martin Curran. When something threatens that, he can turn nasty. It's a defence mechanism. He builds himself up by demeaning someone else. This time, unfortunately, it was you, but you laid yourself open to it.'

'So it's my fault for caring?'

'It's your fault for implying Martin's been taken in by

Dan. He'll come round, but he'll make sure you suffer first.'

Pete looks at me strangely. 'Is that what he does to you?'

I probably should shut up, but I want someone to understand my life. At least I know Pete can keep a secret.

'He has to take out his frustrations somewhere.'

Pete frowns. 'Eliza, are you saying he hurts you?'

I backtrack swiftly. 'No. No, of course not. He just has a nasty tongue on him sometimes.'

'You shouldn't have to put up with that.'

'I'm used to it. He's a good man otherwise. He rewards loyalty.'

'You could have fooled me.'

'You were there for him when he needed you. He won't forget that.'

He sighs, and the atmosphere changes. 'That's another thing we need to talk about.'

The corner where we part company feels a million miles away. 'No, we don't.'

'I hate lying.'

I stop and turn on him. 'For God's sake. If the subject doesn't come up, if they don't come straight out and ask us, then technically, we aren't lying.'

'Technically, that's beside the point. I find it hard to square the person I am now with the man who was capable of doing something like that.'

Fury rises in me with shocking speed. 'That's enough! I do not want to discuss this with you. I don't care if it's hard for you; you have to deal with it. You have Ali and the kids to consider. If you can't cope with being around me because I make you feel bad about yourself, then don't run after me in the street, don't wait for me outside school.'

'You act like what happened between us came out of nowhere.'

'It did.'

'Well, you continue to tell yourself that, if it makes you feel better.'

He makes me so angry. Everything is about him; relationships, in Pete's mind at least, revolve around him. He takes umbrage easily and is equally easily soothed with flattery. His feelings around the betrayal of his friend are about himself, not about me or Martin. It's his guilt, his turmoil, his wretchedness; as if no one else has a conscience. But he's wrong, I hadn't been hankering after him. It was timing, that was all, like everything else. If I hadn't been in that evening, if he hadn't rung my doorbell when I was at breaking point, it never would have happened.

'I saw the look on your face when Dan made that stupid comment about a hiding place for your secrets,' Pete says. 'He touched a nerve. You kept the letter, didn't you? So don't tell me what happened back then didn't mean anything.'

12

Back home, I find Isabel itching to leave for her English class. I apologize for the delay, and put my head round Martin's door. He's deep in conversation. What Pete said has scared me. What if Martin remembers Dan's off-the-cuff comment? He can't access the wardrobe but I wouldn't put it past him to get help. If he really wants to check I'm not hiding anything up there, he'll find a way.

Aurora is sitting at the kitchen table colouring in. Do I dare? Martin won't appear till lunch and Aurora is happily engaged in her task, her yellow pencil scratching across the soft paper.

'Mummy's going to run upstairs, darling. I'll be two minutes.'

She pokes her tongue between her teeth in concentration. She won't even realize I've gone.

In the bedroom, I carry a stool to the dressing room, press the button and wait for the metal arm to complete its elegant arc. Then I climb up and stretch my hand past the mechanics. The first thing I touch is a bottle and for one terrifying moment I'm lost, my brain slipping off its tracks. I curl my fingers round the neck and imagine the alcohol flowing through my veins. Then I pinch my lips together hard and loosen my fingers. I feel actual pain when I let it go, pain that almost chokes me. I take a breath and reach further, my fingers searching the space for a folded slip of paper. I touch it. It's there. I slip it into the back pocket of my jeans and close the cupboard.

Downstairs Aurora is still engrossed in her colouring, and doesn't notice me tearing up the letter into the peelings bin. I slip past her, out into the garden, walk down to the compost heap and fork it deep into the decomposing vegetable matter.

As I retrace my steps, I feel no regret, only shame. I should have disposed of it years ago. It was schoolgirlish of me to keep it.

I enter the kitchen to find Martin comforting a sobbing Aurora. He glares at me.

'Aurora, sweetie? Tell Mummy what happened.' I take her from him and look her over but there doesn't appear to be anything wrong. My daughter can be a drama queen, especially when her father is around.

She pushes her nose into my armpit, a sure sign that she's feeling guilty.

'What were you doing?' Martin asks me.

I lift the hand that's carrying the bin. 'It needed emptying.'

He gives me the quizzical look I have learnt to dread. 'Come here.'

I step towards him. He takes my arm and pulls me down so that my face is close to his. Aurora clings to me.

'Breathe,' he whispers.

I breathe out so he can check for the smell of alcohol. 'You should have more faith.'

He shrugs and lets me go, satisfied. I cuddle Aurora.

'What happened, sweetheart?'

'I wanted somefing.'

'She pulled out the drawers to climb up to the biscuit tin. She couldn't get down so she started yelling. Good thing I heard her.'

'I was only outside for a minute or two.'

'Whatever, I'm supposed to be working. You do your job, I'll do mine.'

He sails back into his office. I hug Aurora close to me. She holds out a hand, her fingers wrapped round a crumbling cookie.

Kate drops Leonie over so she can help Ali clean the house in preparation for the new arrival, and the girls are in their own little world, making fairy perfume out of petals, soil and water. I watch from the kitchen, smiling. It's scenes like this that make everything worthwhile.

'Come and have a look,' Martin says. 'Dan's sent a link to the place he was talking about on Saturday night.'

I'd forgotten all about that. Holding a mug of coffee, I look over his shoulder at a semi-rural aerial view of the Thames. There are a handful of properties scattered along it. One of them has its perimeter outlined in red.

'Don't hover,' Martin says. 'Sit down.'

I draw up a chair and he turns the screen towards me. Martin clicks through the photographs. There aren't many, because it's an auction catalogue. There's a close-up of a boxy flat-roofed one-storey house, probably sixties built, with an arched doorway. There are some internal shots. One taken from the back, showing the wide lawn edged by overgrown shrubs, running down to a mooring with a small wooden pontoon. There's also a floor plan of the building. Martin clicks on the satellite image and zooms in as far as he can go. At the front of the house is a gravelled forecourt with weeds sprouting through it, and a separate garage. The house bears the grandiose name of Gideon Grove. Vacant possession. Dan's description was pretty accurate.

It reminds me of the house we demolished to build Winterfell. That too was a neglected sixties bungalow with little to recommend it but the land it was sitting on.

Martin clicks on the virtual tour, and suddenly we're inside, moving around, and it's someone else's life. Papers on the desk, books on the shelves, beds with their bedding still on, one stripped down to unwashed sheets, one covered by a pink candlewick bedspread. There is medication in the bathroom, a newspaper on the coffee table. A dead plant on the kitchen windowsill.

'Not bad, eh,' Martin says.

'It's wonderful. With that view, and such a big garden – you could do something incredible with it.'

Something I can see myself getting my teeth into. Not just to have reasons to spend time away from Winterfell, but to have a sense of purpose again. I want to project manage. I relish the challenge. I know it was Dan's idea, but I envisage him behind his PC while I do the hands-on work. We'd be a team, a collaboration. The thought gives me a thrill. We would have to work closely with Pete too, of course, which is unfortunate because Dan rubs him up the wrong way, but Ali would never let Martin get away with using a different architect. They'll just have to learn to tolerate each other. The world suddenly feels full of possibilities and my depressed spirits rise. It'll make life bearable.

'What do you think of Dan?' Martin asks.

The question comes out of the blue and my mind scrambles for the correct response. 'He's all right. Why?'

'No particular reason,' he says, before giving one. 'I haven't got to the bottom of him.'

'Do you need to?'

'Pete had a point, didn't he? Why is he still renting? Why doesn't he have a girlfriend?'

'Isabel is his girlfriend.'

'I mean, a woman he could conceivably commit to, not some twenty-one-year-old he's banging.'

I fling up my hands. 'Oh, please. I had this from Pete at the school gates this morning. You don't know that he's "banging" her, as you so delicately put it. They barely know each other. What is it with you two and that girl? I'm beginning to think you're obsessed.'

'You know perfectly well that I've never looked at anyone else since I met you. You are and always will be the only girl for me.' Martin yawns, then adds laconically, 'You've made more of an effort with your appearance today.'

I don't hesitate. 'You told me to, remember?'

Martin pulls his phone towards him. While he scrolls

through his emails, I try to find some tenderness within myself, some echo of what I once felt. I think about what he's been through, what he's made of himself, how he's put a roof over his family's heads and taken care of us. I should be more grateful, but I just want it all to end. Dan Jones shouldn't be the answer. I should be able to find that myself, and yet I feel a change in the way I perceive Martin since meeting him. I don't know why it should be, but Martin seems diminished; as though Dan has given me perspective, made Martin seem more manageable, less frightening. Or maybe it's just that he's made me aware that I possess more strength than I realized.

Martin glances up, catches me looking at him. 'What?'

'Nothing.'

His mouth thins. 'Why do I get the feeling I wouldn't like what's going on in your head?'

'Guilty conscience?'

He smiles. 'Why should I feel guilty, Eliza? I'm not the one with blood on my hands.'

13

To my relief, Martin goes out. He has a meeting with his financial advisor. It's just me and the little girls for an hour or so. Bliss.

My phone rings. It's Sam. Despite everything, it's nice to hear my twin's voice.

'Hi.' I wander into the garden and sit on one of the cushioned sun loungers, stretching my legs out, enjoying the heat on my bare skin.

'Is Martin in?' he asks.

'Not at the moment.'

'Great. Can I come round?'

A cloud inches across the sun, casting the garden into shade. I sit up and cross my legs, resting my elbows on my thighs. 'Has something happened?'

'Why does something need to have happened before I come and see my darling sister?'

I roll my eyes. 'Where are you now?'

'Outside your gate. I was passing, and I thought, hey, maybe Lyzie's at a loose end.'

'Yeah, right. You could have given me some warning.'

'Just let me in. Please.'

I go inside, buzz him in, go to the door, and he strides up the slope towards me, grinning. I can't resist him. He gives me a hug and I wrap my arms around him. The glimmer of hope that this really is a regular visit dims when I breathe in the smell of weed that I remember so clearly from his teenage bedroom. When I let him go and step back, I notice his eyes are bloodshot. Not again, I think with despair.

'Sam . . .'

He walks ahead of me, through the kitchen and into the garden. Seeing her uncle, Aurora runs over and throws herself at him, ecstatic. He picks her up and plants a kiss on her cheek.

'My favourite person in the whole wide world.'

She pushes her fingers through his hair then hugs him hard. She's always adored him, always trusted him.

'Whose Sam am I?' Sam asks her.

'My Sam!'

'Forever and ever?'

'Forwever and ever,' she repeats.

He puts her down and she runs back to Leonie. We watch the girls as they crouch on the grass, their heads together; little conspirators. Sam and I were like that once.

'You've taken something,' I say.

'Don't be judgy.'

'I'm not, but you know I don't like you coming round here when you've been smoking weed or whatever it is you've been doing. What if Martin comes home? He'll be livid.'

'Shame you had to marry our father. I hope the life of luxury is worth it.'

'Who's being judgy now?'

Sam peers at my face. 'You look tired. And unhappy.'

My eyes prick, my face beginning to redden. Sam could always see right through me.

'Don't go there,' I say, indicating the girls with a tilt of my head.

Sam grunts. 'This is ridiculous. Why don't you leave him? Take him to the cleaners. We'd both be fine then. We could live together. I could help raise Lucas and Aurora. They love their Uncle Sam. We could have a cottage in the country.'

'I'm not leaving Martin.'

'You almost did though, didn't you?' he urges. 'You were all set to go a couple of years ago, but you backed out at the last minute. You never did tell me why.'

'It's none of your business.' I've never had the courage to tell Sam that Martin knows our secret and that he's been holding it over my head like an axe ever since I told him, ready to let it fall if I make a bid for freedom. He would never forgive me.

'I'm bored of this conversation. You can get repetitive when you're high.'

He regards me for a moment, his jaw working. 'You're scared of what it would mean to be without all this.' He waves his hand around, indicating our huge house, our landscaped garden. 'You don't have to be. All we need is a bit of money. He's got millions stashed away. Take it and run, before he sucks out what's left of your spirit.'

I smile uncomfortably. 'Don't be ridiculous.'

'It's not ridiculous. If you loved him, you wouldn't have—'

'Shut up, Sam. You're in no position to judge my choices, and I will not be emotionally blackmailed by you.'

'How can you say that after everything we went through? We looked out for each other.'

That's his version of events. Mostly I looked out for him. Sam will never admit it. In his head we have always been equals.

'And now, when you have everything you need, because you're prepared to put up with your sociopath of a husband, suddenly I'm inconvenient.'

Aurora lifts her head and watches us, unsure. How easily children pick up on ripples in the atmosphere. I lower my voice.

'Don't.'

Sam senses my struggle and takes my hand. 'I'm sorry, I didn't mean it. It's the stress. I've run into trouble.'

My heart sinks. I am sympathetic, but there are only so many of these stories I can hear, without them losing their ability to move me. It used to be that he would make his mark in the world, but with each passing year the likelihood of that diminishes. He's thirty-three. This September he turns thirty-four. His window of opportunity is receding, along with his hair.

'What kind of trouble?'

He scratches a spot on his hand. 'Financial. Look, I need a short-term loan. Five grand. That's the lot. I won't ask for anything else.'

He never repaid the last short-term loan. I had to dip into my savings for that.

'Five thousand pounds! What on earth for?'

'It was stupid. I got involved with this girl last year. I thought she was the real thing, but she was scamming me. There's a debt collection agency on my back. If I don't pay up, I'll lose my flat, and get a county court judgment. I'll basically be homeless.'

I look at him closely. He doesn't blink. He's lying. He's got some money-making scheme that he knows I won't approve of. Sam lied from necessity as a child, as did I, but he's never grown out of it. It's true that I still tell lies from time to time, but my lies are to protect myself from Martin; his are to avoid the stark reality of his life. There's always someone or something else to blame for his failure to progress.

'Sam,' I say. 'Come on. Can't you get a job?'

He laughs. 'You know perfectly well I'm unemployable. Too selfish for teamwork. I need to be running my own business, but that takes cash.'

So, I was right. There was no scam. 'No, it doesn't. I'm sorry if this comes as a surprise, but it takes focus and planning, research and knowledge to run a successful business. Getting cash is simple. You're lazy, that's your problem, and you give up too easily.'

The last time I gave in to Sam, Martin was furious. He said all I was doing was enabling him. He was right, but it's hard.

'You know why that is.'

'Of course I do, but at some point you have to stop harking back to what happened and move on with your life. Otherwise Dad wins.'

He sticks his chin out, reminding me of the little boy

he once was. I put my hand over his, pressing my fingers between his.

'I don't have it,' I say. 'I'm sorry, but I can't help you this time.'

He drags his hand from under mine and folds his arms. 'Can't or won't?'

Isabel arrives home before I have time to answer. She waits to be introduced, running her fingers through her hair. I do the honours, and Isabel smiles sweetly, but when she gets no reaction from Sam beyond a cursory acknowledgement, she goes back inside.

Sam drums his fingers on the rough surface of the table. I'm scared. I've never said an outright no to him before, I've always given in or compromised, and it feels like a huge milestone in our relationship. I could lose his trust. I chew my lip. Even though we fight, he's the one person who truly knows me, our roots entangled through twinship and a violent childhood. I might pretend otherwise to Martin, Pete and Ali, but I need Sam. Not as much as he needs me, but enough to make this incredibly hard. But in my heart I know what I have to do, for Sam's sake as well as my own, and that's stand my ground and force my brother to sort his own problems out.

'Bit of a risk, isn't it?' Sam says.

For a moment I think he's talking about my refusal to accommodate him, but then I realize he means Isabel. I'm getting a little fed up with the insinuation that I should feel threatened by the presence of a young and pretty Frenchwoman in my house. People joke about it, but really they're issuing a subtle warning, as if I'm too blind or naive to have noticed that she is attractive.

I shift in my chair so I can see her. She's leaning non-chalantly against the island, playing with her phone, but I feel her awareness of me. The fact is, she watches me even more than Martin does, as though I'm an animal in a zoo. She has a student's fascination with her subject. It was a mistake to invite her for a meal with our friends. It's blurred the lines.

'I think I'm pretty safe,' I say. 'I doubt she'd be interested in a thirty-six-year-old man in a wheelchair, and anyway, she's got a boyfriend. One of our tenants.' Saying it out loud makes me feel a little sick.

'I'm only teasing you. You don't have anything to worry about.'

'I'm not worried, Sam.' I scowl at him.

The girls run across the garden, giggling. Aurora climbs onto Sam's lap. She puts her hands on his shoulders and brings her face very close to his. I can't help laughing in spite of myself.

'Sam can play with us,' Aurora announces.

'Sam has to go, sweetie.'

She pouts. 'No, he doesn't.'

Sam mouths something over her shoulder. We used to have a silent language, born of necessity. Sam is telling me he needs help, but he's adding a warning.

You have to help me, or you will fall too.

That might have been true when we were children. If one of us went down, the other fell with them. But not now we're grown-ups, I tell myself. We are autonomous, responsible for ourselves alone. I have too much to lose now. I shake my head. Sam gets up and deposits Aurora on the grass.

'I'll see you soon, baby girl. I promise.'

He straightens up, a last appeal in his eyes. I don't move a muscle.

'Just remember,' he murmurs. 'When you criticize me, you're not whiter than white, Lyzie.'

My mouth drops open. I'm acutely aware of the thread between us fraying a little more. 'I'm hardly likely to forget, am I?'

He strides back into the house, shoulder bumping Isabel as she comes out. She looks round at him and shouts something rude in French. I hear the door slam. I let out my breath.

Aurora looks up, her lip wobbling. 'Want Sam. Don't want you.'

14

Martin's study door is open, the fan whirring, Dan sitting with his legs outstretched, his arms behind his head, laughter never far from his lips, best mates. Every so often I wander past Martin's line of sight as I move between the playroom and the kitchen, but he never catches my eye. I could almost believe that leaving the door ajar and not inviting me to join them is some kind of elaborate torture.

Dan appears in the kitchen in search of coffee, and bumbles round me, like an overgrown schoolboy. Because I've thought about him so much, I can't act naturally. I talk like an idiot, while his eyes linger on my face. I get him down a mug and he takes it from me, his fingers brushing mine as he smiles and holds my gaze a fraction too long.

Disconcerted, I pick up a cloth, run hot water through it and squeeze it out. I take it to the table to wipe where Aurora has spilled milk and smeared Weetabix and, in my clumsiness, knock her spoon onto the floor. She giggles and puts her sticky hand in my hair when I bend to pick it up.

'We're off in ten minutes,' Dan says.

I clean the spoon under the tap and hand it back to her. 'We can't leave until Isabel is back from dropping off Lucas. They won't be long.'

'Oh, great.' His smile widens. 'I didn't realize you were coming.'

That throws me. 'Of course I am.'

Martin pushes himself in. 'You don't have to. I thought I'd give you some peace.'

I regard him silently, then wash my hands and dry them on a tea towel. 'I wouldn't miss it for the world.'

Dan gets into the front of Martin's car and soon regrets it, his face a picture of restrained dismay. Martin is an aggressive driver who rarely respects the speed limit and gets a kick out of running the lights. Dan grips the side of the seat and casts nervous glances his way.

'Problem?' Martin asks.

'I don't have one if you don't, dude.'

Martin laughs. 'Good man.'

There's a light-hearted, mildly hysterical vibe to the journey, the chemistry between Martin and Dan tangible. Now I get why Martin didn't want me to come. Three's a crowd. It's a bromance. They are very different, but Dan, unlike a lot of people we know, has no fear of Martin, even if his reaction to Martin's driving technique suggests otherwise. He's willing to disagree, even to tell Martin he's a fool, and Martin laps it up like he's been thirsty for confrontation of this sort for years. It's taken this to make me realize how much my husband despises people who bend over backwards to win

94

his esteem. Dan gives as good as he gets. I enjoy listening to the back and forth of their conversation, but I take no part in it, except occasionally leaning forward, my hand on the shoulder of Martin's seat, to ask a question.

'So what happened?' Dan says at one stage. 'I mean, I know it was a motorbike accident – Isabel told me – but was it a collision, or what?'

Behind Martin I hold my breath. Not many people ask him directly, especially as it was so long ago. It used to depend on Martin's mood; he could be open and unflinching or he could shut the conversation down with a terse, *I was knocked off my motorbike.* Today he seems inclined to be open.

'A crap combination of rain, drunk woman driver and an unlit country lane.'

'Fuck,' Dan says. 'I bet it hurt.'

Martin momentarily takes his eyes off the road to glance at Dan. 'I have no idea. My mind and body had temporarily parted company. I remember seeing headlights in my wing mirror and a car overtaking me at speed and swerving, but that's it. I woke up from the coma two weeks later and I knew.' Martin's voice breaks, and he coughs. 'I knew I was paralysed.'

I catch his eye in the rear-view mirror, and he grimaces back at me. I feel an unexpected surge of warmth towards him.

'Jesus,' Dan says. 'Bad luck. At least your head was all right.'

'Not quite. I had some swelling – that happens when your skull stops moving and your brain doesn't . . .'

Dan flinches. Martin seems to be enjoying his reaction.

'They stabilized me and thankfully the long-term effects have been minimal – though I'm shorter tempered and less patient than before the accident. Or so my wife tells me.'

He laughs at that and I respond as I'm expected to, reaching to give his shoulder a brief squeeze. 'You're not so bad, darling.'

We had both been warned to expect increased irritability and I could cope with that. What has proved harder to manage, partly because Martin refuses to admit to it, is the subtle exaggeration of some of the more negative aspects of his personality; the judging, the controlling, the jealousy. I suspect that they aren't solely due to the head injury, but also to do with becoming a wheelchair user. If he was judgemental, controlling and jealous where I was concerned before, it's not altogether surprising that he would be more so now.

'What happened to the driver?' Dan asks. 'Did you prosecute?'

Martin stops at the traffic lights, and his thumbs drum against the steering wheel. A sign of impatience.

'She left the scene but she turned herself in the next day. She said she felt guilty, but I think it was more to do with fear that they'd track her down anyway and her punishment would be worse. I got a hefty payout. Enough to build Winterfell, in fact.'

'But at what cost?' Dan says. 'It's a high price to pay for a house.'

'True, but it's not all bad,' Martin says, pulling away.

'In fact, I honestly believe that I'm better off for what happened. I've reached a point in my life where I wouldn't change it. I was doing well, enjoying the job, recently married, but I would have coasted smoothly upwards without even noticing. As it is, life has been a battle that I'm proud to have won. I'm insanely grateful for the strength it's given me. It's made me appreciate what I have so much more than scaling the corporate ladder would have done.'

Uncharacteristically emotional, he reaches back and I take his hand, just for a few seconds before he withdraws it.

'So, let's get this straight,' Dan says. 'Given the choice, you wouldn't rewind the clock and call a cab that night?'

'No, mate,' Martin says with a smile. 'I genuinely wouldn't.'

Does Dan believe him? I know it's not strictly true. It's just part of the myth my husband has created around himself.

When we draw up outside the property, Martin switches off the engine and turns to me with a grin.

'Wait till you see the other side.'

The surveyor, Gregory Davis, is already there. He gets out of his car and gives us a wave, then tries not to look surprised when I take Martin's wheelchair out of the boot. I push it round to the driver's side, then we walk over to Gregory and have a chat about our journey while Martin transfers himself from the driver's seat. He doesn't appreciate an audience.

The door has already been unlocked. There's a lip on

the threshold and as Martin approaches, Gregory takes a step towards him.

'Do not help me,' Martin snaps.

Gregory flushes. Martin takes a run-up to the door, lifts his front wheels, grabs the door frame with both hands and pulls himself through.

'Don't worry,' I say to Gregory, who looks mortified. 'It wasn't your fault.'

The house's widowed octogenarian owner has gone into care and the place tells a familiar story of loneliness and neglect. The men make disparaging comments, but I restrain myself. Someone lived here. They rose from their beds every morning, went into their kitchen and while waiting for the kettle to boil, looked out of the window, saw the morning sun glittering on the river. There are numerous bird boxes and a bird table in the garden. The birds would have swooped in for food from the shrubs and trees. He would have felt as though he knew them individually. By the looks of it, the birds were the only company the old boy had left.

I like this place. Ugly though it unarguably is, I feel at home. I imagine what we could do with it. The kitchen window and patio doors to the sitting room are mean and don't come anywhere near making the most of the view. The new house would be all about the outside. I imagine standing behind a vast pane of glass with my morning coffee, enjoying the dawn. Or in the evening, watching the sunset cast its cloak of colour on the river. And bad weather would be dramatic, not dismal, rain-drops making circles on the water's surface.

'So?' Martin says.

'It's stunning.'

'A challenge, but we like those, don't we?'

'We do,' I say, touching the kitchen worktop then drawing my fingers away swiftly. It feels sticky. 'It's sad though, tearing down a house that's been someone's life.'

'You can't afford to be sentimental.'

'I suppose not.' I smile, energized. 'It's very exciting, Martin. It's a dream project. Linden Road was such fun to do, but this would be on another scale altogether.'

I could do this; I know I could. Martin would be more involved than he was with Linden Road, obviously, and Dan would be a big part of it, but it would still essentially be my job. I imagine dropping Aurora off at Little Beans and Lucas at Highfields and dashing over here in the car to check on deliveries and progress, or sitting beside Dan, our shoulders brushing as he shows me his 3D plans.

'Like Winterfell,' Martin says, breaking my thoughts. 'But even better.'

Leaving Dan and Martin probing Gregory about potential competition, I wander down to the riverbank on my own, and lower myself onto the old wooden pontoon. A pair of ducks swim by, pausing in their dignified progress to nose amongst the reeds at the bank. On the far side of the river, a man waters what looks like a vegetable garden on the roof of his narrowboat.

Hearing a sound, I turn to find Dan making his way down the crazy-paved path towards me. I glance back up at the house. Martin is still talking to the surveyor.

Dan sits down, leaving a demure gap between us. I'm so aware of him that my nerves tingle. I listen to the sound of the water lapping at the edge of the pontoon and find myself thinking about the children, wondering whether I could remove them from their father's house. He'll never let that happen. It's just a dream. And the idea of wandering off into the sunset with Dan is frankly ridiculous. He's attracted to me, but I can't kid myself that it's serious with him; he certainly wouldn't want to be saddled with my children and my problems and neither would I want that. The silence grows so big, I have to break it.

'Well done for finding this place,' I say. 'It was clever of you.'

'Do you mean clever finding it, or clever finding a way into Martin's good graces?'

I smile. 'Was that your intention?'

He shrugs. We watch a motorboat pass. Dan leans forward and dips his fingers in the water. Seeing his reflection reminds me of Narcissus in the Greek myth. Echo pined for Narcissus, I think. Until she turned to dust.

'How's it going with Isabel?' I don't know why I ask, except to provoke a reaction. I can't help myself, even though I feel like I'm worrying at my own wounds. 'Is it love's young dream?'

He shades his eyes with his hand and looks downriver where a group of rowers, schoolboys I think, are being followed by a man in a small motorboat.

'I'm not interested in her in that way. She's just a friend.'

I smile, relieved. 'What does she think about that?'

'She thinks I'm the perfect gentleman.' The corners of his lips curl into a smile. He drops his hand and turns to me. The rowers pass us, their oars cutting quietly through the water. 'The only reason I befriended her was to give me a legitimate reason to come to Winterfell and see you. Don't pretend you didn't know that.'

'Don't be daft.'

'Why is that daft?' He leans back on his arms, soaking in the sun, his eyes closed.

A delicious shiver runs through me. It's hard not to break into a wide smile. 'It just is. You should leave me alone.'

'Nah. It's too much fun seeing you blush.'

'Can we change the subject?'

'If you like. Ali's a good friend to you, isn't she?'

'Yes. We're very close.'

'And Pete?'

'Him too, but he's more Martin's friend.'

'Yeah. I suppose after what happened to Martin you find out who your friends really are.'

'I suppose so,' I say, wondering where we're going with this. 'Some people inevitably fell away, but other friendships became stronger. The Gordons are family too, so that makes a difference.'

'Do you think it's true, what Martin said? That given the choice he wouldn't go back to how he was?'

I smile. 'Yes and no. To be honest, I think he says that for effect. Of course he wishes the accident hadn't happened, but he's proud of what he's done since. He's made a lot of money, built a house. He's shown he can take care of his family.'

'Impressive,' Dan says. 'To have come through an experience like that and not feel angry . . .'

'It's not that simple. He is angry. But the driver has to live with the guilt. That's a punishment in itself.'

He slips his shoes off, rolls up his jeans and drops his feet over the side into the water. 'Guilt's a funny thing. Some people feel it, others don't.'

'Psychopaths, you mean?'

He smiles and his eyes crinkle. 'Is that true, do you think? That only psychopaths feel no guilt?'

'Psychopaths don't have empathy, and if someone doesn't have empathy, surely that precludes them from feeling guilt and shame.'

'We all know someone like that.'

'Do we?'

'Yeah, you know the type. Successful, powerful, but deep down they don't care about anyone else's feelings. They get off on hurting weaker people.'

'If you're hinting that Martin—'

Martin does feel shame about some things. I can't think what at the moment, but he's no psychopath. If I need proof of that, I only have to remind myself how much people like him, how much he gives to charity, how he is with his children, especially Aurora. It's only me he enjoys hurting and I have to take the blame for at least part of that.

'I'm not,' Dan says. 'I don't know how we got onto the subject.'

'Do you feel guilt?' I smile and raise my eyebrows so that he knows I'm joking.

'All the time,' he says. 'You?'

'Same.'

We share a smile that deepens to awkwardness.

Dan pulls his feet up, lies back on the warm wood and pillows his head on his arms. Where his shirt meets his jeans, there's a small triangle of bare flesh showing, scattered with black hairs. I feel an urge to pluck a blade of grass and tickle him with it.

'I think about you all the time,' he says quietly.

Up at the house, Martin suddenly laughs and I'm jolted back to reality. A duck dives below the water. I watch the ripples diminish before he reappears several yards upstream, flutters his wing tips and settles once again.

'I'm married,' I remind him.

He rolls over onto his elbow and looks up at me. 'Yeah. I know. But your marriage doesn't add up. It's his preening sense of ownership. Like you're a possession he doesn't want anyone else to touch, but he expects men to want you, and wants them to know he's the one in control; that they don't have a hope in hell.'

'Right,' I say, disappointed. 'So this is about challenging Martin? A man thing. My dick is bigger than yours.'

'No! You've got to understand,' Dan says. 'Falling in love was the last thing I expected. I was fed up after I broke up with my ex, I honestly didn't want to meet someone else. I needed a break. But there you were, smiling at me, and that was that.'

Martin is making his way down the path. We get to our feet. Dan shields his eyes from the sun with his hand, for all the world a man at his ease. Falling in love. He said *falling in love*.

'Meet me,' Dan mutters. 'So we can talk.'

'I can't.'

'Why not?' he says in a quick, urgent whisper.

There's no time to explain that it's not possible, that Martin tracks my movements outside the house. I'm not sure I want him to know anyway; not yet at least.

'Hi, darling.' I step towards Martin. 'Are you ready to go?'

'What were you two talking about?' Martin asks.

'Demolition,' I say with a smile. 'This place is magic. You couldn't have a more idyllic spot.'

'I need to get an independent surveyor to take a look at it.'

'And Pete,' I add, with a swift smile.

'Your pet architect, you mean?'

'No, I don't mean that,' I say, surprised at his tone. 'But surely Pete is the obvious choice?'

Dan has returned to the edge of the pontoon, and is standing with his hands on his hips, feet apart, as if he's at the prow of a ship.

'Jesus, this is beautiful,' he says, turning to us. 'I mean, who wouldn't want to live here?'

'I know,' I say. 'It's to die for.'

'How much do you want it, Martin?' Dan asks. 'On a scale of one to ten.'

Martin doesn't hesitate. 'Ten. And I won't be the only one.'

'So we see off the competition.'

That startles me. 'We?'

I look back up at the house, where the surveyor is sitting on the bench, waiting for us, thumbs flicking across his screen. I suspect he's playing a game.

'Oh, didn't Dan tell you?' Martin says. 'If we get it, he's going to project manage the whole thing, start to finish.'

'But, Martin,' I stammer, 'I'd be working on it too, wouldn't I? I managed Linden Road. I don't expect to run the entire project but I would like to be part of it.'

Martin's smile is patronizing. 'Giving you free rein over a two-bed flat is one thing, but I wouldn't want to burden you with a project this big. There's far too much involved. You're not cut out for it.'

Dan turns and looks at Martin in the way my school-friends would sometimes look at my father, with surprise and barely concealed embarrassment. I just think, You've given me one more reason to hate you, Martin Curran. One more reason to stray.

'Speaking of Linden Road,' Dan says hurriedly. 'I almost forgot. There's a small damp patch on the ceiling above one of the windows. Shall I call someone out, or will you organize something? It's probably just a leak in the guttering, but it's best to catch those things before they get worse.'

'Is there?' I say. 'How odd. Perhaps I'd better take a look. I've got a few things to do for the other flats next week, but I'll make the time. Monday would work for me.'

'Monday, I'll be out from nine and won't be back till late afternoon. Sorry, it's a nuisance, I know.'

'Not your fault, mate,' Martin says.

'You don't need to be there,' I say, 'if you don't mind me letting myself in. I've got a key.'

'Fine, then,' Dan says easily. 'I'll make sure I leave the place tidy.'

'If I get it, how do you fancy working from Winterfell, Dan?' Martin asks, as we go back to the car. 'We can set up another desk in my study. There's plenty of room.'

My jaw drops.

'Well . . .' Dan hesitates. Behind Martin's back he glances at me.

'It would be part-time hours,' Martin says. He opens the door and transfers himself into the car. 'But I'd rather have you with me to bounce ideas off than do it remotely.'

For a second I think Dan is going to turn him down. Then he shrugs. 'Yeah. Why not? We could certainly give it a go.'

I put the wheelchair into the boot and get in. Is he doing this for me? Or is Pete right in his assessment of Dan and he's self-serving? But then Dan turns, and the smile he sends me is full of reassurance and love.

15

Dan said he'd be out, but I ring his doorbell as a precaution, wait ten seconds before putting the key in the lock then jerk my hand back when I hear feet pounding down the stairs. Dan opens the door with a big grin on his face. I gaze back at him, frozen to the spot.

'Hi,' he says. 'You look confused.'

I find my voice. 'You said you weren't going to be here.'

'You didn't realize it was a ruse?'

I honestly didn't. 'No.'

'Idiot. Come on up. I've just made coffee.'

I hesitate, then follow him. The landing is cramped because it accommodates his bicycle. I decide not to mention the light scuffing on the wall caused by the handlebar. Otherwise the flat is in good order, the kitchen surfaces gleaming. I suspect he's tidied up for me.

His movements are a little jerky. He's nervous and that surprises me. My mouth has gone dry. This feels too soon, and unexpected, although it shouldn't have been. Down by the river he said he was falling in love with me. I didn't answer him; I didn't get a chance to because Martin was making his way over to us. I wouldn't have known what to answer; I still don't. And now here he is, making assumptions with his usual lack of self-doubt, almost as though if he just ploughs ahead, everything else will fall into line. I want to get out but, at the same time, I want to stay.

'Dan,' I say hesitantly. 'I don't think I should be here.'

'You're trembling. Are you scared?'

'Of you? No.'

He smiles, curls a lock of my hair behind my ear and brushes my cheek with his fingertips. 'Of what then? Give yourself a break.'

I step back. 'Is that what this is? A break?'

'You know I didn't mean it like that.'

He takes my hands. I pull them away and he catches them again, this time moving them behind my back, drawing me in close. I raise my head to protest but he kisses me, absorbing the words I meant to say. His kiss isn't deep, but exploratory.

'So . . .?' he says.

I hold back, then something breaks inside me and it's me who kisses him hungrily, and I hear the sound at the back of his throat, somewhere between a chuckle and a groan.

'Let me show you the damp patch,' he murmurs as his lips move to my neck. 'It's in the bedroom.'

'That is so cheesy.'

'I get cheesy when I'm scared.' His eyes grow serious. 'You take my breath away, you know. You have done from the moment I saw you speckled with paint.'

108

'You have low standards,' I say, the corners of my lips twitching. I refuse to smile.

He holds out his hand and after a hesitation I take it and he leads me down the corridor. I'm not sure why it should be, but it doesn't feel right. With Martin that first time, we had talked so much that I felt I knew him. With Dan, we haven't done a lot of talking yet, just a couple of stolen moments. I want to know him, really know him. It worries me that I'm thinking this even as he pulls me into his embrace and my bag slides from my shoulder and onto the floor beside his bed.

I panic. I'm not twenty-one years old; I have too much going on in my life to fling myself into the unknown. It feels so wrong to sleep with my tenant in broad daylight. It's not romantic. It's not even dangerous. It's just desperate.

Dan must have seen the doubt in my eyes, because he lets me go. 'I'm sorry, I thought . . .'

'No, I'm sorry. It's my fault. This is all happening too fast. There's a lot at stake for me.'

Shaking, I straighten my shirt and stoop to pick up my bag, and something bright catches my eye. A fine gold chain caught at the edge of the bed between the mattress and the headboard. My eyes widen. Last time I saw this, it was round Isabel's neat ankle. I tease it out and close my fingers over it.

'You are unbelievable.' I show him the chain, curled snake-like on my palm. 'This belongs to Isabel.'

I don't know who I'm most disappointed with; Dan for lying, or me for falling for his lies and getting myself into what, on the face of it, is a pretty tacky situation. The tenant and the landlady, for God's sake.

His hands go to his hair. 'I don't know how that got there.'

'What are you, ten? You sound like you've been caught filching someone else's sweets.'

'OK. Sorry. Isabel has been here,' he says urgently. 'But she was with a friend. They dropped in. I promise you, Eliza. I have not slept with her. I don't want to.' He looks at the chain in my hand, frowning. 'She must have left it here on purpose.'

'For what possible reason?'

His brow knits. 'She could have seen or heard something to make her suspect we're having an affair. She wanted you to find it.'

'I doubt that. But if it's true, you have to put her right. Tell her there is nothing going on between us. I can't have her telling tales to Martin. She'll wreck my marriage.'

'Would that be such a disaster? You're not happy.'

He sounds like Sam. 'You don't know me well enough to say that.'

There's a silence. The deep brown eyes that a minute ago I was sinking into grow cold and flat.

'I know what I see in that soulless house of yours,' he says. 'It reeks of unhappiness. You deserve better.'

'Spare me the clichés. What are you doing? Trying to draw me into an affair? Do you have some kind of weird agenda? You come into my life, you wrap my au pair and my husband around your little finger, and now you're trying to get me into bed. It's like you're ticking us off on your list.'

'No.' He reaches for my hand, then seems to think twice. 'You've got me all wrong. I thought you . . . shit. I'm not good at this stuff. What I want to say is that I can't stop thinking about you. I thought you felt the same.'

'Stop playing games.'

I'm not ready to forgive. The Dan I know is back, full of warmth and remorse, but the change in him is disorientating. I don't mind hot anger, it's the coldness I find so hard to deal with. My father's way; Martin's too. Fury is an adrenaline rush, something I can fight; calculated emotion is deadening.

'I'm not,' he says.

'Yes, you are. It's what you do. It's what you did when you rang the doorbell that morning. It's what you're doing with Isabel, and now it's what you're doing with me. It's so simple for you, isn't it?'

'Eliza, I promise you, I have no interest in Isabel. I thought you knew that.'

'You're more interested in a married woman? Is that because I'm unattainable?'

'No.' He practically shouts in frustration. 'You don't love Martin.'

'Our situation is complicated.'

'I don't see why you have to put up with a bad relationship. People divorce every day. Children get used to it.' He narrows his eyes. 'Unless it's about the money.'

'How dare you.'

He is as bad as my brother. Why are they so one-track-minded? Why do they see a woman in an unhappy marriage and assume she stays because she enjoys the

111

perks that come with a wealthy husband? I would give up every penny of Martin's to be free of him.

'What is it about then?'

'None of your business.' I push past him and make for the door.

He shakes his head slowly, and calls after me. 'It's all built on sand, isn't it? Your privileged life. Martin and his achievements. One day you're going to wake up and it'll all be gone.'

The row leaves me shaken, and questioning everything about the world that I've built. Dan was wrong about my reasons for staying, but he cut through all the bullshit lies I tell myself to keep this family together. That night I look at Martin's naked shoulder, the nape of his neck, and I imagine that it belongs to Dan, that if I rest my hand there, he'll roll over and smile at me, smooth a hand over my hip and pull me close. Would I be any happier?

Nope, I tell myself, squeezing my eyes shut. Not going to happen.

In the morning I have a message from Dan, apologizing. I don't know how to respond because I'm still smarting from the humiliation, so I delete it without replying. Martin doesn't allow me to password-protect my phone.

16

It's Sports Day at Highfields School. Arriving at the playing fields, I look for Pete and Ali and spot them picking their way across the parched grass close to where the classes are lined up. Ali is unmissable in a burnt-orange linen maternity dress and straw hat. Pete is in his habitual uniform of chinos and white shirt, with added baseball cap. He's carrying Leonie, who wriggles out of his arms when she spots Aurora. We meet on the side-lines in time to catch the older children being rounded up, ready to race. Lucas sees me and breaks into a shy grin, waving his hand at his chest. My family. I shake when I think about the near miss I had with Dan. All this would have been gone in an instant.

The school playing fields are a riot of colour, the children wearing red, yellow, green or blue bibs, women in summer dresses, men in blazers; not a T-shirt or pair of shorts to be seen. Parents are expected to make an effort, to pretend we're at a smart garden party, that we won't be yelling like fishwives at our offspring. We bring our own picnics, families outdoing themselves with hampers. There's a stall selling Pimm's, which Pete and Martin avail themselves of, while Ali and I make do with water. I try not to stare at the men's drinks.

'They're starting,' Pete says.

We shout our heads off. Briony and Lucas have been practising their three-legged partnership for several days, the grazes on their knees and elbows a testament to their dedication. Briony is an absolute saint to have paired up with Lucas, who inevitably loses his rhythm. They come second from last. Not bad, though Martin remarks that they could have done better, that they lost half a second when Briony straightened her red T-shirt as the whistle blew.

'You know where you can stick your half-second,' Ali tells him.

Martin rocks back his head and laughs out loud.

After that, we stroll across the field to watch them in the egg and spoon race. Ali and I have our arms around each other's waists, and I feel a spark of joy when I see Amanda Kelsey glancing our way with a look of irritation. Ali and Martin have always been my ticket to social acceptance round here. Not that I'm intrinsically unlikeable. It's just that without them, I don't add up to much. I'm pretty to look at, but I'm cagey and uninterested in gossiping. I don't invite confidences or give them. I don't trust easily. Keeping schtum about what goes on behind closed doors is something that was drummed into me thoroughly as a child. It's proven good grounding for life with Martin.

Briony marches towards a triumphant finish. I'm pleased about that, since she sacrificed glory for friendship in the three-legged race. She is the only child not staring fixedly at her egg. Lucas drops his several times. Aurora claps him enthusiastically. Martin sighs. A proficient sportsman in his time, it's disappointing for him that his son is so useless at it.

Pete hasn't spoken to me since our initial greeting. He's been talking to Martin and I've stayed at Ali's side. But when the Head's speech has been made and the rosettes and certificates doled out, it falls to Pete and me to fetch the food, picnic blankets and Ali's fold-up chair from the car, while Ali and Martin find a shady spot at the edge of the playing field.

Pete and I talk about our children, and I play along, thinking I've got away with it, that there isn't going to be any reference to our last conversation, but he has other ideas. As he pushes down the door to the boot and humps the heavy freezer bag over his shoulder, he coughs, clearing his throat.

'I'm sorry about the other day.'

'Oh, it doesn't matter.'

'It does. It was uncalled for. I should have trusted you.'

'Pete—'

'Please let me speak.'

I don't like it, but I shut my mouth.

'I was frustrated and to be honest, Eliza, I'm worried. Work's thin on the ground and what with the baby on the way, it's going to be a struggle.'

'Have you told Ali?'

'I didn't want to, but there was no way to avoid it. She has a way of winkling things out of me.'

'Will you be all right?'

115

'Eventually, yes, but in the short term . . . It's a question of holding out. There are things in the pipeline but the only confirmed contract is too small to make that much difference.'

We walk along. I'm not sure whether to mention Gideon Grove; after all, Martin has not categorically said he's going to use Pete. But if Pete isn't forewarned, how can he build a case? It wouldn't hurt, surely, to give him a hint.

'There might be something,' I say. 'I mean, it's not guaranteed or anything, but Martin is looking at the property Dan suggested. It's a good one.'

'Really?' Pete says dubiously. Nothing Dan suggests is ever going to be good as far as he's concerned.

'Yes. We've been to see it. It's actually a fantastic spot. It has a large garden with a mooring.'

Pete nods, thoughtful. 'I'd like to take a look, obviously.'

'Yes, of course. But Martin will put it out to tender, you know, so don't get too excited.'

'That's normal. He'll need to get different quotes. But we can match anyone else's.' He hesitates, breaking his step. 'You won't tell Martin what I told you about our finances, will you? It's not a good look when you're bidding on a job.'

'Of course not.' I walk quicker, anxious to get back to the others, fearing that Martin would not approve if he knew what I've been saying. He would have told Pete himself if he'd wanted him to know. On the other hand, why shouldn't Pete have a heads-up? That's what friends are for.

* * *

The early afternoon sun beats down, conversation slows; we are replete and drowsy. The older children are off somewhere with their friends, having grown bored with us adults, the younger ones playing where we can see them. Pete's foot accidentally nudges mine. I shift. He wipes the sweat from his brow and brushes a crumb off his thigh. There's still enough shade for Ali to be out of full sunlight, but the sun is moving over the trees and soon even that reprieve will be gone. She is sound asleep, her head resting on her arm, her hat covering her face.

Pete's arms hang loosely round his knees. Martin stifles a yawn.

'So,' Pete says, scratching the side of his neck. 'I gather you're taking Dan's idea seriously?'

'I'm not dismissing it,' Martin responds.

'You will be careful?'

I frown at Pete – why is he doing this now? He refuses to meet my eye.

'What is it you want me to be careful of, particularly?' Martin asks.

His tone is light, but the tell-tale deepening of the lines around his mouth tells a different story.

Pete appears to be putting some thought into what he's going to say. I wish he'd think about shutting up.

'What I see, from the outside, is a chancer sensing an opportunity.'

'Huh,' Martin says. 'Interesting. And why exactly shouldn't a young man with big ideas chance his luck?'

'Well, for a start, I wouldn't call Dan a young man. Secondly, what does he know about building and design?'

'He hasn't actually said he knows anything. He's not offering architectural expertise, he's offering creative support for a venture that excites him. It's up to me, the client, and whoever we commission, to come up with the designs.'

In the pause that follows, Aurora and Leonie come running up wanting a drink of water. It feels as though we are encased in silence, cut off from the world by tension. I want to say something to encourage the girls to stay, but they glug their water down and are gone before I can form a sentence.

'This is not about me,' Pete says. 'I'm not touting for business, or trying to get one over on Dan – I'm sure he's a nice enough guy – but I don't think any of us have his measure yet. He's your tenant, but he wants to be your friend, and now all of a sudden he wants to be your business partner in some cock-eyed venture he's pulled out of thin air. Build homes for the disabled rich? He must think you're made of money.'

Martin leans forward and pushes the brim of his hat up. 'What is your problem? Do you think I can't work things out? Do you think being unable to walk means I've lost my instincts?'

Pete looks horrified. 'I don't mean any of that. I'm just suggesting you should back up a bit. Slow down on this until you know the guy better. What's in it for him, do you think? I saw the way he looked at Eliza. Did you miss that completely? He wants what you have, and if you can't see that, then more fool you.'

'Pete,' I say. 'Can we not talk about this here?'

'It's all right, Eliza,' Martin says. 'The trouble is,

Pete, you underestimate me. I'm not unobservant. I know when other men fancy my wife. She's a beautiful woman, isn't she?' He waits, then repeats, 'Isn't she?'

I hold my breath. Pete's face turns puce.

'Eliza is gorgeous,' he stammers.

'Oh, for heaven's sake.' I glance down at Ali, wishing she'd wake up and put a stop to this. 'I'm not an object.'

Martin puts his hand on my shoulder. It feels hot and damp and I long to shake it off, but I grit my teeth and resist.

'So you trust him?' Pete blunders on. 'Despite knowing nothing about him? Frankly, I wouldn't work with someone like that. He's an amateur, a big ideas man who couldn't possibly follow anything through on his own, who needs to sponge off someone who isn't scared of risk, someone who doesn't turn and run when the going gets tough. He's a shit, Martin. And if you had any sense you'd tell him to fuck off.'

He's right; Dan is a shit, I think. Trying to do business with a man while attempting to seduce his wife, not to mention sleeping with the family's au pair. Pete was right about him all along. I am still furious, I realize. Maybe that's a good thing. Maybe it'll help wean me off him.

There's a heavy silence. Ali shifts and starts to wake up.

Martin's voice drops to a menacing whisper. 'How dare you suggest I don't have the wit to know who and what I'm dealing with, or that Eliza would be weak enough to fall for a man like that. You needn't worry, I understand Dan perfectly. I can see his greed and hunger. I can smell it. But I also know that I can use it.'

'OK. Well, it's your funeral.' Pete pauses, pretends to

be looking for something in his pocket. 'So, I'd like to see the site.'

'The site?'

'Yes. The one by the river.'

Martin leaves a brief, and telling, pause before answering. 'Of course, if you're interested. It's coming up for auction next week, but there's still time. Get in touch with the agent. It's not mine yet. You do realize that?'

'Yes, but if you are keen I'd like to walk round it, get a feel for the environment. See what the other properties are like, what we can get away with.'

'Pete, mate,' Martin says smoothly. 'I don't know where you got the idea from, but there is no "we". You're more than welcome to submit designs if I manage to acquire it, which isn't a given, but things move on. I want a fresh vision for Gideon Grove.'

I watch Pete's face stiffen. 'I can give you that.'

Martin cricks his neck. He looks Pete straight in the eye. 'Actually, I don't want you involved in this.'

'Martin,' I say, but he lifts his hand to shut me up.

'For what reason?' Pete asks. He sounds as though he's speaking through his teeth.

'I don't need a reason but if you insist, I need an architect with a name people recognize. You can't keep riding on my coattails.'

Pete pales and scrambles up. 'Don't count on me when things go wrong. Ali, we're leaving, I'll grab the girls.' He marches off while Ali straightens her straw hat and looks from me to Martin.

'What on earth's going on?'

'Sorry, Ali,' I say. 'Pete will explain.'

Lucas runs over when he sees me stand up.

'Can you get Aurora, darling? It's time to go home.'

'Can't we stay a bit more? We're playing a game.'

'Ali's had too much sun.'

'Can Briony come with us?'

'Not today.'

I glance at Pete. He has Leonie on his hip and is holding Briony's hand. His jaw is set, his eyes blazing when he looks back at me. I shake my head slowly. This is his fault. If he'd known when to shut up, Ali and I could have managed Martin between us. But he had to go charging in, self-righteous and defensive. He's an idiot.

17

'He pissed me off,' Martin says. 'He just assumed he'd be part of it. Like I can't do anything without including him. That's not how it works.'

Even though I'm annoyed with Pete, I feel I should at least attempt to make his case, for Ali's sake if nothing else.

'Maybe not. But you have to see it from his point of view.' I promised Pete I wouldn't tell Martin the company was having financial difficulties. 'Dan comes on the scene and all of a sudden he's feeling excluded. How do you expect him to react?'

'Like a professional.'

'Well, I'm going to call Ali.'

'You do that. Knowing Ali, she'll be unreceptive.'

Martin is proved right. I try Ali's mobile, but it goes straight to voicemail. I call the Gordons' landline. It rings out. They will know it's me, of course. I imagine Ali with the phone in her hand, waiting for it to stop. I'm hurt and alarmed, but I'm sure by morning she'll want to talk. She and Martin have had their spats in the past, but they've always made up. Usually it's Ali who makes the first move, but not always. Martin has had his moments of humility.

I still have Isabel's anklet. I don't know why. I could have so easily slipped it into her bag. I doubt she'd have noticed, it's so full of clutter. But I've left it too late, and anyway, I want to talk to her. I need to know if Dan was telling the truth.

Isabel hasn't gone out this evening. She's in the annexe doing whatever young women do; watching something on her laptop or FaceTiming her friends. I go outside and round to the side door and listen. No sound. I knock.

'Who is it?'

'It's Eliza.'

Who did she think it was going to be? I push the door open. She's sitting on her bed in a pair of knickers and nothing else, cross-legged. She doesn't even attempt to cover up.

'Oh, sorry.' I look away in embarrassment.

'It's OK.'

She gets off the bed and crosses the room, picks a T-shirt up off the floor and pulls it over her head. 'There. That is better, no?'

I'm stunned. I was never that confident.

'It's fine. I didn't mean to invade your privacy.' I open my palm so that she can see the chain. 'I found this when I went round to Linden Road to inspect the damp. It's yours, isn't it?'

'Yes, thank you.' She laughs. 'I did not notice.'

I wait, and she looks at me.

'It bothers you that I was there, with Dan?'

'No, not at all. You're an adult, you can do what you want. But Isabel, I did just want to reassure myself that Dan hasn't put you under any pressure.'

'You are always worried about this. I am not a virgin, Eliza. I don't want to marry him, but we have fun together.'

'Fun as in sex?'

There is an infinitesimal pause before she answers. 'That is personal.'

'I only mean—'

'He is in love with me.' Her expression is sullen. She doesn't like anyone doubting her ability to attract and keep her man.

'Men say that—'

'I understand about men. There is no pressure.' Her gaze narrows. 'What were you doing in Dan's bedroom?'

She still hasn't told me whether they've slept together or not. It's all I want to know.

'That's where the damp patch is.'

'Oh.' She's unsure. 'Were you jealous when you found it?'

'Don't be silly, I was concerned for you.'

'*Bof.* You don't need to be. And I have not been to bed with him yet. You should never sleep with a man too soon, you know. Men like Dan, they like a challenge.'

If I wasn't so irritated, I would smile. Dan wasn't lying. 'Thanks for the advice.'

She laughs like I've said something riotously funny when I meant the sarcasm to sting. I can hear her laughing as I walk back round to the main house. I have a feeling I've weakened myself in her eyes, but I don't care. I've got what I came for.

Later, I try to reason with Martin again. 'Please, will you speak to Pete?'

Martin shakes his head. 'No, let him stew.'

'Did you mean it about the build? That you won't use him? It'll be the end of your friendship. You do know that, don't you?'

'Eliza,' Martin says, his voice ice cold. 'I don't even have the bloody place yet and at this rate I might just forget the whole thing, if it's going to cause this much aggro. Much as I love my sister, I cannot run a business to suit her husband. She'll understand.'

'What about our children? They're used to living in each other's pockets. It's unfair on them.'

How will our lives work? How will we cope? How can I possibly make Lucas and Aurora understand that they can't see their friends? Our children should not be made to suffer because their parents have fallen out. What kind of lesson does that teach them, when we are constantly telling them to kiss and make up?

It's going to be just as hard for Ali, especially once she's had the baby. I would have taken the girls off her hands at the drop of a hat, no notice required.

'Don't turn this into something it isn't,' Martin says. 'I don't want to work with Pete on this, and there is no reason why I should have to. Being related does not obligate me in any way.'

'Evidently not.'

'You know as well as I do that sentiment and business don't mix.'

'You hurt his pride.'

'Tough.'

'He idolizes you. And when you cut him out in favour of a fresh face, naturally he's going to feel threatened.'

'Why do you care so much about Pete?' Martin counters. 'I thought it was Ali you were worried about.'

'It is. Are you going to tell me what's turned you against him?'

'It's a matter of trust.'

He doesn't know what happened. He can't do. I've destroyed that letter.

'What do you mean?'

'He's been lying to me about the state of the Pitfield Group's finances. They've been in trouble for the last three years. I can't work with an architect firm that might go bankrupt at any moment. If he'd come clean it would be another matter.'

'If he hasn't told you, how do you know?'

'Companies House.'

I call Ali when Martin goes back to work, not expecting a miracle, but hoping. To my surprise she picks up.

'Ali—'

'I'm sorry.' Her voice is so gentle, it scares me. 'I know this is hurtful, and I wish it could be different, but you need to stop trying to contact me for a while. Pete and I feel it would be best if we put some distance between us. I'm sure you understand.'

'But Ali, this could all be over nothing. Martin might be outbid.'

'That's hardly the point. I don't know what my brother thinks he's doing, but he's going to end up with no friends if he isn't careful. He's not the man I thought he was. There is more to this, Eliza.'

My hand grips the phone. 'More?'

'I don't think Pete's told me everything. I'm going to get to the bottom of it. But in the meantime, we could do with a bit of space. Living so close to family, it can get a bit intense. Martin is being a manipulative bully, and I won't stand for it. Pete is my priority.'

'But it doesn't mean that we shouldn't see each other. Surely. And what about the children?'

'Eliza.' Ali is growing impatient. 'I have an angry husband, I'm about to have a baby, and there's the dog. My house is a tip and I don't have the luxury of a cleaner. I have more than enough to deal with. Please, just leave me alone. I'll get back in touch if anything changes.'

She means if Martin apologizes and changes his mind about Gideon Grove. I can feel the ground beneath me slipping away. I don't have another friend, not a proper one.

I dash a tear away with the back of my hand. 'Ali, I'll talk to him . . .'

The line goes dead. Ali has hung up on me. I'm stunned. Thank God Isabel has taken the children to the playground, because I cannot stop crying.

18

Can we have a chat? I type.

My fingers hover over the backspace icon. After our last encounter I doubt Dan will want to speak to me, but I have to try. It isn't his fault that we've fallen out with our friends, and yet it wouldn't have happened without him. I can fix this situation, at least; explain to Dan why he needs to walk away from Martin's offer. That's what I tell myself, before I tap send. I also owe him an apology, but that can wait till I see him.

He replies immediately. *I have to be in London later. But that's fine. I can meet you at 10.*

Thanks. Nico's.

I deliberately leave my phone behind, deleting the conversation with Dan beforehand and switching it off. I'm upset and on edge, and when I'm on edge, I get forgetful. Martin is not tracking me today.

On the walk to Boundary Road I give myself a stern talking to. I'm doing this because of the Gordons. I will apologize to Dan for lashing out at him when he hadn't

128

done anything wrong, but I will not succumb to his charm. This is not the time to turn my life upside down. I might fantasize about leaving Martin, but I'm not deluded enough to think I can make it work with Dan. Pete's words still scratch at me, like a label inside the collar of a shirt. *You're all taken in by his shiny smile. Even my wife.* I'm not about to jeopardize my relationship with my children for a pie-in-the-sky romance with a man I do not completely trust. Anything is worth putting up with to save Aurora and Lucas the pain and mortification of finding out what their mother is capable of. An affair with Dan Jones is out of the question.

Dan is sitting beside the window when I arrive, the sight of him making me smile broadly regardless of my internal pep talk. I raise my hand in greeting, go up to the counter, and await my turn behind a trio of Irish builders. Nico's is old-fashioned. It's been run by the same family for thirty-five years and has resisted the pressure to compete with the trendier start-ups. There are no leather armchairs or books leaning at jaunty angles on shelves painted in heritage shades, just good solid chairs and tables ranged against walls hung with sepia images of Boundary Road in the days when horses pulled their loaded carts along the muddied highway. Nico's coffee is authentically Italian, and its pastries and panini are as good as you'd get anywhere else. Best of all, it's not overrun by mums from the local schools. They prefer the much larger Costa where they can manoeuvre their prams more easily.

The builders pick up their takeaway cups and leave.

Dan has put down his phone and is watching me, making me so nervous I fluff my order and have to repeat it.

I sit down. Dan leans his chin on his clasped hands and rubs his teeth against his knuckles. I want to reach over and pull his hand away. Instead I glance out of the window. A bus has stopped in traffic and a couple of passengers look in at us. I wish I'd asked Dan to sit further in, but that would have suggested I wanted it to be romantic, which I don't. I simply want to straighten things out before they get any worse.

'To what do I owe this honour?' he asks.

'Don't,' I say, smiling uncertainly. 'I'm aware I owe you an apology, but that's not what this is about.'

'Shall we get the apology over first then?' There's a hard glint in his eye. He's as resolved to resist me as I am to resist him.

'I know you didn't sleep with Isabel. She told me.'

'You asked her? Wow.'

'Well, not directly; but yes. I asked.'

He sighs. 'OK. Apology accepted in the spirit it was given.'

I look into his eyes. 'Meaning?'

'Meaning, it's conditional.'

I don't know what to say to that. It's true. I feel miserable, as if I've broken something between us, even though it's something I don't even want. Isn't that what kids do? Reject a toy then have a meltdown when it breaks?

'So why did you want to see me?'

I bite my lip. 'It's awkward.'

'You're here now. Best get it over with.' He leans back and folds his arms across his chest. 'I'm all yours.'

I smile at that. 'I have to ask you something.'

'OK.'

'Your involvement with Martin is creating problems. I need you to back off.'

'You're talking about Pete?'

'Yes.' I'm surprised he leapt to that conclusion so quickly. 'But Ali as well. Their friendship is important to me, to both of us. Even if Martin is dismissive of Pete at the moment, he owes a lot to him and deep down he knows it. They're very different characters but their bond is incredibly strong.'

'Then surely nothing I can do can break it.'

'You can damage it though.' I risk meeting his gaze. 'I'm sorry. You've done nothing wrong. I can't blame you for the way the others are behaving.'

'Well, that's a relief. I want to work with Martin because he's inspirational. He goes for what he wants, a hundred per cent. And I admire his resilience. What happened to him would have broken lesser men.'

So it wasn't because of me. It's always Martin people want to get close to, I think miserably. 'He's not infallible. Things do hurt him.'

'Really?' Dan's face softens. 'I suppose that's reassuring. He's human.'

Before I can ask myself what Martin would think, I describe the humiliation Martin suffered at the hands of the intruder. 'It took him a while to bounce back from that.'

'But he's never given up, has he? Being around him makes me want to achieve more. You wouldn't begrudge me that, would you?'

'Of course not,' I respond, taken aback. 'But what you're doing is at the expense of our relationship with the Gordons. They are family and we've been through so much together over the years.' Even as I say it I can hear the ring of hypocrisy.

'Point taken. I'm the interloper. The new kid.'

'I didn't mean it like that.'

'I know. Listen, Eliza, you're stuck in the middle of a shitty situation. This is about two friends falling out. It was probably due, for all sorts of reasons that don't include me. Isn't it more likely that I was merely the trigger for something that's been brewing for a while? Martin and Pete won't stay angry. As you say, they need each other. And to be frank, if Ali is blanking you because of this, then I don't call that friendship.'

'She isn't like that. Ali's always been there for me.'

'And now she isn't. She's frozen you out. Can't you see you're being manipulated by the Gordons? Pete hates me because I've upset the balance. I'm like Uber, a disrupter.' He drinks some of his coffee.

I can't help laughing, because it's true.

'What aren't you telling me?' he asks, leaning forward slightly.

I want to push his hair out of his eyes. He seems to read me because he does it himself, raking his fingers through it.

'What do you mean?'

'There's something beyond all this, isn't there? Beyond Martin and the way he treats you.'

My eyes prick. I look down at my mug.

'Hey,' he says, tipping my chin up with his hand. 'I'm sorry. I didn't mean to touch a nerve.'

I raise my eyebrows and he grins.

'Well, perhaps I did,' he says. 'I want to know what's wrong and I don't think it's just that your husband can be a bastard, because you're still with him after all. I want to know what keeps you there, what stops you coming to me.'

I look into his eyes and imagine telling him everything, explaining what happened to Dad, explaining what makes Sam who he is, and me who I am. I keep looking, keep thinking, then I close it down, shake my head and push my cup away, indicating that I'm ready to leave.

'One day you'll tell me,' Dan says.

'One day.' My smile is crooked.

Then without warning he leans across the table, cups my head with a hand and kisses me long and hard on the lips.

When he lets me go, there's a figure outside the window, looking in, her mouth hanging open. Ali.

19

I burst through the door after her. 'Ali, please stop.'

'I don't want to talk to you.'

She strides along the pavement, her hand supporting her belly, but she can't keep up the pace for more than a few yards. She stops and steadies herself against a lamp-post. Her forehead is beaded with sweat.

'Are you OK?' I reach for her but she jerks away.

She looks at me pityingly. 'I have so misjudged you. My brother loves you. After everything he's been through, you have an affair with your tenant? Jesus Christ.'

'We are not having an affair. He just kissed me.'

She narrows her eyes. 'I thought you had integrity, but you're just a bored housewife, falling for the first man to show an interest.'

I feel conspicuous. Passers-by are watching, interested in the row between two middle-class housewives. I'm surprised no one's filming us for Instagram.

'You betrayed my brother. He works his arse off to keep you in luxury. Everything that man does is for you. He's put you on a pedestal for years. He's never said a bad word about you to anyone. I hear it all the time, husbands and wives belittling each other. Martin has never done that. He is loyal. He took a vow, and like everything else he does, he sticks to it. You don't deserve a man like that, Eliza. I'm disappointed in you.'

My eyes are getting wider and wider. Can she have been completely blind all this time? Martin is always putting me down in subtle ways. Maybe they're so subtle no one but me can see them. I wipe my nose, press my fingers into my eye sockets and swallow back the tears. 'Martin is not as perfect as you make him out to be.'

She tuts.

'You think it's simply a question of bad wife, good husband, but it's not like that. Martin and I . . .' I sniff. 'Our relationship hasn't been great for a long time now. Years actually. He controls everything I do. It's stifling. Your brother is a bully, and I've tried so hard, I've hidden it from everyone, but I just can't any more.' I can't quite get myself over the last hurdle; telling her he physically lashes out at me. It would destroy her.

'I don't believe you.'

'I knew you wouldn't, but I can prove it. There's an app that tracks my movements.' I rifle through my bag frantically.

'Why would any woman who isn't a total doormat agree to that? And why wouldn't you have told me?'

'I agreed because Martin's psychiatrist suggested it, because in the months after he left hospital, not knowing where I was at all times was making him very difficult; and by difficult I mean unreasonably angry and cruel. I didn't tell you because I find it humiliating. I didn't want you to know that I'm that weak.' I groan under my breath. 'Shit. I forgot. I left my phone at home.'

She shakes her head. 'So that he couldn't see where you were going? So you could meet your lover?'

'No! I—'

'Stop lying, Eliza.'

'I met Dan because he's a friend and I needed someone to talk to.'

'You could have talked to me.'

'You asked me to stay away, remember?'

She lets that go. 'You say my brother is cruel to you, and yet you stay. Why? Is the fancy house and expensive car your reward for putting up with him? I didn't take you for a gold-digger.'

'I would have left but it's in his power to make sure I lose the children. I've done things in the past I'm not proud of, things he knows about. He'll use them. Are you . . .' I swallow hard. 'Are you going to tell him?'

'I don't know.' Her voice is stiff but she sounds uncertain.

'Please don't. Nothing has happened with Dan, apart from him kissing me just now, and that was totally unexpected. Nothing is going to happen.'

'From where I'm standing, that man is systematically taking down your life. Why can't you see it?'

She turns away, leaving me gaping, but then stops and looks back. She seems to struggle with herself, then blurts out, 'There's something I need to ask you. I want you to tell me the truth.'

I wait, promising nothing.

'Did you sleep with Pete when Martin was in hospital?'

The shock makes my vision blur. 'What? No, of course not.'

Seconds pass where she doesn't break eye contact. 'Someone pushed this through the door.' She takes a folded-up envelope out of her bag, opens it and pulls out a piece of paper.

You should know what Eliza did with Pete when your brother was in a coma.

I can barely breathe. 'It's not true. I have no idea what . . .'

'Even when I give you the chance to come clean, you still lie to my face. And you claim to be my best friend? There's no point denying it, Pete told me everything.'

I close my eyes in shame. 'Oh my god . . . Ali . . .'

Her face reddens. 'You are toxic, Eliza. Stay away from me.'

20

I stumble back the way I came. I can't help wondering what exactly Pete's *everything* was. No doubt it involved my womanly wiles and his temporarily weakened defences. Dan comes out of the cafe, but I shake my head and keep walking.

'Wait,' he says. He puts his hand on my shoulder.

'Please, Dan, leave me alone.'

'You can't just dash off like this,' he says, sounding genuinely concerned. 'Come back inside and sit down. You're as white as a sheet.'

'I'll be fine. You go to your meeting. I don't want to make you late.' I turn away, not wanting him to see how close I am to crying.

'Eliza—'

'Just go!'

He backs off abruptly, holding up his hands, wincing at my tone. 'OK. No problem. You've got my number. Call me if you need me.'

I start to run, only slowing down when I get far enough away, then I walk, head bowed, barely looking where I'm going, until I reach the less well-to-do end of Boundary Road about half a mile west of the station. Dad used to call me toxic when I was a teenager and attempting to give as good as I got, like there was something wrong with me, not him; like it was me and my behaviour that was poisoning our household. If I'd known how Ali felt about Pete at the time, I never would have slept with him. I would have urged him to shed his tears on her shoulder instead of mine. What a mess.

How did I let it come to this? I wasn't *happy*, but at least I knew how to handle my life. Now everything has spiralled out of control. Have I always stood on the edge of a precipice? It would be so easy to blame this on Dan's arrival, but I let this happen. He only wanted to help. He only kissed me because he sensed I wanted it. And because, I admit silently, after that uncomfortable scene in his bedroom, there is unfinished business between us.

There's a pub on a busy crossing point. I spot it and don't stop to consider what I'm doing. My legs take me confidently to the bar, and my lips order a double vodka before they've engaged with my brain. And then it's too late to turn around and go back to the safety of the street. The barman pours my drink without comment and I tap my card on the reader. I look around and pick a table in a dimly lit corner.

It turns out it's one of those old-school pubs that don't have a trendy menu, just crisps and nuts. The floor is carpeted in patterned maroon, the windows are draped with bottle-green curtains, the tables and chairs dark with varnish. I breathe in the smell and hunch over my glass, absurdly self-conscious considering the place is almost empty.

I've been sober for eight years. I'm proud of every day. When I met Martin I was drinking heavily; I was nineteen, my father had been dead four years, and my mother had died three years after him, leaving me and Sam alone in a heavily mortgaged house with debts that mopped up the bulk of her estate. All I kept was a pair of diamond and emerald earrings, which I've never worn. I'll give them to Aurora when she's twenty-one. I missed Sam, who had gone with a gang of friends to explore Europe by train, and was drinking myself into addiction with masochistic determination. I found if I drank enough I could obliterate the memories. I went to India with a naive idea that I could draw a line under the past, but it just made it easier to drink because no one noticed. Everyone was young and either high on drugs, pissed or asleep. When Martin worked it out, he helped me stop. He was incredible: patient, loving and firm.

After we married and things began to go wrong, I started again, getting into the habit of drinking wine after work, then letting it become part of my day as well, falling back into my old ways, hoping alcohol would give me the courage to make a break with the man I loved but who was slowly chipping away at my confidence. I worked in a finance company where 70 per cent of the staff were male. He didn't like that. And then he had the accident and I couldn't leave.

The long-term psychological effects of the brain injury he sustained were barely noticeable to anyone who didn't live with Martin day to day. Kate and Ali knew that there were issues but were unaware of their extent, and they didn't ask. That made me feel lonely and scared. After the months of rehabilitation and intense therapy came to an end, Martin shut those conversations down entirely. He makes jokes about his short temper, but as far as he is concerned, the accident hasn't measurably altered him except in ways that make him stronger. That is his narrative.

After a bender that turned into a terrifying lost weekend, I cleaned up and made promises to my husband. We found a way to progress, discovered that our sexual life was not at an end, and tried to find each other again. The desire for a baby meant that I stayed dry, and when, after one gruelling round of IVF, I fell pregnant with our first child, those promises were sealed with joy. Until now.

The first taste makes my head spin. I drink quickly, then order another before it enters my bloodstream. Then another. I don't remember alcohol ever hitting me so hard, so fast, but I was younger then.

I look up to find the barman watching me.

'Everything all right?' he asks.

I nod, or I think I do. My head bobs up and down. 'One more.'

'Are you sure about that, love?' His voice is kind.

'Yup. One more.'

I hold up my glass, but it slips through my fingers and bounces on the table before he can come round the bar and take it off me. I laugh and it turns into a sob.

'Bad day?'

'Could say that.'

'It's quiet in here, if you want to talk.'

'Are you a psychiatrist?'

He smiles. He's a big man, with salt and pepper hair, dressed in black jeans and a T-shirt with a faded picture of a tree on the front. His stomach bulges over his waistband.

I lean on my hand. 'I had an argument with my best friend.'

'Ah, well,' he says. 'Arguments can be patched up.'

'Not this one. I slept with her husband.'

He nods, pursing his lips. 'Not a great move.'

'I know. Oh God.' I tuck my head under my clasped hands.

After a second or two he moves back behind the bar. He sees people like me every day. I imagine he thinks we're rather pathetic, buying drinks to dull the pain.

I stay a little longer, because I have nowhere to go. I can't call anyone because I don't have my phone. I could borrow the landlord's, but there's a limit to the numbers I know by heart and anyway, who would I call? My mother-in-law? Would Kate come and get me after what I've done to her family? The idea of her frosty silence on the journey home is chilling.

'Would you like me to order you a cab?' the bartender asks.

'Yes, please.' I throw him a look of abject gratitude.

'Where to?'

'Don't know. I'll decide in a minute.' I put my hand in my bag, looking for a hanky, and find my keys and that brings a burst of inspiration. Linden Road. I have a key.

Dan said he'd be out all afternoon. 'Actually, doesn't matter. I'll go to a friend's place.'

I can see his doubt.

'He's just round the corner,' I add, 'I'll be fine.'

I get up unsteadily and totter to the door. I can feel his eyes on my back, but someone walks in as I leave, so he doesn't come after me. I doubt he would have anyway. His interest ends at the exit.

21

I remember fuzzily, as I step off the kerb and get honked at by a moron in an SUV, that my kind of drunk is the drunk that loses her appreciation of risk. I don't get belligerent or maudlin, I just don't follow the Green Cross Code. This is not good. I pull my shoulders back, lift my chin and wait for the green man with the obedience of a small child, then cross the road behind a woman in a flowery dress, following her steady trajectory. I concentrate on not stumbling when I reach the opposite pavement.

I make it to the entrance to the local supermarket, hesitate, then go in, my heart racing. I don't remove my sunglasses. I pick up a bottle of vodka, ducking backwards behind the shelves when I see Amanda Kelsey. She's holding one of those plastic baskets you pull. I knock my shoulder against a shelf, something wobbles, and I spin round and grab a tin of custard before it falls. If I wasn't so panicked, I'd be impressed that my reflexes still work.

'Eliza,' Amanda says, appearing at the end of the aisle. 'Fancy seeing you here.'

'Hi.' I raise my hand. The one holding the tin. The other one, the one holding the bottle, I keep behind me.

She looks wary. 'Are you all right?'

I barely trust myself to walk in a straight line, let alone speak, but she's waiting.

'I'm fine. It's the heat.'

'Gosh, yes. It does that to me sometimes. Well, I'd better go. I'm having the Gordon kids round for tea, to give darling Ali a break. Honestly, I had to insist. The sooner that baby arrives the better.'

I have no response to any of this, and she gives me an insincere smile. I turn up the corners of my mouth and she goes on her way.

I grab a can of tonic water and pay for my purchases, shoving them into my bag and forcing the zip shut over them. Once outside it's a matter of switching my brain to autopilot. It leads me down one Victorian terrace and up another. The sun beats down, the heat radiating from the pavement and the brick walls. I keep walking, sweat prickling under my arms, anxiety bubbling. I hate Amanda Kelsey because she can see right through me. She senses I'm a fraud, and she's jealous that despite that, I have so much more than her. Not for long though. By this evening she'll know that Ali's not speaking to me, if she doesn't already. Not one to miss an opportunity, she'll cement her position by making herself indispensable, because Ali, despite her big personality, needs people around her to help keep things chugging along.

I don't see anyone else I know, and if I don't see them, maybe they can't see me. I pass Ali's house, walking on the other side of the road, raising my hand to hide my face in case one of the Gordons happens to be in the front room. Then it's left, right and left again, and I release a sigh. Linden Road. Number 42. Sanctuary. I stab at the lock with the key, scratching the paintwork. I lick my finger and try to polish the scratch away, but it remains, a stubborn witness to my disaster. I don't think Dan will notice. Most men don't notice little things like that.

The staircase is moving in an odd way; my elbow scuffs the wall. I grip the banister, find my equilibrium, haul myself to the top, swaying like I'm on a rope bridge. I'm reassured by the absence of Dan's bike. This place still feels like mine, even though it's his. Why did I meet him today? I didn't need to. It was asking for trouble.

I wander in and out of the rooms. The kitchen is passable, some dirty dishes in the sink. The bathroom is clean and there are no damp towels or discarded clothes on the floor. The bedroom is tidy, the bed made, a few clothes left out, but nothing more than I'd expect. I gaze longingly at the bed, tempted to sprawl across it and cushion my slowly revolving brain on Dan's pillows.

In the spare bedroom the single bed is covered with an Indian throw printed with birds, bright red flowers and blue-green leaves. It's gorgeous. I run my hand over it, wanting it. I pick it up and wrap it round my shoulders. Winterfell is so neutral. Soulless, Dan described the house. That stung, but it's only what I think myself.

I leave the room, catching my shoulder painfully on the door frame and snagging the blanket. Whoops. I put it back and try to tuck the snag between the mattress and the wall. Smooth it out. I hope he doesn't notice.

Back in the kitchen I mix my drink and look down into his narrow slice of garden. I'm developing a headache so I decide against going outside. Instead I take my

146

shoes off and sink into the sofa, trying to work out how I'm going to explain to Martin what's happened.

I could say the need just came over me. A combination of stress and the row with Ali and Pete. I'll promise to go back to AA. He'll approve of that. I'll be proactive, one of his favourite words. Just hope he hasn't sent out a search party. Oh God, please don't let him have sent out a search party. Who would it consist of? Isabel and Martin in his car roaming the streets? He'd call Kate to see if I was there. Hell, he might even work his way through the class list.

I drain the glass, put it down on the floor and lean back into the cushions. An hour and I'll be fine. Dan will never know I've been here. The windows are closed and it's hot. The sofa is deep and comfortable. My eyes grow heavy and I let them close, let the need to sleep overwhelm me. I open them once before it drags me down and out.

I'm sitting beside the river at Gideon Grove, dangling my legs in the water, watching the swans, Martin standing beside me. I ask him how he's able to stand. He says something about not realizing he could until a few minutes ago, that he'd been given the wrong information by the doctors. I'm ashamed of my disappointment. He can tell, and reaches down to shake me hard.

'Eliza.'

'Ungh.'

I pull a cushion over my head. It's gently removed, a familiar voice penetrating the fog.

'Eliza, wake up.'

22

I open my eyes. Dan is standing over me.

'Oh shit!' I scramble up off the sofa and sway as the room spins. Dan catches me.

'Whoa. Steady there.'

'Where am I?'

'You're in my flat.' He looks into my face. 'What're you doing here?'

'I . . . I needed to check something.'

I barely make it to the bathroom, collapsing to my knees and vomiting into the loo. Dan holds back my hair, a broad hand on my back. My eyes stream. I sit up on my heels. He wrings a flannel out under the tap, then wipes my face with it. I am a strange mix of mortified adult wishing herself a million miles away and upset child hoping to be hugged.

'Why are you being so kind?'

'Why shouldn't I be?'

He rinses the flannel again, then uses it to cool my forehead. His calmness is reassuring. I reach up and grasp his wrist. It feels so warm and firm, the sinews moving as he dabs at my flushed face.

'I'm not a very nice person.'

'That's OK.'

I can recognize humour when I hear it. Why won't he take me seriously? He should know what he's dealing with.

'I've done bad things.' I adjust my voice, concentrating on getting the syllables out correctly. 'No one believes girls with pretty faces can be bad, but I've hurt people. I'm not pretty inside.'

'You're not that pretty on the outside at the moment either. Come on, up you get.'

He helps me up and lowers me onto the loo.

'Sorry,' I mumble.

'About being here, or about vomiting?'

I give him what I hope is a rueful smile. 'Both. I was only going to stay long enough to get my head together.'

'Well, no apology is necessary. It was my fault, kissing you like that, in full view of the street. I don't know what came over me. And I shouldn't have let you rush off. You were in a state.'

My head is so heavy I have to rest it on my hands. 'I wish you had stopped me. Why didn't you?'

'I didn't want to cause you any more problems.'

I peer at him through my fingers.

'And I had the meeting to get to.' He looks slightly shame-faced at the admission that I wasn't his number one priority. 'A potential client. I didn't want to turn up late and risk screwing everything up. I need as much work as I can get. I'm a bit short at the moment.'

'I thought you were doing OK.'

'I am. I've just spent too much this month.'

'Not on your clothes,' I say, and splutter with laughter. 'What do you spend it on? Cigars? Fine wine? French girls?'

'Come on.' He pulls me up and I fall against his chest. He turns me round and gives me a gentle shove. 'Go and sit down. I'll clean this up.'

I walk back into the sitting room with as much dignity as I can muster and stagger to the mirror above the mantelpiece. I look revolting, my face covered in a sheen of sweat, my lips and eyes puffy, a strand of hair glued to my cheek. I turn away in disgust and dump myself onto the sofa, which immediately starts to sway.

'What time is it?' I call.

'Four.'

I sit bolt upright. Oh my god. Martin's lunch. He'll be going berserk. 'Shit. I've got to go.'

Dan wanders in and stands over me. 'You can't go home in this state. At least let me make you a coffee.'

I hesitate then nod. I don't suppose it matters whether I get home now or in half an hour, the outcome will be the same. I'll get a bollocking from Martin, but he won't hit me in front of the children and if I apologize abjectly enough there's a slim chance he won't save it for later.

Dan goes into the kitchen. I doze until he comes back in.

'What did Ali say to you?' He places the coffee and a plate of toast on the low, bleached wood table.

I sit up and apply myself to it. 'Nothing repeatable.'

'Surely you told her you didn't ask for that kiss, that it was my fault. It would have been true.'

'Maybe, but it isn't just that.' I look down at my lap, screwing my mouth up.

150

'Tell me,' Dan says. He wanders over to the window and leans against it, so that I have to squint to look at him because the sun is in my eyes. He hooks his thumbs into his pockets. 'It'll help to get it off your chest.'

I want to tell him. Not everything, but a lot of it. I want him to know who I really am, then see if he still wants me. I drop my gaze to my knees and Dan comes over and sits down.

'She had discovered something that happened years ago.' I take a steadying breath. 'I had a fling with Pete – before they were going out, but even so.' My face heats. 'Martin was in hospital at the time.' I fish in my bag for a hanky and blow my nose. 'You won't tell anyone else, will you?' A small voice chimes in my ear, but its message is too late. Never tell your secrets when you're drunk.

'You can trust me, Eliza. You must know that by now. How did she find out?'

'Someone sent a letter. Anonymous of course.'

He gives a low whistle. 'Any idea who might have done it?'

'No. No one else knows.'

Except that's not true. Sam knows. He'd practically caught us at it. But Sam wouldn't do that to me, would he? He might be angry because I wouldn't bail him out, but he's never been vindictive.

'What's in your head?' Dan asks.

'I shouldn't involve you in my dramas.'

He rubs the back of my neck. It's absurdly comforting and I lean into him.

'I'm glad you feel you can talk to me.'

'You're just being friendly, aren't you?'

'Yup,' he says. 'I don't seduce drunk women.'

'That's good because I'm comfy here.' It's a long time since Martin and I have snuggled up on a sofa like this. 'Sam, my brother, knew.'

'Ah. Your twin. I remember you saying you don't see as much of him as you used to.'

'We grew apart.'

'Makes sense.' He pauses, as though making a calculation. 'It's an odd thing with twins. When they grow up, life encourages them to forge separate existences and I guess sometimes one twin can feel left behind, even incomplete.'

'Wow.' I stare at him. 'It's exactly like that. How did you know?' I put my hand on his thigh but because I'm not seeing straight, it slips between his legs. I speedily remove it. 'Sorry.'

'Don't worry. I know because I'm a twin.'

'No!' I fall back into the cushions, covering my mouth with my hands.

He laughs at my reaction. 'It's the truth.'

'Why didn't you tell me?'

He pauses and then says quietly, 'Because I lost her.'

'Oh, Dan. That's terrible.' I take his hand and rub my thumb over his knuckles.

'She was twenty-one when she died,' he says, lifting my hand to his lips and kissing it. 'I find that when I tell people, they want to get inside my head, so I don't. Listen, your brother might be everything Martin says he is, but it's a relationship you'll never replicate if you allow

152

your husband to drive a wedge between you. You'll always feel as though part of you is missing; like I do. Jesus. I'm sorry. I didn't mean to go all deep and meaningful on you.'

'I like deep and meaningful.'

He smiles.

'We're both twins,' I say wonderingly. 'It explains why we instantly connected.'

'We knew without knowing.'

'Yes.'

He props his chin on my head. 'Soulmates.'

I squirm. 'Don't be daft.'

'So your brother – hypothetically if it was him, what reason would he have?'

I hesitate. 'He asked me to lend him money, but with Sam lending is just another word for giving. I told him that I didn't have it. He didn't believe me and he was pissed off, but I don't think he would stoop so low. He wouldn't gain anything from it, apart from potentially wrecking my marriage.'

'And would he want to do that?'

'He thinks I'll do it myself eventually.'

'I know what Martin thinks of Sam, but what about what Sam thinks of Martin?'

I roll my eyes. 'That's easy. He thinks he's a sociopath.'

'They could both be right.'

'Don't.'

'I'm sorry. That was cheap. Siblings can be jealous. What he sees is his sister married to a rich man when he's struggling. And maybe he resents the way you've been absorbed into Martin's family. Maybe he's seen the writing on the wall; he's getting older and he has nothing to show for it. If he convinced himself you needed his protection, he would feel better. Without Martin and Ali to get in the way, you would be his purpose in life.'

I shake my head. 'That's not what this is about. It's just . . . it's hard to explain.'

'You don't owe me an explanation.'

'No,' I say. 'I want to tell you. Our father's gone now, but he was abusive and my mother didn't defend us. We learnt to look out for ourselves and to lie, but the thing I'm most ashamed of is that we learnt not to care if someone else suffered so that we didn't have to. It took the birth of my children to shake off the belief that others don't matter as much as me. I don't think Sam has come close to achieving that, or ever will. Dad's gone but it's still about survival for him.' I chew at my thumbnail.

'I understand that,' Dan says. 'You've had it tough, both of you.'

'You must think we're awful.'

'I don't. I admire your honesty. When you say your father's gone, do you mean gone out of your lives, or that he's dead?'

'He's dead. He died when Sam and I were fifteen. He was horrible and vicious and I didn't love him or have any respect for him.' I swallow hard. 'I didn't cry when he died.'

'I don't blame you.' Dan pushes his fingers through his hair. 'You feel protective towards Sam, but I don't think you should discount him. As the only boy, the

154

damage might have gone deeper with him; the feeling that he failed you and your mother.'

'I don't want it to be Sam who gave me away.'

'I know.'

'But Martin doesn't know, and there was no one else around at the time, just Pete, me and Sam. Can we talk about something else, please? Tell me about your twin. Were you very close?'

His chin is resting on my head, so I can feel the words. I'm too warm, but it's so comfortable tucked in under his arm like this that I'm reluctant to move.

'We were as children. Then when we were older she had problems and it became difficult, but before she died we'd started seeing more of each other. I thought she was better. I was telling myself what I wanted to hear; that it had been hormones and she'd grown out of it. Tragically, I missed what was happening to her. I wish I'd looked closer, listened harder.'

'You mean . . . Did she kill herself?'

He scratches at a mark on the table with his thumbnail.

'Dan, I'm so sorry.'

'It was an overdose. I don't believe she meant to die.'

I twist my hand so that my fingers interlock with his. 'That must have been desperately hard for you and your family. You poor thing.'

'Yeah. I lost my parents too, in a way. They blamed me. Since Clare and I had been inseparable as children, they were surprised I didn't know what was in her head. That was my fault apparently.' He breathes out. 'Time is supposed to heal, but it doesn't.'

'I don't think time has anything to do with it. No one's watching the clock, waiting for you to tell them you're all right.'

'You'd be surprised.' He hugs me a little tighter.

'Have you spoken to your family about the way you feel?'

'Oh yes, we've had words. They can't see it and I can't make them. Maybe one day.'

'I don't know why I asked that; I never told my mother how I felt.'

'Why not?'

I sigh. 'Because it would have put her in a position where she had to choose between me and Sam, and Dad, and I couldn't be sure that she would choose us.'

'That's the saddest thing I've ever heard.'

My throat closes. 'Never mind. They're both dead now.'

'But you never gave her the chance to explain?'

'He hurt us. She did nothing. We were her children. It doesn't need an explanation.'

Dan orders me a cab, and when it arrives he accompanies me out into the street. I don't even care that someone might see us. I turn to him before getting in.

'Thank you.'

'I'm glad I could help. I'm sorry about earlier. I mean, I'm not sorry for kissing you, but I'm sorry it's caused you trouble.'

I smile. 'I'd caused myself trouble long before today.'

'Are you going to be all right? Is Martin going to be difficult?'

'If he is, I'll deal with it.'

'Listen,' he says. 'Take my advice and give him back what he metes out. Bullies hate that. Guaranteed he'll back down.' He takes hold of my upper arms when I wrinkle my nose. 'Or I can come with you, explain things.'

'That's the worst idea you've had all day, Mr Jones.'

'Seriously, Eliza, if you ever need help, you know where I am. Just call.'

I get into the cab and sit back. The coffee helped, but only in clarifying things enough in my head so that I'm able to see how bad this is.

23

I find Martin sitting on his own in the kitchen, one hand resting lightly on the table. There is a sour taste in my mouth, and a sour look on his face.

'You've been drinking,' he says.

There's no point in lying. He must be able to smell it a mile away. 'Yes.' I look around. 'Where are the children?'

'Mum came to get them. Isabel's gone with her.'

'What did you tell them?'

'I made something up. Why did you go out without your phone, Eliza?'

I sit down. I have a speech ready. I'm not going to pull my punches this time. The hour spent with Dan has bolstered me, and even without that, I'm really not feeling well enough to be careful.

'I never feel like I'm on my own.' I lift my chin. 'I know it's to help you, but it makes me feel trapped. I've had a crappy few days and I needed the space.'

'You agreed to the app,' Martin says. 'No one forced you.'

'And normally it's fine. But I've tried to tell you that

158

I'm not coping with what's happened with Ali and Pete, and you won't do anything to help. You don't listen. I miss Ali, I need her.'

'And that's what made you drink? Didn't you think about your children?'

'Of course I did. But you should think about them too, Martin. Think about the message you're sending your daughter when you treat her mother like a door-mat. Don't you want Aurora to grow up to be a strong woman? And what about Lucas? He's going to hate you when he's old enough to understand.'

'What on earth are you talking about? It's up to you to make sure your children respect you. I can't do that for you. If you drink and act erratically, you're going to be the one who lets them down, not me. I do everything I can to protect them from the truth about their mother, and you from yourself, for that matter. You should be grateful, not pointing the finger of blame. I had to lie to my mother so that she wouldn't despise you. And that Kelsey woman.'

'Amanda?' I say, caught off guard. 'What's she got to do with this?' I suddenly remember; I saw her in Sains-bury's, or rather she saw me – looking shifty as I tried to hide a bottle of vodka.

'She called, wanting to check you'd got home in one piece, because you seemed a little "off colour". She was very tactful, but I knew what she meant.' There's a thin smile playing on Martin's face, a sneer in the arch of his eyebrows. 'You've been out for hours. Where've you been?'

'In a pub.' My courage seems to have evaporated. I've

exposed myself to the neighbours. Amanda will tell everyone. She'll act all concerned, but she'll enjoy every moment. *I'm worried about Eliza. She was all over the place.*

'Which pub?' Martin asks.

I feel a screw tighten beneath my ribcage. 'I don't remember. Somewhere down the lower end of Boundary Road.'

My head hurts so much. I get up and rummage around the cupboard for a packet of paracetamol, pop two out and swallow them down with water straight from the tap.

Martin pulls over the iPad and types. He swivels it towards me and leans back.

He's searched for *Pubs Boundary Road, Hasleford.* I read through the list, checking the names against the map. 'The Two Brewers. I was there for about two hours.'

'And after that?'

I hesitate for a fraction of a second. 'I walked. I stopped for coffee a couple of times.'

'For three hours?'

'I wanted to sober up before I came home.'

'Or you were with a man,' he shoots back.

'Seriously?'

'You walking the streets pissed for three hours does not add up. I want to know where you went and who you were with.'

'I wasn't with anyone. I walked around. I sat in the park. I fell asleep in the sun for a bit. I don't know . . . time just went.'

He looks at my face. 'No sunburn. You were lucky.'

'I sat under a tree.'

'So with all this walking, you couldn't have walked home?'

'I was tired and I'd ended up in Flaxmere. It felt too far and it was getting late.'

He peers at me. 'How did you book the cab without your phone?'

'I didn't. I took a cab from the station. Martin, you don't have to give me the third degree. I admit I've made a mess of things. I feel disgusting. I just want to have a bath and put this behind me.' I pause, then force myself to say it. 'I'm sorry I let you down.'

'I don't care about me,' he says coldly. 'The children were worried about you. I can't believe you would put them through that. It was unforgivably selfish.'

'Do you think I don't know that? I'll make it up to them.'

A tic flutters beneath Martin's right eye. 'That's what all drunk mothers say. You're a disgrace.'

He's gone too far. I did my best to keep things civilized, to make my case without getting hysterical, but that is too much and my simmering resentment boils over. 'You don't get to call me that. You are so self-righteous it's sickening. And as far as that bloody app is concerned, I don't agree any more. You have to take responsibility for yourself. It's not up to me to make all the sacrifices. I'm taking it off my phone.'

'Don't you fucking dare.'

He grabs my arm, swings me round and slaps me hard. I reel backwards, my hand to my cheek. There he is. The real Martin Curran.

161

'Why do you think I was with a man?' I sob. 'Why's that stuck in your head? I'll tell you why, it's because you know you give me enough provocation. You say you love me, and then you do the opposite. You're a bully who takes his petty frustrations out on his wife. I got out of my head today because I'd had enough of you. You should take a look at yourself. Being disabled does not give you permission to be a shit.'

'Speech over?' Under his eye the tic flutters manically, like something's trying to get out. 'You evil bitch. After everything I've done for you, you think you can just wander off and forget your responsibilities? You have always put yourself first. I wouldn't be surprised if you lied to me about the abuse. You and that useless twat of a brother of yours. The twins from hell. Murderous little goblins.' The colour in his face drains as his voice rises. 'You don't get it,' he yells, spittle flying. 'You think because I'm like this, I can't see what's in front of my nose. I see you looking . . . looking . . .'

His face is in spasm, his shoulders up round his ears, his eyes boggling. He's having some sort of fit, the top half of his body flailing, out of control, his head jerking from side to side.

I take hold of his shoulders, but he's so strong I'm thrown to the floor. I scramble to my feet and grab the phone, dialling 999.

'My husband's having a seizure,' I tell the operator when I'm put through. 'He's a paraplegic. I don't know what to do.'

24

'It's not uncommon for someone who's experienced an early post-traumatic seizure after a head injury to experience further seizures years later,' Martin's surgeon Mr Amner explains. 'We need to keep an eye on things, but there's no reason to believe your husband will have another if he's careful. I see from the notes that you were advised at the time of his recovery about the importance of Martin not getting over-excited, or losing his temper.'

'I feel really bad about the row.' It was a terrifying wake-up call. I should have walked away, not provoked him.

'Well,' Amner says, with a benign smile, 'ten years of keeping your temper; that takes saintly behaviour from both of you. However, it cannot happen again. I can't stress that enough. I'll speak to Martin before he leaves us, but if you have any worries, I recommend anger management classes.'

'I don't think Martin will want to do that.'

'It's not the law, Mrs Curran, it's merely my advice. It's up to you and Martin to take it or not as you see fit. But the main thing is a calm environment.'

* * *

They are keeping him in overnight, so I go home in a cab and put together a bag, then return to the hospital after calling Kate. She drops the children and Isabel while I'm with Martin, then comes to see him. I sense no reproach, so it's probable Ali hasn't told her about the kiss she witnessed, or my fling with Pete. I leave them together and go for a walk to clear my head. When I come back, Martin is sitting up and Kate has left. He has his phone out and he's typing a text.

'How're you feeling?' I ask.

He chucks the phone down on the bed. 'Right as rain. The sooner I can get out of here the better. I'd go home tonight if that bloody doctor would let me.'

He doesn't sound as right as rain, but that's because he bit his tongue during the seizure and it's distorting his speech. His face is a mess; there's a bruise on his cheek, a welt on his forehead, and a red graze on the side of his hand where he must have caught it on the table or his wheelchair.

Neither of us has mentioned the altercation that caused the fit, and I don't think Martin will. He might even have forgotten some of it; Mr Amner warned that might be the case. I hope he has, or at least continues to pretend he has. It doesn't make either of us look good.

'The doctor's right to keep you in.'

Martin rolls his eyes. 'I don't know how they think I'm supposed to sleep. It's like a sodding departures lounge in here.'

On cue, a nurse clatters in with his drug trolley,

greeting his patients with slightly over-pitched joviality. Martin sighs.

'I'll see you in the morning then.' I bend to kiss him, but he doesn't kiss me back. Evidently he's forgotten nothing.

'Sure. Fine. Can you get me a copy of *The Economist* first?'

I call Sam from the main entrance of the hospital.

'Did you send Ali a note?' I say, dispensing with any pleasantries.

'Hello to you too. What kind of note?'

'Implying that Pete and I had an affair after Martin's accident.'

He snorts. 'Your little peccadillo? No. Who said I did?'

'No one, but you were the only other person who knew. Ali is furious with me. It's done so much damage.'

'Well, someone else must have known about it, because I wouldn't do something like that.'

I can feel him rolling his eyes, but I'm not sure I believe him. 'We argued last time we saw each other.'

'If you're capable of thinking I'd ruin your precious friendship out of spite, then I don't know who you are any more. But maybe, just maybe, I'm not the one who's the fuck-up of the two of us.'

I press my fingers against my head. This hangover is a humdinger. 'I didn't mean to offend you. I'm just trying to get to the bottom of it. I pissed you off by not lending you the money.'

'Yes, you did. You have so much, you've forgotten

what it's like not to have any. You have no grip on what other people are going through. Look at Ali. Look at me, and stop making assumptions about us. Try to imagine what being flat broke feels like.'

He hangs up. I stand there, feeling stunned, trying to remember what on earth I'm doing here. Then I remember and go into the shop, pick up Martin's magazine and queue at the till.

'Eliza.'

I turn to find Ali standing behind me and struggle with my expression. I want to smile, to show her I'm pleased and relieved to see her, but she doesn't look friendly.

'Hi.'

'How is he?'

'Bad tempered,' I say. 'Telling everyone there's nothing wrong with him.'

Someone sighs audibly and I realize I'm holding up the line. I pay for my purchase and get out of the way.

'What happened?' Ali asks.

'We had a row and he lost his temper. After I saw you I . . . um, I went on a bender basically. I hadn't told him where I was and he was worried. When I got home he went ballistic.'

She sucks at her bottom lip, an Ali habit I know well.

'Amanda told me she saw you acting strangely. I thought you might have been drinking, but I didn't want to believe you would be that irresponsible.'

I bristle. 'This is the first time since before the children were born. I was distraught after our row, and I didn't want Martin and Isabel to see me like that. There was a pub. I went in and I caved.'

166

'Ah,' she says. 'So this is all down to me, is it? I hold a mirror up in front of you and you can't cope with what you see. Well, I'm sorry if anything I said to you got under your skin, but you know what, finding out my best friend cheated on my brother and with my own husband – I think I can be forgiven for reacting badly.'

'Why is it all so black and white to you? Pete was involved too. I didn't force him. You weren't even together at the time and we were both in a bad way. We had a drink and one thing led to another. Can't you understand that?'

'I'm not even going to try. Pete wasn't married. Do you know how guilty he's felt all these years? He was crying, for God's sake.'

'Oh, spare me that,' I mutter.

Her face falls. 'Can't you see it from my point of view? I was in love with him and we were finally connecting, even if it was in the worst of circumstances. And all the time, you were . . . it's humiliating.'

'I had no idea you felt that way about him. I thought it all happened after the accident.'

'No,' she says miserably. 'I'd had a crush on Pete for years.'

'In that case, I am truly sorry. It was just once and it meant nothing to either of us, I promise.'

Pete has gone so far down in my estimation that I can't even bring myself to pity him. The truth is, he came to me, I didn't come to him. He had already had a few beers, and was emotional. I had a drink or three to keep him company. I listened to him tell me about when he and Martin were boys. We put the television on and watched a film, and I dozed off. I woke because Pete was stroking my hair. It was dark, and I felt far away from everything, somewhere normal life had been paused. He was sitting on the floor, his face close to mine, his hand moving from my head, down my neck, between my shoulder blades. It was hypnotic. He kissed me. I should have said no and politely got rid of him, but I was hazy with sleep and alcohol and I fell into it, like I was falling into a well of warm water.

'Why don't you take this up to Martin? I'm going home.' I keep hold of the magazine when she takes it. 'The consultant said it mustn't happen again. He's not allowed to get overwrought. He mustn't find out what happened between me and Pete.'

'Convenient for you,' she says.

'It might be, but that doesn't make it any less true.'

I let go of the magazine and she tucks it under her arm.

'Fine,' she says. 'It won't be me who tells him what kind of woman he's married to. But you should think about that; whoever sent that note doesn't like you. They may go a step further.'

I hadn't thought that far ahead. I hug myself tightly. I don't feel safe any more.

'Any idea who it was?' Ali asks when I don't say anything.

I swallow hard. 'I don't know, but I think it might have been Sam. He was the only other person who knew it had happened.'

'Oh, Christ. That is brilliant. Your flipping brother.'

'I don't know for sure. I've asked him and he denies it.'

She presses her hand into her back. 'Well, he's your problem. I'm sure you can work something out.'

I can, I think, as she walks towards the lifts and I leave the hospital. But it'll cost me five grand.

25

Martin has been back two days when I find myself locked in. I try the door again, wrenching the brushed-steel lever. He glances up when I walk into his study.

'I can't open the front door.'

'Where are you off to?'

'The shops. We need milk.'

'Do we?'

'Yes, we do,' I say irritably. 'What's going on?'

'Sit down.'

I sit. He leans back and I feel my flesh crawl under his scrutiny. Something tells me he's been looking forward to this moment, anticipating it all morning.

'There are going to be some changes round here. Please understand that it's for your own good.'

I try not to panic. 'I told you it wouldn't happen again.'

He picks up a pen, taps it on his desk. 'I believe that you believe that, but I think it's too great a risk at the moment. I've seen this pattern with you before. Do you remember, after we were married? You lasted for a year before you started drinking again.'

'You know why that was.'

'Yes, I do. You were under a great deal of stress, as you appear to be now. It didn't make any difference that I needed you to be strong. You gave up. You showed a lack of willpower when it was needed most. You let me down, and you let yourself down.'

'Martin—'

'I haven't finished speaking.'

I close my mouth tight.

'You told me you had it under control, but you were secretly drinking right up until you started IVF treatment. To give you your due, you've done very well since then. Eight years dry.' He sighs. 'All spoilt in a single afternoon. If I'd realized just how much you relied on my sister to keep you on the straight and narrow, I'd have insisted you went back to AA. It's partly my fault. I should have known how fragile you were. From now on, you don't move from this house without my say so. You'll have to earn that privilege by showing me that you care about us.' He picks up a letter and casts his eye over it. 'See it as an intervention.'

'You can't do this, Martin. You can't police every minute of my life; in fact, I'm sure it's against the law. I'll go where I like, when I like. I'm not your prisoner. Open the front door now.'

He screws up the letter and throws it into the bin. His voice is no longer friendly and reasonable; it's cold and calculating. 'If you leave, you are not coming back. Do you understand?'

'You have no right.'

He laughs. 'Eliza, darling. Rights don't come into it.'

'I'll leave you, Martin. I swear I will. You can't treat me like this.'

'If you think you're going to walk out on me, you can think again. Don't forget, I know your secrets. If I choose to tell, any sensible judge will agree that you're a danger to the children.'

'You swore you wouldn't.'

'Of course I did. And I meant it. But Lucas and Aurora come first.'

'You know I'd never let anything bad happen to them.'

'Do I?' He eyes me curiously. 'I don't know, I think there's room for doubt there.'

'It's the summer holidays. It's not practical.'

'You have their class contact lists. You can line up some playdates. Their friends can come here. If you want groceries, you can order online. We'll go out together, so you won't be stuck inside all the time. I'm not unreasonable. We can go out as a family. Life will go on pretty much as normal.'

'There is nothing normal about this.'

'I don't want to force you to do anything.' He slips back with ease into his wise husband persona. 'I'm trying to help. I know what addiction is; I've seen you in the grip of it before. Two or three weeks of restricted freedom will get you through the worst of it. I'm suggesting you do this for the sake of the children, not because it gives me pleasure. I love you, but I need you to be strong. Think about it.'

He pushes himself round the desk. 'Three weeks.' He cups my chin in his hand and smiles into my eyes. 'Let's get through this together. You know it's for the best. What do you say? Do we have a bargain?'

I stand up. I hate him and suspect his motives, but I can't deny what he says makes sense. After that binge last week I've barely thought about anything but alcohol. Martin was hospitalized because of me. It's driven the message home. I don't like his methods but I don't want to be a drunk and I know from experience that I can't do this on my own.

'All right,' I say eventually. 'I agree.'

'Good girl,' he says. 'I knew you'd see sense.'

I'll manage, I tell myself.

26

'Lot 35, Gideon Grove. A two-bedroom one-storey detached freehold property occupying a one-acre plot with private mooring, in need of modernization. Development potential depending on permissions. By order of the executors. Who'd like to give me a starter?'

The summer holiday has ground on and it's late August. After three weeks all but confined to the house, it's a treat to be out. It's been difficult for all of us. It's made the children starkly aware that they aren't seeing as much as they would normally of their friends, just joining them in the park with Isabel and Kate. They don't understand why Ali doesn't come round; they are so used to her plonking herself down on our sofa and putting her feet up. I tell them it's because the baby's due any minute and she needs to be at home, but they still sense something is being kept from them. The grown-ups are lying.

I have been very lonely. As lonely as I was when I was a child. I was too embarrassed and humiliated by my father's behaviour round them, his over-the-top friendliness and creepily misjudged compliments, to invite friends to our house. It comes over me in waves, as does the need to drink those feelings away. But with Martin's encouragement, I stay the course.

The auctioneer scans the room. It's so hot in here that people are fanning themselves with the stapled pages of the brochure. Dan is wearing a pale pink shirt with the sleeves pushed up his arms and I keep flicking glances at him. After what happened, after we opened up to each other, I feel as though we've crossed a line. It's charged the energy between us, creating a static that I'm surprised Martin can't feel.

Beside me Martin doesn't even blink. I can feel tension radiating off the two men. Me as well. I am overly aware of Dan's presence. At the moment he's leaning forward, chewing his thumbnail. His fingers snap as we wait for someone to place the first bid. I reach down for my bag and turn my head. He catches my eye and winks. Something pent up releases inside me and I feel lighter.

If things go Martin's way, Dan will be working from Winterfell. There will be opportunities, and traps. I won't let anything happen because Martin does not make empty threats. But it's not just the fear of what Martin could do if he found out, it's the potential for mortification. There's a voice in my head, and it's urging me not to be stupid, cruelly pointing out that the pangs of adolescence are sweet but the pangs of a thirty-something mother hankering after a man who isn't her husband are not.

But it is an awakening. I am not dead inside. I am, as the cliché goes, all of a flutter.

'Lot 35,' the auctioneer repeats. 'Who'll give me three hundred thousand? Three hundred I've got.' He's slick, eagle-eyed, with a ready smile and a charismatic presence. Dressed in tweeds, his longish hair brushed back, he looks for all the world like a country squire. 'Four hundred. I have four hundred. Four-fifty. Five hundred anywhere? The gentleman on the right. Thank you. Five hundred. We have five hundred. That's cheap for a gem like this! Have a think about it. Five-fifty, gentleman in the black shirt.'

Martin waits, poised to pounce. I sit up straighter and look round, trying to work out who's bidding against us and how many of them there are. Most people here today are men, pretending not to be in the slightest bit interested in the competition, some succeeding better than others. I hold my breath. The auction room is packed, the atmosphere electric. Everyone is waiting for something, pumped up, anxious. Martin is no exception.

Dan is still leaning forward, utterly focused. He has an attractive profile; a strong chin, a straight nose and long lashes. I allow myself another covert glance as I scan the room. When I meet his eyes again, his are gleaming. To my surprise there are beads of sweat on his forehead. I know of course that he very much wants this to work out, but his behaviour suggests there is a lot more riding on it than any of us realize.

'Six hundred. I have six hundred. Seven hundred. Gentleman in the flat cap on my left.'

That's Martin breaking cover. When we bought Linden Road at auction, the auctioneer struggled over his description. Martin didn't like that. Since then he's worn a hat to these kinds of events.

'That's seven hundred.' He waits a brief moment. 'Eight hundred.'

Beside me Martin grunts in annoyance and lifts his hand. Dan's foot taps the floorboards.

'Nine hundred from the gentleman in the flat cap again. Nine-fifty.'

'For fuck's sake,' Martin mutters. He raises his hand.

'Is it worth it?' I ask under my breath. It's more than he wanted to spend. Last night he said his limit would be eight hundred thousand.

'One million for Lot 35. Anybody else?'

The air goes still, as if the entire room has stopped breathing. I can hear the pulse of blood in my veins. I dart a glance at Dan's hands, where they rest on his thighs. His fingers twitch.

'If not, it's one million for the first, one million for the second, one million for the third and final time. Sold to the gentleman in the flat cap for one million pounds.' The gavel hits the lectern.

'Yes!' Dan erupts out of his chair, hitting his fist into his palm.

I throw my arms round Martin's neck and kiss his cheek. Dan shakes his hand. Then I stand up, and Dan reaches over Martin to embrace me. When he lets me go, his eyes hold mine in a way that makes me quiver with desire.

Oblivious, Martin beams as an assistant hurries over with a form. 'Let's celebrate,' he says once he's signed. 'Lunch is on me.' He laughs out loud. 'This is a good day. I am bloody well over the moon.'

* * *

Isabel greets us when we arrive back at the house. She seems excited, and at first I assume it's because of Dan. He hovers beside me but he's not coming in because he needs to go home and work. As I ease past Isabel into the hall, she takes me by the arm. She never usually touches me, and it gives me a small jolt.

'Isn't it wonderful about Ali?'

In the instant before I collect myself, I show my shock. Ali has had the baby and no one told us. Isabel has understood my reaction, and cannot contain her glee.

I realize I haven't responded. 'Absolutely wonderful,' I say, then feel myself reddening.

'She went into labour at two o'clock in the morning,' Isabel says, looking at me pointedly. 'It's a little boy. Isn't it wonderful?'

'It is,' I say, not trusting myself to expand on that simple statement. The shock goes deep. I hurt in ways I didn't know I could hurt. This removes me from my friend like nothing else could. 'How did you find out?'

I instantly regret asking because she gives a little smirk. 'My friend lives opposite them. She saw them coming home.'

Ah, yes. The very efficient au pair grapevine. Never knowingly behind on the gossip. By now Martin has joined us.

'Another reason to celebrate,' Dan says. 'It's a good day.'

Martin raises his eyebrows. 'What's that then?'

'You've got a nephew.'

Martin nods slowly, then pushes himself into the hall and through to his study.

Isabel smiles at me, smug as a cat. She wanted to be the one to tell us. She wanted to see me struggle to hide my feelings. She is malicious and sadistic, and she hates me. Dan, Martin, even Pete, they don't know how close to the edge I am, but I think Isabel has understood this about me instinctively, and I think she's enjoying it. But Isabel isn't as clever as she thinks she is, and one day, I predict, she will get her fingers burned.

'I'll be off then,' Dan says.

Isabel makes a small moue of disappointment and rests her hand on his forearm, raising her head for a kiss. I try not to look but I can't help it. He submits to a hug, looking at me over her shoulder, a hint of derision in his gaze. I wonder about that, but only for a moment, because I have more important things on my mind.

We did not know.

I feel the starkness of the message from our friends. The previous times Ali went into labour, Pete had rung Martin, and Ali had called to tell me all the gory details as soon as she was capable of stringing a sentence together.

'Did you enjoy that?' I hiss at Isabel as she walks back inside.

'I don't know what you mean. How could I know they did not tell you yet?'

'Oh, you knew. What is it with you? Are you so insecure you have to get at me? Make me feel small?'

She shrugs. 'That is your problem, Eliza. You are the one who is insecure. And while we are talking, can I give you some advice?'

'No, thank you.' I walk away.

'I am concerned about you,' she says, coming after me. I keep moving.

'It is not good, you know, for someone your age to show they are so desperate. I am telling you this to help you. Leave Dan alone, you are embarrassing yourself.'

She flounces across the hall, through the kitchen and into the garden, leaving me staring after her, shaking with pent-up fury. This cannot be allowed to go on. I've had more than enough of Isabel Gardin. I run myself a glass of water and take a headache pill, then follow Martin into his study. He is not avoiding a conversation about what's happened today. I close the door and stand with my back to it.

'They hate us.'

'You're over-reacting,' he says.

'And you're under-reacting.' I know we shouldn't row, so I speak very calmly. 'Surely you care that we had to get the news from Isabel.'

Martin pushes himself behind his desk and shuffles some papers around. 'Why are you so worked up? Of course it would have upset me if it had been her first baby, but with the third, it's no big deal.'

I look at him closely, trying to see past his air of detachment.

'That's not the point.'

'If Pete thinks he can emotionally blackmail me into handing him a contract I don't want him for, then he's deluding himself. If I do that, he'll assume I'll do anything to keep the peace. Ali won't put up with it. Once she's back on her feet, she'll see what an idiot her husband's being, and she'll sort it out.'

'I'm not so sure.'

He frowns. 'Eliza, is there some other reason Ali's turned against you?'

'No,' I say, too quickly. 'I just think that you under-estimate her loyalty to Pete.' I pace the room. 'I think we should make the first move. I'm going to buy them a present. I can give it to Kate to pass on.'

'I don't think that's a good idea. You'll only be rebuffed.'

'That doesn't matter. I want them to know that we care about them.'

'It's a little manipulative.'

I falter. Is it manipulative to tell Pete and Ali that I'm thinking of them despite what's happened? Will they think I'm implying they're being childish and petulant? Surely Ali knows me better than that.

'Ali would take a call from you, Martin. However angry she is. She won't ignore you.'

He strokes his lip with his forefinger, regarding me speculatively. 'You're tired and emotional. Leave it be.'

I hold his gaze. 'I can't. And I don't like the way you're behaving; like you're untouchable, like nothing can get to you. Your family has been everything to you. I can't believe you're prepared to throw all that away.'

Martin yawns. 'So I have to carry them all, your brother included, just in case I need them one day. Have I ever asked a single one of them for help, financial or otherwise? That's a joke.'

'You're forgetting the support Ali and Pete gave you after your accident. They were there for you every single day. They made sacrifices.'

181

'Well, of course I'm grateful for that,' he blusters. 'But they don't have to hold it over my head for my entire life.'

'You know that's not true.'

'Sure. Ali would move heaven and earth if I asked her, but I wouldn't do that, not if it means bailing Pete out. He has to learn. If the business isn't working, then he'll have to mothball it and get a job with another architect firm. I'm not throwing good money after bad. Sometimes, I feel as though I'm surrounded by idiots.'

27

We're expecting Kate and the girls that afternoon, and when the doorbell rings my kids fly into the hall, push past me to open the door and drag their cousins inside. Kate kisses my cheek and bends to kiss Martin. She's managed somehow to maintain a fine balance between her children, refusing to openly take sides, but today something is up. She seems more impatient as she plonks her handbag down on the kitchen table and goes out into the garden, Martin and I hurrying after her.

'The children are about to go back to school,' she says. 'You won't be able to avoid your friends. Don't you think it's time to patch up this silly quarrel?'

'Would you like something to drink, Kate?' I ask, hoping to be out of the way while Martin deals with this. I don't know what to say.

'In a minute, dear.'

I sit down and brace myself.

'It's a complicated situation, Mum,' Martin says. 'Don't get involved.'

'I can't very well help it when I can see how unhappy you and your sister are.'

'I'm not unhappy,' Martin says. 'I'm not sure Ali is either.'

Kate frowns. I sense that his response was not in her script. 'And then there's your and Eliza's birthday party. It all feels a little awkward. If I go, they'll think I'm siding with you two. If I stay behind, then I'm siding with them.'

'I can't make that choice for you,' Martin says.

She looks like she'd been hoping he would. Kate is not like her children. She's a quiet character and dislikes confrontation. I was fond of Martin's father but he could be domineering. He liked a good debate. Weekends at the rectory, when Ali was home from university, could be explosive. Kate and I would fade into the background. She will have worked herself up to this, probably run the entire conversation in her mind.

I remember when I first met them. Martin and I had been back in the UK for three days, and were still on a high with it, still beautiful with our tans and sun-bleached hair. Kate picked us up from the station. Martin sat in the front of the car and I remember she kept turning to include me in the conversation. The front door flew open as we drove up and Ali ran out shrieking, throwing herself at Martin. She smiled at me over his shoulder, eyes up, eyes down; avidly curious. I guessed what she was thinking: is this one worth getting to know? Martin had told me he'd had several girl-friends, intense relationships that petered out after about three months. I'd been with him for just over two. At that moment I felt the ground shift under my feet. But

I've always been determined. Martin cared what his family thought, so I would make them like me. I would be what they wanted me to be.

Martin released Ali from the bear hug when his father appeared, and reached for my hand, his smile full of pride as he introduced us.

'Eliza, this is my sister Ali,' he said, grinning. 'She's a nightmare.'

'Don't be a dick, Martin. It's lovely to meet you, Eliza. Come on in.'

Ali owned the space in the same way that Martin and his father did, in a way that I never will. That's what security and predictability do for a child. I had a wobble then, but I wouldn't let it show. It was my problem, not theirs.

Martin and Ali quarrelling is painful to Kate. It's not how her world works. Her children and grandchildren are her certainty. For her, a family falling apart is terrifying.

'Can't you talk to Ali, Eliza? Sometimes men find it hard to apologize or compromise. Their pride gets in the way. I'm sure if you two got together, you could have it sorted out in no time.'

'I'd love to, Kate, but the suggestion would have to come from Ali.'

'Why? Will someone please tell me what's going on? I don't see how I can help if I'm kept in the dark.'

'Mother,' Martin says. 'It's kind of you, but Ali will do as she pleases. I've no intention of putting work Pete's way just to keep the peace. If he failed to use

Winterfell as a springboard for his career, that's his problem. What he and Ali don't understand is that I wouldn't be doing Pete any favours if I did. He needs to grow some balls.'

'Kate,' I interrupt before Martin can say anything worse. 'I hope it'll blow over at some point, for all our sakes. But whatever happens, we want you at the party. It won't be the same without you, so please come.'

'I'm not sure. I'd be much happier if you at least spoke to them.'

Martin knits his brows together, then grunts. 'OK. Fine. I'll call Pete and I'll do my best to find a compromise, but on one condition. If the call doesn't go well, you still come to the party.'

Kate and I clear away the tea things, while Martin puts a stack of photograph albums on the coffee table. The children scramble onto chairs, squeezing up to each other; all except Aurora, who takes her rightful place on Martin's knee.

Leonie leans against me and I pull her onto my lap. I've missed them so much. If only Ali were here, it would be perfect.

Where have the years gone? There's Aurora as a newborn, Lucas and Briony as toddlers, their arms around each other, cheeks rosy. Me neatly pregnant with Lucas, Martin and I on honeymoon in Anguilla. Martin, long-legged and bronzed lying beside a pool, squinting up at me as I snap him with my camera. Me in a dark-pink bikini standing on a tropical beach in front of a spectacular sunset. Martin diving into an outside pool, his body lithe and elegant as he arcs through the air, the spray curving upwards as he hits the water.

'Daddy can't do that now,' Aurora announces, and he kisses her head.

'That's right, sweetheart.'

We have never sugar-coated Martin's disability for the children, never hidden pictures of Martin before the accident. For them it's as normal as pictures of me a stone lighter and with longer hair.

The photographs from our time in India bring back the tastes and smells of Goa, the colours and sounds, the vibrancy of everything. I wandered around in a state of wonder.

'Mummy, you were beautiful,' Lucas says.

'She still is,' Martin responds, patting me on the knee.

Aurora twists round and hugs him hard, overwhelmed by the romance of it. Over her shoulder Lucas turns the page to reveal another picture. Martin this time, in a whitewashed hostel bedroom. Behind him is a section of a low bed, covered by a brightly coloured blanket of the type you could buy in the local market. Something snags, a sense of déjà vu, but I can't put my finger on it. There are clothes scattered on the floor. He's grinning, a sarong around his waist. I don't recognize the scene; I didn't take this photo, though Martin will have forgotten that. It was probably taken by my predecessor. I expect he kept it because he looks so good in it. He's a vain man.

Martin opens another album. This one of him and Ali enjoying an idyllic childhood; summer days in the rectory garden, snowball fights and toboggans in the winter.

Kate answers the children's questions; questions they've asked a hundred times.

But I'm not listening any more. Something is nagging at me; a sense of recognition, a spark lighting up in some dark and dusty corner of my mind. I saw something that didn't sit right as we pored over the photographs and it's bothering me.

28

Martin pushes himself into the kitchen. His face is like thunder. I put the knife I've been using to chop onions down slowly and wait to see what he wants. He's been on the phone to Pete, as he promised Kate he would. I take it the conversation did not go well.

'How dare you,' he begins softly, almost casually, 'tell Pete lies about me.'

'What do you mean? I haven't told him anything.'

'I explained how things stood, but he kicked off with a load of cod-psychology about how he knows how scared I am; how you told him that fear makes me behave like a shit to people who are close to me; how he understands where it's coming from, but can't condone the way I treat you. What the fuck did you tell him, Eliza?'

Heat suffuses my neck and face. Was Pete standing up for me? Or deliberately stirring in order to punish me for not taking his side?

'I didn't tell him anything. I was just trying to make him feel better about the way you were behaving. I didn't expect him to repeat it back to you.'

'But you think it's true? You think I'm so scared of not being Mr Big that I bully people further down in the pecking order?'

'Fundamentally, yes.' I stand taller even though my stomach is churning. I remember what Dan said. Bullies don't like it if you fight back. 'It explains the otherwise unexplainable. You say you love me, but you put me down. If I didn't know that fear was at the root of your behaviour, I'd report you.'

'Report what and to who?' he sneers.

I shrug.

'You go whining about our private life to my friend, the husband of my sister. What did you hope to achieve, Eliza? Were you playing the poor defenceless victim by making me look like a monster? If you imagine anyone's going to think better of you because you share your pathetic little problems with them, you're wrong. Ali is not going to take your side. She never will. She doesn't even particularly like you.'

He pauses for breath, his hand going to his shoulder, kneading it.

'Or are you trying to make me lose my rag? Is that it? It would be the perfect way to get rid of me. A convenient seizure. You'd like that, wouldn't you? Well, I'm sorry to disappoint you, but I have no intention of blowing a gasket.'

'You're paranoid,' I say, turning on my heel and walking out of the room.

'Getting repetitive, darling.'

I won't leave him, because I believe his threats to use what he knows about my father to take Aurora and

Lucas away from me, but I don't have to pretend any more. I go upstairs and put the children to bed, trying not to shorten their bathtime or cheat them out of a chapter of the book we're reading, trying to enjoy them and not let them see I'm upset.

Isabel is in the kitchen when I come back down. Martin is nowhere to be seen. He's probably working off his bad mood in the pool. Isabel helps herself to a coke from the fridge.

The more I think about this girl, the more I realize I cannot stand her and her arch smugness. Today was the final straw. She enjoyed my dismay at hearing about the baby from her. The bad feeling between us is clearly mutual, and I strongly suspect it's to do with Dan.

'I need to talk to you,' I say. 'About what you said to me earlier.'

'Ah, that.' She brushes it off as though it was nothing. 'I wanted to help you.'

'Well, I can do without that kind of help, thank you very much. I employ you to look after my children, not to subject me to unprovoked personal attacks. I want you out of here.'

'You are sacking me?'

I almost laugh at the disbelief on her face. 'Yes, of course I am. What on earth did you expect? I can't have someone in my house who speaks to me like that.'

'This is because of Dan. You are jealous.'

I sigh. 'You must know that your relationship with Dan is doomed. You're much too young for him, and besides, you're going back to France at the end of the year. This infatuation you have doesn't alter either of

191

those things. Pack your bags. I want you gone tomorrow morning.'

'I know what you are,' she says. 'You think you can have secrets from me? All the au pairs, we have a good look through our hostess's things. We find so much that is interesting. What do you think we do when we have the house to ourselves? You think we just do your ironing? You think we are fond of you when we tidy your mess? Ha ha ha.' Her voice becomes sing-song. 'Clean your fridges, sort out the washing, like good girls. Well, you do not pay us enough to respect your privacy. So fuck you, Mrs Curran.'

'Out,' I say. 'Get out of my house, and don't come back.'

She wrinkles her nose. 'I will go to Dan. You are a sad old woman. You hate me because I am young and I have what you want.'

I roll my eyes but as soon as she's slammed out of the house I run up to my bedroom, pull over the stool and get myself a drink from the bottle in the wardrobe. One slug is nowhere near enough to blunt the sting of Isabel's words, but I remind myself that the children are at home and screw the lid back on. How will Dan react to this latest development? I wonder. Isabel will want to move in with him, at least temporarily; I smirk picturing how apoplectic she will go when he says no. Will she come crawling back here?

I throw myself down on the sofa in the drawing room and switch on the news, barely taking in the day's disasters. What is Martin going to say? He is already furious about Pete. This is not a great time, when the kids are on holiday and we're throwing a party, to be without childcare. The lift doors open. I brace myself.

Martin comes in. I suddenly don't feel quite so confident about what I've done. Even if his swim has calmed him down, he's going to be furious when he finds out I've made a decision that affects the whole family without consulting him.

'I heard the door slam,' he says. 'What's going on?'

'Isabel's gone, I've sacked her.'

'You've done what? Why?'

'I had to tell her off about something,' I say, using an excuse I concocted a few minutes ago. 'And she took it the wrong way. She was insulting and rude.'

'What did you tell her off about?'

'She's been in our bedroom, trying on my clothes and snooping around. I gently reprimanded her, expecting us to have a conversation about respecting each other's personal space, and for her to apologize, but she went completely mad and all this venom started spewing out. It was shocking.'

He massages the back of his neck. 'For God's sake. This is the last thing we need. Get her back.'

Fury rises in me. 'I'm not doing that. She was vicious, Martin. I can't believe you're taking her side. She's causing so much tension round here.'

'You're just looking for someone to blame, Eliza. The tension is your fault. You're neurotic and irrational.'

193

The unfairness of his words shocks me into silence. Martin palms his mobile.

'What are you doing?'

'Phoning Isabel, of course. We can't just throw her out of the house and wash our hands of her. She has to come back here, serve out her two weeks' notice. We're going to do this properly.'

'Please, don't,' I beg. 'It'll be awful.'

He ignores me and calls her, puts the phone on speaker and rests it on his knee. Had it been the landline or my mobile, I doubt she would have picked up, but because it's Martin she does.

'Isabel,' he says smoothly. 'I'm sorry to hear there's been a disagreement between you and Eliza.'

'Your wife was very impolite to me. She was disgusting. I don't want to say anything else. I will talk to my agency in the morning.'

'Talk to me first, will you?'

He pushes himself out of the drawing room and shuts himself in his study. I get up and listen at the door, hoping to hear Martin give her a dressing down, but he doesn't raise his voice so I go into the kitchen and start cleaning surfaces that are already clean. I scrub the sink, then drop the cloth and press my hands against my face. I'm the one who is going to be left feeling embarrassed and small over this incident, not Isabel. That's the way Martin will play it.

He comes to find me, and I wait for him to tell me how it went.

'Isabel has been very gracious. She's agreed to come back tomorrow morning.'

'Wonderful. Thanks for backing me up.'

His face is devoid of sympathy. 'You have only yourself to blame. If you'd thought before you opened your mouth, you wouldn't have got yourself into this situation and I wouldn't have to clear up your mess.'

'Don't. Just don't.'

Livid, I set my chin and walk out of the room. Minutes later I get a message from Isabel.

I don't take offence. We can be friends. Your husband is a good man. As he says, your children need me.

29

It almost doesn't matter that Martin is keeping me inside, because social invitations dwindle. A lunch is cancelled. The hostess emails to say that she isn't feeling well and could we reschedule? She doesn't suggest any dates. I email back that I'm sorry and hope she feels better soon, but I know. People are starting to take sides.

And another thing: Lucas was invited to a birthday party. He still is. The only difference being that one of the other parents has offered to pick him up and drop him off, because she's 'passing my house anyway'. The lie is a kind one, but the result is the same. I am not welcome. Parents will hang around at the end of the afternoon catching up with those they haven't seen during the holidays. My presence would only make them feel awkward.

I wonder what Ali's actually said. I can't believe she would tell anyone about the long-ago fling with Pete, because it would reflect badly on him, but she might hint that I'm not what I seem.

Why do our friends believe her without listening to what I have to say? I suppose the answer is obvious, I think despondently. It's Ali people are drawn to, not me. And she's just had a baby, so she's more worthy of compassion as well as being easier company. But then she can afford to be that way. She has nothing to hide. She isn't married to Martin. She grew up in a loving environment.

I am in the car, with Martin's permission, on my way to the supermarket to pick up a few last-minute items for the party this evening, and Isabel has come along to make sure I don't go crazy in the wine and spirits aisle. I picture myself doing a supermarket sweep, racing my trolley up and down, chased by Isabel as I grab indiscriminately at bottles of wine, spirits, beer; bottles smashing on the floor as my clumsy, desperate fingers slip.

Martin is at home overseeing the men erecting the marquee and stringing the garden with fairy lights. Kate has arrived early to keep the children out from under our feet. As she's brought Leonie and Briony, I have no doubt they will have reached a fever pitch of excitement before Isabel and I get home. I dread to think what they'll be like by the time we kick off.

The first couple of times we threw a party to celebrate our birthdays, people arrived at four and the last stragglers didn't leave until well into the small hours. Somehow I can't see that happening today. Only the children are in the mood.

Beside me, Isabel scrolls through Instagram, her feet up on the dashboard. She's wearing denim dungarees, a yellow tee and espadrilles, and her hair is unwashed and scrunched up. I remember when I picked her up at the airport she was dressed like this, but her demeanour was different. I spotted her pushing her luggage trolley through the doors, looking around anxiously. We had FaceTimed, but she was different in the flesh, less sure of herself. When I waved to catch her attention she'd looked so relieved, a huge smile breaking out across her face. I had the children with me and they chatted all the way home. I remember thinking that I'd made the right decision when I employed her, that she was going to enhance our lives, bring joy and colour to Winterfell. She's changed in the months she's been with us, become more self-aware. No doubt I have Dan to thank for that. Martin too, in a way. Male attention is crucial to that girl's sense of self.

And this is where we are now. A sullen young woman with her dirty feet up on my dashboard.

'Why are you still here?' I ask. 'Tell me. I want to understand.'

'Because Martin asked me to stay. I was happy to go, but he was very persuasive. He is worried about you.'

'Ah. I see. So you're here as his spy? And does "very persuasive" mean he pays you more?'

'He gave me a small pay rise, yes. He knows I deserve it after all you have put me through. And I am not his spy, but you do need looking after. Round alcohol you are embarrassing. Martin is right to keep you inside where you cannot get into trouble.'

The supermarket is on the edge of town. I turn into the car park and drive up and down until I find a space. Isabel gets out. I grab a couple of large shopping bags off the back seat. It's horrible living with someone who has told you exactly what they think of you. There is no coming back from that. Isabel knows it too and doesn't even try.

She tracks me up the fruit and veg aisle, her thumbs moving like pistons across her phone, eyes glued to the screen. It's so irritating. How can Dan stand it? Maybe she leaves off when she's with him. The only conversation we have is about pizzas. The kids have been promised them in an attempt to encourage good behaviour. A forlorn hope.

Isabel lets me out of her sight only once, to get the bits and pieces she needs. When she joins me again, I glance at her basket. Anti-perspirant, shampoo, moisturizer, a pack of five Crunchie bars, tampons and a bottle of pearlescent pink nail varnish. She checks the contents of my trolley for smuggled goods.

There was no point thinking about it. Even if I had tucked a small bottle discreetly under the other items, Isabel would see it when we went to pay, and knowing her she would say something condescending in front of everyone else as she took it out. *Eliza, that was so silly of you. I'll put it back. I won't tell Martin.* There's a whole afternoon and evening of unlimited champagne to endure, so I'm almost grateful to have Martin's little spy dogging my footsteps. If I've any chance of being forgiven by Ali, I have to rediscover the woman I was at the beginning of this awful summer. The one with self-respect. I still hope she and Pete will change their minds and come this afternoon. It won't be the same without them.

Ali haunts me. Sometimes I scroll back through our

199

conversations out of sheer masochism. She sends me funny videos, messages spitting with irritation about other parents from the school or about their teachers. She says, *Can you come round right now? I'm bored out of my brain.* A lot of LOLs. A lot of emojis. Smut that made me snort with laughter. There is so much fun and affection and trust there, it's unbearable to think I've ruined it.

I make my way to a till. Isabel wanders over to the self-checkout. I think nothing of it as I place my shopping on the belt and fish for my debit card.

Two minutes later, Isabel is waiting at the entrance for me. She's smiling, but she doesn't say anything until we've heaved the bags into the car and I've returned the trolley to the bay, and then she just says, 'Ça va?'

I push the power button, put the car into reverse and switch the radio on. It's tuned to a music station, which suits me fine. I'm in no mood to talk. After a moment, Isabel bends down and takes something out of the shopping bag she's settled between her feet. I glance at her and grip the wheel tighter when I realize what it is. A can of ready-mixed gin and tonic. She pulls the tab and lifts it to her lips, and the air seems to stiffen around us.

'What do you think you're doing?' I say. I hope she can't hear the shortness of my breath.

'I wanted a drink.'

'Now?'

'To get me in a good mood for the party. There's one for you too.'

'Why would you do that, Isabel?'

200

She pouts. 'I wanted to give you something to say I am sorry for being rude.'

Stopped at the traffic lights, I turn and stare at her. 'No, you didn't. You wanted to cause trouble.'

'You have caused trouble for me.'

'And how precisely have I done that?'

'I came here to learn to speak good English and to look after your children, and now I am in a house where my hosts hate each other. It is not *convenable*. I have to come with you to the shops. It is ridiculous. Your husband is not right in here, I think.' She taps her head.

'He had a brain injury.' I leap to Martin's defence, even though she's not wrong, and then wonder why I'm being protective. It's not as if he needs me in his corner.

Isabel stretches over and turns the volume down on the radio. 'Tonight will be fun,' she says.

'Will it?'

'Of course. Dan will be there. I think tonight I will let him make love to me.' She takes another slug from the can as I wince, and smacks her lips. 'It is so good.'

'It's warm, Isabel. I should think it's vile. If you want to make a point, just say it, don't play stupid games.'

She chuckles and wedges the can between her slim thighs. Everything she does feels like a challenge. She pulls down the visor and checks her reflection, then sits back and sighs. 'I wonder what he will be like in bed?'

That makes two of us. I try not to imagine Dan's body covering Isabel's, her fingertips pressing into his tensing muscles. I should trust to what I know of him. He is in love with me, not Isabel. She is a distraction, a sleight of hand to keep Martin from suspecting the truth. I turn the volume back up and ignore her.

When we get home, she reaches into the bag again and places the other can in the cup holder, then gets out and goes round to the boot to take out the shopping bags. I look at the can. I look at Martin's office window. I breathe deeply. It's very unlikely he's lurking in there. He'll be busy with Kate and the children. Before I know it, I've opened it and the unpleasantly warm, fizzy liquid is pulsing too quickly down my throat and into my stomach where it swishes nauseatingly. I tuck the empty can under the seat to dispose of later, and wipe my mouth. Warm gin and tonic; I am plumbing new depths.

It isn't enough to satisfy, or even to go to my head, but it's more than enough to fling open a door that I was already struggling to keep shut. I could cry with despair and guilt. Isabel has made sure today is going to be even harder for me, and she's done it out of mischief. She won't succeed. There are five and a half hours to go before our guests start arriving. I can pull myself together by then.

30

The crowd in our garden is thinner than last year, there's no disputing that. We invited one hundred and ten guests plus their assorted children and teens, and I reckon two thirds of them are here, though people are still arriving. Most are old friends and colleagues of Martin's from his pre-accident days, but a handful of our local friends have shown up. People round here have huge respect for Martin, so it's down to him that some mutual friends of the Gordons have turned out. Still, it doesn't feel as joyous as it has done in past years.

Sam said he'd come, but I wouldn't put it past him to forget or find someone else to celebrate with. I feel guilty about not including him, but Martin and I did that once and it wasn't a success. Our different sets of friends had nothing in common and Sam obviously felt resentful when any credit there was, was lavished on Martin. But Martin had paid for everything. At any rate, it wasn't suggested again.

Kate of course has been here all day. Dan arrived ten minutes ago, his hair combed into submission. He's wearing a blue linen shirt which looks great with his tan. I can't stop staring at him, and after a moment he turns and his gaze lingers on mine before he looks away. I cling to this because it's a clue of sorts. I'm so confused about where I stand with him. We've kissed, but we're not lovers. We've talked about things that are important to us, revealed something of ourselves, but made no promises. It's causing me both anxiety and excitement. I don't want to tear my family apart, but the fact that I could conceivably do so makes me feel as though I have a shred of power left, something that belongs to me and that Martin can't spoil.

The dress code is smart. I've had several panicked emails asking what that means, and I've told people evening dresses for the women, to make it more of an occasion, no jeans or T-shirts for the men. I'm wearing a long blue sleeveless dress in viscose satin that flows across my skin like water, with a split in the side that rises to the top of my thigh. It makes me appear poised and elegant, and requires high heels to pull off. Mine are strappy and silver; more strap than shoe. I am aware of heads turning, and that makes me feel better until I realize it's more likely to be because of the rift between two well-regarded local families. That kind of thing fascinates people.

Now there is only the small matter of the champagne to negotiate. There is grit in me. I can do this.

So that heels don't sink into the lawn, it's been covered by temporary flooring that has itself been covered in realistic fake grass. The bouncy castle is up and running, manned by a couple of local teenage boys, the sons of guests. Martin heeded my advice and is spending

204

money to make sure the children don't break any bones. The lads didn't impress when they slouched in looking like they would rather be anywhere else than a house full of their parents' friends and their snot-nosed brats. The Saturday evening they're missing out on probably involves loitering in the park or in a friend's basement. But Martin spoke to them and, to my surprise, they switched their phones off. They appear to be having as much fun as the kids, so I don't feel bad. As long as they don't drink and get off their heads before the families with small children have taken them home, they'll be OK. Lucas is holding hands with one of the smallest as they bounce, the little ones bobbing around on their bottoms shrieking with hysterical laughter.

I'm chatting to Robert and Sarah Field, who Martin's known since university. Earlier I found them gazing enviously at the house. The kitchen is lit up like a stage behind floor-to-ceiling windows that have been opened to their full extent. The house is already very wide, designed with lateral living in mind, but the windows exaggerate the effect. It is an impressive-looking place, I have to concede.

Isabel makes her grand entrance. There's a hush. A waiter approaches her with a tray of champagne flutes, and she takes one, smiling sweetly at him. He blushes. The teenage boys stop bouncing and stare at her, slack-jawed. She looks incredible. I've seen her smartened up to go out with Dan or her girlfriends, and she always looks fresh and pretty, but today she is stunning, poured into a shimmering, diaphanous slip of a dress, split up both sides and with a draped neckline that draws the eye to her breasts. If you stare, you can make out the shape of her nipples. Heads might have turned momentarily for me, but they literally swivel for Isabel Gardin.

Ignoring lesser mortals, she floats towards Martin, bends over and kisses him on both cheeks, her hair swinging down and brushing his face. Dan walks over to greet her.

Robert Field laughs. 'Blimey. Who is that?'

'That's Isabel, our au pair.'

'Oh my god,' Sarah breathes. 'I wouldn't have her in my house.'

'Thanks for the vote of confidence,' Robert says.

'She doesn't normally look like that,' I say. 'She usually dresses quite conservatively. She's from a tiny village.' Why did I add that? Am I trying to lessen her impact?

'It's the attitude though, isn't it?' Sarah says. 'It doesn't really matter what they look like, if they've got that come-to-bed thing going on. Bloody hell.'

'Is that her boyfriend?' Robert asks, nodding in Dan's direction.

'No . . . yes. Well, I don't know precisely what their relationship is.'

Robert raises his eyebrows. 'I think I know what he'd like it to be.'

I laugh, but the voyeuristic nature of the conversation is making me uncomfortable. I study Dan, trying to interpret the way he's looking at her. He is being attentive. It's all an act, I tell myself. I mutter something about checking on the caterers and move away. A waiter glides past me with his tray, and I follow him with my eyes. My sparkling water gives me little comfort.

Conversation burbles around me; someone taps me on the arm as I pass and draws me into their circle. They are smiling at me, wishing me a happy birthday. There are more pointed allusions to the dangers of gorgeous au pairs, more laughter about not putting temptation in front of husbands after ten years of marriage. I take it all with good grace.

'I'm so sorry that you and Ali have had a falling out,' Amanda Kelsey says. 'You were so close. You must be devastated.'

I'm surprised to see her here, but I presume her special friendship with Ali isn't worth missing a glitzy party for. 'It isn't fun,' I say curtly. 'But I'd rather not talk about it, if you don't mind.'

'Of course. I understand. Sometimes friends can be more precious than husbands. Jack is gorgeous. You haven't seen him yet, have you? He has the funniest little button nose.'

'Sorry, Amanda, someone's arrived. I must—'

'So, which one is Dan?' she interrupts.

I sigh and point him out. He's left Isabel's side and is talking to Sonia Metzger, a tall, bespectacled woman whose little boy, Alfie, is a good friend of Lucas's.

'You must introduce me. Come on. I insist.' She tucks her arm through mine and steers me towards them.

Dan and Sonia smile as we approach. I make the introductions, and Amanda taps Dan on the arm.

'So you're the famous Dan?' she trills. I think she's a bit drunk.

'Am I famous?' he asks, his hand rising to the back of his neck.

'You absolutely are. I hope you're worth all the trouble you've caused.'

'It seems I'm everyone's scapegoat. I should be flattered.'

She doesn't appear to notice the dry tone, or the bemused way he's looking at her. But I notice everything about Dan. Out of the corner of my eye I see that Sam has arrived. He's over by the bouncy castle, Aurora pulling on his arm. He gives me a friendly wave. He looks good. I don't think he's on anything. He'd better not be, not after I gave him the money he wanted. It wasn't easy to find it without asking Martin. I had to sell the earrings that were meant for Aurora. I don't think I got anything like what they were worth. Nothing was said about why I changed my mind. I couldn't bear to spell it out. But he knows.

'It's lovely to finally meet you in person, Dan,' Amanda gushes. 'I've heard so much about you from Pete and Ali. I do hope Martin comes to his senses soon. He and Pete have such a strong bond.' She pauses. 'Their friendship goes back a very long way.'

'Yes,' Dan says, glancing at me for help. I widen my eyes in response and his lips quirk. 'So I understand. But a man can have more than one friend, I assume, without the other feeling threatened.'

'Well, perhaps Pete is a little insecure,' Amanda agrees. 'So tell me, what is it exactly that you're doing for Martin?'

Poor Dan. I grab this moment as my cue to go, and walk off before either of them can stop me. I like the way my skirt ripples away from my right leg as I move. I feel like an actress on the red carpet.

'Eliza.'

I look round, and find Sonia Metzger behind me.

'Lovely party,' she says. 'I wanted a chance to talk to you, and to say I'm sorry about what's been going on. I try not to listen to gossip.' She twists her mouth in a gesture of mock despair. 'But you know what Amanda's like. For what it's worth, I don't believe in painting one person black and the other white. It's never that simple.'

I smile, grateful to her. 'Don't you have to, in your line of work?' Sonia is a lawyer.

'Yes, I suppose I do. But when I'm not at work I acknowledge the grey areas. Oh lord. I recognize him.'

I turn my head. Her attention has been caught by Andrew Joliffe, Martin's lawyer. This is a man who manages to convey the impression that he knows what's in my heart and would be prepared to use it. I dislike him but he and Martin have known each other forever. Andrew's father worked for Martin's, and Edward paid for Andrew to study law at Cambridge. Andrew is about ten years older than Martin, but they are as close as two men can be who don't live in the same town and only see each other on rare occasions. They're talking intently, along with Henry, the schoolfriend Martin was travelling around Goa with when we first met. Henry is a lovely man; very different from Martin.

'Do you know Andrew?' I ask.

'He's crossed my path. He's an arrogant misogynist.' She smiles swiftly. 'Sorry, he's a friend of yours. I shouldn't be rude.'

I laugh. 'Be as rude as you like. He's never been a friend of mine.'

I glance over at Joliffe again as I leave Sonia, and in that instant he catches my eye, his lip curling slightly, as if he knows I've been talking about him. I feel a sense of foreboding, and shiver.

31

'Happy birthday, sis,' Sam says.

'Happy birthday to you too. Have you had a nice day?'

'All right. I'm afraid I took you at your word and didn't bring a present, unlike everyone else.'

'I wish they hadn't,' I say. The drawing room side table is heaving with beautifully wrapped gifts. 'I haven't got anything for you either.'

'No, but you've helped me. I appreciate it.'

'I'm sorry about what I said.'

'Forget about it. It's all fine.'

'How are things going?'

'Early days,' he says. 'Early days. So, where's Martin? I'd better catch him before he's drunk too much. He's always kinder to me when he's sober. Less unfiltered.'

I laugh and wander inside to check on the caterers. Sam can handle himself, and Martin will be civil.

My kitchen is a whirlwind of activity. Trays are being loaded with tasty-looking canapés. A pan steams on the hob, sizzling prawns are shuffled off their baking tray onto a platter and arranged around a bowl of sweet chilli jelly, finishing touches are put to tiny creations. Waiters dart in and out, replenishing their trays with fresh glasses. The champagne has relaxed inhibitions and there are frequent bursts of laughter. Male voices have got louder. There are more than enough people here for it to feel like a success. Martin will be pleased.

I take a breath and cross the hall, and I'm within arm's reach of a drinks tray when three children run inside and scoot past me, sliding socked feet on the polished floor before charging upstairs. Lucas, Briony and Lola Kelsey, Amanda's daughter, up to mischief. They've been told upstairs is out of bounds. I go after them and find them bouncing on the bed in the master bedroom.

'OK. All of you out. You know you're not allowed in here.'

I'm not cross, and I try very hard not to sound it because it's important not to upset Briony. I'm so grateful that the Gordon children have been allowed to come. Lucas and Briony obediently get off the bed. Lola keeps bouncing. She's a pretty little thing, and knows it.

'Come on, Lola darling. You need to go outside and play with the other children.'

'Why aren't you friends with Briony's mum?' she asks, once she's somersaulted the length of the bed.

That's a tough one. I wonder what she's overheard.

'I'm still her friend. Sometimes people argue though and have to wait a while until they feel kinder towards each other. Then they can be friends again.'

'But my mum said it was a relief.' She looks up at me

with big eyes. 'Does that mean Briony's mum didn't like you before?'

'You shouldn't listen to grown-up conversations, Lola. You can get the wrong end of the stick.'

She picks at the sequinned motif on her shirt. 'But Mum talks all the time, so I have to listen.'

She wrinkles her nose, then slips past me and runs downstairs. I follow her slowly, my skin prickling. What did that mean? That Ali was only my friend because I married her brother? That she found it difficult to like me and was glad of the excuse to divest herself of an unpleasant duty? My throat aches. A waiter pops the cork on a new bottle of champagne. I grab two glasses and hold them out to be filled then turn away quickly, swallowing back stinging tears. I mustn't fall into the trap of feeling sorry for myself. It's childish. When we were young Sam was always the popular one, but that was because I allowed him to act the part of the fun twin, leading others into mischief and mayhem, while I did the worrying and carried the anger. I still carry anger. I suppose that's what Amanda and her ilk sense. Something about me alienates them.

As I cross the hall, Andrew Joliffe comes out of the cloakroom. We both hesitate.

'You look upset,' he says. 'Anything I can do to help?'

'No, thank you. I'm fine.'

'Does Martin know about that?' He points to the glasses.

'It's none of your business. Now, if you don't mind . . .' I start to turn away but he steps in front of me.

'If I was your husband, I'd keep a better eye on you. All that beauty and no morals.'

'Fuck off, Andrew.'

He laughs, but he doesn't move. Instead he bends and whispers in my ear, 'I hear you've been up to no good.'

I try to get away, but he grips my upper arm, making me spill some of the champagne. A splash hits my bare toes.

'Should I be worried for my friend?'

'Let. Me. Go,' I say between clenched teeth. My knees threaten to buckle.

He obliges, laughing again, puts his hands in his pockets and whistles as he saunters off.

I'm trembling violently when I slip into the playroom and close the door. No one will come in here. The drawing room with its comfortable sofas and sliding glass doors open onto the garden is a more tempting prospect to those wanting to take the weight off their feet.

I sit down and slip my shoes off. Then I drink both glasses. I can't go back outside now. In fact, I don't think I can move at all. I grip my knees, trying to still the shudders ripping through me, and stare at my reflection in the television's empty screen. What was he hinting at? What exactly does that horrible man know about me? My secrets feel as though they are oozing through fissures in my skin, grey as puddle water.

I take several deep breaths but I don't feel any calmer. I must go back to my guests. I'll count to ten, then I'll go. I count backwards, but when I get to four, the door opens. Embarrassed, I grab a shoe and try to pull it on but it flips on its heel, wrenching my foot.

'Just taking a break,' I say, rubbing my ankle. 'I'll be out in a sec.'

'So this is where you've been hiding.'

Dan comes over and gets down on the floor in front of me. Sitting back on his heels, he extends a hand and curls a lock of my hair behind my ear. I raise my eyes to his.

'Hey,' he says. 'What's up?'

His scrutiny is intense. I look away and have another stab at getting my feet into my shoes. He takes them from me and sets them down, heel to heel, toe to toe, then joins me on the sofa.

'You're shaking,' he says. 'What's happened?'

I can't tell him about Joliffe. 'Could you get me a drink?'

'I can get you some water.'

'I don't want water. I want champagne. Please, Dan. I can't go out there yet. Just get me something, anything.'

He cups his hand around my cheek and turns my head so that I'm forced to look into his eyes.

'That's not going to do any good, is it? You'll be all right. I'll stay with you until you're ready to go back out there, but don't have any more champagne.'

I shove his hand away. 'Get me a fucking drink.'

I see his expression change, almost as if his vision has suddenly cleared and he knows what I am.

'I'm sorry,' I say. 'I'm so sorry.'

He leans back into the sofa cushions with a sigh and pushes his hands through his hair. 'No, I'm the one who should apologize. I didn't realize it was so bad.'

'Well, now you do. I just want to know who told Ali

about me and Pete. Who would want to destroy me like that?'

'Sam?' he suggests.

'More likely Isabel.'

'But you hadn't fallen out with her then.'

I shrug. 'I think things had been bubbling under the surface for a while.' I sniff and update him on recent events, giving him my side of the story, knowing if she's already told him all this, her version would have been very different. I describe the humiliation of being forced by Martin to accept her back into the house after I'd sacked her, and about the gin and tonic she bought me this morning.

His forehead creases. 'Eliza, that's not what Isabel says happened. She said she'd only let you out of her sight for a moment, that you produced the can after you got into the car. She tried to persuade you to give it to her, but you refused. She asked me if she should mention it to Martin. I told her not to.'

'But it's not true! You don't believe her, do you?'

'Not really.' He rubs his face. 'Isabel isn't the most sisterly woman I've met.'

'Seriously, Dan. She's lying. She bought two cans and gave me one. If you don't believe me, I can show you my receipt. They're not on it.'

'You don't have to do that.'

I release my breath. 'I don't know why she'd lie to you about it. She didn't have to bring the subject up at all.'

'She talks about you a lot. She's a bit obsessed.'

216

I laugh bitterly. 'Why? It's not as though I have anything she wants.'

'Don't you look at yourself in the mirror? You're beautiful.'

'Thanks. But she's twelve years younger than me, and a lot more confident than I was at that age. You've seen the impact she's had tonight. The men can't keep their eyes off her, or their wives for that matter. If she's obsessed with me, it's not because of my looks.'

'I dispute that,' he grins. Then his expression turns serious. 'It's because you have me, and she knows deep down that she'll never touch me in the way you have. She's jealous and it's eating her up. I don't think she wanted my advice about whether to tell Martin, I think she just wanted me to think less of you. It didn't work,' he adds softly, stroking my cheek.

I look into his eyes, trying to read him. He's so guileless, but that could be an act.

'Try to forget about it, and enjoy your party. Come on. I won't be the only one who's noticed the hostess is missing.'

He leans forward and takes one of my shoes in his hand, and with the other lifts my foot. He slips my shoe on, pulls the narrow strap over my heel, then does the other one. It feels nice to be taken care of.

Dan jumps up and holds out his hands. After a hesitation, I take them and he pulls me to my feet. I stand against him, the backs of my calves pressed against the sofa. I can hear my breath enter and leave my lungs, my blood pulsing through my veins. After a moment I can't take the tension any more, and rest my head in the crook of his shoulder so that I can't see his eyes.

'I need a drink,' I mutter, half laughing. I'm so nervous.

'I know you do,' he soothes, stroking my back.

Then he winds his hands into my hair and tugs lightly. There is a second, perhaps two, when I could stop this, but I allow the opportunity to slip away. His head dips and his mouth is on mine, and we kiss first softly, exploratively, then fiercely, his hands sliding down the slippery fabric of my dress, cupping my bottom.

I don't hear the door open behind me, but Dan releases me abruptly, and I twist round.

Isabel is standing in the doorway, her face contorted with fury.

32

Isabel rushes off, slamming the door. Dan looks at me, then mumbles, 'Stay here, I'll deal with this,' before running after her, leaving me wondering if he's gone to apologize or remonstrate. Why didn't he stay with me? I'm staring at the door feeling as though I'm the guilty party, while he's raced off to comfort my deranged au pair like some kind of hen-pecked husband.

Slipping back into the kitchen I filch another glass of champagne, and I've drunk it by the time I've wound my way through my guests to the bouncy castle. I stay there, making awkward conversation with the older boys, while the children bounce. A little girl from Aurora's nursery somehow ends up between two larger children and lets out a frightened wail. One of the boys dutifully extricates her. They give me a curious glance. Some of the women have slipped their shoes off; I do the same. I don't care if it earns me a reprimand from Martin.

Dan comes out through the drawing room doors and starts talking to Henry, who leans into him, swaying slightly, but there's no sign of Isabel. Maybe she's gone to her room to lick her wounds, having finally had the message driven home. There's a kind of triumph, particularly after the way she's acted towards me, but there's also fear for the same reason. What if she tells Martin?

An hour passes. Most of the guests are too drunk to notice that I am. I smile until my face aches. I make sure I talk to everyone, even Amanda. I talk about Lucas's school and Aurora's nursery, about the local environmental efforts, about who went where for the holidays. I fulfil my role as hostess to the best of my ability, while inside I am churning with anxiety, wary of the damage Isabel could cause.

I'm reckless. Twice I sneak inside and carry a drink into the loo; one of those times I don't even bother with a glass.

I spot Sam loitering at the shady end of the garden, so I wander along the path to join him. He's sitting on the climbing frame, his legs dangling, a cigarette in one hand, a bottled beer in the other.

'Hey, Lyzie,' he says. 'Come on up.'

He pats the space beside him and shifts over as I gingerly climb the ladder, praying my dress doesn't snag on a rough piece of wood. I settle myself and rest my head against his shoulder.

'I wish they'd all go,' I say.

'Party pooper. You should be pleased everyone's having a good time.'

I think of Isabel and pull a face. 'Not quite everyone.'

'You're not enjoying your own party?'

I laugh. 'I know, OK. Do you remember the parties we used to sneak out to when we were teenagers?'

'Dad sitting in the dark on the stairs waiting for us

220

when we got home late? Christ, he was terrifying. It was worth it though.'

'For you maybe.'

Sam puts an arm around my shoulders and kisses my cheek. 'I'm sorry I didn't know how to help you back then.'

'What's brought this on?'

He releases me and drops his head. 'I feel like I'm going to keep failing.'

'Because of Dad?'

'No. I grew out of that a long time ago.'

I'm not sure I believe him.

'I have ideas,' he says. 'But nothing seems to come off. I can't carry through. Fear of failure, I suppose.'

It's the first time he's admitted this and my heart goes out to him.

'Sam, why don't you get a job? Forget being an entrepreneur, you're not cut out for it. You would be great working in a team. You're fun. With a bit of structure, you could turn things round quickly.'

He stretches his arms up and behind him. 'Too late for that.'

'No, it isn't.'

'I'm unhappy.'

My eyes prick. 'Me too.'

'But we stagger on.' He sighs then grabs the bar, swings himself round and climbs down. 'Time to rejoin the human race.'

Isabel is still nowhere to be seen. The caterers have begun to pack up. I help them locate stray glasses round

221

the garden, and in doing so manage to knock back a glass of warm champagne someone has left sitting on the birdbath. I experience a head rush and tell myself it's time to stop.

The people with small children have left, but no one else seems in much hurry to end the night. Some of our guests are dancing to the soundtrack of our youth, noughties hits; Girls Aloud and the Black Eyed Peas; Kings of Leon and the Arctic Monkeys. Others are loudly discussing politics, Martin among them. A trill of laughter rises from a group of women. I wish I was in on the joke. Perhaps I am the joke.

I mustn't think like that. I go up to them and they make room for me, but after a while I wander off, having contributed virtually nothing. I can't seem to connect with anyone and find myself edging backwards, seeking out one of the few dark spots at the edge of the house, letting the shadows swallow me. From there I'm content to watch. I see Dan look around, scanning the garden.

For me or for Isabel? She's not outside.

Then someone calls him over and he joins their conversation. Dan is so at ease with strangers. He's a chameleon, able to change his stripes to suit his company. It's so hard to know whether I can trust him, but the way he kissed me, that mixture of exploration and passion, makes me want to believe in him; not as my saviour but as someone who will help me save myself.

The music stops and a movement catches my eye. Isabel has come out onto the terrace outside our bedroom. I frown. She's lit by the exterior uplighting, her blonde hair cascading about her bare shoulders. She leans over the toughened glass balustrade, looking for someone. I shrink back. People begin to notice; conversations slow to a trickle. Someone laughs nervously.

'Hey,' she shouts. 'Are you having a nice time?'

Oh lord. She's even more drunk than I am. It's in the way she's holding her head, the way she tips forward then back.

'Come down from there,' Martin barks.

'*But, soft! What light through yonder window breaks?*' Henry shouts facetiously. '*It is the east, and Juliet is the sun.*'

'Shut up, Henry.' Martin moves closer to the house. 'What are you doing, Isabel?'

'What am I doing? I'm here to tell everyone the truth!' she yells. 'About your bitch of a wife. Do you people want to know why Ali and Pete did not come? It's because Eliza screwed Pete. I have proof.' She laughs hysterically, waving her phone. 'You want to read it?'

I am frozen with horror.

'Shut the fuck up,' Martin shouts. There is no mistaking the shock in his voice. 'Go back inside right now.'

'I can do what I like. You do not own me.'

I pick up my skirts and run through the empty drawing room into the hall. I take the stairs two at a time, tripping, pulling myself up by the banister. I tear out onto the terrace where Isabel is in full flow, reading out Pete's letter from a photo on her phone. I press her back against the balustrade, and try to grab the phone from her.

Time grinds to a halt, then speeds up.

Isabel is spitting fury, scratching me, kicking my shin. Her skin is soft and feminine. I'm not used to holding a woman like this, like we're wrestling or making love, and I find it repellent. I don't want to touch her but she's hurt my family. She's a threat. As she continues her onslaught of hissed insults, her face becomes my father's, her sharp eyes are his eyes, her twisting mouth is his mouth, and I push her harder, hearing myself grunt with the effort, like an animal. She stumbles and falls against the rail, clutching my dress, ripping it. Over her shoulder, I'm aware of our remaining guests staring up at us with pale, horrified faces.

A woman screams, 'Somebody do something! She's going to push her over!'

Martin roars, 'Eliza, stop it, you fucking maniac!'

Someone grasps me by the shoulders and pulls me back. My fingers are wrenched from Isabel's wrists and her collapsing body is caught in my brother's arms. Dan puts his arm around my waist and turns me towards the bedroom.

'Let go of me!' I lash out, hurling my fists at his chest and shoulders.

'Stop it!'

My face is slapped hard, just once, and I'm so shocked the fight drains out of me.

'Show's over,' Sam shouts across the garden. 'Everyone go home.'

Dan is panting. He slides down the wall beside me and rubs his mouth with his hand. I hug my legs, pressing my face against my knees. Sam helps Isabel to her feet. I look up, then swiftly drop my gaze. Her dress is ripped; she's holding it up against her breast. Sam pats my shoulder briefly and takes her away.

'Can you get up?' Dan asks.

I nod and allow him to help me. He escorts me inside. I collapse onto the bed and curl up in a tight ball and sob. Feet pad around the room, the blinds are lowered. I feel him stop beside me. He sighs. Then the door is quietly closed.

33

Light seeps through the blinds and my eyelids. I squint at the clock, feeling grim. Nine. Why did no one wake me? There's a small person nestled against my back. Aurora must have come in and fallen asleep; she would have been barely awake anyway. Martin isn't here, and I'm relieved because I feel like shit, my head pounding, my mouth tasting of stale alcohol and bile. I don't remember if he even came up to bed. He might have slept in the guest room if he didn't want to disturb me, or didn't fancy being anywhere near me. I sit up and massage my temples. There's a pint glass of water beside the bed. I drink it all.

When I get up my body protests, my shoulders and neck aching and patches of skin stinging where the edge of the duvet brushes them. I stagger into the bathroom and look in the mirror. Scratches lace my arms and shoulders; there's a bruise under my right eye and a gouge mark under my collar bone. As I grip the side of the basin and stare at the streaks of mascara and smudged eyeliner, I remember three things with painful clarity.

Dan kissing me and Isabel walking in.

Isabel on the balcony.

Attacking her. Wanting to hurt her.

I cover my face with my hands and gasp. I could have killed her. Oh my god. No matter what the provocation, it was appalling and unforgivable. I have to apologize and as soon as possible, even though it's the last thing I feel like doing. I doubt she will apologize for what she has done.

It's obvious how she found out about me and Pete. I don't know why I didn't click ages ago. On the night of the supper party back in July, she had chased Aurora into the bedroom and was there when Dan made that ill-judged remark about me hiding my secrets. I bet she was on the stool, her hand groping round the cupboard, the moment she had the house to herself. She would have found Pete's letter, the one telling me he was sorry, that it would never happen again. She must have photographed it and put it back. I underestimated her cunning, and her dislike. And then she wrote anonymously to Ali. I blamed it on Sam, when it makes much more sense that it was her; the au pair flayed with jealousy.

And then when Ali didn't tell Martin, which was probably what she expected to happen, she chose her moment of maximum impact and did it herself. She made me drop my mask and behave like a wild animal. It was as if she had stripped me naked.

Perhaps this isn't a complete disaster, I think suddenly. It's terrible, but perhaps in the long run I'll be glad it happened. Surely Martin won't want to be married to me any more? As long as he shares custody of the children, it needn't be messy. Within seconds I dismiss the idea. Martin isn't like that. Martin only wins. If I go, I'll lose them. And maybe he's right. I don't deserve my children after the stunt I pulled.

Aurora is still sleeping soundly, unsurprisingly. The children stayed up well beyond their bedtime. At least they weren't awake to witness my disgrace. My robe is draped over the end of the bed. I put it on, tie the sash and tiptoe along the landing to check on Lucas. He's asleep too. I back out of the room, pull the door closed. I peek into the spare bedroom. The bed has been used, the duvet thrown back, one of the pillows still dipped in the middle.

It feels odd that there's no one around; no Isabel brewing coffee in the kitchen, no Martin listening to Radio 4 pundits discussing the contents of the Sunday papers. Hardly a surprise in the circumstances. I go downstairs and cross the hall. Martin isn't in his office either and his computer is switched off. Usually he'll check the markets, even on a Sunday, anxious not to miss a single fluctuation. Through the window I can see that both cars are there, mine where I tucked it right into the side to make space for the catering van. Martin must be in the pool or the gym. That's good, because if Isabel is here, I can talk to her before he gets to me.

The caterers have left the kitchen spotless. I drink two glasses of water, then slide open the doors and step barefoot onto the terrace. There are a few beer bottles lying around, but the place isn't too bad considering. I skirt round the house to the annexe entrance. It seems less intrusive than using the internal door. The blinds are down.

I knock softly. There's no response so I knock harder, then pull the handle down and push. My eyes adjust to the dim light. Isabel is lying on her side, a sheet over her naked body, an arm and leg stretched out, her hair covering her face.

'Isabel,' I whisper.

She rolls over, groans and cracks open an eye. 'What do you want?'

'To apologize for last night.'

She pushes herself up and pulls the sheet round her. 'Dan was drunk, you know.'

'Yes, he was,' I say. 'We both were.'

'He wanted me to come home with him. He begged me, but I refused.'

No way did that happen. She's as deluded as ever.

'It's stupid to forgive men too easily,' she mutters.

'Well, I wanted to tell you how sorry I am for what happened on the balcony,' I say, opting to ignore the provocation. 'I was furious about what you did, but my behaviour was inexcusable. We can talk about it again later, if you want to. Once you're awake properly. I'll make breakfast,' I add as an extra olive branch. 'Scrambled eggs and smoked salmon.'

'No.'

'Oh. OK. Well, I'll leave you to go back to sleep.'

She squints through her untidy fall of hair and pushes

229

it away from her face. 'I think you will lose everything because you do not understand men.'

I really don't need another of Isabel's life lessons. 'And you do?'

'Of course. You do the wrong thing, you say the wrong thing. You are fucked up.'

She lies down again and pulls the sheet over her head, and I leave the annexe. Neither of us covered ourselves in glory last night, but at least I've apologized and can hold my head higher. Or I would if it didn't hurt so much.

Back in the kitchen, Martin comes at me so fast I don't have a chance to escape. He wraps his hand around my wrist, twists it and yanks me forward. When I lose my balance, grasping for the table to steady myself, he slaps me hard across the face. It's a clumsy, misdirected slap, but I end up on the floor, my robe askew, pushing myself backwards to get away from his wheels.

'Do you have any idea how mortifying last night was for me?' he says.

'Of course I do.' I hold the lapels of my dressing gown together. 'It was mortifying for me as well.'

'Oh yes, let's not forget about you. Poor Eliza.'

'I didn't mean that.'

'You've humiliated me, and yourself. I doubt you have any friends left.'

I swipe a tear away. 'If people knew what you were really like, they might not like you that much either.'

'There's nothing wrong with me. You, on the other hand, are pathetic and weak. I loved that about you once. I wanted to look after you and protect you. I would have done anything for you. But something happens to me, and what do you do? You fuck my best friend because you're sad and stressed. Well, Christ, I'm sad and stressed right now. Will you fuck me?'

I wish I could stop crying, but the tears keep welling up and spilling over no matter what I do. 'It didn't mean anything. It only happened once, when you were in the coma. I was going through hell. We both were. I've regretted it ever since and so has Pete.'

'Do I disgust you?' he asks.

'Of course you don't.'

'Why should I believe you? You lie all the time. I am not unreasonable, or under any illusions. I understand. Of course you look at other men. I don't mind that.'

That's a lie.

'But screwing Pete? That's betrayal.'

I feel a trickle from my nose and wipe it on the back of my hand. It leaves a streak of blood. If Martin has noticed, which he must have, he doesn't comment.

'Nothing to say?' He looks down at me. 'That's not like you.'

'It was a mistake and it was a long time ago and I didn't leave you, did I? I could have done, but I didn't because I still loved you.' It was almost true; there was still something left of what he had once meant to me, mixed up with compassion for a wounded beast. 'I hated what happened with Pete, really hated it. I still despise myself. I was so ashamed that I didn't want to see him, but he was your friend and you needed him.'

'I don't need him any more.' Martin presses his steepled fingers against his lips.

'What about me?' I whisper. 'Do you not need me any more either? Do you want me to leave?'

He waits a long time before he responds. 'No.'

'But why not? Why do we have to stay together when neither of us is happy? You don't like me and you'll never forgive me for what I did. Don't you want to move on? I don't need much; a small house with room for the children. I can get a job once Aurora is at school full-time. We can share custody fifty-fifty. There is no reason we can't have an amicable divorce. You must realize that it'll be better for everyone in the long term.'

'What would you do without me?' Martin responds. 'I'm interested. You can try to get money out of me, but you're not getting the children, so without an evidenced need for child maintenance you'd have very little leverage, especially when the truth about you comes out.' He pauses, raising an eyebrow, and sneers. 'Daddy's little girl.'

'You wouldn't dare.'

'Fine. Go your own way. But when the children have been told what their mother really is, they won't want you. The only person who might possibly stand by you is Sam, and even he'll soon get tired of providing his sister with emotional support once he realizes there's no money.'

I lose the conciliatory tone. 'So what's your ideal scenario, Martin? That we stay together and live a lie? Or that I leave you and the children and they spend the rest of their lives believing they've been abandoned by their mother, that she didn't love them enough?'

'There's a price to be paid for the choices we make.'

'God, that's cold. Does that include their happiness and emotional wellbeing? When I'm gone, will you treat them like you treat me? Will you undermine them and control them? Restrict their freedom?'

'Of course not. They're good kids, we've brought them up well.'

I wipe my nose again as I pull myself up onto a chair. More blood. 'It'll happen. You can't control that side of your personality.'

Martin yawns. 'They would be safe and happy with me, I assure you. But it's irrelevant because you're going nowhere. If anyone's going to wash their hands of this marriage it'll be me, at a time of my choosing. I don't want it to come to this, but if necessary, I will tell the police what I know about you.'

'I'll deny it.'

'Ah, will you?' He strokes his jaw. 'It would be enough to sow doubt though, don't you think? In the mind of a family court judge? No social worker would risk leaving children in the hands of a murderer with a drink problem, not when the alternative is me.'

I lean forward and hit him. For the first time in our lives together I physically assault my disabled husband. My ears ring with the sound of the slap, the skin of my palm stings and tingles. A red flush suffuses his cheek and his earlobe. There's a moment when I think he's going to lash back, when I wish he would, to break the sudden, awful tension, but his hands remain in his lap. He swallows hard.

'I am willing to forgive you for that, Eliza, and put it down to the heat of the moment, but you'll have your

233

work cut out if you're going to repair the damage you've done.'

I don't trust myself to say anything, but I feel such despair that I could literally throw up. He has me backed into a corner and he knows it. He pulls me awkwardly into a kiss. My knees land between his legs, against the edge of the seat. I grab his shoulder to stop myself collapsing on top of him. Our mouths and teeth clash, his tongue forces apart my teeth and invades my mouth. His free hand slides inside my robe and closes round a breast. I am a mess of saliva and tears and pain. And loathing. And then, miraculously, we hear little feet running down the stairs and Martin releases me. I grab a napkin from the pile left over from last night and press it to my nose.

'Daddy!' Aurora runs to him. Not to me. She climbs onto his knee and kisses his face. 'I'm hungry.'

'Well, we must do something about that,' he says.

I move towards the door.

'Where're you going?' he asks sharply.

'Nowhere. I just need to clean up.'

I lock myself in the cloakroom and wash my face. I look awful, worse than I did when I first woke up. The bruising seems to have deepened, or maybe I've become paler. Only my lips are red where his mouth crushed them. I sit down hard on the loo and press my knuckles against my teeth. How do I get through this? I can't get Dan out of my head, but he is not the answer; he is not worth a life deprived of my children. I imagine waking in the morning to a quiet flat with no Aurora to snuggle in beside me, no Lucas to bounce around the room. My throat aches.

I want out of this prison, but while Martin is alive and the children are too young for the truth, that isn't going to happen. I wish he was dead.

34

Isabel doesn't appear, but I know she's gone out, sneaking through the side gate, because I checked her room. And of course, there's the note she left for me.

> *Dear Eliza*
> *I will be out today and I am leaving in the morning. I do not want to see you. I feel sorry for Martin, being married to you. I have never liked you. You are a cold person.*
>
> *I am willing not to report your assault to the police, but in return for this favour, I will expect to see £10,000 in my bank account by tomorrow morning. You can afford it.*
>
> *Please give my love to Aurora and Lucas, and tell them I will miss them.*
> *Isabel*

I sit at the top of the stairs, leaning against the wall, my hands draped between my thighs, holding the letter. I remember sitting like this as a child, listening to the house, trying to gauge my father's mood from his foot-steps, the way he closed doors, his tone of voice. If he was angry, his voice would drip with scorn. My mother's breath would get heavier when she was anxious and because it was a small house it was audible. My father would read the paper, slapping over the pages if he was in a bad mood, letting them flop down if he was calm. If he was particularly cheerful he would be manic, unstable and a little bit frightening. If he was building up to violence a pulsing silence would descend on the house, sucking out the oxygen. Unlike Martin, he had no head injury to blame his behaviour on.

Now, when I think back, it's clear that Dad had an undiagnosed psychopathy. If he'd spoken to an expert and attained some knowledge of his condition, maybe our lives would have turned out differently. But he'd never have done that because it would have been impossible for him to admit that there was anything wrong with him.

Martin pushes himself out of the kitchen, Lucas and Aurora following him like lambs. I feel terrible that they are all that stands between me and their father's violence. It's this awareness that forces me to recognize that I have to go. It is grossly unfair on the children to use them as a shield. Lucas is old enough to sense it, and it won't be long before Aurora does too.

I try not to move my head too abruptly. I have a dreadful hangover, but I still need to think. I check my phone. There are no messages from Dan. Maybe he's still asleep.

Ten thousand pounds. How on earth do I come up with that? The answer is, I don't. I can't. I'll call him. I'll ask him to talk to her – if anyone can drill some sense into that girl, he can. He doesn't answer his phone. What would I have said to him anyway? This is not his problem.

After a big breakfast that I can barely get down, Martin insists we take the children out, so we drive to an area far enough away that we are unlikely to meet anyone who was at Winterfell last night. There's a park with woodland, deer and a huge playground. For the children it's bliss. I have no idea what's going through Martin's mind because he is playing the ideal father; fun, noisy, ready to say yes to anything, his wallet whipped out to buy ice creams.

While the children are absorbed we talk, Isabel's letter burning a hole in my coat pocket.

'This is what you want to throw away,' Martin says, adjusting his baseball cap to keep the sun out of his eyes. 'We were the perfect family. It's a shame.'

I turn my head in surprise. 'We weren't perfect.'

'Oh, yes we were. I loved our life.'

I expel a breath.

'I saw you talking to Sonia Metzger last night,' he says. 'Were you asking her for advice?'

'We were just chatting.'

'I don't believe you.'

'That's your problem. But it's not a bad idea. Maybe I will talk through my options with her.'

Martin laughs. 'Are you going to tell her what you did? Or shall I?'

Instead of answering, I take Isabel's note out of my pocket and hand it to him, then get up and walk over to the slide. Aurora is about to launch herself down it. I crouch at the bottom, holding my arms out, and she flies into them and hugs me hard. I breathe in the scent of baby shampoo and vanilla ice cream, then she wriggles and I put her down and watch her run round to the ladder again, noting that she's grown over the summer.

I have another discreet look at my phone. Still no response from Dan. I'm surprised and hurt. After what happened yesterday, I'd expect him at least to show some concern for me.

I have no weapons to use against Martin. He is wealthy and surrounded by a strong, loving family who can provide him with support. I have an unemployed, weed-smoking brother, a drink problem and a murky past. Why did I tell Martin what happened to my father? It was a stupid thing to do.

But I was in love. I look back at that sultry night in Goa with a sense of horror and incredulity. How could I have been so naive? Arms around each other, heads together, we had been drinking but not heavily, and Martin had said, *No secrets. We tell each other everything while we're here. We go home with a clean slate.*

Martin told me things about himself, minor things he was ashamed of. Then he took a deep breath and told me what the worst thing was. He had said nothing to me at the time, but he had heard two weeks previously that the girl he had dumped for me had killed herself. He drained his beer before he admitted that he hadn't written to her family, or done anything at all. He'd pretended none of it had happened, hoping it would go away. He was having the time of his life and didn't want to be involved in some other family's mess.

While she was alive he hadn't returned her calls, or offered her an apology, or even acknowledged that they had meant anything to each other. He had, he told me, discarded her like a piece of unwanted rubbish. It was his friend Henry who told him. He'd seen it on Facebook.

Now I wonder about all this. Martin implied that he hadn't had the guts to approach her parents, but Martin possesses guts in abundance. I suspect it didn't occur to him. He simply didn't care and her death hasn't haunted him. But at the time, I believed every word of it; it's only in hindsight that I can see how callous his behaviour was.

In return for his honesty, I revealed my secrets and told him what I had done.

Martin flicks his finger against the letter. 'She's got a nerve.'

I shrug.

'I'm not paying her.'

'Where does that leave me?'

'I'll deal with it.'

'Thank you.'

'In the meantime, the best thing you can do is to spend some time in Lowndes Place.'

I blink at him, unsure if I've heard him correctly.

Lowndes Place is a privately run rehabilitation hospital about five miles from us. It has a reputation for hosting celebrities and is rumoured to be extremely expensive.

'What on earth for?'

'For your own good. It's the best thing for you and for the children. It's all arranged. They're expecting you at nine tomorrow morning.'

'You can't do that. I won't go.'

'Yes, you will. You need to be seen to be actively addressing your problems, or you are always going to be vulnerable to people like Isabel. It's pointless hiding what you've become – fifty-odd people witnessed your lunacy last night. You're going in tomorrow morning whether you like it or not. When you're well, we'll discuss what happens next.'

A man picks up his toddler and throws her in the air. Her happy squeals cut through to my heart.

'Martin, I can't.'

Now I realize why he's insisted we go out; it's so that he can inform me of his decision somewhere I can't make a scene. A playground full of well-dressed people enjoying a Sunday afternoon with their children.

'We put the children first,' Martin says. 'You know it's the right thing to do, just as you know in your heart that they aren't safe with you when you're like this. Six weeks at Lowndes—'

'Six weeks!'

'It should be enough to get you back on the straight and narrow. Then we can be a family again.' He sighs.

'Right. Let's deal with Isabel.'

He spreads the letter on his lap and takes a picture, then makes the call.

'Andrew,' he says, and briefly explains the situation. 'She's leaving the house tomorrow morning, and possibly the country for all I know. Nip this in the bud, would you? . . . Thanks, mate. I'll forward her contact details and a copy of the letter.'

35

Martin seems almost content after we get home, which is more than can be said for me. I have to do something. I am not being incarcerated in what amounts to an expensive prison. I might have agreed to a week, but six? Six weeks in the life of a small child is the psychological equivalent of six months in the life of an adult. Lucas and Aurora will think I've abandoned them. And who's to say Martin will allow me back afterwards? I only have his word for it.

That evening I give the children fish fingers and baked beans and begin the process of getting them to bed. It takes a little longer than usual because they're over-tired and I still have a lingering headache. Aurora is tearful, Lucas unusually quiet. Aurora falls asleep while I'm reading to them. Lucas climbs into his own bed and clings to me as if he never wants to let me go.

'Is everything OK, darling?'

He shakes his head against my shoulder.

'What is it? You can tell me.'

'I don't want you and Daddy to get divorced.'

My gut tightens. 'Who said anything about divorce?'

'Lola,' he mumbles.

I hesitate, not wanting to lie to him. 'Lola has been listening to grown-ups gossiping and they don't know anything, because they don't live with us.'

'Promise you won't go away?'

'I'll never leave you, Lucas.'

We are going, but I can't tell him that now. I need him to go to sleep while I prepare.

I pack my overnight bag and squeeze in a change of clothes for the children before hiding it at the bottom of my wardrobe. Everything else will have to wait. I haven't had time to think further ahead, but my immediate plan is for us to spend tonight in Sam's flat. He's the one person I know who won't shut the door in my face.

In Martin's bathroom, I find the medication he was prescribed after his seizure. I pop three of the capsules out of their packet, and pocket them.

Martin reads the business section of the Sunday papers while I chop onions and mushrooms, dissolve a stock cube in boiling water and measure out the rice for a risotto. There's champagne in the fridge, three bottles left over from last night. It's tormenting me.

His phone rings. It's probably Kate. She's the only person likely to call on a Sunday evening.

'Right,' Martin says. 'That's great. Let's speak again tomorrow.' He laughs. 'Yeah. That should do it.'

Or maybe not his mother. That isn't how he speaks to her.

'Who was that?' I ask when he hangs up.

'Andrew. He's spoken to Isabel. I doubt we'll have any more trouble from her.'

I shudder inwardly. 'What did he say?'

He smiles. 'Best you don't know. He can be a scary bastard when it suits him.'

Sounds familiar, I think.

Once the risotto is ready, I wilt in a generous handful of rocket to disguise any residual bitterness, divide it between two bowls, crack open the capsules, shake their contents into one of them and stir thoroughly. I drop the empty capsules into the waste disposal unit. The drugs can cause dizziness and drowsiness. Three should guarantee Martin falls asleep.

'How about a glass of champagne?' Martin says.

I stare at him in surprise. 'You are joking, aren't you?'

Martin closes the newspaper, folds it and swivels round.

'Relax. You're going into rehab tomorrow. Let's have a last hurrah. We can put all this behind us and start afresh. You want that, don't you?' He waits.

My fingers twitch. I can't say what he wants me to say.

'Don't you?' he presses.

'I don't think it's a good idea for me to drink.'

'Why not? Were you intending to get in your car tonight?'

'Of course not.'

'Then get the glasses and the champagne.' His voice is dangerously quiet. 'I'm not asking again.'

I've been married to him long enough to recognize a warning. I fetch two champagne flutes and the bottle. If he wants to drink, we can drink. I can pace myself. One small sip between mouthfuls of rice, and at least that way he'll eat what's put in front of him. The pop of the cork sets off the inevitable chain reaction in me. Racing pulse, sweating palms, feelings of panic mixed with expectation, self-loathing and rebellion.

'To a new start with my beautiful wife.' Martin raises his glass.

I clink mine against his. I smell it before I taste it. The liquid fizzes over my tongue. It's beautiful, fresh, renewing. I wish I could stop right here, at this first taste, not go on and spoil it.

I eat a forkful of risotto and try not to stare as he does the same. He picks at his food, finishing barely a third of it before he pushes it away.

'What kind of cheese did you put in this? It tastes rank.'

I swallow back a constriction in my throat. 'Just ordinary Parmesan. It's not that bad, is it? Mine's OK.' I eat a mouthful to prove it.

He raises his eyebrows. 'It's inedible. Was there anything decent left over from last night?'

He pushes himself to the fridge without waiting for an answer. The caterers have left a plate of food covered with silver paper. Martin brings it over and uncovers it. He pops a bite-sized croustade of smoked salmon and crème fraîche into his mouth. I drink some more champagne.

I can only pray that he ate enough of the risotto to make him sleepy. I drain my glass and he pours me another. I notice he hasn't drunk much of his, and I try to ignore mine but it glimmers on the periphery of my vision and I can't help it; I curl my fingers around the stem and I drink.

Within half an hour we have polished off the leftover party food and have opened a second bottle of champagne, the offending risotto ignored. Perhaps I could just go. I wanted him asleep because I'm a coward and I don't trust my willpower against his gifts of persuasion. He'll talk me out of it, undermine my confidence, make me feel like I am a criminal and a terrible mother, an emotionally fragile wife who can't function without him. If I can get out of his orbit, it'll be easier to stand up for what I know is right.

If I call his bluff and leave him, it's possible he'll think twice about going to the police. The threat is to scare me into good behaviour, but I don't believe he would actually do it. He doesn't want to damage his children any more than any parent would. If I don't weaken, who knows? He may back down and accept the situation for what it is. The end of a marriage. Then we can proceed in a civilized manner.

My eyelids grow heavy, and I pinch myself awake. If I don't leave soon I'll fall asleep. I dart a covert glance at Martin. His shoulders are rounded. The weekend's events have been physically as well as emotionally hard on him. He would like an early night, I expect, but he won't say it, won't give me the satisfaction of admitting he's exhausted. Even without the drugs, this shouldn't be difficult.

I'm past the point where I can drive; I'll have to take a cab to Sam's then get him to drive me back here in the morning. I can nip in and retrieve my car before Martin has time to do anything about it. I don't know where we'll go, but I'll keep driving until we reach somewhere Martin can't touch us. I am not going to Lowndes Place. I glance at the kitchen clock and push my chair back. It's getting late.

'Where are you going?' Martin demands, snapping his head up.

I feel light-headed as I walk to the door. 'To check on the children.'

'Well, don't conk out up there. I want to talk to you before you go to bed.'

'I thought we'd said all there is to say.'

'Not quite. If this is going to be a new start, I need to know everything.'

In the bedroom I use an app to order a cab, then put my phone on silent so that Martin won't be alerted by the text when it arrives. I won't wake the children until the very last moment. I carry my bag downstairs, leaving it tucked out of sight in the hall, take my boots and the children's trainers out of the cupboard and place them beside the bag.

When I join him, Martin has refilled our glasses. I take mine but remain standing.

'Expecting a message?' Martin asks, catching me glancing surreptitiously at my phone.

'I wanted to know the time.'

'It's nine o'clock. Drink your champagne.'

I set my glass down on the island. 'I don't want any more.'

'So now you find your limit? Just drink the damn stuff. You're less inhibited when you're pissed. I want to know what happened with Pete – who instigated it, who ended it, what was said afterwards.'

'Why torture yourself?'

'It's worse not knowing. Come and sit down.'

'I'd rather stand.'

He clicks his fingers at me and points to a chair. 'Get over here now.'

I shrug and do as he asks.

Martin holds out his hand. 'Give me your phone. I'd like to see your messages.'

I shake my head. Where is that cab?

'Eliza, if you don't give me your phone I'm going to book you into Lowndes Place for three months not six weeks.'

I consider my options, then I hand it over.

'Thank you. I think there's some cheese in the fridge. Can you wrap one in a slice of bread for me?'

I rush the job, desperate in case the driver messages, clumsily smearing butter onto the bread. My palms are sweating and I feel unsteady on my feet. I clatter the buttery knife into the sink and turn round. Martin is scrolling through my messages. My chest feels tight. I should go. I should leave the house and wait for the cab outside the gates.

'Found anything to interest you?' I ask, putting the plate in front of him.

'Only how few people you seem to speak to. I cancelled your cab, by the way.' He slides the phone across the table towards me.

I feel the blood drain from my face. 'I want to leave.'

'And I've already told you, that is not happening.

Nice try with the risotto. What did you put in it? A crushed-up sleeping pill?'

I raise my chin. 'Your medication. I only wanted to knock you out. But it doesn't matter, I'm leaving tonight whether you like it or not.'

I scrape the chair back and stagger to my feet.

'You are not going anywhere,' Martin says. 'Sit down, for God's sake. You're making a fool of yourself.'

'Stop telling me what to do!'

Martin shakes his head slowly. He pushes himself away from the table and I shrink back, thinking he's coming for me, but he goes to the door and blocks it.

'You really are a mess, aren't you, Eliza? You can't possibly go anywhere like that. Now be a good girl, settle down and we'll talk this over. You know that I've only ever wanted what's best for you. Things have gone downhill so fast, I'm honestly worried for your mental health, not to mention the children's. They need to know their mother is making an effort to get herself better.'

'You'll turn them against me.'

'Don't be silly. I know you love them. You need support, darling, and you won't get that by isolating yourself with two confused and unhappy children. They need us to be strong and together. Wait until morning, when you don't feel so rotten, and then make your decision. I promise we'll talk about it.'

'I'm not waiting another minute. I'm going now.'

He laughs. 'I'd like to see you try.'

I try to pull him but he's applied the brakes. He wasn't expecting me to get physical though, and it puts him at a disadvantage.

'Eliza!'

'I'm not listening to you.'

I clamber over him. He lets out a grunt of annoyance, and grasps my arm and one of my legs. I press my hand against his head, my fingers in his eyes, digging until he's forced to let go. I catch my clothes on his chair as I jump down, and tumble awkwardly, hands and knees connecting with concrete. I flounder to my feet, cradling my arm as Martin manoeuvres himself round. He is white with anger.

'You ungrateful bitch. I found you, I cleaned you up, I worked my arse off to make you happy. Christ, you're not even good for sex these days. But you don't know how to love, do you? It's all about looking out for number one. You're a borderline psychopath.'

I hold myself together with difficulty. My head is too sluggish to do verbal battle with my husband. I just want to kill him. 'I'm leaving you.'

'Are you sure about that, dear?'

There is a chink of light; my growing sense of self. The idea that I can determine my own outcome takes root. Face the music and be shot of this once and for all.

'Absolutely sure. Because I'm going to tell my story. And for what it's worth, when they're old enough, the children will understand. So you can just fuck off, Martin. You've lost.'

Martin holds out his phone, swipes his thumb across it and taps. I react swiftly and run for the front door. But I'm too late. The shutters come down, covering the handle before I can get to it. As I tear back across the hall I sense something move above me, a shadowy form in the darkness at the top of the stairs. It distracts me in that instant, and I slip on the polished concrete, my foot skidding out from under me. The floor comes up to meet me. The crack of my skull against the sharp edge of the stairs is the last thing I hear before the world goes dark.

36

The birds are singing, daylight sidling through the edges of the blinds. Aurora is kneeling on the bed, her face close to mine as I blink awake. Her sleepy breath is warm against my cheek. I feel like shit.

'Let Mummy sleep,' I mumble.

She gets under the duvet and curls up against my back, one small hand on my upper arm. I am dragged down as though I have a boulder tied to my legs, drowning in a fog of disorientation laced with nausea and pain.

I dream about being chased by my father, who then turns into Sam, then Dan, and wake up relieved neither of them are here. I peel my eyes open. It takes an extraordinary effort to bring the room into focus, and even then it's only seconds before I'm seeing double. My tongue is furred and dry.

I detach myself from Aurora. There's a sweat patch on my top where our bodies touched. I pluck the damp fabric away from my skin and attempt to stand, holding on to the bedhead. The room spins. I stumble across the room, into the bathroom, and throw up in the loo.

A dishevelled woman with dark circles under her eyes and the pallor of a ghoul looks at me from the mirror. There is a smear of blood across her right cheek and ear. I feel around my scalp and find a bump, the hair attached to it sticky and matted. I frown, puzzled. I'm wearing a vest top and pyjama shorts.

I splash my face with cold water and give my teeth a quick brush. My dressing gown is hanging on a hook on the back of the bathroom door. I slip it on, leave Aurora sleeping and check on Lucas. He is asleep too, the bedroom stuffy and smelling of child. I step out on the landing and close the door quietly. The spare bedroom door is closed. Martin must have slept there again. I can't face him yet.

Behind the stillness the atmosphere pulses strangely. I grip the banister and walk gingerly downstairs, planting my feet firmly and pausing to recalibrate on each step. My limbs feel like they're made of jellied lead. I must have taken a sleeping pill. How much did I drink last night? A bottle of champagne? More? Why?

My bag and boots, and the children's trainers, are at the bottom of the stairs. This confuses me until I remember what I was meaning to do. My shoulders sag. I let the children down. I shouldn't have put them to bed, I shouldn't have made supper. I should have chucked our bags in the car and driven away with them. It would have been that simple.

Glancing over the banister into the atrium, I can see a white towel discarded on the stairs. I go down and pick it up. It's damp. I raise my eyes to the glass wall. Martin is in the water, floating on his front. I stifle a scream and run down, punch in the code and push through the doors as they swing open, stripping off my dressing gown and jumping in.

Beneath Martin, his wheelchair lies abandoned upside down. I drag him to the shallow end and heave him onto his back, but I'm too late and he's dead. Sobbing with shock, I haul myself up the ladder, grab a towel from the stack, dry myself off and throw my dressing gown across my shoulders.

At the top of the stairs I find Lucas looking sleepy and bewildered. I force my damp arms through the dressing-gown sleeves and tie the sash.

'Why's there blood on your face, Mummy?'

I feel around my head, near the hairline, where it stings, then wipe my fingers on my dressing gown.

'I must have hit it.' I have a flash of memory: the shock of falling.

'Where's Dad?'

I take his hand and lead him into the playroom. We sit on the sofa and I face him, this child whose life is about to be torn apart.

'There's been an accident, darling. Dad needs to go to the hospital.'

'Did he fall out of his chair?'

'Yes, I'm afraid he did. I'm going to call an ambulance now. I need you to be brave and go up to my bedroom and stay with Aurora.'

'I want to be with you.'

He looks so miserable I can't bear it. He doesn't deserve this.

I cup his face with my hands. 'You're such a big,

sensible boy. I'll come and find you as soon as the ambulance arrives.'

'What is your emergency?'
   'I need an ambulance. And police.'
   'Can you tell me what's happened?'
   'My husband, he . . . My husband's had an accident.'
   'Is he breathing, madam?'
   'No. He's dead.'
   'What's your name?'
   'Eliza Curran. My husband is Martin Curran.'
   I can hear the staccato tap of her fingers flying across the keyboard as she records the information.
   'Can you check his vital signs for me, Eliza? He may not be dead.'
   'He is. I found him in the pool.'
   'This pool is in your home?'
   'Yes. He's a paraplegic, but he can swim. He can get himself in and out, no trouble. He must have fallen in.'
   'Is it just the two of you in the house?'
   'No. My children are here.'
   I blow my nose and wipe my eyes. Shaking convulsively, I put the children's shoes away and take my overnight bag upstairs. As the siren wails, I hastily throw the clothes into my drawers and return the washbag to the bathroom cabinet.

37

The emergency services arrive, followed swiftly by two young police officers, then fifteen minutes later an unmarked police car disgorges a detective inspector, whose name I immediately forget, and her colleague, DS Wade. Isabel gets home while I'm talking to the DI, and now finds herself confined, with me and the children, to the kitchen, while the house echoes with footsteps, voices and the crackle of police radios. I gauge from the detectives' presence and air of importance that they are not assuming Martin's death was an accident. They've moved swiftly to avoid potential evidence being destroyed, sealing spaces off.

I sit at the table, wearing damp clothes, trying to keep a clear head for the children's sake. I've begged to be allowed to get changed but have been told no, not yet. The state of my body is evidence; the scratches and bruises yet to be photographed and documented. The shaming thing is, I keep thinking about Dan, wishing he was here beside me, his physical presence comforting me. They are terrible, disloyal thoughts, considering what has happened to Martin. I tell myself that it's the shock talking; that later it will be different and it will be Martin who I think of first.

Isabel and I have barely spoken, using Lucas and Aurora as a kind of invisible shield between us. Her reaction when she heard the news was interesting. She looked down at her feet, then shook her head. Then she curled her hair behind her ears and informed the detective that she hadn't been here last night, and could be vouched for by a friend. I was here; there's no disputing that. I'm bruised and bloodied and my husband is dead. Of course they assume I'm involved. I am involved.

Lucas is shaken and pale and hasn't touched his Weetabix. Aurora is fascinated by all the activity, but has no idea what is going on.

'Mrs Curran?'

I look up. It's the DI.

'Perhaps your au pair could take the children while I ask you a few questions?'

I look beyond her to Isabel. Is she still our au pair?

'I can do that,' she says, scooping Aurora up and holding out her hand to Lucas. He looks up at her, then his gaze slides to me, his face reddening.

'I want to stay with Mum.' His voice is fierce, his stance aggressive. Lucas is growing up too fast, too soon.

'Darling,' I say. 'Please go with Isabel. It won't be for long.'

'Do you remember how you got that cut?' the detective asks, as the door closes. She taps the side of her head to indicate where it is on mine. The medics have already taken a look, applying butterfly strips to the wound.

I trail my fingers over my scalp and wince when I find the cut. 'No. It can't have been during the day, because I'd remember, so it must have been in the evening. I'm sorry, but the alcohol and the bang on my head . . . I just can't reach it.'

She gives me a long look. 'Mrs Curran, can you think of any reason why your husband might have taken his own life? Has he been depressed lately? Or had financial difficulties?'

'No. He's been happy. He had a new project on the go. And he's not the type to commit suicide. He has a large ego.' Had.

'That doesn't mean anything. You'd be surprised how many successful men take their own lives.'

She's being gentle with me, deliberately so, I think. I stare at my hands, then imagine a forensics officer inspecting them, getting his tweezers underneath my nails, and pinch them between my legs.

'I wasn't aware of that.'

'Well, it's true. Sometimes the drive for success is a way of fighting back depression. Money can be a sticking plaster, it can help, but sometimes they lose the battle.'

'I would have known,' I say stubbornly. 'Martin wasn't depressed.'

'Did he have any worries that you know of?'

'No.'

'You knew everything about his finances then?'

'Oh . . . well. Up to a point. He was self-employed, so of course there were ups and downs. He bought a property at auction recently, for a great deal of money, but he knew what he was doing. At any rate, there is no way that Martin would allow business pressures to get him down. He would just do something about it.'

'Did Martin have enemies? Anyone with a grudge against him?'

'I don't think so,' I say. I wouldn't call Pete an enemy. 'But Martin could rub people up the wrong way. He was a dynamic character and didn't always care about other people's sensitivities.'

'And what about yours?' she asks, her voice soft.

I raise my eyes to hers. 'Mine?'

She nods encouragingly.

'He could say things that were hurtful, but he loved me.'

'You were with him last night, and this morning you have a cut on your head. Did you have a fight?'

My lips are dry. I lick them. 'I don't know what happened.'

'Have you ever physically assaulted your husband?'

I see my hand connect with his face. 'No.'

'Did you push him into the swimming pool?'

I recoil. 'No! I couldn't do something like that.'

I see his face stark and white, his eyes staring, nostrils slightly flared, hair waving in the eddies that my movements created in the water. Am I the reason he was there?

She smiles. 'We have to look at all possibilities, Mrs Curran. I'm sure you understand that. What kind of day had you had?'

I close my eyes, think back. 'Not great. We were both feeling a bit rough. We had a party here on Saturday.'

260

'What kind of party?'

'A joint birthday celebration for Martin and me.' I realize I'd better tell her what happened before someone else does. 'There was an incident.' I take a deep breath. 'I had a row with our au pair, in front of everyone. It was embarrassing.' Another image assails me. Isabel leaning over the glass balustrade, her hair flowing down.

'Isabel Gardin?' She nods towards the door.

'Yes.' I drop my head into my hands, draw on whatever inner strength I have left and look up at her. 'She got drunk and started shouting from the terrace outside our bedroom; things about me. Personal things.' God, this is difficult. 'I ran up to stop her and we ... um ... we wrestled a bit, then two of the guests, my brother and a friend, pulled us apart. I was drunk. It was horrific. I feel very ashamed.'

'Do you think this had anything to do with what happened to Martin?'

Another deep breath. 'Possibly. Isabel told everyone I'd had an affair with his best friend.'

'And had you?'

'Yes. No. Well, it wasn't an affair exactly. It was years ago. We were both in a bad way after Martin's accident and we kind of reached for each other. It only happened once. I've regretted it ever since.'

Why did I say that? She doesn't care about my regrets.

'His name?'

'Pete. Pete Gordon. He's married to Martin's sister. She knows about it ... now, I mean. She didn't before.' I redden, but the detective doesn't bat an eyelid.

'Go on. What happened yesterday?'

I drag my mind back. 'The children had gone to bed late, so they were tired too. In the afternoon we went to the park, then we came home and I gave them their tea and put them to bed. I cooked supper. That's all I remember.'

'I'm surprised Martin didn't throw you out after your au pair's revelation.' Her voice, probing and firm, seems designed to ease me towards confession. Careful, I think.

'We had to have the conversation but were waiting until the children were in bed.'

'How was your relationship in general?'

'It was good on the whole. Martin was a very supportive husband. He always made me feel loved, and he was a great father. The children adore him. I'm not saying it was perfect, but it was a good marriage. We've been together for over ten years.'

'It seems a little odd then, that he has an app on his phone that tracks yours.'

Sweat prickles under my arms. 'Martin's had problems with paranoia since his accident. The app helped keep it under control.'

She frowns. 'By keeping you under control?' There's a hint of outrage on my behalf in her tone, as though she's aligning herself with me.

'It wasn't like that. It was his psychiatrist's suggestion and I agreed to it. The alternative was anti-psychotics, and he was never anywhere near bad enough for those.'

'What happened when he had one of his paranoid episodes?'

'He would accuse me of seeing other men, of planning to leave him. He wouldn't believe anything I said. He would go through my messages and emails. It was all completely irrational, but he couldn't control it when it got really bad. Being able to know where I was pretty much avoided that.'

'So, on the whole,' she says, 'your marriage wasn't that great.'

I agree with a small nod, unable to meet her eye. 'Sorry. I'm just so used to covering it up.'

'You don't have to be ashamed, Mrs Curran, it wasn't your fault. Did he ever hurt you?'

My mouth dries. I remember the sting of his hand on my cheek. The pain and humiliation. 'He would occasionally slap me if he felt I deserved it, but mostly it was verbal.'

'Do you mean he subjected you to psychological abuse?'

I grimace hearing it put so bluntly. 'Sometimes.'

She makes a note. Underlines it twice. I realize I've just handed her something valuable. Motive.

'I'm sorry to hear it,' she says. 'What would trigger that behaviour?'

'All sorts of things.'

'Things you did?'

'Well, yes, the focus was on me.'

'What about your children? Did Martin ever physically chastise them?'

'No. Certainly not.'

'Were you worried when he didn't come to bed last night?'

'I didn't know anything about it. I'd taken a sleeping pill.'

'You remember doing that?'

'No, but I always feel groggy the next day if I have, like I do now.'

'Do you take them regularly?'

'A couple of times a week. I'm a light sleeper and Martin snores. Snored.'

She appraises me. 'What do you think happened to your husband?'

I'm trembling with cold and shock. I'd almost say anything to be allowed a hot shower. 'I don't know. It's all a blank after supper.'

'Is there anything you do remember?'

'Cooking risotto.'

'That's good. I love risotto. It's soothing to make, isn't it? All that stirring and adding liquid. How much did you have to drink last night?'

I rub the bony nub of skull behind my ear. 'A glass of champagne.'

'I think it's probably more,' she says, in the tone of a teacher suggesting her pupil isn't being entirely honest about the amount of help he's had with his homework. 'You smell of alcohol.'

Now that she's pointed it out, I can smell it myself. 'Yes. Sorry, maybe three or four glasses.'

She lifts her head and smiles at me. 'Why did you lie?'

'Because I'm an alcoholic. If I lapse, I lie. It's just how it is.'

I detect genuine sympathy in the nod of understanding she gives me.

'I think that's all for now. You've been very helpful.'

'Can I ring Martin's family?' I start to stand up.

'Of course. Sorry to have kept you so long.' She closes her notebook and slides it into her leather case. 'Forensics will be dusting for prints, so we'll need a list of people who come to the house regularly, and your guests from Saturday evening. We'll be contacting friends and business associates of your husband's over the next twenty-four hours, so anything you can do to facilitate that would be appreciated.'

I rub my temples. My head is cracking open and the nausea isn't abating. 'I have a copy of the guest list. That has contact details on it. I can give you the number of the caterer as well.'

The detective's name pops into my head then. DI Westcott. Detective Inspector Westcott.

Kate arrives to take the children. My mother-in-law isn't wearing her customary make-up and her eyes are shadowed, her lips pale and pressed tightly together. She hugs me, but when I try to talk to her through my tears, to say I'm sorry, she shakes her head. What she doesn't understand, and I will never tell her, is that my tears are for her, not her son.

It's a painful handover. Lucas clings to me and has to be prised away by a policewoman. Aurora has a full-on tantrum, throwing herself to the floor and kicking anyone who comes close. I pick her up and tell her I'll see her very soon, and hand a snotty, wailing and flailing mess to the officer who follows Kate out of the house. I'm shepherded back into the kitchen by DI Westcott, and the last thing I hear before the door is closed and their cries are muted is Lucas yelling, 'Get off me! Let me go!'

'We'll get you to the station now, to have your DNA taken,' DI Westcott says. 'It won't take long; then you can go. Pack a bag with enough to last you and the children for at least three nights. Do you have anywhere you can stay?'

I lift my head, catching her eye, unsure what she means.

'Somewhere to stay over the next few days,' she says patiently. 'You'll be allowed back into the house as soon as the forensics team has finished with it. We might be able to find a space in a women's hostel, if there's a problem.'

'It's all right,' I say hastily. 'I have somewhere.'

Martin took possession of Gideon Grove on Friday. The house clearance firm are booked in for Thursday morning, but I can cancel them, use the furniture. It's better than nothing.

'That's fine. Get your things. One of my officers will drive you.'

'I can drive myself.'

'That won't be possible, I'm afraid. We're impounding both your cars. And we'll need any mobile phones, tablets and computers, with passcodes, if you have them.'

38

Gideon Grove is filthy. I'll need cleaning things and bed-linen as well as clothes and food. Watched by a police constable, I fill a holdall with sheets, towels and pillow-cases, and stuff duvets and pillows into black bin liners, all the while with a feeling of panic that makes my teeth chatter and hands shake. I pack the kids' favourite books and soft toys. I remember there being a television, but I imagine it'll be pretty basic. I hope we can get CBeebies at least. At the thought that we might not be able to, I sit down hard on the bed and burst into tears. The constable remains impassive, so I pull myself together and close the bags, then tell him I'm ready.

The gates are wide open and several people have gathered on the other side of Foxgrove Avenue, drawn by the spectacle of police officers outside Winterfell. Someone mouths, *Is everything OK?* I know her, but I don't acknowledge her. The answer is obvious.

As we pull away from the kerb, I look back at the house. The forecourt is a hive of activity, forensics officers in white coveralls going in and out, police standing around,

DI Westcott signalling someone to join her. Life is never going to be the same again. I stare straight ahead as I'm driven to the police station. I don't want to talk or make decisions, I want to be given simple instructions. Do this. Go here. Do that. What have I done to my family? I wished Martin dead, and now I wish I could take it back. I didn't mean it. I wanted to be free, but not like this.

Later, once my mouth has been swabbed for cell samples and my fingerprints taken, I'm driven to Kate's to pick up Aurora and Lucas, and then on to Gideon Grove. We arrive and spill out of the car, exhausted and shell-shocked.

I unlock the front door and we're greeted by a warm front of stale, musty air. I step over a dispiriting pile of junk mail and go into the tiny kitchen, take in the peeling linoleum and the dead flies on the windowsill, and feel numb.

'Is this where we have to stay?' Lucas asks. He looks round, curious and wary, at the scattering of someone else's belongings, at the dreary furnishings and grubby walls.

'It'll be an adventure.' I try to sound like I mean it. There is no getting away from the peculiarly pungent smell of neglect.

I test one of the taps and almost collapse with relief when water streams out. The police officer who drove us here flicks the lights on and off. We have electricity. He seems bemused as he troops back out to the car to fetch more of my hastily packed belongings. I imagine he can't understand why I'm here when, from the look of Winterfell, I can afford more luxurious temporary accommodation. Hooper's would have pulled out all the stops and found me somewhere for a week, but I didn't want to alert them to my situation. Even if I approached a different agency, word would spread, if it hasn't already. Hasleford is a small town.

I pick up the telephone receiver and lift it to my ear. It's been disconnected.

'Anything else you need?' The officer stands in the doorway, a black sack in each hand.

I drop my arms in a gesture of resignation. 'I have no car and no phone, and I have two small children. What do you think?'

He acknowledges this truth with a grimace of sympathy. 'We'll get your car back to you as soon as we can. In the meantime . . .'

He doesn't know what else to say. In the meantime two confused, unhappy children and I will try to make the best of things. Martin is dead. If I say it often enough, I'll get used to it. I look at the ink stains on my fingertips and a wave of misery crashes over me, squeezing the breath from my lungs. I don't see a clean end to this, no line drawn under it, no moving on, at least not for me.

'Where's Daddy gone?' Aurora asks, when we go down to the pontoon to feed crumbs to the ducks.

'Sweetie, we talked about this earlier, do you remember? Daddy is in heaven.'

Poor little Aurora. The concept is vast, well beyond what she can process.

'When will he be coming back?'

Lucas starts to cry and I hug them both fiercely.

* * *

269

DI Westcott arrives at the bungalow two days later, while I'm making the children's supper. I hadn't expected to see her again so soon; I thought we had covered everything. A female constable is with her.

I slide chicken nuggets onto two plates, add green beans and mashed potatoes, and put them down in front of the children. I feel drained of energy, hammered into the ground with anxiety about the immediate future and fear of the long term.

'What is it?' I ask.

DI Westcott turns with a nod towards the constable who joins Lucas and Aurora at the table and starts to ask them questions. What have they been doing today? Any good games? Do they like the river? She has a friendly, unthreatening way about her. Aurora ignores her, focused entirely on her food. Lucas turns his bewildered stare from the constable to me.

'Mummy—'

'Hang on, Lucas.'

I send DI Westcott a questioning glance, and she ushers me out into the narrow hall, where the front door is open.

'This is not a good time,' I say. 'If you have any more questions, I can answer them tomorrow.'

'Mrs Curran, I'm afraid I'm going to need you to come to the station with me, for an informal chat.'

'Why? I've told you everything.'

'There's nothing to worry about. It's really just to get your side of the story straightened out. There are a few inconsistencies in your statement.'

I try to think what they might be. I may have left out

one or two small things, but everything I've told them has been true.

'What about the children? Who's going to look after them?'

'That's all taken care of.'

I stiffen. 'I don't want them left with some anonymous social worker. They've been through enough.'

Outside another car turns into the drive and pulls up, and I watch in disbelief as Isabel gets out and gives me a little wave.

'No! Come on, you have to be kidding. I'm not handing over my children to her. Please, you have to stop this. My mother-in-law can take them.'

'Kate Curran is with her daughter,' DI Westcott says. 'She asked for Miss Gardin to take over in her absence. Surely she's preferable to a stranger.'

'So they all know you're arresting me.'

'You're not under arrest, you are helping us with our enquiries. And I'm sorry, but there was no suitable social worker available before tomorrow morning, or we wouldn't have had to resort to this. But at least they're comfortable with Miss Gardin.'

'They will be fine, Eliza,' Isabel says as DI Westcott leads me to her car. 'I can look after them.'

'You can't.' I cast around for an unassailable reason. 'You've nowhere to stay.'

'Of course I have.' She laughs, as if I must be mad to doubt it. 'I am at 42 Linden Road. You know how to find that, don't you?'

39

Before we leave, I call Sonia Metzger from the bathroom for advice. She tells me that there's no such thing as an informal chat, that if the police want to talk to me, it's because they feel they have good cause to suspect me of involvement in Martin's death. 'If DI Westcott is saying that you have nothing to worry about,' Sonia says bluntly, 'she's being disingenuous. I'll meet you at the police station in an hour. Don't say anything until I get there.'

She is all formality and professionalism now, giving no indication, beyond a reassuring smile when DI Westcott is distracted, that we know each other socially. Though of course they will know that; she was on our guest list. Sonia is wearing black trousers and a cream silk shirt with a silver pendant at her throat. Her thick dark hair is drawn back in a low bunch with a tortoiseshell barrette.

DS Wade produces two coffees in white plastic cups and places them on the table in front of us. I drink some of mine, out of politeness. Sonia ignores hers. It's stuffy, and the detective sergeant has taken off his grey jacket and slung it over the back of his chair. His sleeves are rolled up. DI Westcott, by contrast, looks crisp and cool in her tailored powder-blue shirt.

DI Westcott presses record and confirms the time and date, the names and statuses of those present, and lets me know that I'm here voluntarily, which is debatable, to be questioned under caution.

'How are you feeling?' she asks. 'I appreciate this must be a difficult time for you and your family.'

She makes the enquiry sound as though she means it, but there's a studiedness about the way she speaks, the cadence of her words, that makes me instinctively distrust them. Just like she distrusts mine. If she believes I could coolly tip Martin out of his wheelchair and into the pool, and keep him there, then why wouldn't she?

'It's been pretty bad,' I say.

I am so aware of tone, of how my mouth shapes each word, that forming them almost makes me squirm.

'I can imagine. That's why we need to sort this out as quickly as possible. Shall we get on?'

'Yes, let's,' Sonia answers dryly. 'My client is extremely worried about leaving her children with her ex-au pair.' She lays a heavy emphasis on the 'ex'.

'We know that you attempted to drug your husband, Eliza. The drugs were in his system; your prints are all over the packaging. We also know, from the toxicology report, that he didn't take enough to render him unconscious, although the dosage was considerably higher than it should have been, so the intention to harm was clearly there.'

'Martin could have asked Eliza to fetch the pills for

273

him,' Sonia points out. 'I really don't think that's a particularly helpful piece of information.'

'The bowls are being tested, so we should soon know one way or another.'

In the harsh light I notice a hairline scar at the corner of DI Westcott's lip. She sees me staring and I look down.

'Something wrong?' she asks.

I shake my head, embarrassed.

'I only wanted to sedate him so that I could get out of the house with the kids.'

'Good. Thank you. Shall we start again? Take us through the Saturday; from the morning. As much as you can remember, however trivial. Do you think you can do that?'

Her hands are clasped on the table in front of her. I start to talk.

My mouth aches by the time I've finished. DI Westcott and DS Wade have listened without interrupting, DS Wade scribbling the occasional note on a lined pad with a scratchy biro, DI Westcott shifting from time to time, but otherwise perfectly still. Whenever she did move it was a relief, a pinprick in the tension, before it built up again.

'The next thing I remember is waking up in my bed.'

'In a vest top and pyjama shorts?'

'That's right.'

'So either you did regain consciousness at some time during that night, or someone else took you upstairs and

274

got you changed. I'm surprised you didn't surface. I mean, being pulled around like that? It's got to penetrate the fog, surely? I don't imagine it's easy undressing a dead weight.'

I don't blink. 'I didn't wake up.'

'Shall I tell you what I think happened? You hated Martin after years of control and abuse. You wanted to leave your husband, but you were so scared that he would talk you out of it, that you decided to give him an overdose. You became anxious when he wouldn't eat the risotto you had laced with phenobarbital and you changed your plan. You were going to leave if you had to climb over him to do it.'

That startles me. The detective narrows her eyes.

'Are you remembering something?'

'No. Sorry.'

'Somehow you manage to bang your head. When you come to, Martin threatens you, there's an angry altercation. You take him down to the pool, and you drown him.' Her eyes don't leave my face.

'No. I didn't. I swear it. I wanted to leave, but I wouldn't have killed him. Why would I?'

'I'd hazard a guess that it was because Martin was going to make sure you lost everything; your children, your house, your income. He had found out you were unfaithful; a man like Martin wasn't going to let you walk away with half his wealth.' She stops talking and waits. Silence fills the room. I turn to look at the mirror and wonder if there's anyone behind it, if I'm important enough to merit an audience. It's an unnerving idea – that there are hidden people watching you, assessing your body language, your expressions, your tone of voice, your pauses and stutterings.

'Make it easier on yourself, Eliza.'

I drag my gaze back to her face.

'There are mitigating circumstances. People under-stand psychological abuse these days. You might get a shorter sentence if you help us to help you.'

My face feels rigid. It's an effort to speak. 'You're basically saying that I killed a defenceless man. I'm hardly likely to get sympathy and understanding, am I?'

DI Westcott sighs and sits back, turning to glance at DS Wade, who shrugs.

'Detective,' Sonia says, 'my client didn't need to kill her husband. She wanted to drug him in order to get away without a scene because she was scared he'd talk her round. She's been emotionally manipulated by him for years, so it's understandable that she would be worried she wouldn't be mentally strong enough to withstand his arguments.'

'And yet, he died.'

'But you haven't established how he ended up in the swimming pool. And surely you can't rule out other suspects.'

'We can, actually. My officers have looked at the CCTV footage for that evening, and apart from Mr and Mrs Curran and the children arriving home from their outing, no one else enters or exits the house.'

I deflate, slumping back in my chair. 'Then it must have been an accident, because I'd know if I'd killed him.'

'But your memory isn't very reliable at the moment, is it? So I honestly don't see how you can be so sure of that.' She pauses, waiting for me to answer. I don't, so she moves on. 'Our other problem is that my officers have been talking to the guests at your party, and so far none of them have corroborated your version of what happened.'

'Then it's their word against mine,' I say.

DS Wade raises an eyebrow. 'So all your guests, or what remained of them, including Ms Metzger for that matter, colluded in a lie? What reason could they possibly have?'

'I don't know.'

'At any rate,' he says, 'someone filmed it.'

'Who?'

He checks his notes. 'Charlie Pearce.'

Charlie was one of the teenagers paid to look after the children on the bouncy castle. I don't know why I'm shocked. People film everything these days.

'There's a video of Isabel making her little speech. Then you appear and try to force her over the balcony until you're prevented from doing so by Dan Jones and Sam Morley.'

DI Westcott takes up the story. 'Dan disputes your version of the events that led up to the fight. Mr Morley says he didn't see you go into the house, but neither did he see you not go in – very diplomatic of your brother. He maintains he was too transfixed by Ms Gardin's performance to notice what anyone else was doing. You were still there, I understand, Ms Metzger. Did you see anything?'

I turn and look at Sonia. She smiles apologetically. 'I didn't see Eliza until she came out onto the balcony.'

'What did Eliza say in her original statement, Jason?'

DS Wade looks down at his notes and reads. *'I'd been standing in the shadows, avoiding people. I wanted everyone to go home. I'd had enough. Dan had kissed me about an hour and a half earlier, Isabel had been drinking heavily since she walked in on us. She went crazy. She's infatuated with him.'*

'And what about you?' DI Westcott smiles. 'Were you infatuated too? I must say, when I met Dan, I didn't immediately think, animal attraction. He's good-looking though, isn't he? In a non-threatening way. The type you could introduce to your gran.' She pauses. 'So, were you?'

'You don't have to answer that,' Sonia says.

'It wasn't infatuation.'

'Well, they tell it differently,' DI Westcott says. 'Dan Jones has accused you of being a fantasist, and stalking him. He said he came home one day and you'd let yourself into his flat. He said you were blind drunk and had passed out on his sofa.'

I'm so stunned by Dan's betrayal that I lose the power of speech and stare stupidly at her. How could he?

'Eliza?'

'I did do that,' I stammer. 'I needed somewhere to go and I had the keys. It wasn't a problem at the time. If he's saying it was, then that's just weird.'

DI Westcott raises her eyebrows at my tone. 'Why would he lie, do you think?'

'I have no idea.'

'It does seem strange,' she says. 'Why would he want two women to think he was in love with them? Was it about the sex, or what?'

'I haven't had sex with him.'

'That doesn't mean it wasn't about sex though, does it?'

I shrug.

'Can you answer that, Eliza?'

'My client cannot be expected to know what's going on in someone else's mind,' Sonia says.

DI Westcott nods. 'Isabel's story tallies with Dan's.'

'Well, they're obviously in league.' I rub the space between my eyes. I recognize the heaviness in my body, the exhaustion, as low blood sugar. It's hard to think clearly; it's harder not to snap. Moments come back to me, swimming in front of my eyes like floaters. Isabel watching Dan hungrily. Isabel turning on me. 'What did she tell you?'

'Nothing about catching you and Dan kissing. She said she had gone up to your room because you have a long mirror. You saw her through the window and it made you furious. You came up and accused her of trying on your clothes, using your make-up, flirting with your husband.'

I shake my head in disbelief. 'That's not true. I went up when she started yelling from the balcony.'

'I'm only telling you what she told me. According to Isabel, you upset her so much that she went outside and told everyone what she knew. That's when you threw yourself at her. She admits she was very drunk and that she said the things she did out of spite.'

'That might be true; the rest is rubbish. It was nothing to do with the mirror or my clothes. It was the kiss.'

I can see how this looks – my infidelity, my toxic relationship with Martin, the bitter feud with our best friends, my jealous au pair. I expect she's thinking we're a middle-class mess.

'I don't see how any of this is relevant,' Sonia says. 'A drunken squabble over a man would not logically lead to my client murdering her husband. It's merely salacious gossip.'

'Salacious, yes, but I certainly wouldn't call it irrelevant,' DI Westcott says. 'Mr Curran found out about his wife's affair with his best friend that night.'

She leaves that hanging, then screws up her face and turns to her colleague. 'I feel like there's something missing from Eliza's narrative, don't you, Jason?'

Jason leafs through his notes, takes his time. He picks up a sheet of paper, skims through it and hands it to the detective inspector.

'Ah, yes. Here we are. Apparently Mr Curran telephoned Lowndes Place hospital on the morning of the day he died. That's an addiction clinic, isn't it? One of my officers has been to see them. According to their records you were booked in for six weeks.'

'It was what Martin wanted.' I feel so ashamed.

'And you didn't mention this because . . .?'

'I don't know. I suppose I just forgot.'

'But this happened before the bump on your head, during a time which you agree you remember clearly. You can't have it both ways.'

I dip my head and release a breath. When I look up they are both watching me closely. 'I didn't want to tell you.'

'Why not?'

'Because it was the final straw, the reason why I decided I couldn't put off leaving any longer.'

'Is there anything else you've neglected to mention?'

'No.'

'So let's see if I've got this right. You were worried we might perceive Martin's threat as a motive?' She nods to herself. 'It makes sense. A stay in an addiction clinic would be a blot on your copy book when it came to a custody battle.'

I press the tips of my fingers against my skull. 'I wasn't thinking that far ahead.'

'Really?' She fixes her brown eyes on me. 'All right. Going back to that Saturday night, according to Ms Gardin you didn't merely go upstairs to tick her off for being in your bedroom, you – I quote – shot upstairs like a lunatic and started laying into her. She ran onto the balcony to get away from you.' The detective smiles. It's a smile that attempts to imply she's on my side, woman to woman. 'And who can blame you for losing your rag? Your privacy had been invaded. You'd had too much to drink. Your au pair was in a relationship with the man you want. Your husband had found out you'd been unfaithful. All that in one evening – that's a shocker. You lose control and the next day, Martin gives you an ultimatum: go to the clinic or say goodbye to the children and the house. He's a clever man; he's not going to let you get your hands on his money. You don't have a proper job, you rely on him for all your material needs. You've reached the limit that you can endure, you pack a bag and drug his food. He quickly figures out what you've done. Maybe you run. Somehow you manage to fall and hit your head on the stairs. Next thing you know, you're waking up and he's there goading you. You snap and take him down to the pool where you push him in. According to Alison Gordon and Kate Curran, Martin was a strong swimmer despite his disability. He could remain buoyant for extended periods. In fact, he prided himself on it. He would have swum to the side and pulled himself out with relative ease. We have to consider why he didn't do that.'

'There's the damage to his fingers,' DS Wade says.

'Of course there is.' It's as if she hasn't thought about it, when she obviously has. Their choreography is perfect. 'Which would suggest that someone trod on them, possibly to stop him pulling himself onto the side of the pool.'

'I don't . . . I couldn't do something like that.'

'That is pure speculation, detective,' Sonia says with a show of impatience. 'You have no grounds for keeping my client here; you need to let her go.'

'Nearly there, Ms Metzger,' DI Westcott says amiably. 'Just a couple more points. Interestingly, we've spoken to Fortress. Apparently your security shutters were activated at 21:17 precisely. Do you remember that happening, Eliza?'

'No, I don't.'

282

'Martin was trying to stop you leaving the house, wasn't he?'

'He may have been, but as I've said. I don't remember.'

'Fortress say that it was recorded as an error, passcode given, everything above board. The shutters were raised at 21:23. Ring any bells?'

'No.'

'Do you think that could be because the shutters closing made you panic, maybe made you run and slip? That would account for the nasty wound on your head.'

I can feel my heart starting to pound, sweat prickling under my arms. Exhaustion is making it hard to judge the words I use, how I come across. The overhead lighting makes me queasy, and I sway, catching the edge of the table.

'That will do,' Sonia says sharply. 'It's late and my client is clearly exhausted. Mrs Curran needs to be with her children. I can personally guarantee she won't go anywhere.'

DI Westcott sighs, but she ends the interview and switches the recorder off. DS Wade opens the door for us and Sonia accompanies me outside. I'm given my phone back. It's dark and I'm shocked to see that it's almost eleven. My instinct is to go and get the children but when I picture myself at the door, ringing the bell, facing a bleary-eyed Isabel or Dan and having to talk my way in, I decide against it. Much as I hate the thought of leaving Aurora and Lucas with those two, they won't come to any harm. To pick them up now, when I'm close to breaking point, would be to risk traumatizing them even more. I'll fetch them first thing in the morning.

'Keep calm,' Sonia says as I get into my cab. 'It's going to be fine.'

'I'll talk to Dan and see if I can get to the bottom of this. I can't understand why he would lie.'

'Please do not speak to him, Eliza. I mean it. You'll only make things worse.'

40

Lucas and Aurora peer down at me from the sitting room at 42 Linden Road. I wave. Aurora grins and bangs the window with her palms. Lucas looks like he does when he perceives something to be unfair but can't do anything about it, his smile restrained. The door opens and Dan is in front of me, looking sleepy in pyjama bottoms and a sleeveless vest. His physical presence is a shock. Even after I'd absorbed what DI Westcott told me he had said, the enormity of the betrayal hasn't diminished.

'Oh God, Eliza,' Dan says. 'I am so sorry. What a terrible thing to happen. Are you all right?'

When Dad was confirmed dead I had felt numb, while my mother, who had returned from her shopping trip to find an ambulance and a police car outside our respectable pebble-dashed semi, did all the sobbing and wailing neither I nor Sam could manage. I feel the same way now.

'I'm fine.' I look at him bemusedly, taking in his furrowed brow, his sympathetic grimace, then squeeze past him through the door and walk up the narrow staircase into the flat. Lucas and Aurora don't wait until I reach the top of the stairs before they launch themselves at me. I half laugh, half cry as I deposit Aurora on the landing. I hope my children have been a pain in the arse. I cannot think why Isabel would have volunteered to have them, except to spite me.

'Can we go home now?' Lucas asks.

'Not to the dirty house,' Aurora says. 'I didn't like it there, did I, Lucas?'

'It's not so bad,' I say. 'And we'll be back home in a couple of days.'

'With Daddy?' Aurora says.

I catch Lucas's eye over her head.

Isabel comes out of the bedroom dressed in one of Dan's faded T-shirts, the one I first saw him in, and skimpy knickers. She looks rested. You wouldn't think she'd been drunkenly destroying my reputation from a balcony only four nights ago.

'How are you, Eliza?' she says with false sincerity.

She tries to embrace me, but I step back and she slinks her arm around Dan's waist instead. They make a beautiful couple; Dan with the unruly hair he can't help rumpling when he's trying to explain something, Isabel all tousled and sultry.

'Kids,' I say. 'Can you watch the television for five minutes while I talk to Dan and Isabel?'

I haven't forgotten what Sonia said, but I need to speak to them.

We go into the kitchen and I close the door.

'Why did you lie to the police?' I look at Dan. His

286

expression registers bewilderment, but I don't think it's real.

'I answered the detective's questions honestly,' he says. 'Why would I lie?'

'That's what I want to know. I'm confused.' I turn to Isabel. 'You denied walking in on us when we were kissing.'

She pouts. 'Because it did not happen.'

'Oh, please. You might have persuaded the detective to believe you, but you can cut the crap with me. We both know what happened at the party.'

'Do we? You are a fantasist, obsessed with my boyfriend. No one will believe anything you say. Everyone knows you and Martin had problems.'

'Thanks to you.'

I shift my eyes to Dan, pleading.

'Eliza,' he says. 'You were very drunk on Saturday. I didn't kiss you, and we were never alone together. In fact, I made a point of not being alone with you because I didn't want you to get the wrong idea. There is nothing between us. Isabel and I have been together for weeks now. You know that.'

My mouth drops open. 'You've been chasing me ever since we met. You've tried to kiss me before. In your flat, that time you lied about the damp to get me to come round.'

'But there is no damp. You made some spurious excuse about a leaking gutter, and jumped on me.'

'That's not true.'

He gives me a pitying look. 'Martin's death must have

been an appalling shock. And by the looks of it you had a nasty bang on the head. You're not remembering things right. I told you I wasn't interested, remember?'

I shake my head. This isn't right. He knows it. Isabel knows it. Why are they rewriting what happened?

'Do you think I'm a fool?' I burst out.

'Not a fool, just overwrought. Eliza, I'm in love with Isabel. I've never made a secret of it.'

'You were only with her because it gave you an excuse to come to Winterfell and see me, without Martin getting suspicious.'

Isabel bursts out laughing. '*T'es complètement folle*,' she says, tapping her head.

Dan admonishes her with a frown. 'Let me deal with this, babe.'

He pulls out a chair for me. I sit down. He follows suit. Isabel remains standing, leaning against the sink, backlit by the kitchen window.

'Eliza, you've had a tough time recently. I saw the way Martin treated you. I can understand how that might have made you fixate on me.'

'I have not fixated on you. If anything, it's the other way round.'

Dan rubs his jaw then passes his hand through his hair. 'We're going round in circles.'

Isabel steps forward and puts her hand on his shoulder, and he looks up at her and smiles. Is this love? Have I missed the obvious? But he did tell me that Isabel was a decoy, and he did kiss me. I am not imagining that. I can feel his lips, his hand sliding down my back.

I haven't felt this tired since Martin's accident. The

ache of it, the heaviness and nausea, all remind me of that terrible week. Even the birth of my babies didn't leave me feeling this pulverized. At least then I had euphoria to bolster me; now I just feel incredibly sad.

'What happened at the party was not a fantasy.' My voice trembles; it's all becoming painfully clear. 'Ever since the beginning, you've driven a wedge between me and my family. You've turned Ali against me and Martin against Pete.'

'Pete did that himself.'

'Maybe, but Isabel drove the final nail in.'

Isabel shrugs. 'Martin already knew. He was just angry I had told everyone. It embarrassed him.'

I blanch. 'What do you mean?'

'The morning after that supper party, when you were out, he made me look in your wardrobe to see if you were hiding anything there. Who do you think wrote Ali that note?'

'Martin wrote it?' I reel. I had been so certain it was Sam. It's the last thing I'd have expected of my husband. 'Why would he do that?'

'Don't you understand anything? When he found out what you did with Pete, that finished everything for him. He hated you. He wanted to wreck your friendship with his sister and he was going to make sure you never got the children. He told me to buy you the gin at Sainsbury's. He wanted you to drink and make a fool of yourself, and he wanted people to witness it.'

I feel myself pale as I search her face for signs that she's making it up. 'That's not . . . he wouldn't.'

'Of course he would,' Dan says, amused. 'Though of

course the poor guy didn't bank on Isabel broadcasting the family secrets to the entire neighbourhood. That's what tipped him over. The public humiliation. He never meant anyone to know. That was Isabel's mistake; he turned against her then.'

I snap back at him. 'She wouldn't have done it if she hadn't caught you kissing me.'

'Ah, *merde*,' Isabel says, flicking her hand. 'Not that again. You were such a bitch. I lost my temper. Martin was very angry with me.'

Dan's face softens. 'Eliza, look. We understand. Martin was a bastard. Whatever happened on Sunday night, it seems clear that something he did finally broke you. You might not have intended to kill him but that was the consequence. We only want to help you.'

'No.' I raise my hands. 'No, I'm not having it. I don't care what you say, I didn't hurt him.'

'You just don't want to admit the truth.' Dan sighs. 'There's no point pursuing this. The memories will come back, I expect. But in the meantime, stop trying to blame other people. It's unworthy of you.'

I stalk out of the room. I feel let down and alone. I never knew Dan at all. All this time I thought he was on my side, that he cared about me, maybe even loved me, I was a means to an end. He doesn't care that he's humiliated me, or that I'm in deep trouble because of him. Why? What have I ever done to him?

I put my head round the sitting room door. The kids are glued to a Japanese cartoon, Aurora curled up against her brother.

'Hey, you two, we're off. And as for you,' I say,

turning to Isabel, who's followed me out of the kitchen, 'I don't know what it is you're after, what you've told Dan, but you won't get it.'

We only have to wait five minutes for a cab. The driver gets two booster seats out of the boot; I strap the children in and squeeze awkwardly past Aurora's feet to sit between them.

'So how did you like staying with Isabel and Dan?' I ask.

''S'OK,' Lucas says.

'We had Coco Pops,' Aurora says. 'For supper!'

'Wow! What a treat. Was that pudding?'

'No, that was everything,' Lucas says sullenly. 'I'm starving.'

'Ah, well. It was short notice. I'll fix you something proper as soon as we're back.'

'Where did you go?'

'To talk to the police about Dad.' I risk a quick glance at him. His face is set.

'Look at my drawing, Mummy.' Aurora pulls a crumpled piece of paper out of her bag and hands it to me proudly. It's of a woman with blonde hair, in a white dress.

'This is lovely, darling. Who's the lady? Is she a princess?'

'It's Isabel in her marrying dress. She's marrying Dan.'

I glance at Lucas. He's shaking his head, exasperated by his little sister.

'She told me,' Aurora insists.

'Told you,' Lucas says. 'She told you.'

41

We're home. The weather has cooled. More leaves have fallen from the trees, and lie strewn across the lawn waiting for me to rake them up. The marquee company has dismantled the flooring and the marquee, but the fairy lights are still strung along the walls. I've switched them off but haven't had the energy to take them down. I find I like Winterfell less than ever. As soon as I walked through the door, after being at Gideon Grove for five days, I knew I'd put it on the market. It might not be possible for months, but it feels freeing to have made the decision.

There is an unexpected advantage to the bare concrete; the smudges of fingerprint powder are barely visible. I have to squint to find them as I go round the house with a damp cloth and a bottle of washing-up liquid. Everything is horrible, but the cars and iPads were returned yesterday and that has made me feel slightly more human.

I spend a morning on admin. There is a mountain of work to trudge through. I've registered Martin's death and paid for multiple copies of his death certificate, so now I need to work through my list of banks and utilities companies, insurers, mortgage brokers, Martin's various standing orders and the DVLA, download their forms and tick all those things off. One of our tenancies is up for renewal, so I agree a time for the inventory and book a deep clean. Fortunately, the flats are in my name and the rents go into the joint account, which I'm allowed to access. It will be a long time before probate is granted.

Ali and Kate come round after lunch. It was Kate who mediated, insisting, not unreasonably, that we put aside our differences for the children's sake. She will do literally anything not to lose out on a relationship with them, even give her daughter-in-law the benefit of the doubt, although I sometimes find her looking at me strangely, as though she's trying me out for size as a murderer. She's offered to babysit while I attend AA meetings and has been extraordinarily kind, considering how she must be feeling. Joy is curled up at Ali's feet. Every so often her hind legs twitch.

In spite of Kate's efforts, the atmosphere is thick with misery, suspicion and anger. Ali doesn't want to be here and it almost feels as though this is a goodbye. Kate is holding the relationship together by scraps and tendrils that are simply not strong enough.

'What are you going to do with the properties?' she asks. 'You've got that massive mortgage on Gideon Grove. How are you going to cope?'

'I'm not sure yet. Andrew Joliffe is looking into it for me.'

That was an unpleasant telephone call. Joliffe was

patronizing and high-handed. I'm sure he thinks that I am solely responsible for the death of his friend. I certainly don't anticipate any support coming from that direction and just wish I could sack him and have someone else deal with everything, but he is the executor of Martin's will, and there is nothing I can do about that. I keep those conversations short and to the point.

'There are stocks and shares,' I say. 'And the income from the flats covers their mortgages, with enough left over for our living costs if I'm careful. I'm going to sell this place and downsize. I'll use part of Martin's estate to develop Gideon Grove, and the rest I'll invest in a trust for the children's education.'

'Sell Winterfell?' Ali says, outraged. 'But this house was Martin's dream. How can you possibly sell it?'

'Ali, I don't need such an enormous house. Someone else will appreciate this place more than I ever have.'

I realize my slip too late. Her husband and her brother built it, and anything of Martin's is now sacrosanct as far as she is concerned. 'I mean, I like it,' I hasten to add. 'But it was always more Pete and Martin's vision than mine.'

'It'll be hard for the children to leave,' Kate says.

'I know, and of course I'll explain it to them. I'm not going to let his memory die.'

Ali bristles. 'Don't worry, I wouldn't let that happen.'

'I—'

'Will you leave Hasleford?' Kate interrupts swiftly before I can rise to the bait.

Jack gives a little start, his hands flying up starfish-style, his eyes opening. He reminds me of Aurora as a baby, and that in turn reminds me of Martin. I realize I'm already softening, allowing the bad to fade while the good parts of our marriage burn brighter.

'I'm not ready to think that far ahead.'

'No, of course not.' Kate says. 'You don't need to make any decisions yet.'

But I must, because the harsh truth is that everyone hates me after what happened. I slept with my husband's best friend, who also happens to be the husband of my best friend. And Martin, the reason I suspect people welcomed my company in the first place, is no longer around to act as a draw. I shouldn't care but I'm only human, and it hurts when they shut me out. If I go somewhere new, if I start again, I won't escape myself, but I will escape the women who turn their backs on me.

Ali picks up one of the supplements from yesterday's papers and flicks through it. 'About Gideon Grove,' she says, a little too nonchalantly. 'Had Martin already commissioned an architect?'

'He'd had preliminary conversations, but he didn't get as far as putting it out to tender. There wasn't time.' I pause and watch Lucas trying to teach Aurora to do a cartwheel on the lawn. I don't want Ali to know I can sense the anxiety she is trying to hide. 'As far as I'm concerned, if Pete can come in on the money, he's got the job.'

Ali looks away. She takes Jack out of his pram and lays him on his back on her knees. He gazes at her.

'Can I hold him?' I ask.

She only hesitates for a second before she passes him over. I slide my hand under hers to cup his head. I haven't touched my friend in a long time and the contact gives me a shock. I breathe Jack in and his little body melts into mine. He's both heavy and light, completely relaxed. I hold him until he starts to bump his head on my shoulder and mewl, then I pass him back to his mother.

When Kate tactfully wanders outside to join her grandchildren, Ali and I sink into an uneasy silence. Jack provides a distraction, but it's not enough. Ali takes a sip of her tea then puts the mug down.

'I want you to know that I forgive you for what happened with Pete.'

'Thank you.'

'But until we know how Martin died, I'm still going to think you had something to do with it. It doesn't matter how much of this we do.' She indicates the children pulling Kate by the hands towards the path that leads to their treehouse. 'My brother died in this house when you were here. You were taken in for questioning.'

'But not arrested, and they let me go. Ali, I do understand and I'm sorry that I don't remember. When they get the results of the post mortem—'

She flinches. 'I don't want to talk about that.'

'Neither do I, but it's important. If Martin had another seizure, that would suggest it could have been an accident. He was very angry after the party; that could have brought it on.'

'Whose fault is that?'

'Mine.'

Ali holds Jack up in front of her, bringing his eyes level with hers, so that she appears to be talking to him, not me.

296

'The police have spoken to me and Pete,' she says.

I don't know what response she's hoping for so I keep quiet.

'They wanted to know about your relationship with Martin.'

That's no surprise. 'What did you tell them?'

'Only what I saw; that my brother was besotted with you, but I didn't think it was completely reciprocated.'

I press my fingertips into the space between my eyebrows and close my eyes. 'So nothing about what I said to you?'

'No, because I only have your word for that and as far as I could see you were panicking, making excuses for what you'd done. I don't know if it's true. I don't know you very well, Eliza. Do I? Not when it comes down to it.'

'Perhaps you didn't know your brother that well either,' I retort.

The silence between us fills with static. I'm terrified she's going to leave, that I've lost her completely.

'So what about Dan?' she says eventually. 'Is it a thing? Are you together?'

'No. Absolutely not.'

'Then if you're not sleeping with each other, what are you?'

I chew the inside of my mouth. Ali is homing in on the questions I'd prefer to avoid. 'We're not anything.'

'Oh, come on.'

'It's true. There never was anything between us.' It feels momentous to say it out loud when I haven't been able to let go of it yet, despite his behaviour. I cannot have been living in a parallel universe for the last three months. I'm not nuts. 'He says he's in love with Isabel.'

'Yeah, right,' Ali replies as she disentangles Jack's fingers from her hair. 'What do you even know about him?'

'Not a lot,' I concede. I think of something and perk up a bit. 'It turns out he's a fraternal twin, like me.'

'Sweet. So that makes it destiny?' She shakes her head. 'What else?'

'He's had his problems. His sister, the twin, killed herself when they were in their early twenties. I don't think he's ever got over it.'

She looks dismayed, then sceptical. 'He could have been lying about that.'

'I don't think so.'

'Is he even a twin? He might have made it up after he found out that you're one, so that you'd feel connected.' She makes a face as she processes her thoughts. 'Then he told you she'd died so you'd feel sorry for him – it would give him a bit of depth, an excuse for meaningful conversations. You know what, Eliza, I don't think he was ever into either of you; it was all about getting close to my brother and his money. You should get that man out of Linden Road, and get shot of him. He is seriously bad news. Pete agrees. Talk to Andrew Joliffe if he refuses to go.'

I open my mouth to say I wouldn't involve Joliffe if my life depended on it, but we're interrupted by a thud as the front door closes. Joy leaps up and dashes out to the hall. She doesn't bark. I glance at Ali.

'Who's that?' she says.

I shake my head and stand up as Isabel enters the room.

42

Isabel says a breezy *'allo* and goes to the kettle, Joy scampering round her feet.

'That idiot dog has no loyalty,' Ali mutters, before calling her to heel. She catches my eye and for a moment we are conspirators again. Then she drops her gaze to Joy.

Isabel lifts the kettle to check it for water and switches it on. I get up from the table and switch it off.

'What are you doing here?' I ask.

'I live here.'

'No, you don't. Give me your key. I'd like you to leave.'

She laughs. 'I don't think so, Eliza. Dan's flat is very nice, but it is too small and he needs to work. It is better here, I think.' She steps round me. 'I am so pleased to see you, Ali. I am so sorry for your loss.'

'Thank you,' Ali says through her teeth.

'And this is the little one? Can I see? Oh, how cute. He is beautiful. He looks like you, I think. Eliza, doesn't he look like Ali?'

Ali lowers Jack into his pram, buckles him in and stands up. 'We'd better go.'

'You don't have to,' I say. 'Please stay.'

'No, I think we'll leave you to it.'

'I didn't kill Martin,' I whisper, desperate. 'Ali, please believe me.'

She ignores me and attaches Joy's lead, calls Briony and Leonie inside, ignoring their protests, and bundles them through the house. Kate follows without comment, though she does send me a quick smile of reassurance. *Early days*, it seems to say. *Give her time.* I feel a sadness so deep I can't express it, but there is a sense of things ending here and I've failed to say anything I want to say, failed to tell Ali how much she's meant to me over the years. I stand at the door while they walk down the sloping forecourt to the gates, which swing slowly open then close behind them.

Aurora and Lucas come to my side and I put my hands on their shoulders, and we stand on the threshold waiting for something that isn't going to happen, for our friends to run back in and tell us it will get better. I snap out of it and go back into the kitchen to deal with Isabel.

She grins at the kids. 'I am back to look after you. We will have fun.'

Lucas looks anxiously up at me.

'It's OK, darling. She's only joking. Isabel is here to pick up the rest of her things, then she's leaving. Aren't you, Isabel?' I stare straight into her eyes.

She stares back into mine.

'Take Aurora into the playroom, Lucas,' I say.

For once he doesn't argue. I close the kitchen door after them. Isabel pours boiling water over a teabag. The smell of mint wafts over to me.

'I don't know what you think you're doing, but there is no way you're staying here. You've lied to the police about me, you've caused immense damage with your ridiculous outburst. I don't want you or Dan coming near this house or my family again.'

'Relax, Eliza.' Isabel is smiling, but her eyes are steely. 'I like it here. I'm going to stay. And you're going to let me.'

'And why would I do that?'

'Because I know what you did to your husband. I saw it all.'

That makes me hesitate, all of a sudden unsure of my ground. 'What did you see?'

'I came home that night.'

I frown. 'Why? Did Dan kick you out?'

Isabel flushes. 'No, but he was working and it was a bit boring. I came back to do my packing. I wanted to make sure there was nothing lying around in the house, so I came through. I noticed the lights were on in the basement. I heard a shout. I came halfway down the stairs. Martin was in the pool and you would not let him out. You kept him there until he was too tired to help himself. Then you got into the pool and you finished it. After that you pushed his wheelchair in.'

I laugh, it's so far-fetched. 'You're making it up.'

'Not at all. I understand. He was a bad husband, nasty to you. I won't tell, but I will live here. And I think I would prefer your bedroom. You can sleep in the spare. You will strip and change the bed and remove your clothes from the wardrobe.'

She waits, an impertinent smile turning up the corners of her lips.

302

'I don't believe you,' I manage at last. I feel short of breath, my heart racing.

'That is up to you. I know what I saw. You had a bad fall. Maybe you do not remember. Or maybe you do.' Her eyes narrow as she studies my face. 'I do not care.'

'If you were there, then why didn't you step in? You could have stopped it. And why haven't you said any of this to the police?'

'I did not stop you because I thought you might hurt me too. You are crazy when you're drunk.' She shrugs. 'And the police? You are right, I could have told them; I still can. But I feel you have maybe suffered enough, no?' She considers me, a telling glint in her eyes. 'But I want something in return. Forget about the ten thousand pounds, that is not important now. When you sell this house, you will buy one for me. You have the flats and the development. You are a rich woman. There is plenty for you and the little ones.'

I become slightly hysterical. Isabel waits for me to stop laughing, blowing on her drink, watching me over the rim of her mug.

'It would look very strange if suddenly I am here and you are not,' she says. 'So we will make people think we are friends again and I am still your au pair. You will say it is because the children have had enough upset. They are used to me. They will understand that we were both drunk on Saturday. They will see you have made it up with Ali. They will accept the situation.'

When she puts her mug down on the side, I pick it up and pour the contents away. 'It's not happening, Isabel. Do you understand me? You are not moving in here.

You must be mad. I didn't kill Martin. I may not remember what happened, but I know I'm not a killer. I'll talk to the detective. It'll be your word against mine.'

She laughs lightly. 'Oh, really? Who do you think they will believe? Which one of us has a motive? I will say that I witnessed terrible things in this house. A horrible marriage. Now, I think I will have a bath, in your bathroom. You have some lovely candles. You will not mind if I light them.'

43

Despite the tension pressing behind my breastbone, I decide against taking a sleeping pill. With Isabel here, acting like she owns the place, I need to keep a clear head. I am tempted though, when by midnight I'm still wide awake, anxious thoughts on a loop. Why is she waging this campaign against me?

This can't possibly be all down to resentment, although there's no doubt Isabel feels that way towards me. It's something different and it involves Dan. I picture him on the doorstep that June morning, his open face and friendly smile. Had there been something else? Something speculative lurking behind his eyes? I'm beginning to wonder if he was the stranger he appeared to be. Did he and Isabel already know each other? Is that it? Did she tell him about the flat? Did she put him up to the unconventional approach that day? Or is he using her?

Too many questions. I punch my pillow into shape and roll over. It's raining and the persistent sound is dismal. If it wasn't chance, if Dan rang the doorbell knowing exactly who he was going to find behind it, what is our connection? And why would he want to dismantle my life so entirely? We have nothing in common except that we are both fraternal twins.

I close my eyes and doze, only to be woken by a sound. I roll out of bed and open the door a crack. Isabel is leading Dan by his collar. His hair is wet from the rain. He pushes her up against the wall and they kiss long and hard. Isabel breaks the kiss, admonishing him with a finger to his lips before she pulls him into the bedroom and closes the door.

Bastards. I am so angry I'm tempted to burst in and throw a bucket of cold water over them. I pace the room, stopping to peek through the slatted blinds. The rain hits the roofs of our cars and scatters. I chew on a thought before closing the blinds with a snap and crawl back into bed.

My brain will not switch off, and suddenly I'm sitting up, eyes wide open, my body tingling. I jump up and go downstairs to the cabinet in the kitchen, pull out one of the old photo albums and flick slowly through the pictures, trying not to look too closely at Martin and me, head over heels in love, wishing I could warn our younger selves to stay away from each other.

The photo I'm after is the one my mind snagged on when we had the album out a few weeks earlier – the photo I thought might have been taken by the girl he was with before me; Martin in the whitewashed hostel bedroom. But it's not his figure I study closely when I find it, it's the blanket draped over the bed behind him. There was a reason I recognized it. It looks exactly like the one I'd admired in Dan's spare bedroom that lost afternoon.

What if they're the same blanket, not merely the same design? Could our paths have crossed? I was drunk most of that summer, and not just on feni cocktails and beer, on love as well. I wouldn't have noticed other men circling.

I remove the photo from its protective sleeve, go back upstairs and pull on yesterday's clothes. Ignoring the muffled sounds coming from the master bedroom, I walk silently down to the hall, pull on my boots and Martin's black hooded rain jacket, and let myself out into the night. Isabel and Dan won't hear the car door close or its engine start or the gates open, not from the back of the house, not with rain falling, not being so occupied with each other's bodies.

I never got that far with Dan, and now I wonder why not, why he didn't try harder. Ali's words come back to me: *I don't think he was ever into either of you.* She wasn't just trying to hurt me, she was stating a bald fact. I need to know why he pursued me.

I sit on the bed in the tiny spare room at 42 Linden Road with the photo of Martin balanced on my knee, comparing the two blankets; bird for bird, leaf for leaf, petal for petal. They are identical. There's satisfaction in knowing that I'm not going mad. Dan must have been in Goa that summer, and our paths must have crossed. It's true the markets were full of cheap and colourful blankets and any traveller would have been tempted to bring one home as a souvenir, but something tells me this is Martin's blanket. But why would Dan have it? What am I missing? Had Martin and Dan met before I arrived in Goa? But if so, why hadn't either of them said anything?

I look between the blanket in one hand and the photo in the other. I know I didn't take it and I can see that Martin's smile is suggestive; a come-on. I think my guess was right; this must have been taken by his ex-girlfriend.

I swear under my breath as everything falls into place. The blanket wasn't Martin's – it was hers. And if Dan now has it, that can mean only one thing. The girl who Martin dumped after meeting me, the girl who subsequently killed herself, brought it back to the family home. She was Dan's twin. I drop the photo onto the bed and get up.

Dan's laptop is sitting on the desk. I switch it on. It wakes up, but then requests a password. I didn't expect it to let me in, but it doesn't matter because his screensaver gives me the proof I'm looking for. It's a snap of a boy and a girl, about ten years of age. The girl is holding a hose pipe, squirting water at an unseen victim. The boy egging her on is Dan. I recognize his tufty hair and big smile. They're laughing with glee. The sun catches the arc of water from the hose. The bough of an apple tree sections a corner of the picture. I couldn't say with certainty that it's her, because she's so much younger here than she was when she and I briefly crossed paths in India, but she could well be the girl Martin dumped for me. It makes sense. If it is her, then Dan had a motive. Revenge. I switch off the computer, close the lid and smooth the blanket. Now I know, I feel less vulnerable.

* * *

308

There is no evidence of Dan at Winterfell the next morning, and Isabel doesn't mention him. I don't ask. She behaves as though there's nothing wrong, and I bide my time hoping she'll go out. She doesn't. She seems perfectly happy with her feet up on the sofa in the kitchen while I tend to the children. I clear up after breakfast, and she doesn't so much as lift a finger to help.

The children follow me everywhere. Any other time it would have been irritating, but I don't mind them dogging my footsteps if it makes them feel even a degree more secure. This must be so confusing to them. We go upstairs to clean our teeth. We make our beds. Lucas shakes his head at his sister's efforts. I leave them sorting it out, and go to my bedroom, only to find the pair of them right behind me.

The bed hasn't been made; the sheet is rumpled, the duvet flopped over the side like a snow drift. Isabel's underwear is on the floor. In the dressing room, one of my wardrobe doors is standing open. This is so contrary to what they're accustomed to, with their father's strict rules about order, that Lucas bursts into tears and Aurora is so shocked she hides her face in my legs. I take them back to their own room.

'Wait for me here,' I say. 'Don't move.'

Back in my room I survey the chaos and a deep anger settles in my belly. My bathroom, from which she's already evicted any of my toiletries she doesn't want to make use of, is a mess. Her electric toothbrush is gunky, there's a wet flannel on the bottom of the bath and her towel has slipped off the heater. I bundle up her things, march out of the room and fling them over the banister. Clothes, make-up, shoes. The shoes make a lot of noise. A silk shirt floats down, arms spread, and melts onto the floor as silently as a snowflake.

Isabel comes out into the hall and watches me. Then she turns on her heel and closes the kitchen door behind her. My anger spent, I reassure the children. It isn't easy. Aurora has almost as many questions as Lucas.

The low rumble of the gates opening on their tracks has me running to the window. Beyond them Dan is hauling luggage out of the boot of a cab; a large holdall and a suitcase. I run downstairs, followed by the kids and open the front door.

Dan hitches the holdall onto his shoulder and trundles the suitcase up the incline. He passes me with a nod of greeting.

'Phew,' he says, dropping the holdall onto the floor. He takes in the scene, his eyes widening. 'Wow. What's going on here?'

Isabel comes out of the kitchen and kisses his cheek. 'Eliza had a tantrum.'

'OK.' He smirks at me. 'Cool. Hey, kids.'

Lucas looks to me for an explanation, but all I can do is shake my head. He scowls. Aurora peeks at Dan from behind my legs. She doesn't know whether he's friend or foe.

Dan slips an arm around Isabel's waist and kisses her. 'I could murder a coffee,' he says. 'Got any on the go?'

'Make your own,' I say.

He raises his eyebrows but doesn't comment. We all troop into the kitchen. Dan switches the kettle on and sits down while Isabel charms the children over to the sofa with a book. I pull out a chair and fasten my eyes on his face. He looks away, disconcerted. Good.

'It seems a waste of money, paying rent on Linden Road,' he says, 'when there's plenty of space for us all here.'

'There's space for you in Buckingham Palace,' I retort. 'But you wouldn't move in there.'

'You're funny.'

'I don't feel funny.'

He runs a hand through his hair. 'Nonetheless, this is where we are.'

The kettle clicks but he doesn't get up.

'Is it? You still have to pay rent, you know, or you'll be in breach of contract.'

'Ah, you can sort that out. After all, you're the boss now. Call Hooper's, they'll find a new tenant in five minutes. Someone will bite their hand off for that place. You won't lose any money.'

'Dan,' I snap. 'What planet are you living on? You're not staying here.'

'Oh, well, there you'd be wrong. Isabel and I would like to move in together, and where better? You need our help.'

'Don't kid yourself.'

'Don't be ungrateful. We'll get along fine if you behave, which means no running to your friends to complain.'

What friends? I think. 'What exactly do you want from me?'

He leans back and clasps his hands behind his head. 'A little appreciation.'

How could I ever have found this man attractive? I could wipe that smug smile off his face by telling him that I've guessed his link to Martin, but I hold my tongue. I'm so close now, I don't want to show my hand or push Dan too hard, not until I'm sure of my facts.

'I hear congratulations are in order,' I say.

That gets his attention.

'What are you talking about?'

'Aurora drew a sweet picture of Isabel in her wedding dress. Isn't that right, Isabel? She said you told her you were getting married.'

Isabel puts the book down and gets up, flushing. 'I did not say that.'

'I bloody well hope not,' Dan says.

She drapes her arms around his neck and kisses the top of his head. 'You don't want to marry me, *chéri*?'

He unclasps her hands and stands up. 'Not right this moment, no.'

I watch Isabel's face. I feel the prickle of internalized anger radiating from her. She walks out and starts taking her belongings back upstairs.

Later, when I'm with the children in their bedroom, the doorbell rings. We go still, our heads poised like meerkats. Lucas tries to get up but I catch his arm, then go to the window. The gates slide open, and DI Westcott and DS Wade step through them.

'Wait here.'

I leave the room and look down into the hall. Isabel opens the front door. I walk downstairs wondering what fresh horror they're going to throw at me.

'Sorry to disturb you,' DI Westcott says, looking from me to Isabel with sharp interest. 'But we need to ask you a few more questions.'

'No problem,' I say. 'Isabel, could you make sure the children don't come into the drawing room?'

'Of course, Mrs Curran,' she replies, playing her part to perfection.

We sit down, sinking into the sofas. DI Westcott looks around.

'Lovely room. Cosy.'

'Yes, well, I insisted on one comfortable room in this house,' I say. 'How can I help?'

DI Westcott stands up and goes to the window. 'Impressive. It's like a park out there. You could fit three of my garden onto your terrace.'

I shrug, and she comes back and sits down again.

'Can we talk about the part you played in the death of your father?'

44

I don't know why I'm caught on the back foot like this. After all, my father is at the heart of what makes me. It's only understandable that his looming presence should have some bearing on what happens in my life even eighteen years after his death. I wonder what line of enquiry led them to him though. The only person other than Sam I've ever discussed Dad with was Martin. It was DI Westcott's choice of words that threw me.

The part I played?

'I don't understand,' I say, gathering myself. 'My father died of a heart attack a long time ago.'

DS Wade leans forward, his clasped hands between his knees. 'Humour me a moment. Tell me about the day he died.'

I clear my throat, trying to remain calm.

I tell the story I told the paramedics and the police at the time. Mum was at work. I was upstairs, headphones on, listening to the Foo Fighters, doing my homework. Sam was out, loitering in the streets with some friends. I felt a thump resonate through the house, thought it was the front door slamming shut and ignored it. When

I came downstairs, Dad was unconscious. I rang 999 then attempted to resuscitate him, but I couldn't bring him back.

'That's all?'

'That's all. Sorry, what does this have to do with Martin?'

DI Westcott unfolds her slim form and goes over to the side table. She picks up the framed photograph of Martin and me on our wedding day and examines it before putting it down and edging it back into place with the tip of her finger. 'The reason we bring this up is that we've found an email from your husband to his lawyer, asking whether something you told him in confidence could be used as leverage if you ever attempted to remove the children from his care.'

Some sounds penetrate. DS Wade coughs. Lucas yells from somewhere in the house. Raindrops patter outside the window.

'I explained that he was paranoid,' I say, when I'm capable of stringing a sentence together. 'It's all rubbish.'

'Would you like to read it?'

I nod. DI Westcott opens her black leather bag and pulls out a tablet. She opens a file, enlarges it and passes it to DS Wade, who hands it to me. The email is dated two years ago.

Dear Andrew,
This is confidential and must go no further. I would like to know where I would stand, regarding custody of my children, should my wife carry out her threat to

leave me. I'm all too aware that eyebrows would be raised if I were to be granted custody over Eliza, but there are certain things that could sway the balance.

One is that Eliza is an alcoholic. She is on top of it and hasn't had a drink for some years now, but there are no guarantees she will stay that way.

The other thing – and please understand that I have no evidence for this, it was merely a conversation between me and my wife before we were married. A baring of our souls, you could say – is that Eliza told me that she and her brother Sam had suffered years of maltreatment at the hands of their father. They were bullied and there was physical violence, mostly focused on Eliza. There was no sexual element thankfully, but the psychological abuse has left both siblings damaged. Richard Morley died some years before I met Eliza, so I never knew him. All I have is her word.

The crux of the matter is that when Eliza and Sam were fifteen years old, Morley suffered a heart attack. Eliza told me that she sent Sam out of the room, which I certainly believe, and watched her father die. She called the ambulance only when she was certain he was dead. She made no attempt to resuscitate him.

As I say, there's no proof of this happening. Would we be able to use it in extremis?

Yours sincerely,
Martin Curran

I hand the tablet back. 'It isn't true.'

Sam and I created our version of that day's events so long ago that it's more believable to us than the truth.

But, as Martin has so helpfully pointed out, there's no proof, so I'll keep denying it. Our lives were intolerable. I would not go back and change anything about my behaviour that day.

I pushed my brother out of the room and then I closed the door. It took so long. Only when I had checked Dad's pulse, two fingers to his neck, two to his wrist, and was sure he was gone, did I phone the emergency services.

Sam was sitting on the stairs, waiting for me to come out, his face ashen. I made him leave the house. One of us not questioning the thud of my father hitting the floor was understandable, two would raise questions.

I think Mum suspected, but she kept her counsel. She hadn't been able to protect us from Dad while he was alive, so I'm charitable enough to think she was protecting us once he was dead. If so, it would have been to salve her conscience more than as an act of love. If she had really loved us, she would have taken us away from him years before.

I remember the way Dad's eyes had seemed to bore into my soul even after the spark of life had gone, and that makes my stomach clench. When I turned his body over, Martin's flat, dull eyes had stared in the same way.

How could he have written that email? I'll never forgive him. No wonder Joliffe looks at me like he knows me.

'Why didn't you tell us about the abuse by your father?' Westcott asks.

'Because it wasn't relevant.'

'I think it is. Your husband is saying you're capable of watching a man die and not calling for help. I think the reason you kept quiet about your childhood was because you were worried it would draw our attention to the correlation between your father's death and Martin's. You could have saved him and yet you did nothing. Because that's what happened with Martin, isn't it?'

'No!'

'Are you certain about that? You don't remember what happened after you hit your head, so how precisely do you know? The row with Martin could have brought it all back. You saw a way out, just like you did with your father, thus ending years of abuse.'

'No, that's all wrong. I didn't kill Martin and I tried my best to save my dad.'

'Why, when it meant the abuse would carry on?'

'I thought Dad might be grateful,' I say in a rush. 'I spent my life fantasizing about how I could change the way he felt about me. I'd imagined saving him from drowning in the sea, or from a house fire. All I wanted was for him to love me.'

DI Westcott steeples her hands and presses them against her chin. She glances at DS Wade and he gives an almost imperceptible shrug.

'Why would your husband have said it, if it wasn't true?'

I press my fingers to my temples. 'Because he was hell bent on making me look like an unfit mother. He was terrified that I would leave him eventually and wanted to make sure he got custody of Lucas and Aurora. He knew I'd never leave them behind.'

'We haven't found a response from Mr Joliffe, so I'm

presuming it was a telephone call. It would be interesting to know what advice he gave your husband.'

'I have no idea. Whatever he said doesn't change the fact that I tried to resuscitate my father.'

DI Westcott sighs, and makes a move to get up. DS Wade stands.

'Have you been able to remember anything else about Sunday night?' DI Westcott asks.

I shake my head. 'No. Nothing.'

She slips her notebook into her pocket. 'Have you heard the term "selective amnesia"?'

'No, but I can understand what it means.'

'How would you interpret it?' DS Wade asks.

'I suppose it would be your brain choosing to shut down one section in order for you not to remember something really terrible happening.'

'That's about it. Psychologists think it can be caused by trauma, usually during an isolated event. Its most common form is dissociative disorder. It's the mind attempting to shield itself. When you think about the combination of the injury to your head, the excessive amount of alcohol in your bloodstream, the sleeping pills, and the humiliation you endured at your party, the conditions were perfect.'

'And you think that's what happened? That I witnessed something and my mind decided to hide it from me?'

'Possibly. There is of course another alternative,' DS Wade says. 'That you're lying to us and remember everything.'

Behind his glasses, his eyes are a velvety brown and

319

disconcertingly attractive for a plain-faced man. The kind of eyes a writer might describe as melting.

'I'm not lying. I don't remember that night.'

We eye each other for a moment, then he smiles and clicks his neck, swiftly dispelling the magic.

'I see your au pair has moved back in,' DI Westcott says. 'I was under the impression that you two had fallen out big-time.'

I shrug. 'It provides continuity for the children. Dan Jones has moved in as well.'

'He's what?' DS Wade splutters.

'Temporarily,' I add hastily. 'He and Isabel want to be together.'

DI Westcott is frowning, evidently astonished. 'And you're OK with that?'

I hold her gaze. 'Yes, I'm fine. It's a big house and I don't want to be on my own right now. It means I have help with the children, and a happy au pair.'

And an opportunity to discover a little more about my charming tenant.

'God forbid you make Isabel Gardin unhappy,' Westcott says, rolling her eyes.

I smile for the first time since they arrived. We at least agree on one thing. Isabel Gardin is an egotistical troublemaker.

45

It's been a trying morning. Yesterday I took Aurora into Little Beans for her first day and she was fine, skipping along, excited about being a schoolgirl at last, but today her little face is stained with tears and her foot has stamped so much I'm surprised she hasn't worn a hole in her tights. Dan and Isabel haven't dragged themselves from the luxury of my bed by the time we leave, which makes me fizz with irritation even though they are the last people I want to see.

I look round for the Gordons when we reach the nursery, but they have been and gone. Leonie spots us and runs over to Aurora, but when I search the laminated names blu-tacked to the surface of the tables, they haven't been put together. I tell myself it doesn't mean a thing, that it's probably to do with encouraging new friendships, but I can't help wondering if Ali's had a word with their teacher, if she's trying to encourage Leonie to make an alternative best friend. There was no invitation to walk in together this morning, and I didn't dare ask in case the suggestion was greeted with awkward excuses. People are kind, they stop and say hello, but

I'm also aware of the constraint as they try to express their condolences without getting sucked in. It's the same at Highfields.

'I just can't believe what's happened,' someone says. 'You poor thing. Call me if you need to talk.'

I thank her and move on swiftly, suspecting she would be horrified if I took her up on the offer. I look for Sonia Metzger, then remember she's a working mum. She is the one person I could have counted on to offer support without being intrusive.

I can't see Ali or Pete here either, and it's both a relief and a source of misery. Others will be disappointed too, robbed of the chance to see Ali Gordon and Eliza Curran greet, or not greet each other. I know why I'm being avoided like a bad smell. It's common knowledge that Martin's death was not an accident and that I've been questioned more than once. And then, of course, anyone who wasn't at the party will have had a blow-by-blow account of it by now. The au pair who turned toxic – every mother's nightmare. I bet they're secretly regretting turning down the invitation, knowing they missed a classic soap opera moment. They will have their theories: tragic widow or heartless killer? Either way, what do you say to someone like me?

Then someone does approach. Amanda Kelsey.

'How are you?' she says, her hand on my arm. 'I am so, so sorry about Martin.'

'Thank you,' I say stiffly.

'Are you coping?'

'Just about.'

'I understand Isabel is still with you.'

There is no such thing as discretion in Hasleford.

'Yes, she is,' I say.

'Wow. You're very forgiving.'

I trot out the standard line. 'I can't face having to interview anyone new. The children love her and they need continuity right now, so . . .'

'I understand,' Amanda says. 'You're having a tough time. You will let me know when the funeral is, won't you?'

I nod and move away. The doors to the school open and we file in. I have a quick chat with Lucas's teacher, then go to the school office to drop in his after-school club forms and arrange a meeting with the head in two weeks' time. The staff are going to be monitoring Lucas closely.

There's already someone talking to the secretary, an anxious mum explaining her child's allergies and how to avoid triggering them, so I hover by the fixtures list, which is next to the door, to wait my turn. Unfortunately, I tune into a conversation happening in the corridor, recognizing Amanda Kelsey's syrupy tones. Her companion I can't pin down; it could be any of a number of people. They are speaking in deliciously complicit whispers, and at the mention of my name my ears prick up. Acutely embarrassed, I take my phone out of my bag and pretend to be reading emails.

'I'm surprised she's come to school. If it was me, I'd have asked a friend to bring Lucas.'

'I don't think she has any friends,' Amanda says. 'Not real ones at least.'

'You know, when someone told me Martin Curran was dead I almost dropped the baby. What do you think happened? You must know more than most people.'

I imagine Amanda preening at the implication that she is part of Ali's inner circle.

'From what Ali's told me, it's all to do with that man, the lodger.'

'Wasn't he their tenant?'

'Whatever, it's a bit desperate, don't you think? But then she did that to Ali. I mean, Ali, for God's sake, when she's been so lovely to Eliza. Incredible, isn't it? Ali adored Martin and this has devastated her; she's in bits. Personally, I think Eliza should move away. It would be the decent thing to do.'

'At least Ali has you.'

'Yes, well, I understand her.'

I detect a hint of sympathy from the school secretary when I finally get my turn, but you can never be sure. She might be saving all this up for the staffroom. I imagine her saying, *Oh my god, it was SO awkward!*

'Eliza.'

Pete is waiting at the school gate, Joy at his feet. She greets me ecstatically, wagging her tail and turning so many circles she becomes entangled in her lead. I bend to extricate her and look up at Pete.

'No Ali?'

'No, she went on ahead. I wanted to catch you.' He has the grace to look embarrassed.

I straighten up and start to walk. I do not need Pete's problems. I have enough on my plate with my own.

'I need to talk to you,' he says. 'Somewhere private. There's something I want to show you. It's on my phone.'

He moves ahead, seeming to assume I'll follow him. When I don't he stops and turns round, eyebrows raised as he walks back to my side.

'Please don't take this the wrong way,' I say. 'But this is not the time. If you want to show me designs for Gideon Grove, let's do it in a couple of weeks. I'm glad you're excited about it, but it's the last thing I want to think about right now.'

'This has nothing to do with Gideon Grove. This is to do with Dan. I have some information about him.'

I tilt my head, trying to fathom him. 'Why are you doing this?'

'Doing what?' He sounds surprised by the question.

'Being helpful. After everything that's happened.'

'Because I want to get the cunt.'

I catch my breath. 'Pete!'

'Sorry. I just feel so bad about everything that's happened. We might have had our disagreements, but Martin was my oldest friend. And you don't deserve any of what's happened to you. Dan is at the bottom of it.'

'You have no proof of that.'

'I don't need proof. I know it.'

I can't deny I'm curious. I'm also chasing clues about Dan Jones; not least why he went to so much trouble to convince me he was in love with me.

By now we are on the corner of Linden Road. I dig in my bag for my keys and hold them so tight they hurt my palms. Can I bear to go in there? We could go to Nico's, but I dismiss the idea. Too public.

'Come with me.'

I stride down the street, checking behind me. There's no one around, so I stop outside number 42. I don't bother ringing the doorbell.

Pete and I face each other over the kitchen table. I have his phone in my hand and I'm reading a post. After Ali told him about Dan being a twin, Pete trawled LinkedIn, Facebook, Instagram, and any other social networking sites he could think of, and finally tracked down someone who fitted his profile on a forum for people who have lost their twin and are suffering. I agree with him that this is almost certainly our Dan Jones.

Members' Stories

Daniel Jones on 23 October 2012 said:

I lost my twin sister in 2009. She took an overdose of heroin. We were very close growing up. Our parents were keen for us to have separate identities, so we were put in different nurseries for a while, but we were both so miserable that they relented. At primary school we were separated again, but found each other at lunch and breaktime.

We complemented each other. We made up for each other's deficiencies. She was naughty, so I was good. I found it hard to make friends, so she shared hers with me. She wasn't bright academically, but I was and I helped her, coaching her before exams so that she could get a decent pass and not be humiliated, because she wanted so badly to prove herself. As a teenager I was clueless about clothes, so she made sure my jeans were the right cut, my T-shirts had the right designs, my shoes were the right make. I was tidy, she was a mess.

She killed herself because of a man. I don't understand why she did that and I find it hard to forgive. She had me, so why was he so important?

She's left me with a sense that part of me, the part that was her, doesn't function any more. It's as though I have a dead spare part attached to me that I should rip off and throw out, but I can't.

Maybe one day this feeling will ease, and I'll be able to look back at our time together and appreciate it, stop being angry and forgive. I hope it happens soon because I'm pulled down by the weight of her.

I think about Sam and how I would feel if I lost him, and a lump forms in my throat. Even if Dan has lied about everything else, he isn't lying here.

There are many sympathetic responses. One of them asks whereabouts he lives, as there are local support networks throughout the UK. Dan says Sussex, which fits with what he told us.

This led Pete to an article in the *Sussex Express*. There's a photograph, a family gathered outside a house in front of a magnolia in bloom. Mother, father, teenage brother and sister. The boy is unmistakably Dan. The girl is the one brandishing the hose on Dan's screensaver, the girl who I met in Goa. The girl who lost out on Martin.

Tragic Twin Killed Herself

An inquest has found that twenty-one-year-old Clare Jones took her own life on 7 July this year. Her parents, Lewes residents Philip and Celia Jones, have asked for privacy at this time. Her brother has spoken about the loss of his twin and his difficulties in coming to terms with it. 'I've tried so hard to make sense of what she did, but it's impossible. She had so much more to give. I just can't seem to physically separate from her. I can't move on when a part of me has died.'

'I've found his parents,' Pete says. 'I have an address.'

46

The wide tree-lined avenue of detached Edwardian houses with their mature front gardens has an air of solid gentility. The magnolia has grown by a third since the photograph in the *Sussex Express* was taken, but otherwise not much has changed. I can't imagine anything bad happening here, although it must have. Tragedy doesn't discriminate. For a second I wish I'd allowed Pete to come with me; he argued hard enough. But then I pull my shoulders back and ring the doorbell. Dan is my problem. I want to do this on my own.

After what feels like ages I hear someone shout, 'I'll get it,' then footsteps coming towards me. A woman opens the door.

'Sorry,' she says, 'I was in the garden. Can I help you?'

Celia Jones has silver hair that frames a delicately carved face. She's wearing jeans with the hems rolled up and a floaty shirt with a cardigan over it. I look for a resemblance to Dan, but I don't see it.

'I wonder if I could have a word. My name is Eliza Morley. I'm a friend of Daniel's.' On the drive here I decided to use my maiden name, to avoid her connecting me with Martin. His death has been interesting enough to garner column inches in the national press, and I don't want it muddying the waters.

'You'd better come in.'

She opens the door wide, then leads me down a tiled hallway into a pretty kitchen with cream walls, green hand-painted units and a weathered wooden floor. French windows open onto a wide garden with deep borders and mature trees. I think about the brutalist kitchen at Winterfell and shudder. Wasn't it Dan who called the house soulless?

'Did Dan ask you to contact us?'

She doesn't offer me so much as a glass of water, or ask me to sit down. Her expression is closed. This is the woman who blamed her son for the death of his sister. She obviously doesn't want to be reminded of it. I feel a sliver of sympathy for Dan. But only a sliver.

'Not exactly.'

'Let me get my husband.' She leaves the room, calling upstairs. 'Philip. There's someone here about Dan. Could you come down?'

We stand in silence while we wait. Philip enters the room briskly. He's a good-looking man, and, when he passes a hand through his thatch of salt and pepper hair, I catch my breath. The gesture is so familiar. Celia introduces us.

'What's your connection with my son?' he asks.

'I met him when he rented a flat I own.'

'You're his landlady?' Celia's gaze sharpens, making me feel as though I've divulged something much more interesting.

'Well, yes,' I say hesitantly. 'But we've become friendly since then.'

'Oh?'

'Not in the way you're imagining.' I raise my left hand to show her my wedding ring.

'If everything's fine, what is it that you want from us?' Philip asks.

'The thing is,' I say, 'we've had a bit of a rough ride since he arrived on the scene. Things have happened, horrible things that have nothing to do with him. It's probably a coincidence . . .' My voice trails off.

'But?' Philip presses.

I indicate the photograph of a young woman prominent on the dresser. 'Is that Clare?'

'Yes,' Celia says, sounding surprised. 'Did Dan tell you about her?'

'Only that she died,' I say carefully.

Philip picks the photograph up and holds on to it, as though he's protecting it from me. I feel my presence is increasingly unwelcome.

'I'm sorry to intrude, I really am, it's just that something doesn't feel right. On the face of it, Dan is a charming man, he works hard, he's good with people. Extremely good, in fact. But I can't help feeling something's missing. I know that he was devastated by Clare's death and I was wondering whether he talks to anyone about it. Does he talk to you?'

'So let me get this straight,' Philip says. 'You're here because you're concerned about our son's state of mind?'

'Well, not just that—'

'Sorry, I didn't catch your name.'

'Eliza Morley.' I feel my cheeks going pink.

'Well, Eliza, what is it you're after? If he's left you in the lurch, I'm afraid that's your business. Dan isn't our responsibility.'

'Philip,' Celia admonishes. 'We haven't seen Dan in years,' she says, turning to me. 'I'm guessing you're here because you want to know if you can trust him?'

'Something like that.'

She sighs. 'The answer is, we can't guarantee it. Dan did have some emotional difficulties growing up. I don't know whether he's solved them, though I hope so. He and Clare were the kind of twins who cut others out, but with Dan it didn't naturally fade as he grew into adolescence. It seemed to be rooted in him in a way it wasn't with Clare. Even when he was old enough to understand that she was a separate person, I believe he still thought of them both as one entity, whether consciously or not. If Clare hurt, he hurt. On one level, it was a lovely thing to witness. They adored each other. But it wasn't healthy. That's why we encouraged Clare to go travelling at a time when Dan was unable to follow her.'

'Why was that?' It confirms my theory that it was Clare, not Dan, who was the original owner of the embroidered blanket.

'He wanted to, but he'd contracted glandular fever. It hit him hard. He changed, he stopped caring about things. He'd been ambitious, but he became unreliable. He couldn't hold down a job for more than a few weeks. He's our son and we love him, don't get me wrong, but we've found that our lives are easier without him in it. I'm afraid he's the kind of person who blames everyone but himself for whatever problems he encounters.' She gives me a pained smile. 'Everyone meaning us, usually.'

'It's why he moves around so much,' Philip says. 'He fails, but as far as he's concerned, it's other people who have failed him, so he drops out of their lives.'

'He implied that you were estranged because you blamed him for Clare's death.'

Philip shakes his head; a gesture of disappointment, not a rebuttal. 'You seem like a nice person, so I'll give you some advice as regards my son. Don't let your guard down. He only ever truly loved one person, and she took her own life. He's never recovered from that.'

Celia speaks as I move towards the door. 'We certainly didn't blame Dan for what happened to Clare. The reason Dan no longer talks to us is more banal. On Dan and Clare's twenty-first we gave them each a sum of money, enough for a decent deposit towards their first property. Clare died before she could use hers and the money reverted to us. Dan expected to be given his sister's share, in effect to double his, but we said no.'

'Why?' I ask. It doesn't seem particularly shocking or unreasonable. A little grasping perhaps, but not unduly. 'Perhaps he was simply trying to salvage something from the wreckage.'

'You said he's renting off you,' Celia says.

'That's right.'

'That's because he never used the money to buy a flat; he'd burned through it within six months. He gambles, I'm afraid. We didn't want the money we'd saved for

Clare to go the same way, so we told him we would put it into a trust for our future grandchildren. It didn't go down well.'

Her lips tighten, and I see the sadness in her eyes.

'Understatement,' Philip mutters, giving her shoulder an encouraging pat.

I had no clue, but I expect he hides it like I hide my own addiction. You'd think I would have recognized a fellow addict. Then I remember his odd behaviour at the auction for Gideon Grove; the almost manic gleam in his eyes, his twitching fingers. It makes sense now. It was the adrenaline of the race – akin to the feeling I get when I'm close to alcohol.

Before I leave, I scribble my phone number down on the back of a receipt and hand it to Celia.

'Thank you for your time. If you think of anyone else who I could talk to about Dan, who may have seen him more recently than you, please call me.'

I look back once as I walk to my car. I feel sorry for them, hanging on to an enormous house they have no need for, in case that need arises, but their daughter is dead and their son is showing no signs of providing them with grandchildren. More to the point, they may be about to find out that their son has killed. He loved Clare too much, just as Clare loved Martin too much. She came home from India broken, and he might as well have been broken himself. They were, as Celia said, one entity.

If I'm right, will Martin's death be enough for him? It might satisfy him for now, but the need will grow back, putting me and the children in danger.

* * *

I call DI Westcott from the car and she picks up, surprised to hear from me. I tell her what I suspect; that Martin's death was payback for Clare's. Westcott sounds unconvinced, but says they'll look into it.

'He's living in my house,' I say. 'I don't think we're safe.'

'He won't do anything stupid. He knows we're keeping an eye on all of you.'

I don't feel reassured. 'But what if he's dangerous?'

'If you're worried about it, ask him to leave and tell him that you've spoken to me. That might be enough of a threat. Frankly, I was extremely surprised you let him move in in the first place. It was a questionable decision on your part.'

47

I'm laden with Lucas's bookbag and games kit when I get home. Lucas runs straight into the kitchen, perpetually hungry, while I remove my boots. The house has changed since Martin's death. There are clothes and toys on the stairs, footwear in the hall, and the air is laced with Isabel's perfume. A red scarf draped over the end of the banister stands out like a gash against the grey concrete.

Martin's study door is half open, and for a moment I think he's in there and I feel a shot of adrenaline, before the figure behind the computer screen resolves into Dan. He's wearing a white shirt unbuttoned at the neck, the cuffs turned up. It's a much better quality shirt than he normally wears, and I strongly suspect it's one of Martin's. Even in my current mood I can appreciate that it suits him, the bright white against his tanned throat and wrists.

He's on the phone. I push the door open wider and lean against the frame, arms crossed, watching him. He finally notices that he has an audience, finishes his call and rolls the chair back. He stands up and rotates his right arm, his left hand on his shoulder.

'Working hard?' I say.

'Gotta earn a crust.' He smiles then, but I merely lift the corners of my lips.

'Is that Martin's shirt?'

He glances down at it, as if he's checking. 'Is that a problem?'

'You should have asked.'

'You'd have said no.'

I sigh and turn away, wandering into the kitchen. Lucas is making toast; Aurora is playing a game on the iPad. I kiss her head but she barely acknowledges me.

'You did not tell me how long you were going to be,' Isabel says, glaring at me. 'I am not your servant.'

Keep things calm, I think. 'I know, and I'm sorry, but I had to go round to Linden Road with the agent from Hooper's.' The lies flow easily. 'Then there was a problem with one of our other tenants. She's been made redundant. These things take time. But I am sorry if it inconvenienced you.'

'Hm,' she says. 'Next time tell me what is happening.'

There won't be a next time. I'm never leaving her alone with my children again. I wipe the crumbs away from where Lucas has been, then run my eyes over my once pristine kitchen. Dirty dishes, dirty mugs. Sink stained with coffee dregs. On the floor, scraps of food and straggles of fluff caught on hairs have gathered at the base of the units.

'Perhaps you should get a proper cleaner now,' Isabel

says. 'It is not my job. I should not have been doing it anyway. I have talked to my friends, and their hosts all have cleaners. You are mean with your money.'

'Fine,' I say, not caring. 'I'll sort something out. Presumably you'd like room service as well?'

She bangs around. I look at my phone, scroll through emails. After a while I move over to where she's standing, looking sulky.

I keep my back to the children and whisper, 'Isabel, has Dan tried to coerce you into doing anything you are uncomfortable with?'

'I don't know what you mean. I have done nothing wrong. I am staying here. Dan too. We are together and you cannot split us up.'

I could almost cry with frustration. 'He isn't going to stay with you, not in a million years. You're hanging on to this relationship by a thread. You know in your heart that's true. He's using you, Isabel.' I spell it out. 'He wants you to help him cover up Martin's murder.'

The shock on her face convinces me I was right. 'It was you,' she says.

'Come on. I know you made that up. Dan made you say it, didn't he? Because he killed Martin. Can't you see you're being manipulated? You shouldn't protect him.'

She doesn't answer.

'The police will work it out, Isabel, make no mistake. You'll be an accessory. Is this man honestly worth doing time for? Wrecking your life for?'

'I love him.'

She sounds uncertain and I feel bad for twisting the knife, but not enough to stop.

338

'But he doesn't love you. He doesn't love me either, he never did. We've both been played for fools.'

'You, not me. And why would he kill Martin? He was excited to be working with him.'

I deflate slightly. 'I think I've figured it out, but I can't tell you until I'm sure.'

'Ah, well.' She shrugs at me. 'You don't know anything.'

I hear Dan's footsteps in the hall and move away from her before he comes in.

'Something smells good.' He glances at me, then at Isabel, before leaning over Lucas to steal his toast. He pretends to bite into it.

'Hey!' Lucas protests.

Dan laughs and hands it back. 'You were out for a long time,' he says to me.

'I do have a life outside this house.'

'Eliza has been to Linden Road,' Isabel says.

'Oh, right. Yeah, I need to go back and pick up the rest of my things. I'll give the place a clean while I'm about it, then you can return my deposit.'

'Once I've completed the inventory and subtracted the cost of a deep clean and redecoration.'

He raises his eyebrows. 'It doesn't need redecoration. I've only been there a few months.'

'There's damage all the way up the stairs and on the landing, from your bike,' I say, improvising. 'And you've scratched the paintwork on the front door. There's more scuffing where you pushed your feet against the wall under the desk. You should have taken your shoes off.'

'That's just normal wear and tear.'

'I don't think so. You'll receive a copy of the full inventory when it's been done.'

He scowls but I ignore him because my mobile is ringing. I don't recognize the number, but it's a landline, and I have a gut feeling about it. I dart a glance at Isabel and Dan and go out into the hall.

'Eliza? It's Celia Jones.'

'Oh.' I was right, but the sound of her voice still gives me butterflies. I shut myself in the playroom.

'I thought you might want to talk to Dan's ex-girlfriend.'

'I'd love to. Hang on.' I cast around for a felt-tip pen and a scrap of paper. 'Is she the girl he was with until earlier this year?'

'No. This was several years ago. We haven't met any of his more recent girlfriends. I'll send you her contact details. Her name's Gaby Wilder.'

I almost drop the phone. 'Gaby Wilder? Are you sure?'

'Well, she might be married by now, I suppose. Poor Gaby, I felt so sorry for her. She couldn't accept it was over. I'm sure she's fine now, but there was a stage when she was calling us every day. Why? Do you know her?'

'I'm not sure. Possibly.'

I thank her and hang up, stunned. The name might as well have been written in neon lights. Gaby Wilder was the woman who caused the accident that paralysed Martin.

'Who was that?' Dan asks, faux casually, when I re-join them.

'None of your business. I don't need to account to you

for where I go and who I speak to.' I almost add, *You're as bad as Martin*, before I remember my children are in the room.

I call Gaby Wilder from my bedroom after Lucas and Aurora have gone to bed. I even shut myself in my dressing room, just in case Dan is listening at the door. He seemed very interested in my movements earlier.

Gaby picks up so quickly that I don't have time to formulate my response, and I stammer my name.

'Who is this?'

'Sorry. It's Eliza Curran, Martin Curran's wife. Celia Jones gave me your number.'

She takes in a sharp breath. 'I don't want to talk to you. All that's over now.'

'Please. It's not about the accident. I need information about Dan.'

There's a long silence. Then she swears under her breath.

'I have no contact with him, haven't had in years, so I can't help you. I presume he owes you money.'

'No,' I say, surprised. 'It's not that. It's a bit more complicated. Would you mind if I came to see you? It wouldn't take long. Just half an hour of your time. It's urgent.'

She sighs. 'The weekend's no good, we're away. Although, I suppose you could come on Sunday evening. We'll be back by five.' She pauses. 'I am very sorry about what happened to your husband.'

'Thank you.'

'I saw it in the paper. It gave me a terrible shock.'

48

I wake in the small hours of Sunday morning and can't get back to sleep. My mind is wired, I'm so excited and anxious about meeting Gaby. I sit up in bed and hug my knees. Questioning her about Dan could be the key to convincing the police that he's the person they should be looking at in connection with Martin's death, not me. If anyone knows who Dan really is, what he really is, then surely Gaby Wilder does.

I have nothing else, and I need to move things along. My children are suffering. Lucas has clammed up. Aurora doesn't know what the hell is going on but she's lost the daddy she adored, another couple is sleeping in her parents' bed, and another man is working at her father's desk. Her world has been upended, and her mother doesn't appear to have the answers. Hopefully, Gaby will supply some of them.

Sleeplessness makes me hungry. I get out of bed, put my robe on and go downstairs. There's a dim light on in the kitchen. I linger outside it, in two minds. I don't want a conversation with Isabel, but if it's Dan that's different, because Isabel never leaves me alone with him. I push open the door. The light is coming from the strips of LEDs under the wall units. Dan is standing with his back to me, looking out at the darkened garden. He's not wearing a top, and I stare helplessly at his bare back.

He turns. 'Can't sleep either?'

I open the larder cupboard and find a packet of Jaffa Cakes, tear it open and hold it out to him.

'No, thanks.'

He moves away from the window and sits down. I pour myself a glass of milk and join him.

'What's kept you awake?' I ask. 'Guilty conscience?'

He shrugs and I wait for him to rake his fingers through his hair. After a moment he obliges.

'I don't understand what's going on,' I say. 'What are you doing here?'

'I don't really know.'

I raise my eyebrows and, in response, he screws up his face.

'It wasn't my idea. The last thing I want is to live with all this.' He gestures at the house. 'Your family. Isabel.'

'I can imagine. So why move in?'

He smiles. 'Isabel can be persuasive.'

'But you're no pushover.'

He rubs his nose with the back of his hand, a curiously childish gesture. 'Perhaps I am.'

'Did you kill Martin? I only ask,' I add dryly, 'because I was knocked unconscious and when I woke up the next morning he was dead.'

'Why on earth would I kill him? You need to face things, Eliza. You're the only one here with a motive.'

'Am I? I keep asking myself why you came to Linden Road. If you knew me from somewhere else.'

'I met you for the first time that day.'

I bite into a biscuit and chew thoughtfully. 'What about Martin?'

'What about him?'

'Had you met him before?'

'No.'

'And what about what happened between you and me? Was there ever a connection between us?'

'I'm sorry, but no. There wasn't.'

Despite understanding that he isn't the man I thought I was getting to know, that's a surprisingly painful thing to hear.

'You can't deny that you kissed me that time in Nico's. Ali saw you.'

'No, I can't deny that. You were so desperate for it, I took pity on you. It was a mistake.'

I look steadily into his eyes, trying to gauge his innocence or guilt from his expression. I'm getting closer to the truth, better able to read him. His eyes betray nothing except mild amusement, but he can't fool me any more. There's a strategic mind behind them, problem solving, trying to keep one step ahead of me.

I sense a movement and look beyond his shoulder. Isabel is reflected in the darkened glass. I twist round in my chair as she walks into the room, reasonably decent in pyjama shorts and a spaghetti-strap top. She comes up to the table and sits on Dan's knee, and pulls him in for a deep kiss that seems to drag on. When she finally stops to draw breath, she tosses her hair back and looks, catlike, at me.

'Fuck off, Eliza,' she says. 'I want to make love to my man.'

In bed I replay that moment, especially the look on Dan's face. He hadn't been delighted, he'd been irritated. The manipulator is being manipulated and he doesn't like it one little bit. Theirs is not a healthy relationship. Really, all I have to do is sit back and wait for it to implode.

49

This time I'm better prepared and arrange for Kate to have the children. I drop them off before driving the two hours to Gaby Wilder's house. Gaby has married and is now Gaby Lee. Her house is in the countryside and part of a new-build estate. It's large, detached and designed to recall a Palladian mansion. There are pillars outside the front door.

The honey-coloured wood floor of the room into which she shows me is covered by an enormous, patterned rug. The huge cream sofas are threaded with gold. A chandelier glitters above us. The curtains are swagged, framing windows onto a wide, lawned garden with a weeping willow at the end.

Gaby is dressed in a pair of jeans sparkling with diamanté studs, and a crisp pink shirt with the collar turned up. Hanging from a platinum chain, a diamond heart nestles at her throat, her blonde hair is brushed to a shine and her earrings are small diamond clusters. I feel scruffy beside her in my faded black Uniqlo jeggings and dove-grey high street sweater. When I took my boots off in the hall, at her request, I felt ashamed of my socks.

Her husband Terry, who I reckon must be at least fifteen years older than her, brings in a tray laden with porcelain cups and saucers and a matching teapot. He sets it down in front of us and leaves, waggling his fingers. Gaby ignores him.

'So. Dan,' she says, getting down to business. 'What's he been up to?'

I'm happy to dispense with small talk too. 'I'm not sure. It's all the little things that don't add up.'

'Go on,' Gaby says.

'Things have gone wrong for my family ever since he turned up.'

'Now there's a surprise. Are you wealthy?'

My phone rings. I take it out of my pocket and switch it off. It was Sonia. I feel a niggle of fear. What does she want?

'We're well-off, yes. Would that matter to him?'

'You bet.' Gaby pours the tea and lifts the jug of milk, raising her eyebrows. I nod.

'Terry and I talked after I spoke to you. He's a lawyer, in property, but he's generally up to speed with other aspects of law. He said since the case was over and I'd fulfilled my, um, obligations' – Gaby had done community service at the time – 'I'm entitled to say what I like.' She finishes on a defensive note.

I nod encouragingly.

'I need to have your word that this won't go any further. I do not want to go back to court, or ever see or hear from Dan again, or you for that matter. And certainly not Martin's lawyer. Misogynist prick. No offence.'

'None taken.'

'I've had therapy and I've dealt with it. I'll tell you the truth only because you need to know who you're dealing with. But that's it.' She fixes her pale blue eyes on mine. 'None of this goes on record, OK? I have not said it. If you ask me to make an official statement to the police, I won't do it.'

'I understand.'

'I wasn't driving that night.' She ignores my sharp intake of breath and carries on. 'Dan was. We'd been to the pub, and I'd had more to drink than he had. He said the motorbike came out of nowhere. Dan drove away. I was hysterical. Then the next morning he got worried because chances are the car was caught on CCTV somewhere. He persuaded me to say I was driving. He had points on his licence and mine was clean. He said that because I was a young woman the judge would be lenient. It had been pitch dark in the lane and raining hard, so he reckoned we would get away with it, since they would be less likely to go to the trouble and expense of searching for footage and examining it if someone had already confessed. I turned myself in and told the police that I'd left the scene because I panicked, but then felt terrible and decided to face up to what I had done and try to make amends. It helped in court.'

To my dismay a tear rolls down her cheek. She wipes it away.

'Sorry. I can't tell you what a relief it is to talk about this. It's been such a strain, keeping quiet all this time.' She drinks some of her tea. 'I was head over heels in love with Dan. I'd dozed off when he suddenly swerved, so I believed him when he told me it was the motorcyclist's fault. I was convinced that Dan didn't deserve to be punished. I even felt like I was doing a good thing. He said it would ruin his whole future if he was convicted for dangerous driving. I was so naive; I thought that future included me. People hated me for it. I lost my friends and my job. If it hadn't been for darling Terry, I think I would have had a nervous breakdown.'

'Did you ever meet Dan's sister?'

'No, she had died by the time I came on the scene. It was so sad. Dan was really screwed up about it. I think that's what appealed to me at the beginning, the fact that he was a mess. I thought I could help him, that I'd be enough. But . . . well . . .' She hesitates. 'Your husband was part of a rather rowdy group at the pub that night. It might have been a stag do or someone's birthday, but they were shouting over each other and roaring with laughter. Dan was getting more and more wound up. I thought it was because they were a bunch of ex-public schoolboys, bankers, that Dan was pissed off – because they had money and he didn't.'

'Did he tell you he recognized one of them? That Martin was Clare's ex?'

She wrinkles her brow. 'No. I had no idea. That changes everything. I remember Dan grabbed his coat and we left very shortly after Martin did.'

'Knowing what you do now, do you think he might have driven into Martin deliberately?'

She looks genuinely appalled. 'I don't think so. He wouldn't do something that extreme.'

349

'Are you sure about that? What if he was provoked? Maybe the sight of Martin out having a great time with his mates, while his sister was dead, was too much.'

'But Martin had nothing to do with Clare's death.'

'Not in Dan's eyes. He saw his sister come home from India broken. And Martin knew what had happened, but he never got in touch with Dan's family, never expressed sympathy or came to her funeral.'

'What a shit.'

'It would explain why Dan lost it in the pub, why he left straight after him.'

Gaby's eyes swim with tears. 'I expect he only meant to scare him. It was a country lane, not the main road, and there was no traffic around. Your husband was just unlucky.'

'You were right to come,' she says as she sees me to the door. 'There's no way I'd have told you all that over the phone.' She places a beringed hand on my arm. 'Dan is greedy and cowardly, but he isn't evil. Losing his twin screwed him up badly. No relationship's ever going to match the one he had with Clare. I wish I'd understood that earlier, but by the time I did I was in too deep. He will never be happy, you know; it doesn't matter who he's with, because they're not her.' She pats my arm. 'I do hope you're not in love with him.'

'No . . . I—'

Terry comes up behind her and puts his hands on her shoulders. My cue to leave. I have much to think about.

Dan knew exactly who I was when he rang the door-bell at 42 Linden Road. He deliberately inveigled his way into our lives because he's been watching us for years, waiting for the perfect moment. He decided to gamble everything on getting close to us, to avenge his sister. And as a result, Martin is dead. If I'm right, then I need to finish this quickly.

It's twilight. Between the edge of a bank of dark clouds and the horizon, there's a strip of yellowish sky. I feel a drip of rain on my face as I walk down the wide driveway. In the car I switch my phone back on. Sonia has left a voicemail message.

Hi, Eliza. Her voice sounds urgent. *I've had a tip-off from DI Westcott. You need to make arrangements for the children. You're going to be arrested tomorrow morning.*

50

My hands are trembling so much I can barely press the button to call Sonia back. 'What new evidence do they have?' I wipe the mist from the inside of the windscreen with my sleeve.

'Something's come up in the post mortem,' Sonia says. 'But they wouldn't tell me what. Don't worry, Eliza, I'll sort it out.'

The rain drums on the roof and I have to press the phone hard against my ear to hear her properly. Sonia's voice is measured. I imagine she's used to this, to keeping clients calm, not raising the stress level, but I can feel my blood pressure cranking up.

'But they wouldn't arrest me unless they were really sure this time. It would be embarrassing for them if they were seen to have got it wrong.'

'There's no point us speculating until we have the information.'

I grip my phone. 'I swear I didn't kill Martin.'

'I know you didn't. One step at a time. DI Westcott has done you the courtesy of giving you a chance to get childcare organized, which she isn't obliged to, so call who you need to call. I'll see you first thing tomorrow morning. Be brave.'

I disconnect and put the phone on the passenger seat beside me. I'm tired of being brave. I've had to be brave all my life and I'm sick of it. I want to put this whole horrific episode behind me and start again. I imagine picking the children up from Kate's and driving through the night, along miles and miles of motorway. They would be asleep in the back and I would be alone with my thoughts. We'd arrive at some far-off destination in the early hours of the morning. I'd park, get into the back between them, and fall asleep until the morning light woke us. We'd have breakfast in a greasy spoon; the works. Then we'd book into a hotel. I'd tell them we were on an adventure.

And then what?

The sky has darkened while I've been putting off making what will possibly rank as the most shaming phone call of my entire life; telling Kate I can't pick up my children because I'm about to be arrested on suspicion of the murder of their father, her son. And I'll have to ask if she'll keep them for an indefinite amount of time. I don't doubt Sonia's abilities, but I'm not confident that she'll get me out of this nightmare immediately.

Kate picks up and before I can explain, she tells me that the children are with Ali and Pete.

'I'm sorry, Eliza, but Aurora was being very difficult. I've had several tantrums from her, and I really couldn't cope. Pete came and got them. I'll tell Ali you're on your way, shall I?'

I throw the phone down and rest my head on the back of my hands, clutching the steering wheel. Then I straighten up, press the power button, and set off towards Hasleford and Ali and Pete's house.

The journey gives me time to think through what Gaby has told me. Looking at it, I cannot believe that I didn't realize from the off that Dan had an agenda. It occurs to me now that Nico's, where he used to work in the days when he was supposedly sofa-surfing, is opposite Hooper's. He may have been watching me for weeks, or even months, following me around the town, looking for some chink, some back entrance into Martin's life. He would have seen me go in and out of Linden Road, as well as Hooper's, and would have put two and two together. He would have seen that Nico's was my favourite of the local coffee shops and that Ali and I often popped in after dropping off the children. So easy then to use his charm, to wander into the estate agent's and smile at Susie in the lettings department, get her all flustered, wheedle her into suggesting the flat so that she would back up the story he told me.

I was flustered too. Dan knew exactly how to push my buttons. That touch on my face, for instance, scratching off the paint fleck; in doing that he had turned an unhappy wife into a piece of plasticine he could do what he liked with. He took a chance; I could have been furious and offended, but I think he had my measure even then.

Had he had a look at all of us? At Ali and Pete too? And Sam? It was Dan after all who had insinuated that my twin couldn't be trusted, who had talked me into blaming him for Ali finding out what had happened between me and Pete. Had Dan carefully planned how he could systematically undermine the foundations of Martin's relationships, targeting me as his way in, because I was the weakest link? Yes, of course. I played into his hands.

I get to Ali and Pete's road and find a parking space opposite their house. The lights are on in the front bay window, the curtains open. Pete's there, holding the baby on his shoulder. I can't see any of the children so I expect they've been put to bed.

I can't do it. I can't get out of the car and face them. I can't even face my own children. Sick with shame, I drive away, taking a right turn and heading towards Boundary Road. I reach the Two Brewers, the pub where I fetched up like a piece of driftwood after Ali caught Dan kissing me, and find a parking space a few yards down the side street.

I had hoped there would be someone different in tonight, but it's the same bartender and he recognizes me, saying 'Hello again,' when I approach the bar. I brush the rain off my hair with my hand and ask for a double vodka tonic. The table I sat at before is empty, so I take it before anyone else can and lay my phone beside my glass. Ali will be expecting me to ring the doorbell at any moment. I knock the vodka back then make the call.

Ali picks up on the first ring. 'Where the hell are you?'

'Sorry. I had to stop off at home for something.'

The bartender catches my eye and I look away.

'You're at Winterfell? Oh, that's great. I have four children and a baby on my hands, Eliza. You told Mum you were on your way. I'm exhausted.'

'Sorry. It took longer than I expected.' I feel the start of a panic attack and breathe deeply, cupping my hand over the phone so that Ali can't hear.

'You can't just—'

'Listen, Ali,' I say, rushing to get the words out. 'There's a problem and I need the children looked after tonight and tomorrow.' Tears surge up and I choke on them. I can't speak any more.

'Oh Christ,' Ali says, and I hear Pete ask her what's going on.

Through my tears and sniffles, I manage to tell her what Sonia told me. I finish by saying that I didn't kill Martin. 'I swear it, Ali. Please believe me.'

'Eliza, I love your children almost as much as I love mine, but you must see that you've put me in an impossible position. I can't help you.'

'No. No, I understand. I shouldn't have asked. I can leave them with Isabel and hopefully get something sorted.'

'You'd leave them with that girl? Are you mad?'

'I don't have any choice, do I? Ali, please. I'm only asking for one night. Just so they're not with me when the police come. I don't want them to see that.'

The thought that she had been my friend and never would be again makes me cry even harder. God knows what the bartender is thinking. *Got a right one here.*

'I'll call you back,' she says. 'I'm going to talk to Pete.'

I blow my nose and wipe my eyes. My stomach rumbles and I remember that I've had nothing to eat since lunchtime, so I buy a packet of crisps and wolf them down while I wait. After about ten minutes, my phone rings and I grab it. It's Pete.

'Eliza, look, this is an exceptional situation so we'll help you out tonight, but we're not clearing your mess up after you again, do you understand?'

'Yes.' The word has to be forced from my throat.

'OK.' Pete's voice softens. 'You need to stay calm. Ali is going to take Jack and go to Kate's. I'll keep the older kids here and I'll speak to you tomorrow. We'll sort something out once we know what's going on. There's not a lot we can do till then, except get a decent night's sleep.'

'I'm so sorry.' My nose is running. I smear it clumsily with my sleeve.

'This whole situation is horrific,' he says. 'I cannot believe what's happened to our lives in the last three months. I told Martin to be wary of Dan. He should have bloody well listened to me.'

'I know you did,' I say. 'You were right. I should have listened too.'

'What have the police said?'

'Only that the post mortem's thrown something up. Pete, what will happen to the children if they keep me inside? I can't let them go into care.'

'We would never let that happen. They are family.'

I don't want to go home to Dan and Isabel and the atmosphere they create, but if I stay here I'll only get drunk, and I mustn't give in to that. There's Linden Road. I could stay there tonight and go to the police station in the morning. I visualize myself climbing the stairs to the empty flat, curling up on the bed and falling asleep, temporarily unburdened of responsibility.

It's tempting, but something better occurs to me. I pull the hood of my coat over my head and go outside. My car is about ten yards away. I set off, the water on the pavement splashing my boots. The downpour feels biblical. I rifle through my bag for my keys, half aware of a man approaching, chin to his chest, bony shoulders hunched. There's something familiar about him and I feel a twinge of anxiety; more than a twinge. But it's too late and as he passes, he takes hold of my arm. I twist round, crying out in shock, knowing suddenly who this skinny creature with the lank hair is. He clamps his hand over my mouth and hustles me into the alley behind the pub. I struggle, but he smashes his elbow hard into my midriff so that I bend double. Then he hits me again, this time sending me flying against the bins.

'I can give you money.' I drag in a painful breath. 'Just don't hurt me.'

Under his sodden fringe his eyes have a look of intent. He hauls me up and I scream as his hand covers my nose and mouth. This time, I can't see a way out; this time there's no Dan to come running out of Nico's, no passers-by, just him and me and the rain clattering on the bin lids.

I writhe desperately, trying to catch a breath, knowing I'm suffocating. His body crushes my bag between us. I squeeze my hand in and my fingers close around the rape alarm. The ear-splitting siren that goes off when I yank the strap shocks him into letting go of me. I turn and run, my hand in my pocket pressing the button on my key fob. The car responds with a friendly blink of its rear lights, and I throw myself in and lock the door just as he grabs the handle, his other hand slamming against the window. I shove the car into reverse, then wrench the steering wheel round and pull out, the tyres screeching on wet tarmac.

My heart races as I head back to Winterfell, windscreen wipers on their fastest setting, rainwater flying off in sheets of rippling grey. I can smell him on me. Stale sweat, beer and cigarettes.

51

The television is on in the drawing room; an action movie by the sounds of it. I go straight up to the bathroom and swap my wet clothes for dry, then assess the damage to my appearance in the mirror above the basin. It's not good. My hair is bedraggled, there's red bruising round my neck, my make-up has run, and a nasty scratch stretches from under my left ear to my throat. My fingers tremble as I slowly tug a hairbrush through my hair.

Replaying what happened, I'm whisked back to a morning in June, walking along Boundary Road with a heavily pregnant Ali. It had seemed such a delightful coincidence that Dan had been sitting in the window of Nico's when my bag was snatched, ready to play the hero at the exact moment Ali and I were passing. But was it really? Could he have set the whole thing up so that Martin and I would owe him a favour and rent him the flat? Had he been manipulating me even then? Dissuading me from pressing charges without seeming to do so.

But if that was the case, and this second attack was

also pre-arranged by Dan, this time with much more serious intent, how on earth did he find me?

I check my phone screen, but I've already deleted the tracking app. Dan could have replaced it, I suppose, but there are other ways without having recourse to my phone; DIY tracking systems for the car, for instance. But how he managed it isn't important right now. What *is*, is that he knows where I've been.

On impulse I transfer my personal alarm from my bag to my jeans pocket, then I set my phone to record and go downstairs, where I find him on his own. He doesn't acknowledge me until I walk in front of him and drop down on the armchair.

'Where's Isabel?' I ask.

He pauses the action just as a motorcycle flips on its side and slides under a jack-knifed truck, sparks flying. He shows no surprise at seeing me alive and well, albeit bruised.

'Gone out for a drink with her friends.'

'Didn't fancy joining them?'

'No.'

'I've just been to see an ex of yours,' I say. 'Gaby Wilder. But you already knew that, didn't you?'

He shrugs.

'How did you know? Have you tampered with my phone? Or will I find something attached to the underside of my car?'

His eyes flicker and I nod, satisfied.

'How did you find her?' he asks.

'Don't you know? I thought you'd been keeping an eye on my movements.'

'Only since Friday evening. You were being shifty. I wanted to know what you were up to.'

'You had a GPS tracker just knocking around? That was handy.'

'Next day delivery.'

'Wow. Well, I met your parents. Pete tracked them down.'

He makes a dismissive face. Pete is nothing to him. 'Believe me, you can't rely on those two to be unbiased. They don't rate me very highly. My sister always came first.'

'According to them, Clare went to India to get away from you. That's when she met Martin and fell in love. That's what led to this, to Martin's death.'

Dan goes quiet, then he suddenly leans forward, jabbing his finger at me. 'Clare died. She fucking died because of you two. Your husband made her think he was in love with her, then you homed in on him and he just tossed her aside.'

I feel a buzz of anger. 'Romances go wrong when you're young,' I snap. 'You get dumped. Heartbreak is part of life. Most people chalk it up to experience.'

'Clare wasn't most people. Martin had a lot to answer for. He sloughed my sister off like dead skin. She was devastated. And you didn't give a shit, did you?'

'I didn't get a chance to know her.' Does anyone truly care about their lover's exes? I decide it's probably wiser not to voice this unsisterly thought.

'What happened when she came home?' I ask.

'She became withdrawn. She wouldn't talk to any

of us or see her therapist. She started smoking weed again.'

'Again? Had it happened before?'

He looks quizzically at me. 'Would it make you feel less guilty if it had?'

'I don't feel guilty.'

'Oh, yeah. You and Sam look after number one, even if it means someone else suffers.'

I flinch. I told him that.

'Clare had suffered from depression on and off,' he says, 'and had used drugs as a teenager, but she was not beyond help. Martin should not have encouraged her to lean on him, then taken away the support. He was a coward when things got difficult.' He looks me up and down. 'I'm only surprised he took you on. I wouldn't have thought he'd have had the patience for an addict.'

'Apparently he did.' There's a long silence. I can hear us both breathing. 'I expect that's why you set your nasty little friend on me,' I say. 'You were worried about what Gaby might have said. Well, you were right to be worried. She told me she took the blame for the crash.'

'Gaby agreed to the switch.'

He has himself back under control; shoulders straight, chin slightly forward when he's normally so physically relaxed. I wonder about my own body language and sit taller.

'She agreed because she was madly in love with you, and she didn't realize it hadn't been an accident. You put my husband in a wheelchair, but that wasn't enough, was it? You came to Hasleford to finish the job.'

'Is she going to the police?' He's rattled.

'No,' I say, after a pause while I contemplate winding him up. 'She doesn't want to be involved; she's moved on. She's happy.'

'Good on her. I'll hold my hand up to causing the collision. I was angry and not thinking straight. It was a stupid risk to take. I didn't expect to hurt him that badly. But if I'm being honest . . .'

'That would be a start.'

He smiles at my tone. 'I thought, great, he's lost the use of his legs, his life is fucked. It's a kind of karma. What goes around comes around. But it wasn't like that, was it? He thrived. My sister took her own life, and he didn't give her a second thought. She wasn't even on his conscience. I wanted him to pay, but I didn't come here with the intention of killing him. I didn't kill him,' he adds, in case I've misunderstood.

I emit a sceptical groan. 'What brought you here then?'

'I was following Martin's career from a distance. I wanted to see if I could do anything to ruin things for him. For you as well. When I realized how bad your marriage was, it was easy. You were easy.'

'I was,' I admit. 'You knew how to get to me.'

'I only wanted to rock your smug little boat.'

'Well, congratulations, you succeeded.' Even though I'm being flip, I find it hard to meet his eyes. Looking at his mouth is worse. I'm still perversely drawn to him. 'Tell me something. How long did you stand at the side of the pool watching Martin run out of energy? It must have taken ages; with his level of fitness and upper body

364

strength, he could stay afloat with no problem for well over an hour. Or maybe it didn't last anything like that long. Maybe you pushed him under and kept him there.'

He laughs. 'Nice try. You either have a vivid imagination, or that bang on the head dislodged something, because you were the one who brought him down to the pool. Isabel witnessed you pushing him in. I expect you were off your head.'

'Isabel was lying – for you; just like Gaby did. I can't have killed Martin if I was out cold on the hall floor, could I? What really happened, Dan? Tell me now, when there's no one else to hear. I need to know how Martin died.' I hesitate. 'For closure.'

'Closure,' he repeats. 'Huh.' He stiffens, his eyes narrowing. 'Hand it over.'

My mouth dries. 'Hand what over?'

He raises his eyebrows, then gets up off the sofa and leans over me. I squirm frantically as his fingers rove my body. He steps back with my phone in his hand.

'Recording. Very clever.' He deletes it, shoves my mobile into his back pocket and sits down again.

I gaze at his face, wondering what it was that had drawn me to him so violently, when in the end there is nothing solid there. Dan Jones is a construct; cheerful, open, attractive. That construct seems almost broken now, what lurks beneath becoming increasingly clear. I wonder if I'll ever know where the truth ends and his lies start.

'So what did happen to Martin?' I ask. 'No one's recording you now.'

He shrugs. 'Isabel came over. She was completely hyper,

storming round the flat. She'd had a call from your husband's lawyer pal. When she told me what he'd said, I remembered. After Clare died, my parents tried to get in touch with Martin. They didn't blame him, but they wanted to know what had happened in India. Martin walked away from it all but my parents wouldn't let it go. Eventually they received a cease and desist letter from Andrew Joliffe.'

My eyes widen. Andrew must have convinced Martin it would be ruinous for his future career to get involved, especially as Clare's death was drug-related. Martin was driven enough to listen to him. How cynical.

'Andrew Joliffe would barely have been qualified back then,' I say.

'Doesn't matter. You don't have to be a lawyer to write one; but he sent it on letterhead from the law firm where he was doing his training contract, which happened to have a reputation for being one of the most ruthless in the country. My mother was almost broken by that.' He breathes out slowly, then smiles. 'I decided we should pay Martin a visit. Isabel still had her set of keys and the code to the gate.'

I frown. 'But you weren't caught on CCTV.'

'Do you know how easy it is to hack into someone's Smart system if you know what you're doing? For someone like me, it's child's play. I'd already connected up to yours, to test it for weak points. I thought it might prove useful.'

Of course he had. Dan is a planner, prepared to wait, to defer pleasure, happy to serve his revenge cold.

'People don't have a clue how vulnerable they are,' he

says. 'I can manipulate the cameras from my phone. We were already in the house when the shutters came down. We didn't see you fall, but we heard it. Martin was just sitting there, staring at you. I checked you over. You were alive, but I pretended I couldn't find a pulse. I told him you were dead.'

I close my eyes, picturing Dan leaning into me, feeling my vital signs, my warmth, then turning to look up at Martin and shaking his head sorrowfully.

'What did he say?' I whisper.

Dan grunts dismissively. 'He said, "What do I do?" Again, the man couldn't give a shit about anyone but himself. It's the only time I've ever felt sorry for you. I was so angry, my blood was boiling. I told him who I was and what I thought of him. He didn't react, literally did not bat an eyelid. I needed a reaction from him; I wanted him to piss himself, basically.'

I flinch. That is not the way I want to remember Martin. 'Where was Isabel while all this was going on?'

'Upstairs. I told her to wait outside the children's bedroom in case one of them woke up. I got him into the lift, took him down to the pool and pushed him in. He reacted then. I've never heard anyone bellow with rage like that. I was going to leave him there to savour his humiliation, but as I walked away he started laughing. I asked him what he was laughing about, and he said I was pathetic, using the excuse of avenging my sister to disguise the fact that my life hasn't amounted to anything. He described Clare as a nonentity, manufacturing emotional problems to make herself more interesting. So I lost it.'

Even under threat, Martin was determined to win back a measure of dignity.

'Why did you stop him getting out of the pool?'

He looks at me as though I'm stupid. 'Because of Clare, of course. Because I couldn't see any other way of ending the pain. It's like being trapped in a bubble. I wanted to burst it.'

My blood chills. 'So you murdered a defenceless man?'

He hesitates, as though he hasn't thought about it in such stark terms before. 'I allowed him to drown.'

'You trod on his fingers.'

'You're glad he's dead.' His voice drips with contempt. 'I did you a favour.'

'And Isabel?' I ask. 'Does she know what you did? Has she been lying to protect you?'

'No. I convinced her it was an accident. She wanted to believe me so she did.'

He looks very tired and I have a sense that he wishes he had never started any of this, that events have snowballed to such an extent that he is no longer controlling what happens. And that is a frightening scenario for both of us. I know what it feels like not to be able to go back, to know that you've gone too far.

A phone starts ringing and I recognize Isabel's ringtone. I stare at Dan. It rings on and on, echoing through the house, and then it stops, leaving a brutal silence.

52

Isabel would not go out without her phone, and if she was here, she would have answered it. She's claustrophobic, so if she was locked up and conscious she'd be screaming blue murder. My mind hurtles through possibilities. Is she injured in some way? Trapped somewhere in the house? To me her silence can only mean one thing. Dan has done something bad.

I leap up, but he's quicker than me and blocks my exit. I launch myself at him with a yell of fury and he reacts by throwing a punch, hitting me so hard that I stagger, crashing against the side table, knocking over a small bronze statuette of the minotaur. I straighten and gasp, pressing a hand to my burning jaw.

'Just let me check she's all right.'

Dan rubs his knuckles. 'If she isn't, it's your fault. Why did you have to interfere?'

'I don't know what you mean.'

His eyes darken as he scowls. 'You told her she'd be an accessory, so of course she's been on the internet. She read about some high-profile cases and went into full meltdown. She threatened to walk away, not testify against you in court.'

'Do you mean she wouldn't risk her future for you? Oh dear.'

'Don't mock me, Eliza. You'll regret it.'

'Like Isabel?'

No reaction.

'Where is she?' I ask.

He doesn't speak but his eyes flick downwards. In that moment I reach for the statuette, but he clocks my intent and roughly grabs my arm before I can curl my fingers round it. I dig in my pocket, pull out the alarm and shoot my hand to his ear. It emits its high-pitched scream for the second time that night and Dan lurches away, yelling, 'Fuck!' I push past him, open the door and run. He is only seconds behind me.

Isabel is lying on her side about a metre from the edge of the pool, her knees pulled up, her hands pressed against a cut above her right hip from which blood pulses, spreading across the floor, a smooth red tide.

I drop down beside her and place my fingers against her neck but my hands are shaking, and before I can find her pulse Dan hauls me to my feet. I can feel the tension in the arms that lock me against him; he's so much stronger than me, but I am just as desperate. I work my body round, ramming my elbow into his midriff, then sink my teeth into his upper arm. He doesn't let go, so I tuck my leg between his and hook my ankle around his calf. We lose our balance and start to fall. The pool comes up to meet us, and we enter the water.

My eye is caught by something glinting at the bottom of the pool. A knife. I swim down but Dan grabs hold of my waistband and pulls me back. He winds his fingers through my hair and forces my head underwater. I struggle, trying to push myself up with his shoulders, clawing at his face, my nails catching on his ears, but he keeps me under, ramming me down. My lungs scream for oxygen.

What happens next has a dreamlike quality. There's a movement beyond Dan, beyond the bubbles and his pedalling legs. Trailing tendrils of blood like smoke from a cigarette, a blurry figure dives for the knife. Everything goes black, and then I'm suddenly released and I break the surface coughing and spluttering, my lungs heaving as I drag in mouthfuls of oxygen. Blood clouds the water, getting into my mouth and nose. I try not to swallow but it trickles down the back of my throat, making me cough. I swim backwards, windmilling my arms, but Dan has lost interest in me and I realize he's hurt. He makes it to the ladder, clutching his side, flings the knife so that it skitters across the floor, and hauls himself out. There's a moment when I think he's going to come back for us, but he folds in on himself and crumples like a discarded piece of clothing.

Isabel is floating face down in the water. I get her onto her back, then hook my right arm around her middle and pull her to the shallow end. She's a dead weight and slippery, and I have to strain every muscle to heft her torso over the edge.

'Isabel?' I get out, pull her clear and roll her over. 'Oh God.'

I try to remember what to do from what I've absorbed over the years. Tip her head back, open her mouth. I'm not sure how many breaths to give her so I do three, then two more for good measure. I straighten up, splay my hands one on top of the other over the middle of her chest, and compress hard and fast, my voice pleading in time to the rhythm of my pumping arms. 'Please, Isabel, please.'

She coughs up water and I sit back on my calves with a gasp of relief. I get her into the recovery position, then grab a folded towel from the stack and press it against the knife wound.

'You're going to be OK,' I say, hoping it's true. She's lost so much blood, I can't believe she's still alive.

I pull my stretch top over my head and get it underneath her and around her waist, apologizing when she moans with pain. I knot the sleeves tightly to hold the towel in place, keeping up a stream of one-sided conversation about how much she has to look forward to, how brave she's been, and eventually her eyes swivel towards me, her pupils so widely dilated that the irises look black. She makes an attempt to grip my arm, but her fingers are weak and her hand slips to the floor.

After that I see to Dan, roughly sandwiching a towel between his arm and his waist. His wet clothes have absorbed a lot of the blood. It's mingled with the puddles, wet footprints and snaking trails. The poolroom looks like a slaughterhouse. I make the calls I need to, then go upstairs to open the gates and front door. When I return, Isabel's skin is clammy and cold to the touch. Should she be breathing as fast as this? I shake her shoulder and tap her cheek to keep her awake, worried that her body is going into shock and that if she slips into a coma I could lose her. I think of her parents and shake her harder, eliciting a moan.

'Stay with me, Isabel,' I say. 'Please. Don't go to sleep now. Help is on its way.'

The ambulance is taking forever, seconds feeling like minutes. I glance at Dan. His eyes are closed. I shout his name and he opens them slowly, then closes them again.

As soon as the wail of sirens hails the approach of an ambulance, I sprint upstairs and into the fresh night air. I run down to the gates and out into the street, where I stop and look about me, perplexed by the peace and quiet after the chaos and fury of my house. It's almost scary how normal our street seems; lights on in the other houses, cars parked on driveways. A cat comes out from under one of them and crosses the road. It's funny how you expect the world to look different when you've been through a trauma.

Seconds ahead of the ambulance, a car races up our road and screeches to a halt. I feel oddly detached as DI Westcott jumps out and hurries towards me. I catch her shocked expression before she rearranges her features. There is blood all over me; soaked into my bra and my dripping wet jeans, on my hands and feet. Rivulets diluted by pool water make a pattern like the channels of an estuary on my midriff. I raise my eyes to the detective's face and beam at her. It's over.

53

November

The garden is still covered in frost this morning, the sky clear, the ripples catching the morning light on the river. Outside, a carpenter is constructing a picket fence at the river's edge so that I can keep the children safe while we're here. We are going to stay until the bungalow is demolished in the summer to make way for the new house Pete is designing. My two stipulations are that it's zero carbon and zero concrete, but otherwise I've given him free rein. Pete is very excited; he thinks it will establish him. I hope so. Winterfell has a buyer lined up already. With the money from the sale and the income from the flats, I can afford to build our future.

In the meantime, I'm happily engaged in whitewashing Gideon Grove. The kitchen and bathroom are dated and tired, but everything works. We'll have Christmas here.

We scattered Martin's ashes in Kate's garden. I'd wanted to do it at Winterfell, especially since that's where we held the wake after the funeral, but Kate was adamant, and who am I to part a mother from her son?

The radio is on. 'Common People' by Pulp is playing. I love the nineties stuff; the music my father didn't like. I sing along as I work my way round the room with my trusty roller. This place is my sanctuary for now.

Aurora and Lucas will be starting at new schools in January. We are going to get a puppy and a kitten, it's going to be chaotic, but it's the best thing I can do. I imagine going for walks with the Gordons at the weekend.

If I picture it vividly enough, it might even happen.

I miss Martin despite everything; he was an amazing man. I've found the bad memories are fading, though sometimes I get confused between him and my father in my dreams. That's all done now, I've drawn a line. I will never speak badly of him to his children, but I'm much happier without him. Dan was right about that.

The new evidence that DI Westcott felt justified my arrest, until of course it was superseded by the bloodbath at Winterfell, was that Martin's head injury was consistent with him being pushed into the pool and twisting his body to the side to prevent it. Forensics found traces of Martin's blood at the edge of the pool. It convinced her that her theory was correct. After Martin threatened me with Lowndes Place I drugged his food, thinking I'd make my escape with the children while he was sedated. He caught on and closed the security shutters. In my haste to get to the door I slipped, hitting my head on the sharp edge of the stairs. I may have been unconscious, or I may not have been. At any rate, when I came to, he threatened to tell the authorities about my father's death and make sure I never saw the children again. I took him down to the pool where, in the struggle to tip him in, he sustained a head injury. Still conscious, but woozy, he tried to get out. I trod on his hands to prevent him from doing that. It hurt that DI Westcott would think that of me, because those would have been the actions of someone very cold and calculating.

But anger is a pointless waste of energy.

I am inclined to believe that Dan didn't set out to kill. He lost Clare and he wanted to blame someone, so he blamed me and Martin. He saw ruining our lives as our just deserts, but he went too far, and Isabel became involved and complicated things. Her love for Dan was obsessive, jealous and dangerous, but when her vision cleared and she could no longer delude herself that she was anything other than a pawn in his campaign against me and Martin, she wanted nothing more than to bring him down.

Martin died because he had no respect for the young woman he'd briefly fallen for one long-ago summer. He shouldn't have mocked Dan, but he underestimated the damage the loss of Dan's twin did to his psyche and the longevity of his grief. Martin died because of his arrogance. Dan failed for the same reason; because he thought he knew our weaknesses, and didn't take into account our strengths.

It was Dan's idea to make me think that I'd killed Martin when he realized that I had no memory of that night. He knew the police probably wouldn't believe me, that I would be the obvious suspect, so all Dan had to do was deny there ever was a relationship between us. At that point Isabel was still infatuated enough to accept his reason for making me think he was in love with me; revenge, which was true, though it pains me to accept it. She wasn't the only infatuated woman at Winterfell; although I like to think the scales dropped from my eyes a hell of a lot sooner than they did from hers.

Dan lost control of the situation when she turned against him. He swears blind he had no intention of killing her.

Isabel lived to spin her side of the story. In her eyes, she was the young ingénue seduced by an experienced manipulator. She portrayed Dan as some kind of mind-bending guru. That evening she had been fuming about the call from Joliffe, full of self-righteous indignation about me and Martin and our behaviour towards her. Dan encouraged her to view herself as a victim and him as her knight in shining armour, upholding her honour against the evil Currans; so when he suggested they confront Martin, she was all for it. They entered the house via the annexe and she stood guard outside the children's bedroom while Dan tore a strip off him, or so she alleges. She swears that she did not know that I was hurt, and that Dan was lying when he said she witnessed everything and even helped put me to bed. Since I was unconscious and have no memory of what ensued, I can't corroborate her statement. It's her word against Dan's.

She says she heard some of the row between Dan and Martin but she didn't come downstairs. According to her, she put her headphones on because she couldn't bear to listen. Dan told her there had been an accident, and that if questioned she should say they had been together in Linden Road watching television all evening and had spent the night there.

It's up to a judge and jury to decide who to believe, but I think they'll choose Isabel. After all, she has a livid scar to prove that she was the victim of a warped and desperate man. I will stand in the witness box and tell them my version of the truth; that I don't know what happened that night, only what I had discovered about Dan's connection with Martin and me, and what he told me later. All the evidence points to him, so I think I'll be more of an object of interest than suspicion. The unfaithful wife and wealthy widow. Even that notoriety will be short-lived.

And what of my memories of those events? Is there a chance they'll return? No, they will not. They don't need to because they never disappeared. Once you've watched one man die and done nothing to stop it, the second time is so much easier. When my father died, I watched with a sick but exultant feeling in my stomach. It wasn't quite the same with Martin but I did feel sick. Of course, that was partly down to the bang on my head.

I regained consciousness to the sound of the lift descending. I don't have a clear memory, but I think I must have pushed myself up. Downstairs, the lift door opened and closed. I sat hugging my knees for a minute or two, trying to pull the strands together: the row; my attempt to leave; the shutters closing. Well, they were open now. I felt around the bump on my head and my fingers came away sticky with blood. I needed to know what was happening.

I descended the stairs on my bottom, so that I was hidden by the concrete sweep of the banister, and peered over the edge, catching my breath when Dan tipped Martin into the pool. I suppose Martin must have given him the code to the poolroom at some point; most of our friends knew it. Martin swam to the side and Dan trod on his fingers. I cried out once, but he didn't hear me. My voice was too weak. And then I got scared; if Dan knew I'd seen him, I would be next. I crawled back up on my hands and knees and lay down again, resting my head on the pool of congealed blood and closing my eyes. I was nauseous, cold and in pain, but I kept still, even when I heard Dan and Isabel discussing what to do with me. Somehow I managed to remain slumped, a dead weight, when they dragged me into the lift, took me upstairs and put me to bed. It was Isabel who changed my clothes; I thought it more realistic to be seen to surface then, mumbling and half opening my eyes before I was soothed back to sleep by a soft 'shh' from Isabel. It was Dan who picked up the controls from my bedside cabinet and lowered the blinds. I could smell him close to me.

Even so, if I had really wanted to, I could have called the police and intervened before it was too late, but I didn't. Martin should not have called me a psychopath.

There was a time when I wished it had never happened, but I've got over that. I am better off without him. I can make better choices. I can be a good role model to my children. When I feel guilty, I remind myself that Lucas and Aurora would have grown up watching their father treat their mother with contempt and cruelty, and they would have been irreparably damaged by that, their adult lives as fractured as mine. So I'm not going to let the guilt gnaw. Only sometimes, in the small hours of the night, does it get to me. That's when I see Martin's face merging with my father's.

And what of our friends and family? My relationship with my mother-in-law has been damaged. She blames me, but she's so scared of losing her grandchildren that she pretends. Her position is safe; I have no intention of depriving either her or Lucas and Aurora of a precious relationship. I want to be compassionate, so I also pretend, and actually, pretending can become real if you try hard enough.

And Ali. She is always in my thoughts. I suspect she believes that giving Pete the contract for Gideon Grove was some kind of bribe, a down-payment for a route back into her life. I can't deny it was part of the motivation. My life has less colour without her. The children see each other regularly, but it's a dump and run, no lingering for a cup of tea. I don't think she can hold out long though. Amanda Kelsey has got her feet under the Gordons' table, but I know for a fact that Pete doesn't like her, because he's told me. He's also said that when Lola has been round to play, Ali is literally popping with stress by the time she leaves. I'm patient. She'll need my help when she goes back to work. By the time summer comes round, we will have found our groove again.

Oh, and Sam is getting married! His fiancée is from Liverpool; her father is a builder and has offered him a job. Sam is currently training to be a plumber. He's much happier now that he's discovered he enjoys using his hands to make a living. He has also finally accepted that he's not cut out to run his own business. For the time being, at least.

Are you in the market for a well-appointed flat to rent in Hasleford? 42 Linden Road is back in Hooper's window, smartened up and looking extremely desirable, available immediately. Susie asked me if I wanted to meet potential tenants. I've told her no, that I trust her instincts more than I trust mine.

Acknowledgements

Thank you to my amazing agent Becky Ritchie and my equally amazing editor Tash Barsby. I feel very lucky to work with two such talented women. At Transworld, a big thanks to Imogen Nelson for providing a fresh eye on the manuscript, to my publicist Izzie Ghaffari-Parker, and to Lilly Cox and Ella Horne in Marketing. Thanks also to eagle-eyed freelance copy-editor Claire Gatzen and production editor Vivien Thompson, and to Black Sheep for the brilliant cover design. A huge thank you to Dr Clare Williams, sensitivity reader, who has made doubly sure that my portrayal of Martin's disability is accurate.

I couldn't do without the Petersham Writers Group: Ellen Alpsten, Georgie Boheim and Jill Whitehouse – I'm always happy to while away a morning talking to you. To Susie Lynes and Nicola Rayner for the friendship and the WhatsApp messages that have kept me giggling through lockdown. To Lauren North for keeping in touch during a tough writing year. To the Prime Writers who have been there for me since I took my first wobbly footsteps into life as a published author, to the

PSAA for cheering on psychological suspense authors, and to the remarkable authors who have been generous enough to read and review this book.

Thank you to the book bloggers who requested, read and reviewed advance proofs. You are such an important cog in the wheel.

Enormous thanks to everyone who has bought *Invite Me In*, borrowed it from their local library, downloaded it to their ebook or listened to the audio version.

Thanks to Steve, Max and Lulu. I'm very grateful my family are so lovely and not at all like the people I write about.

Thank you to my friend John Caute for reading and critiquing an early draft. Your opinion is always highly valued.

And finally, to my friend Liz Glendenning, whose story about the stranger who knocked on the door of her buy-to-let flat and declared, 'I'm your new tenant,' sparked the idea for *Invite Me In*.

Emma Curtis was born in Brighton and now lives in London with her husband. After raising two children and working various jobs, her fascination with the darker side of domestic life inspired her to write her acclaimed psychological suspense thrillers *One Little Mistake*, *When I Find You*, *The Night You Left* and *Keep Her Quiet*. Find her on Twitter: 🐦emmacurtisbooks

You trusted your best friend. You shouldn't have.

Vicky Seagrave is blessed: three beautiful children,
a successful, doting husband, great friends and a
job she loves. She should be perfectly happy.

When she makes a split-second decision that risks
everything she holds dear, there's only one person
she trusts enough to turn to.

But Vicky is about to learn that one mistake is all it
takes; that if you're careless with those you love,
you don't deserve to keep them . . .

**'A compelling page-turner which kept me
reading well into the night'**
Jane Corry

AVAILABLE NOW IN PAPERBACK AND EBOOK

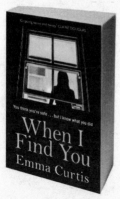

**What do you do when someone takes advantage
of your greatest weakness?**

When Laura wakes up the morning after her office
Christmas party and sees a man's shirt on the floor, she is
horrified. But this is no ordinary one-night-stand regret.

Laura suffers from severe face-blindness, a condition that
means she is completely unable to identify and remember
faces. So the man she spent all night dancing with
and kissing – the man she thought she'd brought
home – was 'Pink Shirt'.

But the shirt on her floor is blue.

And now Laura must go to work every day, and face
the man who took advantage of her condition.
The man she has no way of recognizing.

She doesn't know who he is . . . but she'll make him pay.

'Gripping, tense and twisty'
Claire Douglas

AVAILABLE NOW IN PAPERBACK AND EBOOK

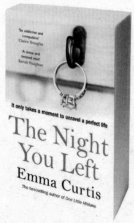

It only takes a moment to unravel a perfect life . . .

When Grace's fiancé vanishes without a trace the night
after proposing, her life is turned upside down. But has
Nick walked out on her, or is he in danger?

As Grace desperately searches for answers, it soon
becomes clear that Nick wasn't the uncomplicated
man she thought she knew. And when she uncovers a hidden
tragedy from his childhood, she realizes an awful truth: that
you can run from your past – but your secrets will always
catch up with you . . .

**'Another breathtakingly brilliant thriller . . .
Psychological suspense at its best'**
Nuala Ellwood

AVAILABLE NOW IN PAPERBACK AND EBOOK

When your life is a lie, the truth can destroy you.

Jenny has just given birth to the baby she's always
wanted. She's never been this happy.

Her husband, Leo, knows this baby girl can't be his.
He's never felt so betrayed.

The same night, a vulnerable young woman, Hannah,
wakes to find her newborn lifeless beside her.
She's crazed with grief.

When chance throws Hannah into Leo's path, they make
a plan that will have shattering consequences for all of them.

Years later, a sixteen-year-old girl reads an article in a
newspaper, and embarks on a journey to uncover the truth
about herself. But what she learns will put everything she
has ever known – and her own life – in grave danger.
Because some people will go to desperate lengths
to protect the secrets their lives are built on . . .

'Will keep you reading long into the night.
I absolutely loved it.'
Lesley Kara, author of *The Rumour*

AVAILABLE IN PAPERBACK AND EBOOK